Short Stories by

MARJORIE KINNAN RAWLINGS

University Press of Florida

Gainesville/Tallahassee/Tampa/Boca Raton/Pensacola/Orlando/Miami/Jacksonville

Short Stories by  **MARJORIE**

 **KINNAN**

 **RAWLINGS**

Edited by Rodger L. Tarr

F
Ra
#89425

Library of Congress Cataloging-in-Publication Data
Rawlings, Marjorie Kinnan, 1896–1953.
Short stories / by Marjorie Kinnan Rawlings; edited by Rodger L. Tarr.
p. cm.
A collection of most of her short stories.
Includes bibliographical references.
ISBN 0-8130-1252-X (cloth). — ISBN 0-8130-1253-8 (paper)
I. Tarr, Rodger L.   II. Title.
PS3535.A845A6   1994
813'.52—dc20   93-30649

In loving memory of my mother
Sara Gaugh Tarr

CONTENTS

PREFACE

ALL of Marjorie Kinnan Rawlings's short fiction published during her so-called Florida period (1928–53), except for two works, is collected here for the first time. *Mountain Prelude*, a serialized novella, is not included because of its length. *The Secret River*, a children's story published in book form, is omitted because of copyright complications. Her juvenilia, written while she was in high school and college, are also not included. The copy texts for the stories in this volume have been taken from the first publication of each story, except for "Lord Bill of the Suwannee River," which is the second publication and only complete text. They appear in chronological order, as they were published, except for the two posthumously published stories, "Lord Bill" and "Fish Fry and Fireworks," which are placed in the year or period in which they were written. No attempt has been made to alter the texts for consistency. Rawlings's spelling, especially of dialect, differs on occasion from story to story, as does the spelling of proper names such as Quincey/Quincy. In this collection, the uniqueness of each story is preserved. However, obvious spelling and printing errors are silently corrected. Otherwise, the stories are not edited in any way.

I am especially grateful to Norton S. Baskin, executor of the Rawlings estate, for his encouragement and assistance. I am also indebted to Philip S. May, Jr., the son of Rawlings's attorney, for answering my innumerable questions and for his spirit of negotiation. My special thanks to Gloria May, who has with kindest heart put up with me. For their invaluable suggestions, I gratefully acknowledge David J. Nordloh and Peggy Whitman Prenshaw. For her faithful work in typing the manuscript, I thank my graduate assistant, Michelle Anderson. My special thanks for their many kindnesses go to Jean F. Preston, former curator of manuscripts, and staff at the Princeton University Library; and to Mary Ellen Brooks, curator of rare books, and staff at the University of Georgia Library. I also acknowledge the splendid assistance of Carmen Russell Hurff, curator of the Rawlings Collection at the University of Florida. Finally, my full appreciation to those at Illinois State University who administer grants and support research. This project could not have been completed without their consideration. The staff at the University Press of Florida is to be commended in every way, with very special acknowledgment to George Bedell, Walda Metcalf, and Deidre Bryan.

Rodger L. Tarr

Short Stories by
MARJORIE KINNAN RAWLINGS

INTRODUCTION

I T is not generally known that Marjorie Kinnan Rawlings considered her short fiction a sustaining part of her career. Even enthusiasts are startled when told that she wrote extensively outside the genre of the novel, and they are even more surprised to learn that her short fiction was held in esteem by her contemporaries. Maxwell Perkins, the famous editor at Charles Scribner's Sons, saw in Rawlings's short fiction a preciseness of detail and a power of observation not altogether common in American letters. As her mentor and later close friend, Perkins encouraged Rawlings to write short fiction and then to use it as a foundation for her novels. It was her first short fiction, "Cracker Chidlings," that prepared the way for her first novel, *South Moon Under* (1933), just as it was her introspective "Gal Young Un" that set the tone for her psychological novel *Golden Apples* (1935). And, of course, much of the realism found in her portrayal of remote Florida in "Jacob's Ladder" found its way into her Pulitzer Prize–winning novel *The Yearling* (1938).

Yet the fact remains that Rawlings's achievements in short fiction are seldom acknowledged. Just why the public lost touch with her short stories is a matter of speculation. However, it seems clear that the immense popularity of *The Yearling* was at least in part responsible. When Rawlings received the Pulitzer Prize in 1939, she became an instant celebrity. To be sure, *South Moon Under* and, to a lesser extent, *Golden Apples* gained her a considerable reputation,

3

but the immediate success of *The Yearling* brought new pressures as the expectations of her audience and her publisher increased. The Pulitzer Prize changed everything. For ten years she had enjoyed the relative anonymity she had found at Cross Creek. Now she was in constant demand. *The Yearling* became a part of Americana. In just over a year it went through twenty-one American printings, selling more than 500,000 copies. Authorized and unauthorized translations appeared throughout countries in Europe and South America, not to mention Asian countries like China and Japan.

As always, fame had its drawbacks. In Rawlings's case it took her too often and too far from her adopted central Florida hammock, Cross Creek, the roots of and the inspiration for much of her fiction. This is not to say that Rawlings did not continue to write short fiction. Indeed, half of her output came after the fame *The Yearling* brought her. Yet the audience for her short fiction was in eclipse. She tried to hold her readers through the publication of *When the Whippoorwill* (1940), a reprinting of a selection of her short fiction together with the novel *South Moon Under*. The reprint was cordially received by the critics, but was not especially popular with the public. Her readers wanted more of the sustained portraits found in *The Yearling*. The immense popularity of Jody and his fawn left Rawlings with a difficult decision. Should she capitalize on the story by writing a sequel? She sensed the danger that writing a sequel might pose to her art and avoided the temptation. Thus, at the outset of World War II, she began searching for a different avenue for her creative impulses.

Rawlings found the approach she was looking for in *Cross Creek* (1942), a collection of impressions, part fiction and part fact, that she had been working on for a number of years. Oddly enough, this volume highlighted her ability to create short fiction, here largely autobiographical pieces put together to form a panorama of her beloved Florida. In some ways *Cross Creek* is a monument to the powers of detail and observation that had impressed Perkins a decade before. The novel, if it can be called that, is in the tradition of realism, although the slice-of-life technique and the episodic organization are reminiscent of naturalism. It was an instant success and sold within a short time nearly as many copies as *The Yearling*, which by then was becoming increasingly viewed as a children's novel. *Cross Creek* recaptured Rawlings's adult audience and paved the way for a number of short stories that were to follow. Rawlings continued to be one of Scribner's best-selling authors. *Cross Creek Cookery* (1942), Florida Cracker recipes punctuated by humorous anecdotes, was another strong seller.

World War II, however, took its toll. A staunch patriot since her college days at Wisconsin, Rawlings turned her attention to the war effort, and in consequence the quantity and the quality of her short fiction diminished. Among other things, she sold war bonds, made radio appeals, and became involved in civil defense. Her second husband, Norton Baskin, volunteered for the American Field Service and drove an ambulance in India and Burma. At one point he was declared missing; when found, he was desperately ill. This was a great personal trauma for Rawlings. She wrote to Sigrid Undset about her creative failures: "Part of the trouble is that I cannot get my mind off the war in general and Norton in particular . . ." (unpublished letter, 26 March 1944, May Collection). She later confided to Norman Berg, "Norton's being over-seas absorbed a great deal of creative impulse, in that I felt that I must write him fully, give him of myself, every day in my letters . . ." (4 February 1949, *Selected Letters*, 322). Perhaps the greatest toll came from her efforts on behalf of the American service people. *South Moon Under*, *The Yearling* (two printings), and *Cross Creek* were issued in cheap form, the so-called Armed Service Editions, by the government, and Rawlings gained through them a new audience and a new popularity. She received hundreds of appealing, often distraught letters from service people recounting their experiences. She answered each one with a thoroughness that left her little time for creative periods. Significantly, the few short stories that she was able to write during this period reflect a tone of despair, a feeling of alienation, not found in her earlier writings.

It could be argued that Rawlings sacrificed her career to the war effort, but such an argument would not take into account other factors in her life, not the least of which was her deteriorating health. Then there was the infamous *Cross Creek* trial in 1946, in which her friend Zelma Cason sued her for invasion of privacy for Rawlings's account of Zelma in *Cross Creek*. The trial and the appeals were exhausting for the already fragile Rawlings (Acton, "Effect of the 'Cross Creek' Trial"). The lower court ruling in her favor was overturned by the Florida Supreme Court in 1947, and Rawlings was ordered to pay one dollar in damages. Her complaint to Sigrid Arne is typical of the professional distress she was experiencing during this period: "I am working on a book [*The Sojourner*] and it is lousy. . . . I have done half a dozen short stories that my agent was enthused about, and they all have been rejected" (21 July 1945, *Selected Letters*, 271). Still, her popularity remained relatively undiminished. The Metro-Goldwyn-Mayer production of *The Yearling* in 1946, starring Gregory Peck and Jane Wyman, was a box-office sensation. In an attempt to capitalize on the movie, MGM employed Rawlings to write the screenplay for another movie, using *Mountain Prelude*, later a popular serial in the *Saturday Evening Post*, as the basis for a story about an orphan boy and his dog, on occasion in MGM correspondence referred to as the "last Lassie story." What Rawlings wrote and what MGM finally filmed were only remotely alike. The movie, *The Sun Comes Up*, was turned into a musical to showcase the talents of its star, Jeanette MacDonald. Rawlings's contribution is barely recognizable. In the case of *The Yearling*, Hollywood exploited her talents; in the case of the adaptation of *Mountain Prelude*, Hollywood ignored them.

With the writing of *Mountain Prelude*, Rawlings's endeavors in short fiction were nearly at an end. During her lifetime one more short story, "The Friendship," was published—by the *Saturday Evening Post* in 1949—but it is obviously not an effort to recapture the charm of her past work. She wrote other short stories, but to her dismay they were all rejected. Her artistic sense told her something was wrong. On 30 March 1948 she wrote to Norman Berg, "I am struggling with the re-writing of the short stories I did last summer, and still haven't gotten them right" (unpublished letter, University of Georgia). In response to such disappointments, Rawlings increasingly turned her efforts to writing *The Sojourner* (1953), a chronicle of a New York farm family that is expressly transcendental in theme. The novel attained some popularity and was a Book-of-the-Month Club selection, but never acquired a sustained following. Rawlings died suddenly in 1953, while working on a commissioned biography of Ellen Glasgow. In her papers, entrusted to Julia Scribner, she left behind a children's story, *The Secret River,* published posthumously in 1955, which demonstrates the diversity of her abilities as a writer.

Since her death, Rawlings's place in fiction has steadily declined. She is at present known principally for *The Yearling,* which continues to sell briskly, though largely as a children's book. Like Rudyard Kipling, Robert Louis Stevenson, and Mark Twain before her, Rawlings has become, to a large extent, the purview of children's literature. In a way she would be proud of this, for in the planning stage she and Maxwell Perkins agreed that *The Yearling* was to be written for adults but in a spirit that would appeal to children. Rawlings was forever proud that children loved *The Yearling* and encouraged their devotion by editing a School Book Edition of the novel in 1941. Yet in the end she considered herself a writer of adult fiction and was not altogether happy that her other works seemed of lesser importance in the wake of the success of *The Yearling.* It was a difficult position for her to be in, accepting the adulation of her young readers and at the same time realizing that such adulation made it more difficult for her to be accepted by adult readers.

Most of Rawlings's fiction uses Florida as a backdrop and was written after she moved there in 1928. However, she did serve a long apprenticeship. Even as a young girl, she wrote fiction. From 1907 to 1913, she was a regular contributor to the children's page of the *Washington Post* and in 1912 published a prize-winning story in *McCall's Magazine* (R. Tarr, "*Washington Post,*" 163–68). She continued writing fiction at the University of Wisconsin, where she was an editor of the literary magazine. After she was graduated with honors in English in 1918, Rawlings moved to New York City. While working for the YWCA there, she found time to write fiction but had no success in placing it. After marrying Charles Rawlings, her college sweetheart, in 1919, she wrote features for newspapers, most notably the *Louisville Courier-Journal* and the *Rochester Times-Union.* From 1926 to 1928 she wrote nearly 500 poems for the *Times-Union* under the rubric "Songs of a Housewife." These poems, which went into syndication, displayed her ironic humor and subtle wit. She also managed during this time to write satiric chitchat for the Rochester society weekly *Five O'Clock* (R. Tarr, *"Five O'Clock,"* 83–85). Still, her desire to publish fiction went unfulfilled during the decade following her graduation (Silverthorne, "Early Years"; R. Tarr, "Observations").

However, when she moved to Florida in 1928, her life as a writer of fiction changed dramatically. She found her niche among the Crackers of north central Florida, whose reserved but humorous spirits became the objects for her pen. As Gordon Bigelow puts it, the Crackers as a subject "appealed powerfully to her imagination and allowed her romantic sensibilities fullest exercise" (10). Rawlings did not live entirely apart from her fiction; she did not try to distance herself totally. Instead she became both the narrator and the pilgrim of her own fictive world of rural Florida, what Samuel I. Bellman refers to as her "geographical primitivism" (80). In 1931 her first story was accepted by the prestigious *Scribner's Magazine.* "Cracker Chidlings," subtitled "Real Tales from the Florida Interior," was her first attempt to chronicle the lives of her new-found friends, whom she describes as "people of dignity . . . aloof," but "friendly and neighborly" (*Selected Letters*, 37). It is here that we are introduced to Fatty Blake's squirrel pilau and Brunswick stew; to 'Shiner Tim's chauvinism and illegal corn liquor; to Sam Whitman's wife, whose Georgia heritage nearly costs her her Florida marriage; and to the arrogant Kentucky Colonel Buxton, who is outfoxed by the shrewd Florida Judge Atkinson over the ownership of Silver Springs.

"Cracker Chidlings" brought Rawlings to the attention of Alfred S. Dashiell, editor of *Scribner's Magazine*, and Maxwell Perkins, editor at Charles Scribner's Sons, both of whom encouraged her to write more stories formed upon her experiences with and observations of the unique Florida Cracker character. Regarding the authenticity of her stories, Rawlings wrote to Dashiell, "I have gathered my facts first-hand. Most of the material is to my personal knowledge. The rest has been told me here and there in the locality, and is equally authentic" ([March 1930], *Selected Letters,* 37). Rawlings blended fact into fiction with a deftness that signaled to Scribner's that they had a major talent on their hands. In her Cracker stories she was able to capture the human drama found in a life of deprivation and alienation, to locate tragic heroes in the coarseness of life in the formidable scrub. Rawlings finds a universality of spirit in the most bleak of characters. She records their often epic-like journeys of survival, moving them along the rivers of experience like Conrad and Twain before her (York, passim). Life is not easy for any of Rawlings's Cracker subjects. Much like Dickens's waifs, they exist in a world of little pleasure and considerable pain. For them, hardship is not a thing apart; it is everything. Yet they often give added dimension to this life through their humorous dispositions. For Rawlings, their journeys of sacrifice are also their journeys of renewal. And, significantly, in her short fiction the journeys are often seen through the eyes of the female characters.

Rawlings was not a feminist, at least not in the postmodern sense, but she was a strong-willed woman who detested role playing. Equality of opportunity was paramount to her (*Selected Letters*, 238). As Peggy Whitman Prenshaw concludes, "what Rawlings most deeply resented and found personally debilitating—and fought against all her life—was the powerlessness of the average woman, the powerlessness even of exceptional women in her society" (16). Rawlings had been outspoken on women's causes since her student days at the University of Wisconsin. Her subsequent work at the YWCA in New York and as a feature writer for the Louisville and Rochester newspapers led her repeatedly to the emerging role of women in twentieth-century culture. Her need to understand and to interrogate womanhood led to deep introspection. Her first and still unpublished novel, entitled "Blood of My Blood," written in the late 1920s, eschews aesthetic distance. This intense autobiographical account of her life as a woman and a writer, a work she called "poor Jane Austen," is a stark portrait. No one in it is spared from her satiric pen, least of all her mother.

With this psychological background, it is not surprising that Rawlings's first hero is female. The story in which this character appears is "Jacob's Ladder" (1931), and the hero is a Cracker girl named Florry whose sensitivity is squelched by her abusive father. Indeed, Florry's sensitivity is barely evident until she sets out on an epic quest with her lover, Mart. Both endure the many hardships of learning and living, but it is Florry who emerges as the emblem of strength. She survives in a landscape of male figures and finally triumphs in a largely male-oriented culture. Her triumph of will was suggested by Perkins, who thought Rawlings's original characterization of her was too bleak. Rawlings relented and wrote a romantic ending, even though she knew that such triumph was unlikely. The prototypes for Florry and Mart were once tenants on Rawlings's grove property, and their life, as later described in *Cross Creek* in the chapter "Antses in Tim's Breakfast," was anything but ideal. The real Mart and Florry lived with their newborn baby in appalling squalor, refusing, out of pride, any help, even from Rawlings.

Florry's strength of spirit reappears in "A Crop of Beans" (1932) in the character of Drenna, whose husband, Lige, in spite of being a "bean man," seems unable to make a profitable crop. A freeze inevitably burns him out. Impulsive and prideful, Lige is steadfast in his determination to "make a crop" and thus free himself from the Widow Sellers, whose benevolent authoritarianism saves his family from starvation, but at the price of constant tongue-lashings. Drenna, who is the epitome of Rawlings's belief in the nobility of labor, helps Lige cover the beans in the face of yet another freeze. This time, in large part because of Drenna's labor, the beans survive. Lige is able to sell the crop at a considerable profit of $1,500, which is put in the bank, except for some indulgence money for Lige and fifty dollars for Drenna to buy a fancy new dress. Lige spends his allotment quickly, but Drenna, always frugal, cannot bring herself to spend her fifty dollars. The story hinges on a twist of fate. The bank abruptly closes, and the couple's savings are lost. Lige is distraught, believing that the years of sacrifice have gone for nothing, until he learns that his faithful Drenna has kept back the fifty dollars as insurance for "another crop o' beans." Lige once again is saved from his avarice and pride by Drenna, who is his source of strength and renewal. Drenna's similarity to the prefall Eve of Milton lends intertextual meaning. Drenna is Lige's "unsupported flower."

Rawlings's women are seldom ennobled and idealized as Florry and Drenna are, however. Most suffer repeated indignities, and they are often cursed by a self-imposed role of deference. The most dramatic example of such a loss of dignity is Mattie Syles in "Gal Young Un," a story which gained Rawlings wide attention as an interpreter of the female experience. "Gal Young Un" is Rawlings at her best and at her most feminist. Mattie is a loner who has done well for herself until the entrance of the contemptible Trax, a drifter whom Mattie first befriends and then loves. The tension of the story is heightened through Rawlings's ability to pull the reader into the progression of Mattie's humiliation. From the outset we know what the lonely Mattie is unwilling to see: Trax is an odious male who acquires and then dismisses women as objects of utility. Trax seizes Mattie's wealth, turns it into a profitable moonshine business, and then has Mattie operate the still while he philanders, finally bringing into Mattie's home his "gal young un" named Elly. Elly is the archetypical innocent who looks like and acts like a wounded doe. Rawlings is merciless as she bores in on these two women, both competing for the same man because of their need to be needed, or more important, because of their fear of being alone. Trax, on the other hand, is a utilitarian being who sleeps with Elly and has Mattie cook his meals.

Rawlings's message is clear: those who sacrifice their dignity lose their identity. In the end, however, justice triumphs. Mattie comes to her senses and dispatches Trax in a scene of violent confrontation in which she simultaneously asserts her womanhood and takes Trax's manhood. In the end, the story is saved from the melodrama of revenge by a surprising act of compassion. Mattie, who overcomes her "self-hatred" (Preu, 79), takes into her home the forlorn Elly, who otherwise would have been left to suffer the consequences of her weakness. Interestingly, Alfred Dashiell of *Scribner's Magazine* rejected the story because of what he saw as a bias toward men. He objected especially to the portrait of Trax, finding him unreal, "a feminine conception of what a man of that sort would be like" (unpublished letter, 9 February 1932, Scribner Archive). *Harper's Magazine* immediately accepted the story. "Gal Young Un" was awarded the O. Henry Memorial Prize for the best short story of 1932 and in 1979 was made into an award-winning movie, first shown on PBS in 1981.

Rawlings's depiction of the female experience is not always so serious in tone. In fact, she is often at her best when she turns to light satire and sarcastic humor. Her Quincey Dover stories are examples of her ability to convey a message by appealing to the reader's comedic spirit. Rawlings moves easily from high comedy, formed upon word play and situational irony, to low comedy, found in the dialect and the action of her characters. In many respects Quincey Dover is Rawlings's version of Chaucer's Wife of Bath. They both manage situations by realizing that overt control is impossible. The woman senses what the man misses, the essential absurdity of the human predicament that fosters, against all principle, hierarchical relationships.

In "Cocks Must Crow" (1939), a title that leaves little to the imagination, Quincey is Rawlings's mouthpiece (McLaughlin, "Narratives of Quincey Dover"). "She is," Rawlings confesses, "entirely imaginary, but she is so real to me that I can smell her. She is, of course, *me,* if I had been born in the Florida backwoods and weighed nearly three hundred" (unpublished letter, 14 November 1939, University of Georgia). In "Cocks Must Crow" Quincey learns once again what she already knows too well: "Man-nature is man-nature, and woman's a fool to interfere." Quincey reminds the reader that a man must be given freedom, or at least the illusion of freedom, to assert his manhood. Like Chaucer's rooster Chauntecleer, man must crow. The delightful irony of man, like rooster, ensnaring himself in his own rhetoric is not lost on the reader.

In "Benny and the Bird Dogs" (1933), Quincey Dover is a foil to her friend Benny, a character based on Rawlings's hunting and fishing companion Fred Tompkins. As the resident narrator of the story, she becomes caught in her own testimonial rhetoric. She weaves an outrageously satirical account of the shiftless but loveable Benny, who makes his living by selling his bird dogs to unsuspecting Yankees, knowing all the time that the dogs will come home at their earliest opportunity. Benny is the king in his world of Crackerdom and refuses to be tamed, especially by his shrewish wife, whom he calls the "Old Hen." As if to underwrite Benny's invincibility, Quincey reminds her female audience: "Quarrel with a man and you'll be hornswoggled." Irony is pervasive here, for Quincey argues with Benny at the slightest provocation, as does Benny's "Old Hen." In this farcical tale, comedy dissolves quickly into burlesque. Robert Frost thought "Benny and the Bird Dogs" to be among the best stories of the period and is reported to have fallen off a rocking chair in uncontrolled laughter while listening to Rawlings read from it.

Quincey is not always the hero of her own story, however. In "Fish Fry and Fireworks," written around 1940 and published posthumously, the combative Quincey, through her own comedic machinations, outwits herself with near-tragic consequences. In this story Rawlings explores the notion that women meddle too much. Here Quincey arranges for a defanged rattlesnake to interrupt the political speech of Benny's opponent, with unexpected consequences. The resulting chaos teaches Quincey a hard but fortunately not a fatal lesson on the results of a female's attempting to enter into the male world of politics, where intelligence is seldom a prerequisite. Might, not right, governs Benny's life. Survival is accorded only the fittest. Quincey is fortunate to emerge a wiser woman.

Rawlings's affection for the frustrated Quincey is also evident in "Varmints," which Rawlings called her "mule story" (*Selected Letters*, 118). This "half fact and half fancy" story is founded upon a ridiculous premise, namely that two friends can own and share the use of a tobacco-chewing, rum-drinking, snuff-dipping mule named Snort, while each avoids responsibility for the animal's care (*Selected Letters*, 47). The indomitable Quincey is again caught up in her own intrusions, and her patience is tried when Jim Lee and Luty Higgenbotham abandon any responsibility whatsoever when Snort dies in a sweet-potato patch from both overwork and overindulgence. Unable to reconcile the differences between Jim and Luty, each of whom artfully dodges culpability for the decaying Snort, Quincey sums up her frustration with men: "A man's borned varminty and he dies varminty."

Rawlings intended to write more Quincey Dover stories and at one point proposed to Perkins that they be made into a "whole book" (unpublished letter, 20 May 1936, Scribner Archive). Regrettably, she did not pursue the project beyond "Donny, Get Your Gun," a story left unpublished (*Selected Letters*, 272–73). Instead she continued her examination of women in a man's world in quite another mode. She abandoned comedy and turned toward psychological drama. The plots of the stories in this form vary enormously, but at their center is the frustrated woman who is alienated from her surroundings. Rawlings's psychologically dark perspectives may very well reflect her own frustrations as she moved from budding novelist to international celebrity. Her divorce from Charles Rawlings in 1933, after years of his mental cruelty, was the catalyst for the release of her explosive feelings.

Motherhood, or the lack thereof, became the subject for her most famous story and one of her most autobiographical works, "A Mother in Mannville" (1936). Set in the mountains of North Carolina, this story is about an orphan boy named Jerry, a Wordsworthian innocent, who teaches a visiting writer (clearly Rawlings) about the meaning of loyalty through his devotion to her and to her dog, Pat. Hemingway-like in its simplicity and force, the story hinges upon a surprising revelation at the end, an ironic twist that leaves the reader suspended between joy and sorrow. Jerry gives the impression that he has a loving mother who is alive and well in nearby Mannville. Hurt that she cannot be a mother to Jerry, the writer then learns too late that Jerry's revelation is a fiction the boy has created to hide his embarrassment at being an orphan. The child the writer wanted, the child whom she would have adopted, is now lost to her.

So popular was this story of personal loss that Rawlings, succumbing to the demands of Hollywood, rewrote the story for the movie *The Sun Comes Up*; it was later published as a serial under the title *Mountain Prelude* (1947). However, the power of the human drama is lost in the melodrama necessary for the serial expansion. In *Mountain Prelude*, the woman is not denied the gift of motherhood. In fact, she is not denied anything, once she learns the lesson of patience and understanding. The psychological barriers of motherhood are lowered, and the writer, now a pianist, wins both the boy and a husband. There are flashes of brilliance in *Mountain Prelude*, particularly in the descriptions, but the plot dissolves too often into sentimentality.

Female weakness and vulnerability remained favorite subjects for Rawlings. "The Pelican's Shadow" (1940) presents another view of an ancient problem, submissiveness. In this story Rawlings asks the same questions that Henrik Ibsen asks in *A Doll's House*, but the end is dramatically different. Rawlings's Elsa, unlike Ibsen's Nora, is willing in spite of her resentments to suffer the outrages of her husband, Dr. Tifton, for the comfort and station he provides. Rawlings is so ruthless in her treatment of this marriage, so personal in her portrait of Elsa's failure to extricate herself from her humiliation, that portions of the story must certainly be a retrospective on Rawlings's own long reluctance to act decisively to end her unhappy marriage to Charles Rawlings (McLaughlin and Parry, 57). In fact, Tifton's complaint that Elsa's hollandaise sauce is too thin parallels Charles's throwing the tomato mayonnaise salad at Marjorie because the dinner she had prepared was "inedible" (*Cross Creek*, 206). The violence in the actual event does not take place in the story, although, of course, both women are the subjects of humiliation. Further, Tifton's brag that "editors were grabbing my articles before I knew you [Elsa]" reflects the intense literary rivalry that Charles Rawlings, a struggling writer, created between his wife and himself. And even though Elsa recognizes the limits of her "obnoxious Pelican" husband, who in his condescending, scientific puffery refers to her as "my mouse," she chooses to do nothing about her desperate situation. Elsa has purchased a life of ease at the expense of dignity. The weakness here is the woman's, not just the man's. Rawlings referred to the story as "a perfectly *evil* thing that I loved doing" (unpublished letter, 14 November 1939, University of Georgia).

Although Rawlings's women are often weak and/or vulnerable, they are also of unusual character, like the deliberately unnamed bride in "The Shell" (1944), a poignant account of a young woman whose special presence is like a "south wind blowing over wild roses." Each day she looks out across the ocean in search of her husband, who has been called to war. Terrified by his absence, she seeks the harbor of the Red Cross but is officiously turned away. Confused by her alien surroundings, she has no other recourse than to find her husband on her own. Remembering that he once told her to look to the sea and he would be there, she unwittingly walks into the water in search of him. Her drowning is compared to the empty shell that falls from her hand at death; she was after all in the eyes of society an empty shell herself, mentally retarded since childhood. Rawlings skates carefully here on the edge of blatant social commentary. The integrity of the story is saved through the brevity of description and the power generated by a language that evokes both despair and transcendence. The editors of the *New Yorker* called the story "terribly experimental" (*Selected Letters*, 271).

"The Shell" is Rawlings's last enduring story about a woman's struggle with social alienation and personal affliction. "Miriam's Houses" (1945) and "Miss Moffatt Steps Out" (1946), which Rawlings once referred to as her "'queer' stories" (*Selected Letters*, 272), were written toward the end of her career and are not of the quality of her earlier work, though they are important to any assessment. The former involves the psychological realization of a woman reflecting on her childhood fantasies forty years removed. The narrator, in youth envious because Miriam, her childhood friend, moved from house to house, comes to the realization in adulthood that the moves were in fact necessitated by the life-style of Miriam's mother, an impoverished prostitute. The story is, of course, about the changing perceptions of the narrator. Unfortunately, the plot does not approach its premise. The story is too elemental, too bare. It lacks both tension and credibility, and teaches us little about self-realization through maturation.

"Miss Moffatt Steps Out" is also founded upon a promising premise. Miss Moffatt, an old maid schoolteacher, has always lived life vicariously through her books and through her students. The more she withdraws into her imaginary life, the more vulnerable she becomes. Her tragedy is fear, the fear of experiencing life in the raw. Lonely and frustrated, she finally decides to participate in life directly when the town celebrates the return of the soldiers from World War II. She impulsively books dinner at a local hotel, only to realize that her meager income and meager experience will not buy her a proper meal and the fellowship of a soldier. As the waiter cruelly reminds her, "Madame is alone." Ignored by everyone, Miss Moffatt is forced to return to her insular life. Here again the potential of the story is lost in the telling. In Rawlings's defense, however, it should be said that her title, originally "The Celebration," and portions of the text were altered without her permission (Silverthorne, *Sojourner*, 243).

As committed as she was to the subject of women, Rawlings did not lose her edge when she wrote about men. In fact, in many respects she was more attuned to the world of men. Toward the end of her life she confided to Norman Berg, "I refuse to be *only* a biological female. . . . I was born half-male, understanding the true male, and resenting the . . . hypocrisy, *sneakiness,* of the average woman" (*Selected Letters*, 366–67). When she moved to Florida in 1928 to take over the ownership of an orange grove, Rawlings's agrarian world became decidedly male. And, as she freely admitted, she felt more comfortable with men. At the outset, her male subject was the Cracker. If there is a single difference between Rawlings's Cracker women and Cracker men, it is that the male heroes are less morally upright, more likely to be involved in questionable dealings and shady actions. "Cracker Chidlings" is devoted almost entirely to such men. Her third story, "A Plumb Clare Conscience" (1931), concentrates on the uniqueness of male Cracker morality. For this story Rawlings borrows one of the characters from "Cracker Childlings," 'Shiner Tim, and describes his harrowing attempts to avoid the law. Tim's character was based upon a real moonshiner named Howard, about whom Rawlings "took notes under a table in a dusky room" (unpublished letter, 16 July 1930, Scribner Archive). A small-time moonshiner whose still is necessary for his survival, Tim hides in the swamp among mosquitoes and water moccasins to escape a particularly persistent revenue agent. Frontier morality prevails in this dispute between civil law and Cracker ingenuity. As Rawlings explains to Perkins, "These people are 'lawless' by an anomaly. They are living an entirely natural, and very hard, life, disturbing no one. . . . Yet almost everything they do is illegal. And everything they do is necessary to sustain life . . . (4 November 1931, *Selected Letters*, 49).

The frontier ethic, espoused by characters like the real-life model for 'Shiner Tim, was a source of endless fascination to Rawlings. She clearly admired the fortitude of these characters. They were survivors. Part chauvinist, part humorist, and part thief, Benny of the Quincey Dover stories was her favorite. Her almost stock portrayal of Benny as Cracker extraordinaire is always saved by her injection of comedy into his otherwise amorphous existence. Benny survives, at least in the stories, because he is a foil for Quincey, or perhaps because she is a foil for him. It is difficult to sort out just who, at any given moment, the hero is: Benny in his role as stereotypical Cracker or Quincey in her role as the narrator of Benny's ever-fluctuating existence. Whether he is selling bogus bird dogs in "Benny and the Bird Dogs" or tricking his political enemies in "Fish Fry and Fireworks," Benny is emblematic of the frontier world, where justice is always in the eye of the beholder. His compatriots are found earlier in "Alligators" (1933), a clever narrative experiment described by Rawlings as "awfully funny Cracker alligator experiences" (*Selected Letters*, 47). This compendium of lore about Cracker versus alligator is a thinly disguised retelling of the stories told her by the renowned hunter Fred Tompkins, whom she gave credit as co-author when the story was first published in the *Saturday Evening Post*. In "Alligators," justice can be quickly altered by the snap of a jaw or the force of a tail.

A different view of frontier justice is found in "The Enemy" (1940), a story of confrontation set in the cattle country of central Florida, a subject Rawlings had addressed earlier in *South Moon Under* (1933). The plot reads like a western novel. A new landowner, a wealthy Yankee, fences in his land and as a result denies his neighbors access to the water once available to all. The ritualistic drama that develops is a classic confrontation between the dominant Cracker, Milford, and the interloper Yankee, Dixon, a "quarrel between the old and the new." This familiar story is lent credence by Rawlings's sensitive portraits of the Cracker's son, Tom, who feels compelled to defy his martial father, and his young wife, Doney, who comes to see that "Life [is] the enemy" and that "love [is] a bulwark against the foe." Hate is redefined by love in this story. With the exception of Milford, who admits, "I'm too old a man to begin obeyin' the law," all the characters learn that the territorial imperative of the "open range" has no place in the structured world of "modern law."

One of Rawlings's first attempts at dealing with the frontier ethos came in "Lord Bill of the Suwannee River" written in 1931 and published posthumously. Lord Bill is based upon an actual person, William E. Bell, who because of his extraordinary exploits became a legend in Florida. Rawlings researched her subject carefully, interviewing people who knew Lord Bill. From these interviews grew her own legend of Lord Bill Bell, a foreman for the Atlantic Coastline Railroad, whose appearance and strength caused him to be feared by his enemies and loved by his friends. A white John Henry, Lord Bill ruled his domain, where might was right, with an iron fist and a gentle heart. Rawlings builds here upon the tradition of the oral folk tale, describing Lord Bill as "a Hercules of the Suwannee" who "loved money and power and men and railroads and food and drink and jesting." Interestingly, the editors of *Scribner's Magazine* and the *Atlantic Monthly* rejected the story as too historical, more like a chronicle than a story, they opined, and thus not of interest to them.

Rawlings's interest in the concept of justice and its application to human endeavor had a personal as well as a public context. Her life in Florida led her to one of the most difficult issues she ever faced: racism. As a child growing up in Washington, D.C. and as a student at the University of Wisconsin, she had witnessed first-hand the effects of racial injustice. However, life in the South was quite another thing. There racism was blatant, and it was accepted as a fact of life. When she moved to Florida, Rawlings by her own admission fell into the ethos of racism. It was all around her. Her personal dilemma soon became a professional one as well. If she were to portray accurately the situation and the language of the people she wrote about, if she were to be honest for the sake of historical record, how was she to treat the subject of racism? Her Cracker friends and Cracker characters were, with few exceptions, racists. Her dilemma was not unlike that of any writer whose subject is the Deep South. What was even more traumatic for her was the realization that she herself was often racist in attitude and in the use of language. Yet she had a deep commitment to the presentation and the ennobling of the black culture.

It is true that in the decade leading up to the publication of *The Yearling* in 1938, Rawlings's fiction did not focus on the black culture. It is also true that when blacks were used as background characters in her fiction, they were often stereotyped as "niggers," usually incidental to the story line and hence to the culture. Yet even here sharp distinction should be made between the language of Rawlings the narrator and that of her characters. In "Lord Bill of the Suwannee River," for example, she employs the words *negro* and *black* in her narrative description, while her characters use the word *nigger* in their dialogue. On occasion, however, Rawlings the narrator does fall into stereotyping, as in her description of Mengo, the dwarf in "Lord Bill," as the "little black ape."

Nevertheless, in the years surrounding the publication of *The Yearling*, Rawlings's personal attitudes began to change dramatically, and in consequence so did the language of her fiction. Her largess toward blacks who lived near Cross Creek often put her in conflict with her white neighbors, especially when she raised the salary of her black workers to nearly double the going wage. She also befriended blacks and allowed them to stay, often free of charge, on her place. She made clear to everyone her affection for her black workers. This affection often evolved into genuine love, as in her relationship with her "perfect maid," Idella Parker. Rawlings also became a confidante of the struggling black author Zora Neale Hurston. Their friendship has been explored in *A Tea With Zora and Marjorie*, a drama by Barbara Speisman. In a letter to Rawlings, Hurston calls her "sister," principally because of Rawlings's realistic treatment of the black culture (16 May 1943, Hurston Papers, University of Florida). In effect, then, Rawlings not only experienced the black culture, she became a spokesperson for it.

In 1940 Rawlings turned formally to the subject of racism in her story "In the Heart," based partly upon occurrences at Cross Creek. However, the point of view is shifted from the prejudicial attitudes of whites toward blacks to the prejudicial attitudes of blacks toward blacks. Bat, a heroic figure like Lord Bill of the Suwannee, is rejected by his fellow blacks, the domesticated Joe and Etta, ostensibly because he has just been released from prison. The real reason is even more objectionable. Bat is an expert gardener, a worker of the earth who proclaims proudly, "I got the livin' hand." Joe and Etta are jealous, seeing Bat as a threat to their otherwise secure life of mediocrity. The ignominy suffered by Bat—"All my life. Niggers mis-entrustin'. White folks shuttin' me up"—becomes in the end an object lesson for those who ignore decency and thwart justice as a result of prejudice. This subject is expanded upon in the chapter "Black Shadows" in *Cross Creek*.

By the time *Cross Creek* was published in 1942, Rawlings felt that she had purged racist attitudes from her psyche. In this autobiographical account of her life in the Florida hammock she celebrates the close friendships she has enjoyed with her maids and other workers. One of the most revealing descriptions is of the time she spent with her maid 'Geechee, whose problems with men and alcohol were overshadowed by a loyalty and work ethic Rawlings came to revere. However, one of the most difficult chapters for the contemporary reader in *Cross Creek* is "Black Shadows." In it Rawlings deals extensively with her relationship with blacks, and the picture is not always pleasant. She repeats the platitudinous opinion held by many southern whites of the time: "The Negro is just a child . . . carefree and gay . . . a congenital liar." Rawlings declares these judgments "superficial truths" and asserts that the only difference between the black slave and the black worker is that the "Negro today is paid instead of being rationed." Harsh words and harsh judgments, but spoken from her experience. Rawlings believed that "there is no hope of racial development until racial economics are adjusted" (180–81). The title "Black Shadows" was not without personal meaning to her. As she wrote to Norman Berg, "I have forced myself to take the final mental leap about the Negroes. There is no question . . . that we must go all out for 'full equality', meaningless though the phrase may be. Anything else is the height of hypocrisy" (unpublished letter, 27 November 1943, University of Georgia).

By the mid-1940s Rawlings's distress over the condition of black people resulted in an extraordinary letter to John Temple Graves, a segregationist and editorial writer for the *Florida Times Union* in Jacksonville. After reading a separatist editorial by Graves, Rawlings wrote to him:

> I myself began with an acceptance of segregation. I took it for granted, coming of a preponderantly Southern ancestry. I can only tell you that when long soul-searching and a combination of circumstances delivered me of my last prejudices, there was an exalted sense of liberation. It was not the Negro who became free, but I. I wish and pray for your own liberation. It is almost a religious experience. No man is free as long as another is enslaved. . . .
> (*Selected Letters*, 238)

Rawlings was determined to challenge segregationists in every way she could. She wrote to Sigrid Undset in 1944 about the lecture she had given at predominantly black Fisk University in April: "I asked to stay on the campus, as my own private gesture against segregation, and stayed three days at the president's house. . . . The pig-headedness and inferiority complex of much of the South makes me ill and so ashamed" (unpublished letter, 24 May 1944, May Collection).

In the light of these opinions, Rawlings published her final story on the subject, "Black Secret" (1945), an early draft of which was completed while she was writing *The Yearling* (unpublished letter, 10 May [1937], Scribner Archive). The approach is Faulknerian, the psychology deep and dark. The subject of Rawlings's probe is Dickie Merrill, a seven-year-old who learns through gossip at the barbershop, notably a shop run by a black barber, the "black secret": his favorite uncle fathered a child by a black woman. Dickie, raised in a white culture, feels betrayed. His feeling of betrayal is reinforced by his mother's friend Mrs. Tipton, who, from the point of view of a gossip, concludes, "Women are blind. Women are stupid" and "men are beasts." These statements confuse Dickie as he is forced to abandon his childhood innocence to racist gossip and innuendo. For Dickie, realization brings no cathartic experience; knowledge is despair. "Black Secret" was awarded an O. Henry Prize for short fiction. Prejudice involving children is also found in "The Friendship" (1949), Rawlings's last published short story before her death, but it is about the social prejudice of a spoiled white boy toward his white friends and contains none of the emotive spark found in "Black Secret."

If a strain of hopelessness permeates Rawlings's perception of the black experience, she is often even less sanguine about the white culture. Several of her stories are similar in tone and in subject to those written later by Flannery O'Connor. One of her earliest stories, "The Pardon" (1934), is about a misfit named Adams who is unexpectedly pardoned after spending seven years in prison for a crime he did not commit. Upon release, Adams must confront a situation worse than prison: his wife and his children are living with another man. The psychological drama that follows weaves a brutally frank tale of alienation. However, Rawlings saves the story from inevitable darkness through an act of compassion similar to that of Mattie in

"Gal Young Un." Adams reaches out to and accepts his wife's illegitimate son: "Pore little bastard," he empathizes, "I reckon you wasn't much wanted." The primal need for sympathy and understanding is the message Rawlings adroitly conveys.

How people act under the most stressful of circumstances always intrigued Rawlings. One of her more compelling portraits is a story about a man who is thwarted in his desperate attempt to establish a bond with another man. "Jessamine Springs" (1941) is a psychological study of an itinerant preacher whose rote, meaningless sermons are emblematic of his passive existence: "He was glad to serve." This story of existential despair finds its tragic irony in the spring of Christian brotherhood. The scene focuses on the preacher's visit to a natural spring, where he hopes to experience renewal. There he encounters a businessman with whom he tries to establish a personal bond. However, his expectations are crushed when the businessman recognizes him as a fellow salesman and in consequence rejects his overtures, leaving the preacher to his life of loneliness and despair.

Humanity is not always the vessel of cruelty in Rawlings's view, however. She is quite willing to explore the role of sentiment and its value in a world seemingly devoid of feeling. In "The Provider" (1941) she examines the meaning of charity from the giver's point of view. Joe, a fireman on the No. 9 train, which runs from Jacksonville to Atlanta, defies the utilitarian ethic of commerce without feeling. His eleemosynary spirit becomes a source of self-realization as he extends a hand of compassion to an impoverished mother and her children who live in a cabin near the tracks. Joe first throws coal to them as the train passes and later prepares Christmas presents for them. For his charitable endeavors, which the railroad considers an improper use of its coal and time, Joe is fired. Undaunted, he sets out to find the family he has seen only as a blur from the speeding train. He plans to claim them as his own, only to suffer the shock of learning that they have suddenly moved. Refusing to succumb to the despair this knowledge causes him, Joe continues his quest and hence his journey toward fulfillment.

In all, Rawlings published twenty-three short stories in addition to the serialized novella *Mountain Prelude* and the children's story

The Secret River. As a group, the stories form a literary journal of her career. Just where her short fiction fits in the tradition of the American short story has yet to be determined. A full assessment of her work is badly needed but has until now been impeded by the lack of a full awareness of the extent and the range of her writing. At this point it can be safely said that her finest quality is her ability to tell a story. Rawlings possesses what her master storyteller Penny possesses in *The Yearling,* a flair for the dramatic. Carol A. Tarr points out that "She was aware of her audience always, as she learned how to develop the most action, how to pause, and how to end a story" (23). Gordon Bigelow describes her as a "raconteur, a teller of tales" (136), very much in the tradition of Mark Twain. Rawlings uses sentiment without apology. She makes complicated narrative strategies appear simple, whether her mode is humor or pathos. She appeals unabashedly to the heart and the soul of her reader. The moral configuration of her stories is intentional. She is a writer with a message.

The quality of Rawlings's stories—as is the case with the work of any writer—is uneven. Some are better than others, but none is embarrassing or unworthy of consideration. It is important to remember that most of her stories were published in *Scribner's Magazine* and the *New Yorker,* whose editorial demands were uncompromising. *Harper's Magazine* and the *Saturday Evening Post* were equally discriminating, although the latter appealed to a wider audience. And we should continually remind ourselves that stories sent to these magazines were almost always edited, more often than not with commercial considerations in mind. The editors of *Scribner's Magazine* were especially forthcoming with suggestions, and Rawlings usually adopted them, particularly when they came from Maxwell Perkins. To be sure, the aesthetic, in its broadest sense, was important to her, but in the end it was the general reader who mattered. When she became too esoteric, Perkins would remind her that she should write about what she knew, what was intimate to her. His death in 1947 was a personal tragedy for her, an "unspeakable grief" (*Selected Letters,* 297) from which she as a writer never recovered.

What, then, is Rawlings's contribution to American letters? Certainly her use of humor, which Frost appreciated most in her work, and her precision of description, which Perkins appreciated most, are attributes not to be overlooked. However, there is much more. Rawlings's power of observation is her lasting strength, kindled by an embracing wit and a disarming sentiment. Under her pen, documented fact becomes believable fiction. Her chronicle of the human spirit in transition, particularly that of the Florida Cracker and the Florida black, provides invaluable historical perspective. We come to know her characters as if they were our neighbors. When she abandons Florida for her more introspective stories, little is lost and much is gained; she continues the universality of her message. Her people are not cheap grotesques or remote caricatures lost in endless fictive complexities. They are us. They experience the same hurts and humiliations, the same tragedies and triumphs, that we all do. Though they may be multidimensional, they are uncomplicated representations of the American dream.

Margaret Mitchell, winner of the 1936 Pulitzer Prize for *Gone With the Wind*, wrote an admiring letter to Rawlings in 1940, praising her fiction in general and her short fiction in particular: "Your versatility is a marvelous thing. There is no one today writing the way you write or the type of things you write. There have been all too few writers like you in the past. Yours is truly an American gift. You are just a born perfect storyteller and all of us readers are very lucky because you are willing to let your stories stand on their own feet" (copy, 12 June 1940, Tarr Collection).

Such testimony is typical of the affection and the respect Rawlings drew from her contemporaries. In 1940, at the zenith of her success, the *New Republic* ranked her "among the first ten American story writers today" (Ferguson, 680); the *Atlantic Monthly Press Bookshelf* said she was "one of the two or three *sui generis* storytellers we have" (166); and the *Boston Transcript* placed her at "the forefront of American women writers. . . . [S]he will help to make the American short story a living part of our literature again" (Owens, 11). The esteem in which she was held by her peers is summed up in the words of Wallace Stevens, who, after visiting Cross Creek in 1936, wrote to Philip S. May, "Mrs. Rawlings is a very remarkable woman in her own right as distinct from her literary right" (*Letters,* 308).

Works Cited

Acton, Patricia. *Invasion of Privacy: The "Cross Creek" Trial of Marjorie Kinnan Rawlings*. Gainesville: University of Florida Press, 1988.

——. "The Effect of the 'Cross Creek' Trial on the Writings of Marjorie Kinnan Rawlings." *Marjorie Kinnan Rawlings Journal of Florida Literature* 2 (1989–90): 57–70.

Atlantic Monthly Press Bookshelf (June 1940): 166. Review of *When the Whippoorwill*.

Bellman, Samuel I. "Marjorie Kinnan Rawlings: A Solitary Sojourner in the Florida Backwoods." *Kansas Quarterly* 2 (Spring 1970): 78–87.

Bigelow, Gordon. *Frontier Eden: The Literary Career of Marjorie Kinnan Rawlings*. Gainesville: University of Florida Press, 1966.

Ferguson, Otis. Review of *When the Whippoorwill*. *New Republic* 102.21 (20 May 1940): 679–80.

Florida, University of. Marjorie Kinnan Rawlings Collection, University of Florida Library.

Georgia, University of. Norman Berg Collection, University of Georgia Library.

Hurston Papers. Zora Neale Hurston Collection, University of Florida Library.

May Collection. The Marjorie Kinnan Rawlings Collection of Philip S. May, Jr.

McLaughlin, Robert L. "The 'On-Natural' Narratives of Quincey Dover." *Marjorie Kinnan Rawlings Journal of Florida Literature* 4 (1992): 41–49.

McLaughlin, Robert L., and Sally E. Parry. "Symbolic Divergence: Communication and Alienation in Marjorie Kinnan Rawlings's 'The Pelican's Shadow.'" *Marjorie Kinnan Rawlings Journal of Florida Literature* 3 (1991): 49–58.

Owens, Olga. Review of *When the Whippoorwill*. *Boston Transcript*, 4 May 1940, 11.

Parker, Idella. *Idella: Marjorie Rawlings' "Perfect Maid."* Gainesville: University Press of Florida, 1992.

Prenshaw, Peggy Whitman. "Marjorie Kinnan Rawlings: Woman, Writer, and Resident of Cross Creek." *Rawlings Journal* 1 (1988): 1–17.

Preu, Dana McKinnon. "A Woman of the South: Mattie Syles of *Gal Young Un*." *Southern Quarterly* 22.4 (1984): 71–84.

Rawlings, Marjorie Kinnan. *Cross Creek*. New York: Charles Scribner's Sons, 1942.

——. *Selected Letters of Marjorie Kinnan Rawlings*. Edited by Gordon E.

Bigelow and Laura V. Monti. Gainesville: University Presses of Florida, 1983.

Scribner Archive. The Papers of Charles Scribner's Sons, Princeton University.

Silverthorne, Elizabeth. *Marjorie Kinnan Rawlings: Sojourner at Cross Creek.* Woodstock, N.Y.: Overlook Press, 1988.

————. "Marjorie Kinnan Rawlings: The Early Years." *Rawlings Journal* 1 (1988): 18–28.

Speisman, Barbara. *A Tea With Zora and Marjorie. Rawlings Journal* 1 (1988): 67–100.

Stevens, Wallace. *Letters of Wallace Stevens.* Edited by Holly Stevens. New York: Knopf, 1966.

Tarr, Carol A. "In 'Mystic Company': The Master Storyteller in Marjorie Kinnan Rawlings's *The Yearling." Marjorie Kinnan Rawlings Journal of Florida Literature* 2 (1989–90): 23–34.

Tarr, Rodger L. "Observations on the Bibliographic and Textual World of Marjorie Kinnan Rawlings." *Rawlings Journal* 1 (1988): 41–49.

————. "Marjorie Kinnan Rawlings and the Rochester (NY) Magazine *Five O'Clock." American Periodicals* 1.1 (Fall 1991): 83–85.

————. "Marjorie Kinnan Rawlings and the *Washington Post." Analytical and Enumerative Bibliography,* n.s. 4.4 (1990): 163–68.

Tarr Collection. The Marjorie Kinnan Rawlings Collection of Rodger L. Tarr.

York, Lamar. "Marjorie Kinnan Rawlings's Rivers." *Southern Literary Journal* 9 (1977): 91–107.

CRACKER CHIDLINGS

Real Tales from the Florida Interior

HERE, in the uncivilized Cracker interior of Florida, you insult a man in half-friendly fashion by calling him a damned Georgia Cracker. Nine times out of ten you have hit the mark. Georgia Crackerdom, joined by a thin stream of Carolinians and a still thinner one of Virginians, has flowed lazily into the heart of this State, back in the scrub, in the hammock, along the lakes and rivers, and created Florida Crackerdom.

Georgia Cracker and Florida Cracker have a common ancestor in the vanished driver of oxen, who cracked yards of rawhide whip over his beasts and so came by his name. One hates the other as mothers and daughters sometimes hate. I saw the hate flicker into words at the doings at Anthony.

Squirrel Eyes

Word came that Fatty Blake, snuff and tobacco salesman and Anthony's richest citizen—wealth in Anthony, as elsewhere, is relative—was having a big doin's on a certain Thursday night. The world, it appeared, was invited. Finally Fatty himself drew up in front of Adams's store to verify the advance story. Fatty was inviting two counties to his doin's, and all was free. Squirrel pilau and Brunswick stew. Fatty couldn't likker you, as he would like to do, but if you brought your own 'shine and were quiet about it, why, he'd meet you at the gate for a drink, and God bless you.

28

"I got boys in the woods from can't to can't," Fatty said (from can't-see to can't-see, or "from dawn to dark"), "gettin' me squirrels for that pur-loo. I got me a nigger comin' to stir that pot o' rice all day long. And my wife, God bless her, is walkin' the county, gettin' what she needs for Brunswick stew, the kind her mammy made ahead o' her in Brunswick, Georgia."

Cars and wagons and lone horses and mules began coming in to Anthony long before dark. They brought women in home-made silks and in faded ginghams, men in mail-order store clothes with high stiff collars, and men in the blue pin-checks of the day's work. Children screamed and sprawled all over the swept sand about Fatty's two-story house.

Up and down the forty-foot pine-board table bustled the wives of Anthony, each of whom had brought her contribution, as to a church supper, of potato salad made by stirring cut onion and hard-boiled egg into cold mashed potatoes, of soda biscuits and pepper relish, of pound cake and home-canned blueberry pie. Back of the house a nigger stirred rice in a forty-gallon wash-pot with a paddle as big as an oar. It grew dark and the crowd was hungry. It had not eaten since its high-noon dinner of white bacon, grits, and cornbread.

At seven o'clock Mrs. Jim Butler played three solo hymns on the Blakes' parlor organ, moved out to the front porch for the occasion. Then she lifted her shrill soprano voice in the opening chords of "I know salvation's free," and the crowd joined in with quavering pleasure.

At seven-thirty the Methodist preacher rose to his feet beside the organ. He lauded Fatty Blake as a Christian citizen. He prayed. Here and there a devout old woman cried "Amen!" to taper off his prayer. And then the parson asked that any one so minded contribute his mite to help Brother Blake defray the expense of this great free feast.

"Will Brother Buxton pass the hat?"

Habit was too strong. The parson could not see a multitude gathered together in the name of the Lord or in the name of victuals without giving them a Christian shake-down.

The hat was passed, and as the pennies and nickels clinked into it, Fatty Blake made his address of welcome.

"I've done brought all you folks together," he shouted, "in the name of brotherly love. I want to tell you, all at one great free table, to love one another.

"Don't just stick to your own church," he pleaded. "If you're a Baptist, go to the Methodist church when the Methodists have Preaching Sunday. If you're a Methodist, go help the Baptists when their preacher comes to town.

"Now I want to tell you this meal is free and I had no idea of getting my money back, but as long as our good parson here has mentioned it, I'll say just do what your pocket and your feelings tell you to, and if you feel you want to do your share in this big community feed, why, God bless you.

"Now, folks, we've all enjoyed the entertainment, and I know you're going to enjoy the victuals just as much. There's all you can eat, and eat your fill. Don't hold back for nobody. Get your share of everything. I've had a nigger stirring the pur-loo since sun-up, and it smells the best of any pur-loo I ever smelt. It's got forty squirrels in it, folks, forty squirrels and a big fat hen. And my wife herself done made that Brunswick stew, just like she learned it at her mother's knee in Brunswick, Georgia. Now go to it, folks, but don't rush!"

The crowd packed tight about the table, weaving and milling, two or three hundred hungry Crackers. The pilau and stew were passed around in paper dishes.

The passing hat reached a lean, venerable Cracker just as he had completed a tour of exploration through his pilau.

"No!" he shrilled, with the lustiness of an old man with a grievance.

"No, I ain't goin' to give him nothin'! This here was advertised as a free meal and 'tain't nothin' but a dogged Georgia prayer-meetin'. Get a man here on promises and then go to pickin' his pocket. This food ain't fitten to eat, dogged Georgia rations, Brunswick stew and all. And he's done cooked the squirrel heads in the pur-loo, and that suits a damned Georgia Cracker but it don't suit me.

"I was born and raised in Floridy, and I'm pertickler. I don't want no squirrel eyes lookin' at me out o' my rations!"

Even a Snake

Clem Paxon set off with the Bickley boys one cold night to hunt deer in the scrub. He was only started on his way when he discovered that he had pocketed the wrong box of shells. He and Lige Bickley turned around and went back. When they walked in the door of his one-room cabin, at once he identified the form in the bed as that of his friend Abner Twill. Clem's wife looked up stupidly from where she stirred a low fire on the hearth.

"Damn you, Abner, you ole low-down dog!" roared Clem.

Abner sat up in bed and smoothed the coverlet about him.

"Clem, I'm plumb ashamed o' you," he expostulated, "goin' off a cold night like this'n and not leavin' no wood cut fer yer pore wife here. What do I find when I comes in? Her scrapin' together a few bits o' fat-wood to git herself a leetle ole puny fire agoin'—"

"Damn you, Abner, you pole-cat, git out o' thet bed if you ain't too rabbity to fight—"

"Clem, you was learned to treat women-folks better. Now when I was married to my pore wife what's now in her grave, a corpse, I wouldn't no more o' gone off a cold night like this'n and not cut no wood fer her than I'd spit in my mammy's face. Soon's I got warm, I was fixin' to git right out in the cold and split some wood fer this pore woman—"

"Damn you, Abner, you allus could talk yerself out o' ary hole, but you ain't in no cooter hole now—"

"Now shame to you, Clem—"

"Shut up!" groaned Clem wearily. "You ole snake, you."

"Now, Clem," Abner protested mildly, settling back under the covers, "even a snake likes to git hisself warm."

A 'Shiner's Wife

'Shiner Tim agreed as casually to show us his still as though it were a potato-patch. Except for one slow appraising flicker of his drooping eyelids, he did not inquire whether, aside from having long been patrons of his art, we might prove friend or enemy. He scarcely cared. As a mere common-sense precaution, he would move the still the next day.

He had served a term at paying off the sheriff, handing over his ten dollars a week, for the still was large, to the deputy who clattered up to his cabin door every Monday morning on a motorcycle. He soon found that the pay-off was no protection against the Federal men, who swooped down like chicken-hawks and picked at random from the sheriff's list. He outlawed himself deliberately, trusting to a tri-weekly moving of his apparatus to evade the government agents. Acres of swamp, of branch-fed hammock, of the deep marsh the Cracker calls a prairie, gave him a choice of impenetrable covers. The day of our call, the still lay in the heart of scrub palmetto on a fragmentary island deep in the cypress swamp. The next day it was half a mile removed, its exact location known only to Tim and his wife.

His protection against the sheriff and his deputies is only his readiness to use his shotgun at first sight of them. They respect the fact. He has killed and will kill again. He has the eye of the killer, dispassionate, disinterested, the eyelids heavy as a snake's. He has a trick of swaying his head from side to side, like a moccasin weaving. He drinks his own raw liquor by the cupful, like water. He is never entirely sober but certainly never entirely drunk.

His wife never touches their product, but brews her own pot of tea or chicory. She was apologetic as she refused the white-hot rum Tim had recently run off from a barrel of cane skimmings. She was "proud to have company." She didn't get to see much of women-folks. She listened raptly to my every word. The scantiest news of a larger world moved her to an impersonal wonder. She was friendly in the manner of a dog or child, her eyes bright with her interest. She had a gentle face, freckled like a little girl's. She wore black cotton stockings, neat cheap shoes, and a fresh starched blue gingham dress. She was possessed of an utter quiet of soul.

When Tim said to me, "You can stay on with me. This ain't my wife. It's just a woman been hangin' around," she laughed as good-humoredly as the rest of us.

For the fifteen years that Tim has been making corn liquor, she has been an active partner. She is as clean as clover. She keeps all his vessels and pails immaculate, and moves about the great still, white cloths in hand, with an honest domesticity.

"You can be nasty with whiskey makin', same as anything else," she explained.

She works every run with Tim, and goes with him to make deliveries in a ragged flivver.

"I don't fret none about the worrisome part of the business," she said, "but 'tis better for Tim, do I have him carry me with him. A car with a woman ain't so noticeable-like."

I thanked her for her courtesies.

"I had never seen a still," I explained. "Never anything but a picture."

She nodded understandingly.

"A picture's a false mess," she agreed. " 'Tain't real."

We spoke of the practical inaccessibility of the still-sites in Tim's swamp. The swamp is too full of cypress knees to be traversed by boat or raft. Tim and his wife reach some portions by careful wading in hip-boots.

"You don't need to fear being caught in that stretch of swamp," one of the men said. "Nobody but Christ would try to walk it."

She chuckled pleasantly at the thought.

"I reckon Christ don't pay no attention to us mean rascals," she said.

Georgia Money

Sam Whitman, whose daddy's daddy killed bear and panther on the Ocklawaha, hates a Georgian worse than most Florida Crackers, because he married one.

Sam lived a happy, drunken life until he took the lean spinster, in an outburst of respectability, from her comfortable farm home in the Georgia hills. He 'shined for a living until she caught him at it. He trapped and seined on Lake Lochloosa until an unfriendly game-warden destroyed his traps and seine and had him fined.

With the last of his fishing-money, under the lash of his wife's tongue, he set up at the crossroads in the restaurant business, which the woman, with good Georgia thrift, made almost to pay. Then Sam discovered that in spite of the persecution of the Georgia spouse, life was very simple. For when the till of the little café was full, Sam scooped the contents into his pocket and went on a grand drunk.

The most eagle surveillance of the woman could not keep the profits from him. At last the business was ruined. He had bought supplies on credit and drunk the proceeds until his shelves were bare and his customers gone. His creditors came and nailed the door tight shut.

His wife reviled him. He pitched her garments, her pots and pans and her bed, outside the door. She departed wailing to her Georgia home. Three months later she came back and took up the wrangling thread again. The philosophers of Adams's store, clustered about Sam on the sandy steps, inquired of him what he intended to do, now that a wife's support was again incumbent on him.

"That's her worry," he informed them. "It don't worry me. Her folks sent me a message. Her daddy wants I should start up the restaurant again. He sent her to tell me he'll pay off all my debts and stock me up again, if'n I'll leave the till alone."

"What'd you say, Sam?"

"Say? Why, dogged if I'll let him do it. I didn't miss gettin' her told. It's this-a-way," and he leaned over to pound the steps of the store with his fist.

"I won't be no party to bringin' Georgia money into this State!"

The Jest

When a new youth comes to the hamlet, the adolescent male population plays "the joke" on him. As visitors are rare, and new residents almost unheard of, the jest is staged not more than once or twice a year, and has never lost its tang for the local palate. In many seasons of use, the details have not varied. The female population is supposed to know nothing about it, but a thing as splendid as a town's jest cannot be kept entirely quiet. The word goes around from the women quilting at Aunt Mag's, or meeting on church business.

"Miney and the boys 's playin' the joke to-night—"

I had the liveliest version from behind the withered cupped hand of a respectable elderly Baptist.

For two years Miney Whitman has acted as stage-manager. Miney is lank and sallow from twenty-one years of fat meat and cornbread, with the prestige on him of having once been to Jacksonville and come mighty close to joining up with the Navy.

Miney ingratiates himself with the stranger. He treats him to a Coca-Cola at the filling station at the crossroads, and sometimes to a snort of Dad Chance's 'shine. He draws him back of old man Adams's store with furtive looks, lights a Camel for him, and winks slowly, profoundly.

Miney says: "I'm studyin' to do somepun for you, somepun I got in mind—"

Miney's manner is calculated to accelerate the stranger's pulse. They puff their Camels almost through before he speaks again.

"How 'bout me gittin' you a woman?"

"Women," as implied by Miney, may be new or old to the stranger, or an untold story. In any case, he says cautiously, "Well, I dunno—"

Miney lights a fresh round of cigarettes and goes to work as a creative artist. It isn't every one who could put it over as slick as Miney. He paints a picture of a ravishingly beautiful bad girl who lives back off Crackerneck Road, whose charms and acquiescent nature are not generally known. He saw her in the store that morning, it seems, and saw her glance out at the stranger with every sign of interest. Miney has to go out past her house that very evening, about three o'clock, and if the coast is clear, he'll fix it. It is only a favor to the stranger. Miney himself, he says, is mixed up with a girl near Campville.

The stranger either acquiesces at once, with a pleased, shifty expression, or goes on smoking, scuffling the sand with the toe of his shoe, saying nothing. In the former case, Miney's Thespian antics need now be only perfunctory. In the latter, he suddenly slaps the stranger on the shoulder, says briskly, "All right, I'll go see can I fix it," and unless, as happened once, the stranger rips his shirt half off, stopping him, and "plumb refuses," Miney is off like a martin to a gourd.

Miney calls for the stranger when it is "good dark" and hustles him out Crackerneck Road in his old rattletrap flivver. Any qualms the victim may have developed are whisked out of him with his breath. The girl is waiting and eager, but they must hurry, for she will only be alone until ten o'clock. Miney's flivver bounds through the scrub, over palmetto roots, past whipping wild grapevines. It swoops under the moss from a live oak tree into the clearing about the old Marshall house, where now a dim light in the doorway pricks the tropical darkness.

"I'll stop back for you just before ten," Miney whispers, and dropping his passenger in the clearing, ten yards from the door, roars off into the night.

If the stranger is approaching the assignation with a bold, glad heart, he is the more unprepared for the subsequent events. If he is timorous, the shock comes like a bolt of lightning added to the thunders of his uncertainties.

The door swings partly open. A slim figure in a scanty dress lifts a naked, beckoning arm. The scarlet paint on the lips and cheeks, the painted shadows around the big eyes, give a first impression of startling female beauty. This is little Bill Morrison, who vanishes then out of the flickering kerosene light into the dim recesses of the house, still beckoning.

The stranger steps across the threshold.

Out of the dark there now falls on the visitor the mighty voice of big Tom Turner, roaring curses like the beat of angry surf, on the dogs that try to get to his daughter. Tom leaps into visibility at the same moment, a gray beard waving from his jaw. He lifts a repeating-rifle to his shoulder and lets loose with blank shells.

The stranger, realizing only that he is as yet miraculously unhit, runs as he will never run again. He runs until he is exhausted, or trips and sprawls in the dense palmetto scrub, or becomes conscious that he doesn't know the way out, and that he might wander the rest of his life without finding the road.

At this point in his discomfiture, he whistles softly in the night, or calls helplessly:

"Hey! Miney! Hey! Oh, Miney! Hey!"

The scrub comes to life. From hundreds of yards around emerge male youths, slapping their thighs and laughing like hell.

The Preacher Has His Fun

Gus Teeter and Harry Barnes and a handful more have given their town a bad name. The Methodist preacher on the Hawthorn circuit was warned against it.

"You're going to a town full of niggers," he was told.

Indeed? He had not been informed of that.

"Yes—but you'll find they have white skins."

He never recovered from the initial prejudice. Being a philosopher, he did not seek blind solace in the comfort of the plainly good nor of the hypocrites. Nor did he make more attempt than his first revival week to reach the plainly bad. He simply gave up the whole town as a bad job.

He was never malicious about it. This, too, would pass away. But in the short period of his priesthood he managed to have his fun. The town has forgiven him all but two of his jokes—the first one and the last.

One Sunday night, the pre-sermon hymn sung, he rustled his notes, adjusted his glasses, looked about over the scattered congregation.

"What time is it?" he asked in a conversational tone.

There was a sliding of feet and a fumbled reaching into Sunday pants and vests. Old man Benson got his slick dollar Ingersoll out first.

"It's a quarter to eight, parson," he quavered.

"I got only seven-thirty, parson," Dick Crosby called from a rear pew. He flashed his silver mail-order watch. "I'll guarantee my time's right."

The minister of the Gospel smiled sardonically.

"I have the answer," he said. "It's time to seek God."

A few months later when he announced that he was leaving the circuit for work as a chaplain, they felt uneasily that maybe they hadn't supported him properly. He had always preached a fine sermon, they remembered, and contributions had been small. His final sermon was brief.

"This is my farewell to you," he said solemnly, "my last words to your town. I have only this to say: 'I go to prepare a place for you. Where I am, there ye may be also.' "

The women cried openly and every one gave profound thought to the hereafter.

As he left town, he also left the news that his destination was Raiford, the State penitentiary.

Grampa Hicks

Grampa Hicks lives in a ten-by-twelve palmetto-log shack on the edge of Cross Creek. His brown old face is beardless, and the cracks in his chin wear the rich patina of tobacco-juice. He wears one blue mail-order shirt, "Chieftain" brand—loyalty forbids his buying the cheaper "Big Yank"—and one pair of blue pin-check pants, until they drop from his unlaundered body. He lives, sleeps, and fishes in them.

He is also loyal to "Three Thistles" snuff. "Railroad" is only fitten for niggers and "Buttercup" for women.

He exists by the illegal trapping of fish in Lakes Orange and Lochloosa and by renting other Crackers' rowboats, without permission, to fishermen from Jacksonville. If a customer's outboard motor lacks gas, he shuffles mysteriously to the other side of the narrow bridge across the creek, where lie beached other boats and motors, and returns with fuel. If a stranger to these parts needs liquor, so that, when the fish don't bite, he can spit on his hook, cuss and take a drink, to get them started, Grampa is gone into the underbrush beyond his shack, through the palmetto scrub, under the moss hanging from the live oaks; returning with a catsup bottle of 'shine made from cane skimmings. If catfish are scarce on his own lines, he runs the other fellow's.

Man's law is one thing, God's another.

Last Sunday morning we asked Grampa to go fishing with us. He knew where the bream and perch were biting, and we had had no luck for weeks. He spat.

"I don't fish on Sundays," he said haughtily. "I wa'n't raised up that-a-way."

The Silver River

The Silver River is as beautiful as its name. Dreamlike, it has an invisible source, rising from underground caverns to form Silver Springs, then flowing off into the sparsely populated Cracker hinterland east of Ocala. Like most lovely things, it has caused much squabbling among men.

Thirty years ago, a too foresighted old Cracker named Sylvester Hopkins finished buying from poorer Crackers the last strip of land lying along the river's lovelier banks. He promptly died, leaving a widow already gaunt from the years of privation during which Syl annexed river lands. She had buried her five children, always puny from malnutrition. She starved it out a few years more, when God sent, or so she said at first, Colonel Buxton.

Colonel Buxton was a Kentucky gentleman with money made in Burley-tobacco manipulations. He "bought" her river holdings of the Widow Hopkins, along with rights to Silver Springs, and set about the development of the territory. Two miles beyond the Springs, in still virgin country, there stand to-day the ruins of the pretentious cypress and palmetto-log lodge the Colonel built on the river for his delight. The butler's pantry is the largest of the rooms, since the serving of venison, quail, squirrel, wild turkey, doves and river fish, and especially the serving of drinks, was the *raison d'être* for the establishment.

There is scant reason to believe the Colonel saw the mystic beauty of the diamond-clear, palm-bordered river with anything save a commercial eye. The river landing, below the lodge, is at a bend in the stream. The bank of this bend is carpeted with mint. Cracker legend has it that the Colonel and his friends sat on the landing, waiting for the flat-bottomed river-boat that brought mail and supplies by way of the Ocklawaha River. These comfortable and contented gentlemen sat waiting, sipping mint juleps, and it is believed that the sprigs of mint dropped from their ice-frosted glasses took root on the cool, sandy river-bank.

The Colonel "paid" the Widow Hopkins with worthless certificates in a Silver River Development Company. She lived thenceforth gaunter then ever, and died, on the grudging bounty of a relative who had always sneered at Syl's schemes. The Colonel must have sold many of the same certificates to presumably more alert persons. He departed these regions with pockets well filled. The years passed with nothing heard of him, while the chicken-snakes crawled in and out of the lodge's eaves and the mud-daubers spotted the rafters.

A few years ago one Judge Atkinson, who had risen from a shrewd Cracker-youth to county-wide prominence, resumed the developing activity on the Silver River adjacent to the Springs. Colonel Buxton had been careless about proving title. The Judge had studied law by a fat-wood fire to good purpose. And behold, out of the past arose the prosperous spectre of the Colonel informing the Judge by telegram that he understood the latter was attempting to steal the Silver River from him.

The Judge wrote out his answer in his own laborious hand. A copy of the letter is in his office files to-day.

"Colonel Buxton, dear Sir. I have already stole the Silver River. There is just one difference between you and me. You stole it from a poor widow woman and I stole it from a Goddam rascal."

JACOB'S LADDER

T

I

HE night was sultry for square dancing.
The Florida summer hesitated sullenly between continued heat and
the equinoctial need of change. The dancers in the Jacklin cabin
sweat as they shuffled and wheeled. Tie-tongued Pinny called the
figures in a high minor wail intelligible only to experienced dancers.

" 'hoo' a coo'!"

There were grumblings.

"Dogged if it ain't too hot to shoot the coon."

Alternating couples shot the neighboring girl through to her partner, languidly. The figure was usually danced violently, so that the
lighter girls often sprawled on the rough pine floor, and it was
all a man could do to brace himself to catch his partner if she
were buxom.

The tune was plaintive, "Comin' 'Round the Mountain," and lent
itself to the suffocated daze in which the dancers moved. Feet "sluf-
sluf"-ed flatly. The bellow of a bullbat sounded outside the window, a hoarse bass to the squeak of the fiddle and the whine of
the jew's-harp. Marsh frogs tinkled intermittently like the jangle of
Chinese music.

"Bir' i' a ca'!"

Bird-in-the-cage was always popular. Dull eyes brightened. The
tempo of the dance quickened. The middle-aged men held them-

selves rigidly, shoulders back, chests expanded, moving only their feet and their long arms. The young bloods danced with their heads lowered, reaching belligerently far ahead of their slight bodies, their heels flicking up behind them. In the night's wet heat they sent forth the odor of their own pointer dogs, overlaid with the acridity of plug tobacco, the musk of mules and of the soil, with here and there the sharp sweetness of corn liquor.

Old Jo Leddy was the only man drunk. He claimed that "he couldn't no more go thu a set then a barbecue 'possum, lessen he was good and likkered." His partner to-night was his newest gal, the widow Boone. With the adjacent couple that formed his square, he made a cage about her. She shuffled rhythmically as the other three whirled around her. The cage broke to let her out. Old Jo moved in to take her place. The circling three chanted briskly.

> "Bird out—buzzard in!
> Purty good bird fer the shape he's in!"

They tittered. The figure was amusing when the "buzzard" was drunk.

"Ha-hey!"

The dancers sashayed. The individual couples concentrated on each other, shoulders pressed together like wrestlers. The whole dance was violent, earnest, without levity.

"Sluf-sluf! Shuffle-shuffle! Sluf-sluf!"

The music stopped as abruptly as though the instrument had been struck from the fiddler's hands. The dancers fell away from one another wherever the end of the set found them. Some of the couples loitered out into the sulky moonlight, fanning their hot faces with handkerchiefs and slapping at the mosquitoes. The older women dropped down on the sides of the white iron bed in a far corner of the room, where old lady Jacklin sat sewing pieces for her interminable quilts.

The kerosene lamps flared up sootily as a quick gust of air sucked from window to door. The palmettos rustled their fans a moment above the cypress shingles of the roof. The fiddler tilted back in his splint-bottomed chair and dozed between sets. The men spat in the empty fireplace. Old Jo Leddy passed around a pint, then the night's closeness absorbed even his exuberance.

Suddenly the flickering voices of quarrelling females flashed like lightning in the thick atmosphere. Old Jo's former sweetheart was threatening the widow Boone.

"Celie's fixin' to crawl onto her," commented old lady Jacklin delightedly.

Jo jumped to the doorway, moistening his loose red lips. His eyes hardened. He snarled impartially at both angry women.

A thin girl in a ragged brown calico dress loosened herself from the confused group on the stoop and entered the one-room cabin for the first time. She flattened herself against the wall, as though, like a chameleon, she wished to fade from sight. She was conspicuous for the extreme poverty of her clothing and for her emaciation. Her body had the graceful ease of any thin wild animal. Her chipmunk-colored hair hung loosely about her neck. Her eyes were bright and quick. Above the pointed cheekbones and sharp chin and nose they gave her very much the look of a young squirrel. For all her gauntness, she was not unlovely.

Old Jo stopped to glare at her as he swaggered into the cabin again. He had pushed both Celie and the widow Boone off the steps in the perfect justice of his arbitration.

"Git on outen here, Florry!"

The girl was gone as quietly as she had come.

"Jo!"

Old lady Jacklin shrilled him to her across the twenty feet of cabin. "Who's thet gal?"

"My gal young un. Hain't never carried her nowheres before. Done carried her with me to-night, did I git the notion to git too drunk to go home alone."

"Jo Leddy, you be the sorriest ole Cracker I know. Ain't she a pore leetle puny thing!"

"Jest thin-like. She's strong."

"Unh-unh! Reckon it's true, then, I heern tell you works her loggin' in the cypress swamps, like a man. Up to her shoulders in swamp water, times."

"Shore I works her. Why not? Women-folks is good fer love or fer work, one. My ole woman makes a die of it and don't leave me nothin' but a gal young un. No boys. You bets I've done worked her. Loggin' ain't hurt her none."

The next set was forming. Old lady Jacklin threw insults at his indifferent back.

"Steaden o' spendin' what sorry leetle you makes on liquor an' women, you'd orter buy thet gal some store clothes and carry her to the dances decent-like."

"She wouldn't go noways," he laughed. "She don't favor me none. She's rabbity!"

The dancers were in position. The fiddler struck up the favorite tune, brought to the Florida interior long since by Georgia and Carolina ancestors, "Ten-Cent Cotton."

Old Jo cut a buck-and-wing as he swung toward his partner. He thundered out the opening phrase.

"Ten-cent cotton an' fifty-cent meat!
How in the Hell kin a pore man eat!"

The dancers roared with laughter.

"Old Jo's a sight. He shore kin cut the fool."

The girl Florry looked up from her solitude on the steps at a shadow in the doorway. A young Cracker in torn blue pin-checks, as ragged almost, almost as gaunt, as she, came hesitantly out of the light and music of the room.

"I'll set down by you, if you don't keer," he said. "I don't aim to worry you none. I—I be rabbity, too."

They smiled together a moment.

She was both alarmed and attracted, like all young woods things in their first intimate contact with man. Until this terrifying night, when old Jo had ordered her to follow him the six miles to the dance, she had seen perhaps a dozen white men. None had spoken to her except the sleepy old fellow who drove a team of buff oxen in to their clearing to load their logs; the manager of the lumber mill, splendid, scarcely to be called human, in dark store clothes and driving an automobile; and a fat range rider.

Florry and the youth sat without speech. Their thoughts moved brightly toward each other, like fireflies in the darkness. She decided, as she usually did when anything startled her, that she was not afraid. Fearlessness was her defense against the world. She was conscious neither of happiness nor of unhappiness. She accepted. When any new aspect of the disagreeable presented itself, she asked herself only whether or not it was best to run from it. Against the background of old Jo and the cypress swamp, very few things seemed formidable.

Assuredly, compared with the other things she knew, this lean, tattered young Cracker was nothing to fear. She grew accustomed to the sweaty smell of him beside her, the rise and fall of his breathing, the comfort of his silence. She placed him, the first human being to enter there, in the corner of her mind that contained things definitely pleasing. These were: grits when she was very hungry; wild game, always; Sport, the hound; all flowers; trees in bloom, particularly the sweet bay and the magnolia; facts new to her, that she could be sure she understood; the taste of running branch water, for their well was sulphurous; a lighter'd fire on a cold night; nigger babies—she had never seen a white one; and a certain sort of day, cool and blue and wind-swept; a day in fall, when the summer's heat was done, and the red-bugs and mosquitoes gone.

Such days must be due now. Wet heat like this meant storm. The moon, white as the belly of a dead fish, had a great ring around it. It was a wet moon, a moon of impending change. Out of the night's heat puffed another quick gust of air, fresh and chill. The palms rustled wildly, the tops of the pines lashed a moment, a ribbon of black cloud trailed across the moon. Then the night was still again. A hoot owl sobbed throatily. A whip-poor-will, late or persistent with his courting, sounded his nocturnal mating call uncertainly.

Florry spoke.

"Hit's September a'ready?"

"Yessum!"

The youth's voice was eager. Speech was as difficult for him as for her, but he longed to attempt it.

" 'Bout the fust week. Shore will be good to git the skeeters blowed out. I mean, they's a pain, nights, and days too, places over in the hammock."

"Hit's time fer the high winds?"

"Yessum. Shore is. Wouldn't surprise me none to see 'em beginnin' tomorrer."

"Wouldn't surprise me none," she agreed.

"Yessum. 'Bout crack o' day, mought git up and hear the palmeeters shakin' theirselves to pieces, and the ole pine trees a-crashin', and the rain fair fallin' sidewise, if the high winds has done come."

"Well, I reckon it's time."

"Yessum. Hit's time."

They were silent again. Suddenly the girl knew that this man was not a stranger. He was like herself. More, he was a part of herself. She was a part of him. It was altogether natural that they should be sitting together in the hot, swarming night, while other folk thumped their feet and tossed their heads to fiddle music.

The last set was called and ended. The young Cracker moved cautiously away from the girl, inside the cabin. The fiddler was ready for a snort of old Jo's 'shine, now his night's work was done. Old Jo was reeling. The widow Boone left him and went home with a man who had a mule and wagon.

Florry helped her father down the steps, her mind full of other things. His condition was of no importance. He beat her, drunk, and worked her, sober. The beating was more painful than the logging, but it was sooner over. She accepted old Jo, his 'shine, his women, as part of the general pattern of life. They came and went across her like the heat and the mosquitoes, like the waters of the swamp. She had no more control over them than over the impending hurricane.

They had walked the six miles from their clearing to the Jacklins' in an hour and a half, old Jo leading the way smartly through the familiar piney-woods. Dawn was breaking before they were home again. Florry had to go ahead through territory unknown to her for the first four miles. She picked an instinctive trail, often quitting the dirt wagon road altogether for a northeasterly short-cut through the open flat-woods. Jo stumbled behind her, the effort absorbing all his breath, so that he had none left with which to curse. When he dropped too far behind, she waited without looking back, her eyes strained ahead in the umbrous twilight that was the moon's setting.

When they plunged into the hammock south of the clearing, Florry could move more surely. The gusts of air that had been puffing at them on their way had blended into a long sweep of wind, rising and falling like the surge of surf. As the moon set behind them and the east lightened, the sky showed itself a bedlam of scudding clouds, rushing pell-mell south by west. Birds were stirring sleepily in the clearing. A red-bird trilled richly from a sweet gum. A pair of turtle doves whirred from the long-leafed pine where they had nested for the night. In the cypress swamp to the north, jorees began to crackle. A covey of young quail emerged in single file from the night's shelter of thick brambles back of the cabin. The hound pat-patted his tail on the sand to greet them, but did not lift his sleepy head from his paws.

Old Jo tumbled into the rough pine bed at the side of the main room and snored thickly at once. Florry did not light the lamp in the gray dawn, but walked through the open, covered breezeway to the kitchen at the rear. This was the hour at which they arose when they were getting out logs and she was hungry. Jo was probably at the beginning of a long drunk. At any rate, he would not log to-day nor to-morrow.

There were a few embers of live oak in the small wood stove, but she did not trouble to stir them to life. She poured a cup of thick cold coffee and chicory in a tin cup and drank it, munching a slab of cold gray cornbread, a slice of cold boiled bacon and a few left-over greens. A very little satisfied her, for she was accustomed to working hard on light rations, but somehow she wanted more. She split a leathery biscuit and soaked it with home-made cane syrup. It was last year's boiling and was souring a little. Old Jo would give her the devil if he could see her pouring out so much syrup.

Near the stove was a pallet on the floor, covered with crocus sacks stuffed with black moss. Florry took off her stiff boy's shoes and black cotton stockings, the ragged brown dress, and her drawers made of sugar sacking. She lay down in her short shift of the same material and drew a quilt over her head to keep out the mosquitoes. She was not sleepy. She knew that things awaited her for which she must be prepared with sleep. The pines were hissing. The water-oak scratched long boughs across the cypress shingles of the kitchen roof. High winds were coming. They would sweep across her, move her on. When they were gone, she would not be in this place.

The girl was awakened by the tumult. It was broad day, and the outer perimeter of the hurricane was moving across the section. The yellow-grayness of the sky was tinged with green in the west. The roar of the wind was a train thundering nearer and nearer. The palmettos thrashed their fans in frenzy. Rain was pounding on the roof as though it would beat it open. On the gutters it flailed like bird-shot. The thunder no more than boomed above the down-pour. Beyond the kitchen window, the gray flood was a curtain across the piney-woods. The world outside the cabin was obliterated.

Shingles ripped off with a dry rattle. The winds seemed to be the worst she could remember. This was the first time they had taken the shingles. Good, heavy, hand-hewn cypress, they weren't ready by twenty years to give way. The sugar cane would be flat. They'd have to grind right away to save it, fully ripe or no. Old Jo would have to grind—

Sport darted into the kitchen, his spotted coat blown into bristles. He whimpered. He was always afraid in a storm. She set the plate of cornbread on the floor and he gulped it, his ribs heaving in and out. He came back to her, quivering. She listened for sounds from old Jo. She could hear nothing in the tumult, in any case. He could be screaming for his rations and she didn't believe she could hear him. She opened the kitchen door to get fresh water and the wind lifted it from its make-shift leather hinges as if it were a leaf in her hands. She was all but taken with it as it hopped across the sand. The gale sucked her from the house. She pulled herself back into the confused open kitchen by great effort.

She washed her face and hands in the basin of water she had used last night. She put on her drawers and dress and made a lunge across the breezeway. She couldn't remember ever having to fight so hard across it before. The winds were bad last year, but not like this. Her lean body bent almost at right angles. The last few feet she was lying on the wind, like a swimmer in the water. Her strong bony arms pulled her along. She sprawled breathless into the main cabin. Old

Jo still lay in the sagging bed, his red lips open, his breath rising and falling heavily, too deep in sleep to hear if the roof should fall about his head. Well, she thought, leave him lay.

"I better be fixin' to clean up whilst he's quiet-like."

She was filled with the need of putting the place in order. She brushed the rough pine floor with a broom-grass sweep. The dirt was largely loose sand which she brushed into the fireplace. She picked up old Jo's wide-brimmed black felt Sunday hat from the floor and hung it on a wooden peg on the back of the door. A bunch of yellow daisies from the flat-woods was dead in a coffee can on the bare deal table. She threw them in the fireplace and poured the fetid water on the tin cans of plants on the two window-sills. They were wild ferns and jasmine vines. The rain was beating down too fiercely to set them out in it. Her porch plants in lard pails were being whipped to pieces. Two of them had been knocked over and rolled toward the wall of the cabin, where they thumped and banged. She moved Jo's twelve-gauge shotgun to a corner by the clay fireplace. There was nothing more in the room to put in order. There was indeed nothing more there.

Florry made a rush back to the kitchen. The gale lifted her across the breezeway as though great hands lay under her armpits. Moved by an obscure instinct, she overhauled her wardrobe. She patched the brown calico dress and took a few stitches in her other shift and drawers. The cockroaches had been at her ancient coat. She shook it out and brushed off the summer's white mould.

The young Cracker arrived in the lull of the gale. Like a bird-dog guided by scent, he came direct to the gaping rear door, where he stood hesitant. The rain washed through him from shirt to shoes. He pushed the dripping brown hair back from his eyes.

"I mean, hit's a toad-strangler of a rain," he proffered.

"I mean!" she agreed.

"Reckon your daddy'll keer, me a-follerin' this-a-way?"

"Reckon he mought." She looked him fearlessly in the face. "Hit don't worry me none. You couldn't get you no wetter," she said, "iffen you'll go yonder to the wood-pile and fetch me some lighter'd and a handful o' them turpentine chips, I kin make you a fire to dry you out a leetle."

"I shore will do thet thing."

He dragged back the door and propped it against the opening. The wet wood steamed and popped in the iron stove. Sport stretched luxuriously closer, groaned in his sleep. The smell of the man, the smell of his garments, filled the room in rich waves. Florry sat by him on the pallet.

"Them ole winds didn't waste no time a-comin'," he said.

"Seems like us mought o' brought 'em in, like, a-talkin' of 'em."

He shook his head.

"They was ready to come. I seed the signs."

She nodded.

"I kin feel them things a-comin', a long ways. I could kind o' feel you comin'," she added gravely.

"I studied some you mought be proud to see me."

They listened to the irregular surge of the rain on the shingles. The wind seemed to be picking up again. The chinaberry crackled ominously in its old brittle limbs. The boughs flailed the roof. The storm enclosed them, boxed them in together. It was inconceivable that they had ever been afraid, that they had ever been separate.

"My name be Martin," he said. "I be called mostly Mart."

"Mart," she repeated.

"You want to go off with me?" he asked.

She was not startled. She had sensed its coming, as she had sensed the coming of the gale. It was strangely a part of the storm. It was part of the inevitable change.

"I reckon."

"Git your things. Le's go."

She made a bundle of her belongings.

"What about your daddy?"

"I reckon we'd best jes' ease out. He mought raise up a turrible fuss iffen he knowed I was goin'."

"Kin you write out a letter to leave fer him?" he asked.

"No. I cain't write ary word."

"Nor me," he said.

"I got my name writ out," she suggested eagerly. "Thet Yankee at the sawmill done printed it fer me on a white paper."

"I got no use fer a Yankee," he said dubiously. "Reckon it's writ wrong, or means so'thin' else?"

"I don't think. The range rider kin read, and he said it done spelled 'Florry.' Iffen I leaves it where Pappy kin find it, he'll know it means I done went."

She withdrew the slip from her bundle and smoothed it out on the kitchen table, weighting a corner with the coffee-pot. Mart nodded approvingly. On the step he hesitated.

"Hit don't seem right, takin' you off in sech a wind and rain."

"Hit'll mebbe fair off to-morrer. Hit don't mean nothin' to me, gittin' wetted. Us got to git in the clare whilst Pappy's likkered."

"Thet's right. Us got to git in the clare."

As he turned to replace the door behind them she darted back and set a pan of rain water on the floor for the hound.

"A thirsty animal be so pitee-full," she explained.

The second circle of the hurricane was on them as they fought their way through the piney-woods, riotous with the hissing of pine boughs. The northwest section of the State was only getting the fringe of the great upheaval.

"On the east coast," Mart cried in her ear, "they tell the palmeeters gits flatted smack to the ground, times, like, and over in the scrub they sa-ays the trees 'll done be bended."

They stopped for breath under the comparative shelter of an over-hanging live oak.

"There wa'n't much there," Florry told him, "but I be ashamed, I plumb forgot to git you some rations."

"Don't let it worry you none," he assured her. "I don't eat regular. You got you a long whiles to git me rations in."

His lean brown face was bright with his smile. He grew serious.

"I figgered on gittin' over to Levy County and gittin' us a parson there, mebbe to-night."

She grew anxious.

"Don't it cost money to git married?"

"I reckon."

The subject was delicate.

"Mart, I ain't got me a dime. Have you got ary cash-money?"

Turning his back to the driving rain he emptied his pockets. There were two paper dollars and some loose silver that proved too complicated to count accurately. It did not seem to total another dollar.

"Mart, I ain't too pertickler about standin' up in front of a parson. Hit's sort of a church-business, like, and I don't know nothin' abouten sech things. We could fix to git married some time when you got plenty cash-money."

"I 'druther you'd feel right about it, Florry. Hit shore don't make no difference to me. When we was sittin' together last night with the air so hot and restless-like, I studied then on you and me goin' off. All two of us so kind o' rabbity, like your daddy said. I shore gits lonesome, times, like."

She nodded.

"I shore feels all right about it. I'll be your ole woman and you'll be my ole man, right on. I ain't no leetle mite skeered."

He put one hand on her bony shoulder and peered fiercely at her.

"Leave me tell you," he said, "I ain't studyin' none on quittin' you, no ways, no how—no time—"

They made a new venture into the storm, working always south.

"Iffen we don't make Levy County," he called, "I knows a 'shiner'll put us up. He done borried my gun and I got to git it one time. Mought as well git it now. These high winds this time o' yare is like to last three, four days."

"And then them fine, blue days," she shrilled back. "Jest breezy-like and clare, and no red-bugs or skeeters."

"Thet's right."

They fought on.

"I shore feels mean about leavin' ole Sport," she said. "Pappy'll starve him to death."

"Ain't he a good rabbit dog? Cain't he ketch hisself rabbits?"

"I reckon." She pondered. "I reckon ole Sport kin make out on rabbits."

II

Florry said, "A marsh sho' am the crawlin'est thing."

She was a little homesick for the high piney-woods. The marsh seemed low, as though she were living in a sink-hole. The air was oppressive. The October night when Mart had brought her to the cabin in the lake-side hammock had startled her by its manner of falling. She had been looking idly at the streamers of salmon and gold in the sky above the close-set live oaks and sweet gums. Mart was repairing the sagging square shutters, so that they might be swung to, like casements, and hooked from the inside. The night air must be kept out, for it bred fever.

Suddenly, it was twilight, and in a moment, dark.

A brief panic touched her. The day was gone, and she was unable to see its going. All her life she had watched the sun burn fire-red through the long-leafed pines; drop inch by inch to a discernible oblivion. The close vegetation of the hammock turned the good sun unfriendly, a little treacherous.

She felt, at first, insecure in her footing. The piney-woods had been firm and dry. Following Mart along the marsh, in and out of the swamp, bare-footed, the soft muck gave alarmingly under her. Here and there Mart pointed out a bubbling seepage and warned her of quick-sands. She remembered the cypress swamp, where she had moved carelessly in brown water shoulder-deep. To her memory it had been surer, but she decided that a stranger might have been uneasy there. The cypress waters, amber-brown like a fine clear coffee, had been open. There was no undergrowth. The marsh edge, the very waters of the lake, until they were a half-mile out, were a thick, slippery mass of lilies, marsh-grass and coon-tail. Frogs splashed everywhere. Small fish darted in and out, brushing cool against her bare legs. Water moccasins slid like oil into the water.

In a brief time she grew intimate with the marsh Mart called a prairie. The marsh gave them their living, for in the cool autumn crispness Mart began to trap along its borders. The lake in front, the jungle hammock behind, enclosed them in what came to be a delightful safety. Rations were still scanty at times. Hunger was not new to her belly, but it was on the whole rather unimportant. A deep peace filled her. Sights and sounds and odors moved her as they had not done before. They were all associated with the pleasure of knowing that Mart was there; never more than a mile or two away.

Mart came in with a soft-shell cooter. The turtle was new to her.

It had come out of the marsh to lay its eggs.

"Mart, a thing with a ugly ole haid like thet un, shore ain't fitten to eat."

"I mean, shore is!" he insisted. "Hit's a sight sweeter meat then chicken."

"Hain't it a fishy ole thing?"

"Nary a mite. Go on, Florry, cook it. We ain't had no meat in so long."

He drew out the long leathery neck with a hooked wire and cut off the sharp-beaked head with his knife. He separated the neck and four thick legs deftly from the shell, trimmed off sections of the translucent border, flexible like thin gristle. The female was full of yellow fat and still yellower eggs, some of them encased in paper-white shells, ready for depositing in a hole in the sand.

"Coons and skunks is wild fer cooter eggs," Mart told her. "You kin allus tell when it's fixin' to come a rain, for a cooter's got sense enough to lay jest aforehand, so's the rain'll wash out her tracks and fool the varmints."

"Be cooter eggs fitten fer folks to eat?" she inquired distastefully.

"I mean! And here's a question my daddy allus asked and nobody couldn't never answer. Why do a soft-shell cooter lay a hard-shelled egg, and a hard-shell cooter lay a soft-shelled egg?"

She marvelled duly at the conundrum without an answer.

Mart cut out the heart and the plump liver. The heart continued to beat in its regular rhythm. Florry's eyes widened and Mart laughed silently at her astonishment.

"Jest you wait 'twel you sees what happens in the pan," he chuckled.

In the face of her ignorance, he did the cooking. He boned the pieces of pink and white meat, dipped them in meal and salt, and fried them in the black iron Dutch oven that was their only cooking utensil. The lid vibrated alarmingly and in a few moments he lifted it to show her the heart still beating in the bubbling grease and the muscles of the legs twitching spasmodically.

"Mart," she protested, "dogged iffen I wants to eat anything you has to stand on the lid to keep it from poppin' out o' the pan."

But when the meat was fried golden brown and tender, she agreed, after a first cautious nibbling, that it was plumb noble rations. The left-over pieces, with the shell-less eggs, Mart made into a stew the next day, with a little wild garlic for seasoning. The shell-eggs he boiled in salted water.

"They ain't done thu," Florry declared.

Again he could laugh at her, for the white of a turtle egg will not solidify, not though it be boiled a week and a day. The eggs were slightly musty in flavor, but fine eating. After that, Florry too kept watch for cooters, come on shore to lay. She delighted to poke one with a stick and watch the flat brown pancake body lunge viciously forward and the evil, snake-like head snap futilely. She had to be fast on her feet to run one down before it could reach water ahead of her; quick to flip it on its back.

The cabin, with trapping rights, Mart rented for a percentage of his hides. They went hungry often through December while he acquired a few skins and reinvested them in more traps. A dozen traps were needed to show a profit. Game was plentiful. Cool weather had set in early and the pelts were thick and glossy. In the hammock were 'coons and 'possums, skunks, red foxes and gray, and an occasional wild-cat. In the marsh were mink and a few otters. The mink were of poor quality, but the rare otters were large and fine.

Mart showed Florry an otter slide on a slight clay elevation. She wanted to come and watch the play the next moonlit night. Mart said she was foolish and set his largest trap at the top of the slide. A big trap with inch-long teeth was necessary to hold an otter in the full of his strength.

"Hit don't seem right," Florry said, "a-settin' trapses where a critter plays."

But he trapped one very seldom, and when he received thirty dollars for a fine pelt, in January, she forgot her scruples. That was a powerful piece of cash money for a varmint hide.

They ate 'coon meat only when there was no 'possum. It had a strong taste. Yet a 'coon was clean and a 'possum was a scavenger. But when a 'possum was fat with persimmons and pilfered pinders, his flesh was more succulent than the juiciest young pork. Sometimes

Florry cut one in pieces and smothered it in the Dutch oven. Mart's favorite way was to turn it on a spit over a bed of live-oak coals.

Florry's only quarrel with Mart was over his taking of the skunks. He insisted on bringing them home to skin, as he did the other varmints. Florry swore she was half ill from the stench. Mart seemed indifferent to the odor. In the early spring he found a young skunk caught only by a toe. It enlisted his interest by showing no fear. He brought it home alive. Old nigger Will showed him how to remove the musk. It was a clean and pleasing pet. Florry was beginning to feel a warm surge of pleasure in its white-striped little black form, when a wild-cat made off with it one night, defenseless without its primordial weapon.

She went every morning with Mart to visit the traps. He did the skinning alone, but she helped him tack the hides to cure on the wall of the cabin, or stretch them over shingles. They must be stretched good and tight. All through the winter the unpainted gray walls were covered with drying skins.

Mart had the owner of the cabin send his name to fur houses in New York, St. Louis and New Orleans. Catalogues and post-cards came to him in the mail. The fat prices offered were read off to him. He sent bundles of hides to the various houses, but the money-order sums he received back did not tally with what had been offered. He found he did better at the fur dealer's in Manitopy. He had to walk some miles, fording a shallow river, or rent or borrow old Will's gray mule for the trip. It paid to do it.

Florry walked with him one crisp bright day in February and bought herself some red-spotted percale for a dress. There were many people walking up and down the streets. Some of them stared at her. They looked at her split coarse shoes, her ragged dress and caught-back soft hair. She was panicked, distraught, like a squirrel caught in a room. She could scarcely make the store-keeper in the village dry-goods store understand what she wanted. She picked the material at random, took her change and bundle blindly and scrambled out into the open. Her one thought was to meet Mart quickly and get away again. He came out of the fur dealer's dusty little building to find her crouched against the wall like a frightened dog. He was very little more comfortable than she. He bought snuff and pipe tobacco and they walked home without speaking. She did not go with him again.

It was hard for Mart to keep within boundaries at his trapping. A warm spell in February, with the sun beating down on the chilled hammock ground until it began to steam, brought out an old male rattlesnake for a few days. He caught or frightened away most of the small game in the immediate territory. One week of a diamondback meant a deserted area. Mart looked longingly at the adjacent cultivated field, a Yankee's forty acres. There had been watermelons and corn there through the summer, pinders and chufas through the fall. 'Coons roamed the plot, seeking expectantly the next fresh crop of vegetables.

"Hit won't do no harm jest to work the edge, like," he decided.

Gradually he put his traps further and further in, until one day the Yankee caught him at it and ordered him off.

"Them 'coons shore'll eat up yore next crop," Mart found courage to protest.

"That's my business. I'll do my trapping if I want any done."

"How about trappin' on shares, like?"

The landowner looked distastefully at the youth's brown, unshaven face, at his bare feet with the torn blue breeches turned up above them.

"No. Now get out and stay out."

Mart walked into the cabin with his clear brown eyes clouded with hate. He threw his traps on the bare pine floor.

"Hit don't hurt no man to talk polite," he grieved. "Not a man thet owns forty good turned acres, free and clare, it don't hurt him none."

He breathed heavily with the shock of the encounter.

"Florry," he burst out, "the dogged biggety bastard done sended me off liken I was a nigger!"

She sorrowed with him. He brooded long over it, bitterly.

Cold weather sent the rattler back to his hole and the game returned. Just before the season closed Mart filled his traps several times. Tempted, he trapped on for another ten days, but word came through nigger Will that the game warden was making the rounds.

He hustled his hides to Manitopy. He oiled his traps and put them away in a lean-to back of the cabin.

They had enough money, buried in a glass fruit jar, to last them until trapping should open again the coming November. The fur dealer figured it out for Mart.

Spring was a delicious thing, invested with a new benevolence. It was unreal to have money under the porch. Unreal, to be able to idle all day. No work to do. Grits to cook once or twice a day, white bacon to crisp to otter-brown, fresh-caught fish to fry, late sour oranges to gather from the three wild trees in the hammock, so long hung as to be almost sweetened. No cypress logs, tearing at the muscles. No eddying brown water under the arm-pits. No old Jo.

The lake turned musical over-night. The frogs piped up and down the length of their small silver song. Hoot owls over the marsh boomed with the vibrancy of a bass viol. The cranes and loons cried dissonant, not quite inharmonious. On a night of full moon in April, Mart and Florry sat on the cabin steps. The palms were silver in the moonlight. The new growth of the oaks was white as candles. An odor grew in the stillness, sweeter than breath could endure. It seeped across the marsh like a fog of perfume. It filled the hammock. Yellow jasmine was in bloom.

When in the brightness a mockingbird began to sing, Florry put out her hand to Mart with a quick, awkward motion. In the richness of her content, it was vital to her to touch him. It was as though she needed to be sure that he was there. Deep-sunk in her was a wisdom warning her that beauty was impermanent—safety was not secure—the money under the steps would not be always there. Nothing good stayed forever.

The mosquitoes were bad that summer. They slept with the cabin doors closed, the square shutters swung tight. They sweltered on hot nights on the pine bedstead Mart had hewn by hand and laced back and forth with strips of hide. In July the rains stopped. Both night and day were suffocating.

Florry awoke once at dawn, scarcely able to breathe. In the dim gray light she could see the sweat glistening on Mart's face. She slipped outside for air. Swarms of mosquitoes settled on her like a cloud. When she came down with chills and fever a few weeks later she knew of course that it was because she had exposed herself to the night's vapors.

The ordinary chills, the ordinary fever, striking her like a knife every afternoon, were matters of no particular alarm. Mart went to Manitopy for a bottle of Black Draught. She took it and grew worse. When she came to be out of her head for hours at a time, fighting phantoms, and wasted down to even more skeleton-like a figure than when Mart had taken her away, he lost all caution. He went to Manitopy for the doctor and paid willingly the staggering fee of thirty dollars for the half-dozen trips and the medicine. The iron and quinine took hold and by mid-September Florry was strong again.

The trapping money, however, was gone. The careful allotment of three dollars a week for rations and snuff and tobacco had been useless.

III

The September gales were not so fierce as usual. Summer moved into autumn without harshness. After the first quick distress, Mart and Florry were not disturbed that the money jar was empty. Mart made an alliance with the lake fishermen. They would not be forced to move on. Florry began to plant flowers and ferns and cuttings in tomato cans.

The fishermen were willing to have Mart join them on the terms by which they sold their fish to the storekeeper in the nearest village. He understood that hook and line fishing was only a pretense. A man could not be sure of catching half a dozen fish a day. They trapped and seined. This was illegal. The danger depended on who was county sheriff and who was the local game warden. At present Cap'n Tack, the storekeeper, who peddled the fish to city markets, had the game warden taken care of. A change of wardens would mean trouble.

Cap'n Tack owned the two seines, a hundred and fifty yards in length. They were worth a couple of hundred dollars. He provided the material for traps, a fine-meshed wire which the fishermen made into barrel-like traps with a funnel in each end. The fish swam idly into one of the funnels and seemed content to make no great effort to escape. But if a trap were left unemptied on the lake bottom too long, the fish swam out again. Cap'n Tack allowed the fishermen five cents a pound. He sold the fish for twelve. This did not seem disproportionate to the men. They could not buy seines themselves. When an unfriendly warden pulled up their traps and destroyed them, Cap'n Tack bought new ones.

Mart was allowed fishing shares in a rowboat with the half-grown son of fisherman Boyter. He took Florry with him, half expecting to be told to send her home. No one seemed to object. Most of the time she paddled the boat, leaving Mart and young Boyter free to pull up and empty the traps.

The lake never lost its charm for her. They reached it by way of Crab Creek, two miles of winding channel to the lake. The Creek was a dark, lovely dream leading to the bright open of another world. The hammock pressed close on either side. Sometimes the rowboat scraped against cypress knees. Sometimes the moss-hung boughs of a live oak brushed like hands across it.

The channel was always sweet of odor. In season the jasmine perfumed it, the waxy white magnolias and the smaller blossoms of the sweet bay. In the rare intervals when there was no bloom, the clean smell of pines filled the Creek, or the rank reptilian richness of the marsh. The Creek was always alive with birds. Blue and gray cranes took fright slowly. Often white egrets sat without moving as the boat slid by. In a great dead hickory lived a pair of bald-headed eagles, crying weirdly on moonlit nights. Ahead of the boat the coots took off like clumsy seaplanes, threshing the water with their feet long before the incompetent wings lifted the dark bodies into the air.

The channel passed between rows of tall cat-tails just before it reached open water. The lake came before Florry suddenly. Each time, into the open, she felt its unreality, as though she were transfixed in space. It was of the blue-ness of space. A mile out from shore it was so solitary— The roar of a bull 'gator was like thunder in the heart of solitude. The gray and green and red of the distant hammock merged to form the semblance of tall cliffs, like prehistoric walls. The palms topped them like shaggy heads, far away. The blue sky was illimitable. Except for the rain-like rush of the coots and the dip of the paddle, the lake was a blue pool of silence.

The boat moved here and there about the bonnet patches, in and out among the floating tussocks. It was often difficult to locate the traps. Mart marked the spot where a trap had been dropped into the water, by beating the lily pads with the oar, cutting the edges of the thick green leaves. But time and wind and worms had a trick, too, of eating off the edges. He often groped futilely with a pole with a nail in the end.

When a trap contained many pounds of live fish, it was heavy lifting. It loomed large over the side of the boat and Mart and the boy tugged and toiled to get it in and open the small wire door to empty out the contents. They trapped much stuff for which they had no use, mudfish, eels and jacks. Sometimes Mart took the jackfish in to nigger Will. The jackfish flesh was white and sweet, but only a nigger had the patience to pick out the endless fine bones.

Their main catch was big-mouthed bass, which they knew as trout, perch and bream. There was a brief closed season, but they managed to slip out now and then at night. Cap'n Tack could always sell the catch as coming from Lake George, where there were no restrictions.

Old man Boyter said, "A man cain't stop makin' hisself a livin' jest a-cause the law be meddlesome."

The seining must be done at night. Hauling in the heavy nets was too lengthy a process to risk by daylight. Trapping by day, the movements of strange boats could be watched.

In March Cap'n Tack got drunk and talked freely in the wrong house. The friendly game warden was deposed. Zeke Teeter, from the village, was named in his place. It was not dreamed of that he would attempt to interfere with the local fishing faction. He took his authority seriously. He not only found and destroyed twenty traps his first week, but he began to lie in wait for the fishermen along the shore.

Mart's boat lay alongside that of old man Boyter. They were emptying their traps leisurely when the sudden *put-put* of an out-board motor exploded and Zeke bore down on them. Old Boyter dropped the incriminating traps overboard not so much with dis-cretion as with astonishment. Zeke cut off his motor and faced them a little sheepishly.

"Iffen Mart yere didn't have his wife along, you Zeke you, I shore would git you told!" old Boyter sputtered. "Sneakin' up thet-a-way on fellers you was raised with!"

"I don't keer," Zeke insisted, "I'm inforcin' the law on this lake."

"Well, you go do yer inforcin' some'eres else. You don't belong to be inforcin' it on me."

Zeke withdrew before the old Cracker's wrath, but war was declared. It was agreed that with Zeke acting up it would be just as well to fish the traps by night and avoid trouble. When a campfire was observed of nights on Black Island, opinion was divided as to whether Willy Butler, recently escaped from the penitentiary at Raiford, was in hiding, or whether Zeke was fool enough to be lying there. Strong spiritual necessity alone would put a man in that jungle nest of rattlesnakes.

Old Boyter said, "Hit must be Willy. Zeke knowed there was a nine-foot shed of a rattler seed there lately. A man wants to be on Black Island bad, to risk them things."

But the inhabitant of Black Island proved to be Zeke, set on ingratiating himself with the county authorities by bringing in the lake's offenders.

Trapping by night, Mart refused to let Florry go with him. During a hot spell in April, young Boyter came down one afternoon with an early attack of fever. Mart set out alone that night, paddling softly to the bonnet patch where he had half a dozen traps. There was a murky half-moon. A water turkey, disturbed, flew off with a clatter of wings. Frogs splashed into the water from the lily pads.

As he reached for a bonnet to act as anchor, a boat moved in on him from either side. Quick hands in the darkness turned his boat over. He flailed wildly in the deep water. The two boats moved silently away. He thrashed about, trying to reach his rowboat. Rifle shots flicked across his head. One grazed his knuckles as he put a hand on his boat. He let go and swam in the opposite direction with a strong dog-paddle that was the only stroke he knew. He caught the drift of voices.

"Serve him dogged right iffen he do git drownded."

It was the voice of old man Boyter, in ambush since early morning. Mart understood that alone, he had been mistaken for warden

Zeke. He raised his voice in a Hulloo, declaring himself. After an astonished pause, the two boats came to him. Old Boyter told it in the village as a prodigious joke. It came in due time to Zeke's ears. He was frightened. If they had caught him, he would surely have drowned. He let them alone most of the summer, until his courage oozed back in him, like sap rising again in a tree.

Mart lied to Florry. Some private knowledge of him told her when he came in at dawn that things had gone wrong. She looked at his blood-caked hand.

"A plumb acceedent," he said, and washed it carelessly.

"Hit ain't neither," she said shrewdly. "Did Zeke git you?"

He shook his head.

She had a basic fear of treachery.

"Mart, Boyter and them ain't turned on you?"

"No. Now Florry, don't git worrit up over nothin'. They ain't nary thing the matter."

She could get no further satisfaction. In her isolation from the village life, five miles away, the tale did not reach her.

After a summer of brooding inactivity, Zeke took heart to go after the fishermen. He had a sullen nature, and long pondering through the hot dog days finally inflamed him. He appeared on the lake recklessly, day and night, with an obtrusive shotgun. He had been taunted here and derided there. Cohorts of the fishing faction laughed at him openly. His own friends advised him that it was a job for a man from another part of the county.

Cap'n Tack decided to end the matter once and for all. He drew out his several hundreds of dollars in postal savings and invested in a fast little motorboat for the use of the seiners. Old man Boyter planned the campaign. His headquarters were in the Pocket, a lake-cove deep-indented in the hammock on the north shore. No one could slip in unobserved. Cap'n Tack and old Boyter decided to concentrate. The fishermen gathered in all the traps and piled them high in the Pocket. They would not leave them in the lake for Zeke to pick off, like a chicken-hawk picking off biddies. All the men were assigned to a few boats, and intensive seining was done openly, in the daytime. They dared Zeke to trouble them.

In the unbearable, sultry days of early September Zeke foamed at the mouth. His motor followed the big new one around and around the lake. When old Boyter was through for the day, he shot in to the Pocket, and Zeke, frenzied though he might be, kept out.

The first day of the September gales lashed the lake into the peculiar fury of inland waters. It was impossible to venture out more than a few yards from shore. The wind was followed by a tropical deluge of rain that obscured both water and land. It was agreed by the fishermen that Zeke in his cowardice would be sitting safe by his light-wood hearth fire. They left the Pocket and went home to their own.

"Mart," said Florry, after the rain had lifted, "ain't thet smoke yonder in the Pocket?"

Zeke had gone in by land and made one gigantic bonfire of traps, seines, rowboats and the new motor-boat.

"You buzzards should of knowed better," Cap'n Tack said mildly. "You should of had you some watchment. I'm thu with fishin'. I got no cash money to start you off agin. Go git you a job fer hoe-hands."

IV

Rations had been regular the year Mart fished with Boyter. When a fishing week was lean, Cap'n Tack let them have grits and white bacon and water-ground meal just the same. With plenty of fish and wild mustard greens, they had lived well. Mis' Boyter had a scrub milch cow and sometimes sent Florry a can of clabber-milk. Blackberries were plentiful that summer, and huckleberries and blueberries, for the piney-woods had not been burned over. Long, sweet paw-paws were ripe in August. Florry's lean frame took on a few pounds of flesh. The malaria did not return and her golden-tanned cheeks were like sun-ripened guavas. Her quick squirrel eyes were clear and bright.

Well-nourished, strong, conception took place within her. It was strangely fortuitous. Neither was amorous of nature. Passion for her seized the man as briefly, if as necessitously, as flames that lick the turpentine pines when forest fire moves through. The meagre delights of her sparse body were no more to him than the pleasures of a drink or two of the hot, raw 'shine old Boyter sometimes passed around. If they were together, side by side of pleasant nights on the stoop of the cabin, it was usually comfort enough.

"A young un won't make no pertickler diff'rence, I reckon," Mart said.

He was driven to finding work not so much with conscience toward the coming child, as because, with credit stopped at Cap'n Tack's and Florry on short rations once more, she dropped back rapidly to her old gauntness. She made no complaints. If the growing belly pinched her with hunger, she borrowed a little of Mart's snuff to lip. That satisfied for the time. If it had not been for Cap'n Tack's sardonic injunction to the fishermen to take jobs as hoe-hands, it would perhaps never have occurred to Mart to hire out to another man. He was not of a breed that took to work for others.

He had been thinking over his problem when the Yankee came to him. The man did not seem to recognize Mart as the trapper of two years before, whom he had ordered off his forty acres. Crackers, like niggers, looked much alike to his complacency. The Yankee did not get along well with the negro help. The other unemployed white men had all refused him. His last tenant farmer, a negro, had walked off. He needed a man to live on his place and work his orange grove. He could not pay an inexperienced man very much—four dollars a week, his house, and land to garden for himself.

Mart's impulse was to send the man about his business. Florry's lean face with the quick, wild-animal eyes flashed before him. He accepted the job. He was depressed as he told Florry what he had done. She was in a fiercer panic at the thought of living close to another house; close to Yankees. But a canniness for the child moved her, and she found courage to follow Mart to the dirty tenant house in the orange grove.

The negro family had left the house a sty. The Yankee owner had not troubled himself to determine its condition. In her bare, clean life it was Florry's first experience with filth. She found refuge from her unhappiness the first week in scouring the place from end to end. She ran down cockroaches one by one. The sagging walls were crudely papered by former occupants with newspapers and magazine pages, glued to the wall with a gummy paste made of flour and water. Spiders and roaches were thickly nested behind them. Mart made her a new shucks scrub, dried corn husks inserted in holes in a block of wood, the handle set in at a convenient angle. She took satisfaction in its thick wet swish on floors and walls.

"I kin hear you a-scrubbin' t'other end o' the lot," Mart said.

The Yankee home was occupied from September to May. Cap'n himself was mean and miserly, but his family, headed by a young wife, made holiday through the winter. There was a constant coming and going of high-voiced people. The front gate was just within range from Florry's sagging front porch. Carefully concealed, she watched brightly dressed women get out of automobiles and walk up the path, shrieking with pleasure. The Cracker speech was soft as velvet, low as the rush of running branch water. The foreign voices were a constant alarm.

Florry kept out of sight whenever possible. The sulphur well that supplied the tenant house was a hundred yards away. When she went for water, a pail in either hand, her graceful tread stiffened self-consciously into rigidity. When one of Cap'n's family appeared on the distant side porch facing the tenant house, she darted inside.

The Yankee walked over one day and called them both out of the house.

"Wonder if your missus will take on our washing?" he asked Mart. "I'd expect to pay her extra, of course."

In his first week Mart had learned there were many things the Yankee did not know. He forgave him much for his ignorance. He stifled from expression the hot wave that swept over him.

He wanted to say, "No white woman don't ask another white woman to wash her dirty clothes fer her nor to carry her slops, neither. 'Course, fer a favor, like, a woman'll do most ary thing fer a woman in trouble, sick-a-bed. Or fer her own kin-folks."

He dared not. He shook his head. The Yankee shrugged his shoulders and walked away.

"Hit shore will be a pain, tryin' to work fer thet catbird," Mart said.

"I mean!" Florry agreed. "Hit'll be a pain right on."

Florry marvelled that Mart was able to go out among strangers and talk up to them. It distressed him, but he could force himself to it. He hated the grove work, not because it was hard, but because it was unfamiliar. He could not seem to learn fast enough to please the owner. When he was pruning, the Yankee constantly complained.

As a matter of course, Mart got out his traps, cleaned them up and set them at the far edge of the hammock grove near the lake edge. The Yankee's cow stepped in one and lamed herself a little. The Yankee recognized Mart. He raged just short of firing him. He would not have him trapping on his land and on his time. Mart pointed out that he was up at his traps before dawn. That made no difference.

But the fur money, sheer profit, was too tempting. Mart slipped closer to the lake and set his traps where the Yankee would not find them. Cap'n smelled the hides drying in the tenant house. He railed constantly. Mart's revolt was no more than held in leash.

"Florry, I swear me an' some Yankee's goin' to git mixed up some day," he confided to her. "I jest got no use fer one."

"I knows how you feels," she said. "I gits the same feelin', times."

"After the young un gits borned," he said hopefully, "mebbe we kin git out."

They decided against having a doctor. The last experience had been too financially disastrous. Nigger Will told them his old woman had helped birth many a child. She was better at bringing chillens than any white doctor. It seemed reasonable. It did not occur to them even to mention the matter to Cap'n or his wife. Old black Martha slipped in to stay with Florry when she began to have spells of faintness. She stayed in the house and no one knew she was there. Cap'n would perhaps not have permitted it. The old negress nursed Florry with a kindness that was like warm sun.

"You sho' is po'ly, chile," she said, disturbed, "po'ly as a snake. You wants to eat good and flesh up. You time 'bout come."

"Hit shore don't seem long enough," Florry puzzled.

"Mebbe you's to be took a little soon. Chile," she asked suspiciously, "you isn't done anything to git rid of it?"

Indeed she had not.

"Tha's right." The old woman sighed, relieved. "These days so many ladies don' want they chillen. I's raised all my gal chillens to live right and mind they manners wid de men. But I'se often tole 'em, 'Iffen one o' you does do wrong, now mind, iffen you does, and gits you'se'f in a way you hadn't oughta—why, you be lady enough to bring the chile into the worl'!' "

The child was born on a chill evening in January. The temperature had hung just above freezing all the dank and cloudy day. The Yankee kept Mart hauling wood, to fire the grove at night if necessary. At dusk a changing wind brought that rare phenomenon, a Florida snow. It hissed on the cypress shingles like a shower of pine needles. It blew in under the eaves of the flimsy tenant house and lay in scattered white flakes on the cold floor. Martha had a roaring fire on the hearth in the bedroom, but the other room was bleak and cold. Mart came in after dark. The temperature was still just thirty-two. They would not need to fire. He noticed the light fluff at his feet.

"What you spilt, Marthy," he asked wearily, "meal or salt?"

Weighted as she was with the announcing of his son's birth, she smiled at him.

"Snow new to you, son, ain't it? You don' know its ways. Dat snow on the flo'. Fust snow I'se seed in thutty year. Done come in thu the eaves. Snow's a searchin' thing. Searches in thu the eaves and thu the cracks. You got you a boy-chile, Mist' Mart, but he puny. Po' li'l Mis' Florry too scrambly-scrawny. The chile cain' live too long. You look at that snow good, boy. Snow be's like sorrow—hit searches people out."

The puny boy-child lived all spring and most of the summer. Florry could have been almost content if Mart were not like a wildcat sullen in a cage. Mart hated the grove, but she loved it. Trees were gentle. The sounds they made were lovely sounds. The susurrus of the palms, the sibilance of the pines, the roar and rush of great winds through the oaks and magnolias, were the only music she had known. A holly tree, shining with glossy leaf-points, with green or red berries alive like eyes, was to her a bright friend. When a tree ripped and crashed in a storm, its death was pitiful, like that of an animal. Anywhere among trees she would be at home.

She had known wild oranges. The green richness of the cultivated grove was new to her. There was rhythm to the hexagonal planting, so that whichever way she looked, the trees made straight and marching rows. When the golden globes of fruit were picked, unharmed after the snow, it was as though bright lamps had been turned out around her.

The grove was in bloom when she was first able to sit out on the porch with the baby in her arms. The oranges and tangerines, the spicier grapefruit, the wild-rose-like bloom of the thorny trifoliata, drenched the world with their sweetness. The scent was more powerful at night. As soon as the sun withdrew its dryness, the bloom sent its odor into every nook and cranny of the air. It was inescapable. Still weak and dizzy, for weeks she dropped off to sleep at night, drowning in perfumed waters.

The jasmine was too far away in the hammock for more than a breath to reach her. It was tantalizing to get only a whiff of it. Compensation came in May. A magnolia sixty feet tall shaded the tenant house. It was covered from top to bottom with tall white candles that burst wide into dazzling glories, opening from the top down, like a Christmas tree being slowly lighted. The blossoming was leisurely. The great white blooms were above her head for weeks. Then the white petals began to drop down and turn russet on the ground. The yellow stamens fell. The huge green leaves, brown-faced, drifted down with a soft rattling on the roof. In summer, the white candles shone red. Tall red cones were thick with glistening seeds and the birds rustled in and out among the branches.

The Yankee complained about Mart's clothing. He wanted his hired man to look trim, like a servant. Mart had three sets of blue pin-check pants and blue denim shirts. He changed twice a week. There was no use, he said, in changing every day when he was wet with sweat an hour after he had begun to work. In his brown face and hands and arms, his bare golden chest, in his blue work-clothes, he was like a patch of good loamy soil covered with a mat of blue flowers. He had the smell of earth, with man-sweat and mule-sweat over it.

He handled the mules well. It was one thing Cap'n could not criticise. The negro ahead of him had almost ruined them. He had beaten them about the head, so that it took Mart weeks to make them stand for bridling. Slowly, easily, he gentled the team until they were as amenable as oxen. Cap'n was pleased. When Mart had such a way with the animals, when he was so handy at repairing tools and harness, the Yankee could not understand why he didn't get the hang of the grove work better. Why, when a task was done, he didn't come for further instructions, but went straying off with his wife in the nearby hammock or down to the lake. There was something about him the Yankee could not control, could not quite put his finger on, to make discipline take hold. He was like an old bird-dog, that, when you are not paying attention, goes pattering off, hunting for himself.

Mart had to wear boots at his work. He was in and out among brambles, over the evil cruelty of sand-spurs, in danger of stepping on rattlers and moccasins. He needed their protection, although they chafed his feet and heated his ankles. Cap'n had started him off with an old pair of his own. As Mart saw them wearing out, he tried to save a little each week to send off to the mail-order house for a new pair, but he could not get enough ahead. He had felt obliged to give old Martha five dollars, although she had professed herself willing to help out for nothing. A white man ought to pay a nigger. He had to buy unbleached muslin for sheets and towels and underclothing for Florry and the baby. The baby choked and gagged a great deal and he bought a bottle of colic medicine once a week.

His toes were out of the boots. Cap'n looked at them and laughed.

"Those look like nigger-shoes, Mart," he said. "Tell you what I'll do. I've decided to put in spring beans. If you'll stick by the crop and not go prowling off half the time, I'll stand treat for a new pair of boots."

They made good money on the beans. Mart forced himself to nurse the crop, doing long hours of working and hoeing he felt a nigger should be helping with. He felt some little interest in the rich, quick growth.

"I mean, we made beans," he said proudly to Florry.

Nothing more was said about the boots. The soles were loose. He tied them to the uppers with binder twine, but they continued to flap under him. He decided to speak.

"How abouten them bootses, Cap'n?"

"Oh, yes." The man frowned impatiently.

Matt saw him glancing over the mail-order catalogue. When the boots came, Mart could see they were so flimsy they would not last the summer.

"Them soles is paper," Florry said. "One good wettin', like, 'll jest turn 'em to mush."

Mart drew them on and laced them slowly.

Florry went bare-footed always. When she kept out of the sand-spurs, the light sand was soft under her feet. Her toes were spread wide. Her thin muscular legs were strong and straight. Even when she carried the baby lightly on one shoulder, she walked erect and firm. Her gait had the quality of a trot, so that she seemed to be walking with determination to some certain place.

One afternoon nigger Will stopped by with a post-card addressed to Mart that had been left in his box. It had a picture of a red house and some printing on it. Mart had gone to town with the mules to get feed. He would not be back before dark. It might be something very important. She lipped a little of Mart's snuff and pondered. Better find out. She tucked the baby over one hip, his little wizened head hanging down, and walked over to the side porch of the Yankee house. The Yankee woman saw her coming on her first call. There was something a little alarming in the fixed swing forward, the steady Indian-like tread of the lean body.

Florry said "Evenin'," and thrust out the card.

The woman turned it over, uncomprehending.

"Will you please to read hit?" Florry explained.

The card was an advertisement from a raw fur house. It quoted probable prices for the coming year. Florry listened gravely as the woman read aloud the list of wanted skins.

"Be thet all?"

"The name of the firm and their address."

"Read hit."

Then, "I thanks you." The girl reached out to take the card again and turned to go.

The Yankee woman had a strange feeling of bafflement.

"How are you getting along?" she called to the straight thin back.

Florry half turned.

"Purty good." Then, truthfully, "Nothin' extry."

"Is your house comfortable?"

"Hit'll do, now I got it cleant." She paused. "The antses is bad. I cain't keep the antses out o' Mart's breakfast."

She paced back to the tenant house.

The Yankee's family went north early and in late May he followed. The mosquitoes in the grove were very bad. The tall grass, which Cap'n did not want cut until August, bred them. They came up from the marsh in high-singing droves. All night they sounded like a high-pitched machine. The few old screens in the tenant house were gaping with rusty holes. Florry stuffed the door-cracks with paper and tried to block the paneless windows. But the old house itself was settling, wall from wall, beam from beam, timber from timber. They could see sunlight through the gaps by day and stars by night. They kept smudges going in the yard, but there was no keeping out the mosquitoes.

Mart bought enough mosquito netting to make a little canopy for the baby's pallet on the floor. It would cost more than he could get together to buy enough for their own bed. Cap'n sent him his wages each week by mail, and by the time he bought rations and colic medicine and snuff and tobacco, there was nothing left. He got young Boyter to write him a letter to the Yankee asking for money for a mosquito bar. The Yankee did not answer for a long time. At last he wrote, reminding Mart that he'd never had a mosquito bar in his life and if he indulged him now Mart would expect too much of him.

"First thing you know, Mart," the Cap'n wrote, "your wife'll be wanting running water in the tenant house."

That day Florry saw Mart walking around and around the Yankee house.

"What you lookin' fer?" she asked.

"To see kin I git in. Iffen I kin git in, us'll shore sleep on the floor in there. Us'd jest go in and out to sleep, like, and not do no harm."

But he could not make an entrance without ripping off a door or a barred shutter. Florry was not willing to have him do that.

The mosquitoes were of a feverless variety, but sleeping under covers on the hottest nights to keep away from them, weakened her. She had only begun to be strong again. She had recurrent fever attacks. Her milk grew scant and poor. The under-sized baby had grown very little. It was blue-white in color. The unhappy small face scarcely seemed to recognize the mother. Even its cry was not a lusty one. It whimpered and fretted. In mid-August, Florry was feverish for a week. One morning the baby turned blue, then black, and merely failed to draw again the thread-like breath that all along had been its dubious hold on life.

They had half-expected it to go, but there seemed nothing to do about it. Old Martha had seen it once or twice, had exclaimed "Do, Jesus!" and made it some herb tea. She had assured them there would be no raising it. But when it was actually gone, a dull knife turned over in Florry's vitals and for long months would not give her rest. She stroked the small cold body over and over while Mart sat in a corner, whittling a stick unhappily.

"Well," he said at last, "mought as well go make it a grave."

They had never given it a name. It seemed always too indefinite to need one.

"Dig it where the varmints and the hogs won't git to root it," Florry called.

They decided that back of the house, in the grove itself, would be safest. Mart knocked together a small pine box—it was astonishing how little room the body took—and lined a hole in the sand with bricks from the chimney of an old smoke-house. Florry washed the baby and dressed it in clean clothes. She trembled a little as Mart piled bricks on top of the box and threw in three safe feet of sand. He stood back and looked at her questioningly.

"No need fer to mark it," she said faintly from pale lips. "Cap'n mought not like it and then we'd have fer to dig it up agin."

She dug up some petunias from the Yankee garden and planted them above the pine box.

"They'll seed theirselves, even after the land be ploughed," she explained.

With the rainy season, the vegetation swelled overnight. The red-top was man-high. Dog-fennel lined the roadway like a green wall. The coffee-weed was thick in the pasture lot. Mart mowed hay and stored it in the barn. The citrus sized up rapidly. By late August the grapefruit boughs were bending to the ground. The slim branches of the orange trees were freighted with more than they could bear.

Cap'n came down early in September, just after the high winds had come and gone. Whole sections of trees lay cracked to the ground, a quarter of the crop flat and ruined. Growth conditions had made the limbs too brittle for the immense crop of fruit. He called down frenzied imprecations on Mart's head.

"You Cracker fool," he finished, "when you saw what was happening, why didn't you prop the limbs?"

"I allus reckoned trees could take care of theirselves," Mart said quietly. "I allus thought trees jest takened what comed."

He went to Florry gravely.

"Florry, I got a bait of it. I got eight dollars. Le's us go down to the Gulf and see kin us make us a livin' salt-water fishin'."

She hesitated, her thought on the petunias growing purple and white.

"Hit suits me," she said at last.

They packed their few belongings in cardboard cartons and set off on foot before dawn. The sunrise came on them as they crossed the prairie west of the lake. The waters were rosy and the white egrets circling up from the reeds were tinged with pink. The man and woman cut a little north through a stretch of flat-woods.

"Hit's done been a sorree-full yare," Florry said. "I shore be proud to git shet of it."

V

The wharves of the last westerly town dropped slowly behind Mart and Florry in the rowboat. They set out down-stream at the full of the tide. Mart had bought a sunken boat for fifty cents, raised it and repaired it. It was too make-shift for fishing, but it would take them down the tidal river to the Gulf.

Mart rowed with jerking, powerful strokes. The current was with him, yet it was hard going until the tide should turn. Florry sat in the bow, the high afternoon sun in her face, the river dazzling, flipping its spray over her now and then. The oppression of the town, of the ever-alarming contact with folk, lifted from her. She felt light-headed. She hummed a little, "Jacob's Ladder."

A rush of vital force surged through the man. The escape from the town, the push of the river-current toward new ground, the sound of Florry's small, sweet voice, stirred him. He picked up the song from her.

> "Jacob's ladder's steep an' ta-all—
> *When I lay my burden down!*
> If you try to climb, you boun' to fa-all—
> *When I lay my burden down!*"

There was no burden. The sorrowful year was over and forgotten. The tide was turning. Tide and wind and current were taking them down the river to a deep sea thick with fish. Florry dipped her fingers in the river water and tasted it. It was brackish. They were coming closer to the Gulf.

The river lost its identity reluctantly. Its banks followed it far into deep water. Toward the mouth, the banks broke up into a succession of shell and limestone islands, where Spanish bayonets fought with palmettos for a footing. Cactus showed among the undercover. Cedars twisted and writhed and grew sturdy on bare rock. Florry studied them, like new strange faces.

They reached Alligator Joe's island at sunset. Alligator Joe's name was now only legend, but the high ground of his island home was fine camping. Some other fisherman had been ahead of them, for a camp was built. It was a good sign, warming, like a welcome.

Pine saplings had been nailed together to make the bare framework of a shack. The peaked ridge poles were thatched with palmetto fans. The walls were of palmetto fans, closely overlapping, nailed by the stems upside down, so that no amount of wind or rain could beat through them. Square openings were left for doors and windows. The builder had not camped there long and he was not long gone. The palm fronds had scarcely finished drying. Their gold was still steaked with sage-green. They rustled constantly, for there was a breeze as steady as the Trades. Day and night, the whole shelter murmured as though it were alive. Small gray lizards were already at home in the thatched rustling roof. The rustling of the palmetto fans seemed the voice of the river—the current, the marsh grass and the tides made audible.

Mart made sure his patched boat was safely moored. Florry cooked bacon and grits with a Gulf sunset riotous beyond her. It was fine to see the sun go down again. She waved a thin arm about her.

"Be this Mexico, Mart?"

"Not yit. This be Floridy right on." He pointed. "Yonder, jest out o' sight, down to the end o' the river, be the Mexico Gulf. But Mexico's a furrin country. It be way yonder, across them miles o' waters."

She stared, trying to make out the Gulf, and maybe Mexico.

Sleep was sweeter here than she had ever known it. The cool salt air cradled her. The dried palm leaves' whispering overlaid the suck of the tidal water on the shingle. She roused up once at night, only to breathe deeply of the sibilant peace, to touch Mart gently, to make sure he too was there.

He intended to start off the next morning alone. Florry begged to go.

"They'll be a bait o' times when I won't git to go, when you gits to fishin'," she pleaded. "Hit'll make me feel acquainted-like to go when I kin."

It was not the folk she longed to know, but the river. The small islands were entities with whom she would become familiar. The river seemed uninhabited as they rowed to the mouth. After the wild-life of the piney-woods and the populous hammock, it was strange to see no live things moving, no birds, no small furry faces turned to her for a brief moment. After she had lived on these back-waters of the Gulf for a few weeks, she would know where to look for the few shy birds and animals. She began to distinguish a human habitation here and one there. There was only a handful of families on the lower river. Houses on islands were often sunk out of sight among palms and cedars. Others lay up the winding salt creeks and were not visible from the river.

The chief of the small fishing clan lived up Channel Creek. The creek was no more than a canal connecting two of the tidal rivers. It wound interminably, like a tangled thread. The reeds and grasses were so high, the route so tortuous, that the boat seemed to be making no headway, land-bound and forgotten between flexible green walls.

Cap'n Harper's house sat back in the marsh, reared high on stilts. A swaying plank walk sagged for two hundred yards from wharf to house. The wharf was over an old oyster bed. It was low tide and the shells showed thick in gray muck. A sizable fishing dory with a sturdy in-board motor rocked at the wharf.

Mart was not gone long. He came back to report that Harper had just come in from a night's fishing, sleepy and a little ugly.

"He didn't shore enough promise I could fish fer him," Mart said. "He done tole me to come along an' fish with 'em a whiles, thouten no shares nor wages, to see could I git the hang of it."

"You kin git the hang of it all right," Florry said confidently. "You done good on the lake. You belong to do good at it."

"Hit's all right," Mart said. "He's got to see does my ways suit his ways. He'll likely give me fish and us is got rations fer a while and a leetle more cash money. They ain't no hurry."

"No, they ain't no hurry," Florry agreed comfortably. "No use a-hurryin' no ways, no time."

When Cap'n Harper told them they might stay, Mart rowed Florry in and out among the islands at the mouth of the river, house-hunting. They had their choice of several deserted houses. The island they chose was on the incurve of a cove. High, it still was not visible either from Gulf or river. Florry liked the feeling that no one could look in. No human life came within her vision, but there would be enough to see. Far out she could glimpse the fishing boats. There was never anything else. The steamship lanes were further west.

Her house had once been very fine. It was two tall stories of weathered gray cypress, with gables and chimneys. A broad-columned porch spread across the front, sagging at the corners. There were endless gaunt rooms. The house was sunk almost out of sight in oleanders, shell-pink and fragrant. The gray-limbed bushes grew taller than the roof. The flowers dropped their soft pink petals all over the gray shingles.

Straggling in exotic borders on either side of the path leading to the water, were venerable fig trees. Fat yellow figs hung dripping, like great beads of amber. Some had dried on the trees without falling and these were withered and honey-sweet. Mart and Florry stuffed greedily, hungry for fruit and for sweets.

Florry found a sunken pot of geraniums alive by the back steps. Some one had lived here recently. After they had been in the house a few days, the aromatic smoke of cedar logs curling up from the chimneys, an immense black and brown house-cat emerged from the woods. It skirmished about, watching for hours from the thicket. It had been deserted by the planter of geraniums three years before. It was sleek and fat. Small game was plentiful on the island. When Florry called, it yowled distressingly, as though it would have her understand that it longed, but feared, to come. At last it came to her. It kneaded its paws and beat its head against her.

Harper told them they had chosen a good place. It was even possible, he said, to grow a little garden in the few inches of top-soil above the shell and limestone. The droppings of the live oaks, the cedars, the bay, the palms, and the myrtle, had finally created a layer of humus.

"And they ain't nothin' there to watch out fer," he encouraged them, "exscusin' rattlesnakes. Tell ye what I'll do fer ye. Give ye a leetle shoat fum my new litter. Too many fer the ole sow to nuss. When it grows up it'll clare the place of ary snakeses."

Florry made a pet of the small runty black porker. Wherever she went, the pig trotted behind her, and the immense cat with its tail high in the air.

"I's got me enough comp'ny now to suit anybody," she said.

She raised the pig on cornmeal and water. For lack of milk it did not grow. The blue cedar berries had fallen to the ground, and the live oak acorns. It soon found these and made a living for itself. It slept with the cat under the house. Florry felt as though she had lived here a long time. Now and then she saw a familiar bird, a red-bird in a cedar, a gray or white crane in the marsh. Marsh chickens, smaller than quail, walked daintily on the shore of the island, picking up food in the mucky sand. Mart made spring traps and they caught all they wanted to eat. On the uninhabited islands lived water-turkeys and pelicans and black nigger-geese. The gulls came and went.

Florry thought the army of fiddler crabs at the edge of the water came to know her. When she walked among them they no more than moved out of her way. When Mart came, they rushed to the grasses or into the water. Their movement made a hissing sound, like the rustle of a stiff silk. Sometimes units of them paused, and lifted their single large claws up and down in rhythm. They became an orchestra, sawing without sound on invisible fiddles.

Mart felt a free man again. Taking the fisherman's orders was quite different from laboring under the alien cloud of the Yankee's displeasure. Harper turned over to him a flat-bottomed skiff and a gill net black with age. Mart would have to fish on shares. He had no money for equipment. Even the old rotten net was worth twenty dollars. Mart was assigned Cully Johnson for partner. Cully was a tall youngster of fourteen. The Johnsons were kin to the Harpers. As on the inland lake, Mart was being utilized to help a younger member of the tribe add to the family profits. He was an outsider and he was willing to take what was left. If fishing was good over any considerable length of time, even on third shares he could save up for a net and boat of his own.

He found Cully a good partner. His slim brown body was almost as strong as a man's. He could pull in his share of the great net, loaded with fish, as competently as Mart. There was a trick to paying out the net over the stern of the dory, a trick to handling it in again. On land, it must be spread just so on parallel poles to dry. There was a trick to fanning it—gathering it in folds so that it would dry evenly. It was a matter of rhythm. One man alone could handle the net when he knew his business. Often, when the fish were running, Mart took the boat out alone by night and Cully took it out by day.

After Mart came to feel sure of himself, he took Florry with him when he fished alone. It frightened her a little to pass from the river into the open Gulf. The mouth of the river was an end and a beginning. At a certain point it could be said, "Here, now, the river is alive." A few yards more, past the last wind-beaten cedar, there was no longer any river. There was only the blue horizon. As it is told of a departing life, the river was not ended, but was become part of the sea's infinity.

More than ever at night, the boat was precipitated into a dark eternity of waters. The last receding islands loomed immense. The black heads of the palms towered above the earth. The water was black as Death itself. On moonlit nights the world was silver. Flecks of silver dotted the Gulf as far as Florry could see, so thick, so glittering, it seemed she could gather them by handfuls. The islands behind were silver, and the palm trees. The fish in the net flashed silver.

It was slow work finding the net on dark nights, finding the way in and out of the river. All the work seemed slowed up by a great dark hand. Fishing, day or night, was on the low tide. The boats went from one to four miles out in the Gulf, fishing the flats. Sinkers along the bottom edge, corks along the top, made the long straight nets stand like wavy fences down in the water. In calm weather they stood as erect as though posts held them. The fish swam into them and were hooked by the gills in the small meshes.

The usual catch was an assortment of sheephead, drum, mullet, butter-fish, needle-fish, sea-trout and mackerel in season. Stingarees were a nuisance in the nets. Mart's only complaint was over the painful necessity of removing them. The fat blue crabs were a pest. They tore the nets as if they were feasting on a choice bait. Mart and Florry could not believe it when Harper told them there were people who ate the meat.

"Them spidery things! They cain't be fitten!"

When she was alone, Florry sometimes took the old patched boat and rowed in and out among the winding cross channels. On each inhabited island nets were hung in the sun to dry, cream-colored, tan, gray or black, according to their time of service. Once a porpoise leaped and blew in the river near her. Cully told her a porpoise often came in and fished out the river.

"Reckon this un was jest traipsin' around, a-visitin'," she decided.

She and Cully were good friends. He was solemn and mature. She saved him pieces of corn pone and let him talk to her of what he thought the world was like. The world to him, as to her, was the rest of Florida. He took her one day to visit his family. Florry sat painfully on the steps of their shack and answered questions. The place was dirtier than hers and the family seemed poorer. So many children ate up a heap of rations.

Cully took her around the Johnson island to show her the sights. He led her with pride to a small rectangle planted with vines, with a rickety cross at one end.

"This be Bob's grave," he said. "He got kilt daid by the pneumony."

Florry found herself suddenly weak.

"I got me a grave," she told the boy. "Back yonder to the east I burrit me a young un, a leetle ole baby no bigger'n a cat."

No bigger than a cat, but the old pain was on her.

In the late winter Mart fell into a great piece of luck. Harper's son Eph was away, 'shining, and Mart was given a place in the motor dory for a week, on fourth shares. They ran unexpectedly into huge schools of pompano. The pompano ran for two days and two nights. The slim silvery fish announced their coming half a mile away, raising the surface of the water visibly. The boat was ready for them. The motor was fast enough to throw out one end of the net and circle around the fish, ahead of them. They must be taken quickly, or they were gone forever.

The dory took in hundreds of pounds in the forty-eight hours of the aristocrats' passing. Pompano had been scarce for two years. They brought twenty-five cents a pound at the wholesale market. The whole town came to the dock to see the dory unloaded. Boats put out feverishly from all the tidal rivers, but the pompano had passed.

Mart's share of the big catch was enough to buy the net and rowboat he was using. He was now the capitalist. When Cully fished alone, Mart had half of the catch coming to him. His own catches need no longer be shared. Until early summer he prospered.

Then the fish, of a sudden, simply were not there any more. It was astonishing. Mart and the Johnsons and the Harpers lamented together.

"There ain't ary fish by day nor there ain't ary fish by night."

"Hit's them pound-net fishermen north up the Gulf," Harper decided. "Them big ole pound-nets, with traps in the bottoms, they jest scoops in everything. 'Course, them fellers has the right to make a livin', but it shore makes fishin' sorry down here."

Two or three days often passed without a catch. Times were lean. The fish house paid three cents a pound. When twenty pounds of fish at this price had to be divided two or three ways, there was not enough to buy grits and meal. Mart and Florry were better off than the rest. Johnson said that if fishing did not soon improve, he would have to give away his two younger boys. He could not feed them.

The Johnsons and the Harpers had no gardens on their bare soil.

They could no longer buy greens. They grew sallow from the steady diet of fish and corn pone. Mart had planted a garden back of the old house, where the soil was thickest on the shell. Florry tended it. They had collards and cow-peas and pole beans. They shared as far as they could.

Harper fought the fish house to get four cents a pound.

"This is Saturday," the dealer answered. "If I have to pay you men four cents to-day, the fish house won't open Monday morning."

Fishing would pick up. They knew that. The fish would run again. It was a question of how long they could all hold out.

Perhaps despair made them careless. Harper must have known the signs. He had seen too many September gales drive in across the wide sweep of the Gulf not to know a fuzzykin. In the daytime that mass of black cloud, low-slung in the south, full of wind and thunder, was ominous but not alarming. Time could be gauged, and distance. At night, seeing that certain sign of high winds, Harper should have had the small fleet put in at once.

Wind in the south—and thunder. Especially at night. This time of year. They should have scurried in ahead of it, hell-bent. The first squall caught them from the south-west with the saved-up force of hundreds of miles. The black rain came in sheets. The gale seemed to pile half the Gulf into the two shore-miles. Harper in the motor dory set out for the mouth of the river, calling to the slow boats to follow. Cully wanted to pull an oar but Mart took both.

"This be work fer a man, son."

Mart had not known such effort was in him. He was fighting the Gulf of Mexico, with all the winds of the Caribbean behind it. The wind seemed to move him at a terrific speed, but the waves caught up with him and spat venomously into the flat boat. Cully bailed fiercely. His young wet face, white in the night, showed the sternness of an old man.

Harper looked back. A long flash of lightning showed the small boats foundering. Ten men bailing could not have kept them from swamping. One by one they filled to the gunwales. Harper put back and took the men on board the dory. The dory put into Channel Creek and the men slept that night on the floor of Harper's house.

The next morning, although the gale still raged, he took them to their own islands, working through the maze of cross channels.

Florry had not slept. She had been afraid for Mart for the first time. On the north point of the island she had tried to build a signal fire as a guide for him. It was useless in the roaring downpour. The west end of the porch roof had blown in. She could not have slept long in the din, at best, but whenever she lay down and dozed a moment, she was awakened sharply by a black vision of Mart swimming in the Gulf—then going under. When he landed at the foot of the path below the fig trees, like a phantom in the rain, it was as though he had come back to her from the bottom of the Gulf. She stirred up the fire on the hearth and moved the coffee pot closer to the coals.

"Leetle boats done gone," he said after he had eaten.

"Nets, too?"

"I mean. They was in the boats."

"Won't they float, with all them big corks?"

"Mought. But they'll likely git all tangled up with the boats. Iffen they does float, they'll dreeft on beyant where we could ketch 'em at."

They sat silently by the window with rags stuffed in the broken panes and watched the palm trees bend and the cedars flatten. The Gulf seas thrust long gray claws up the river. The wind roared steadily. Florry shook the sound of it off impatiently. Wind had once been only wind, a good sound in the trees. Now it was something else. A brief moment of resentment against it came over her, like the rare flickers of hate she had once felt for old Jo. Her thoughts came and went uncertainly in her mind, like fish far down in a dark pool.

The high tide was due in mid-afternoon. As the time approached, the Gulf seas swelled to appalling size. The gale was at its height. At three o'clock, with a great heaving and rolling, there came in what is still known on the river as the high salt tide. It writhed up the river like a sea-serpent, in and out among the islands, and flooded land that had never been submerged before.

"Mart," Florry asked, "us kin stay here right on? You kin fish with Harper's? Or the fish-house mebbe credit you on a boat and net?"

Yet she knew the answer. He shook his head.

"Reckon not. Harper cain't no more'n use his own kin-folks in the dory. He's studyin' on movin' down to Cedar Key. Fishin's some better there. The fish-house feller was down to Harper's this mornin'. He's closin' up."

"Us could ketch enough fish fer our own rations," she persisted, "and us got a fine garden comin' on. I seed yestiddy the beans was up, and the cabbage jest comin' thu."

They walked back to the kitchen window to look out at the garden on the low slope back of the house. The high salt tide was on it. The new green sprouts just had their heads above the sucking water. To-morrow the brine would have made black wisps of them. Florry's lips twitched.

"Hit'll be plumb destroyed," she whispered.

Mart looked at her curiously.

"Ain't you gittin' to be a froggy leetle ole thing?" he said. "I got me good plans. Eph Harper ain't been gittin' but seventy-five cents a gallon fer his 'shine. He sa-ays there be good money in 'shine in the right place. He's fixin' to clare out fer Putnam County and start him a still in the scrub. He sa-ays Putnam County likker do bring a fine price, two, three dollars a gallon, if you takes time to run it thu twicet, so it ain't raw. He sa-ays he'd as leave carry me with him as not. I ain't never been in the scrub, but I allus hankered to see it. You'd like it fine."

She pondered.

"Would I jest leave the ole cat here, like I found it?"

"Shore. You cain't tote cats fum one county to another. They allus runs away."

"Kin I carry the pig?"

"Eph wouldn't want no pig messin' up his flivver. Tell you, Florry, we kin barbecue the pig jest afore we starts and carry it fer rations."

"Mart, dogged iffen I could eat ary mouthful o' thet leetle ole critter. The longer I chawed it, the bigger it'd git."

He frowned.

"Hit's take it thet-a-way or leave it, one. Pigs was meant fer eatin'. Hit'll git et some 'eres else iffen we don't eat it. Hit'll jest be pork when it's daid. Now don't you take on, Florry," he soothed her. "Hit don't make no special difference where we goes nor what we does.

Rations be rations, right on. Hit don't make no difference where we squats to eat 'em."

"No," she agreed, reassured. "Hit don't make a mite o' difference, do it?"

VI

The river folk who knew Eph Harper could have warned Mart, if they would, that a year with Eph would be a year of treachery. In the vast silence of the scrub country, with cabins in clearings sometimes twenty miles apart, it would seem that there would be no evil for Eph to do; that two men would cleave together, in any case, for safety. But it was in the man to betray.

Florry was in no danger from him, although at first the three shared a shack in the high region above the Ocklawaha. When Mart's back was turned and Eph made tentative overtures, she did not even understand. He watched her afterward with wonder in his square yellow face, squatting on his haunches, his long arms dangling from his bunchy body, like a frustrated ape. Besides, a different kind of treachery was to his taste. He was a born informer.

Their location was good for liquor making. Eph set up his still on the bank of the river, so deep in saw palmettos that the approach of federal invaders would be announced far off by the loud rattling of the sharp fronds. They were equally safe from the river side. The clear cold river water ran swift under over-hanging buttonwoods and cypresses and swamp laurel. It eddied against banks riotous with wild scarlet hibiscus and white spider lilies.

The shack they lived in was high above, up a steep bank where cooters came to lay their eggs, and skunks and 'coons to dig them out and eat them. The variegated growth along the river gave way, back of the shack, to dense virgin scrub. Scrub oaks and pines stood as close as matches in a box, match-lean, with myrtle and rosemary at their feet. The scrub was always shadowy, except where the deep sand roads cut through in blazing sunlight. Areas that had been burned over by forest fires were shadeless; the scrub naked and exposed, marked only by the tracks of deer and wild-cat.

Mart had not begun to understand that Eph was using him for

the mean work necessary; for the carrying of water; for the setting of the mash; for the long watches when the mash was slow to heat, slow to cook, and the drops of water-clear liquor at the end of the copper coil dripped as slowly as turpentine sap.

Eph found him a red-lipped girl in the scrub, a half-wild thing who would always mate here and there like any rabbit. He moved with her into another shack, five miles down the river, and left Mart with most of the labor of the still. Florry began to help in Eph's place. The arrangement seemed logical enough. Eph owned the still. He had to take what shelter he could find for his girl, and five miles was quite a distance to come to light a fire under the boiler. Eph took the finished liquor to a house some miles east of Palatka, where it was picked up for further relay.

Until uneasiness at being dependent on Eph came over them, Mart and Florry were contented here. No human voices came to startle them. Eph brought their rations with him on his return trips. The shack was on higher ground than they had ever known and it was a treat to look across the river valley to blue and purple distant ridges. The scrub was soft underfoot as a carpet. Pine needles and oak leaves, undisturbed on white sand, gave beneath their bare feet with a delicious yielding. There was game again to eat; wild turkeys, rabbits and 'possums, and young squirrels fat on hickory nuts and pine mast.

Mart shot a 'coon in the early spring. There came snuffling up to the dead body a young one, no more than a few days old. It let Mart pick it up as if it were a baby. When he took it home to Florry it nestled in her lap snugly, then cried to be fed. The creature seemed half-human. The palms of the fore-paws were marked like a child's. When it tussled with Florry a little roughly, and she slapped it in punishment, it ran off whimpering with an un-animal distress. She added canned milk to her list of rations for Eph to bring. It ate the things they ate, more daintily than they.

It washed its face and hands in the wash basin, like a well-trained child. It snuggled as soft in Florry's arms as the baby she had lost. Its pointed face with the black mask peered into hers with a recognizable affection. It liked to sit on her shoulder and rub its soft nose and long pointed hands across her neck. They kept it in the house at night, for fear of wild-cats. It fought persistently to sleep next to Florry in the bed, but Mart found this distasteful.

"Hit's a cute leetle feller," he admitted, "but hit's a varmint right on."

Florry fixed a padded box for it on the floor beside the bed. When Mart was asleep it slipped stealthily under the cover on the edge and lay mouse-still all night, its enigmatic face close to hers on the moss pillow. At daybreak Florry put it in the box again, before Mart wakened. It looked up at him smugly when he arose.

When Mart and Florry went off into the scrub together, they taught it to stay at the house, driving it back with switches. It ran around and around the shack in protest, its longer hind legs giving it an awkward gallop. Then it reared up, its fore-paws in the air, and craned its neck after them. Occasionally it disappeared in the scrub for a few hours. They found they could not eat 'coon meat at all any more. There was enough of other meat, in any case, through the winter season. Twice they had the small black bear of the Florida scrub. The deer seemed scarce and wild.

Old-timers in the scrub said to Mart, "You cain't git no deer in the open season. Them hunters fum all over is a-stirrin' up the woods with their dogs an' their fuss an' their shootin'. They thinks it's a big thing, does a whole camp git 'em a deer. You jest wait 'til the law closes down. Closed season be open season fer us what lives here. The deer gits to be a plumb nuisance in the spring and sum-mer. You cain't make cow-peas, nary a crop, the deer be so crazy fer 'em. They'll lepp ary fence to git to 'em. You kin git all the deer you wants. You jest wait."

It was the venison that gave Eph away. He was ready to get rid of Mart. He had his market for his liquor, his price established. He was ready to move the still close to his own cabin, let his girl do some of the work, and collect the profits instead of sharing them.

Mart had been timorous about shooting deer out of season. The meat was more than they could use before it spoiled. Tales had reached him of the high fines imposed for out-of-season shooting. But in the first heat of May, Florry had not been well. She was languid, without appetite. They had had no fresh meat for some weeks. A young buck paused within range of Mart one afternoon. Before it could show its white scut and flash away, Mart had brought it down. He broiled the choice steaks over live-oak coals. Florry enjoyed it and ate plentifully. She thought it made her feel a little livelier.

The next morning, on his way down the river to help old man Bradson round up hogs, he carried a hindquarter of venison to Eph. He was pleased to bring such a fine gift to his friend. Eph took it with thanks. As later testimony brought out, he and the girl gorged on it that day and the next. Then Eph drove to Waleka, looked up the game warden and turned Mart up. Eph swore to an affidavit that to his personal knowledge one Martin had shot a buck deer on May the eighteenth.

The trial is still talked of. All over the scrub, through Marion and Putnam counties, one man says of another, "He's as good a neighbor as Eph Harper," and it is known at once what depths of treachery are implied.

The lawyer who had volunteered to defend Mart, questioned Eph's girl.

"How can you swear the meat was deer-meat? Venison is very similar to beef."

"Well," she hesitated, "I seed a deer-hair on hit."

The crowded court-room stirred.

A venerable Cracker announced audibly, "Dogged iffen thet ain't purty fine swearin'."

Before Mart was put on the stand, old man Bradson rose majestically in court.

"Somepun's jest come to me," he announced.

The judge rapped for silence.

"Thet affeedavit this yere Harper has sweared to, do I understand the date be May eighteenth of this yare?"

A hunter himself, the judge recognized the river patriarch. He looked at the document before him.

"Yes, Mr. Bradson. Do you wish to testify?"

"I shore do."

"Swear him—. Now then, Mr. Bradson?"

"I got me a Coca-Cola calendar in the kitchen an' I jest happened to be studyin' it this mornin'. Wa'n't the eighteenth a Sat-day?"

"It was."

"Well then, Jedge, I cain't swear I'd know deer-meat by a hair on hit, but I shore kin swear by God A'mighty thet on Sat'day, May the eighteenth, this man Martin was to my house the hull day. He come soon in the mornin' to he'p me round up some hogs an' he worked with me to good-dark. My wife done give him a bite o' supper, seein' as it were so late. He didn't have no gun nor no deer-meat, nor I didn't see no deer-hairs on him. He didn't shoot no gun on the way home, nor pick up no deer, fer I went home with him 'count o' bein' on my way to my son's house fer Sunday."

The record shows that the judge had to silence the roar of delight that shook the court-room. Eph's yellow face was white. Old Bradson's word was unimpeachable. Mart had indeed worked for him on that day. It was only a perfunctory matter for him to testify that he had no means of telling one day from another, but that if the date named on the papers was the date he had worked for Bradson, the papers lied. Eph had made the mistake of assuming that Mart had shot the deer the same morning that he brought him the meat. The case was dismissed.

It was known generally that Mart had shot a deer out of season. Eph's crime was greater. He had broken a frontier law more fundamental than the game rules. Yet Mart's safe return from the hands of the law was to Florry miraculous.

Because neither knew how to change the arrangement, the two men continued to 'shine together. It was their joint livelihood. Mart worked silently, watching Eph constantly for fear of attack. Eph was surly.

"He'd shore be proud to shoot me in the back, behint a clump o' palmeeters," Mart told Florry, "but he ain't got the chidlin's."

Chance probably played into Eph's hands, for he would not have planned to betray Mart at the expense of losing his still. It is certain that the federal men merely nosed out the still. Eph was heading for it when he saw the agents creeping toward the bank where the odor of the sour mash rose strong. Florry caught a glimpse of him running toward home. He did not warn Mart, as he might easily have done. Mart's only escape would have been the river. The agents hand-cuffed him and smashed the still. They allowed him to speak with Florry before they took him away.

"Git on outen here afore Eph gits to harm you," he told her. "Go work fer ole man Bradson whilst I be shut up. I'll come there fer you. Git Bradson to find out how long they puts me in fer. When the time's up, you be ready and us'll git back to the hammock where us fust come, when us went off together. I been studyin' on the way up the hill. Us'll go back to the hammock and go to trappin' agin, come winter."

He was gone.

When he came back on foot a month later, Florry was not at Bradson's. He found her still in the shack above the river, with the 'coon. She was gaunter than he had ever known her.

"I didn't aim to be with folks," she excused herself. "I had me yore gun and I felt safer-like here. I made me some box-traps and caught me rabbits, and I fished some. Eph ain't bothered me."

"Hit wa'n't right," he said slowly, "but it cain't be he'ped now. You ready? Le's go."

"Mart," she pleaded, "I don't aim to worry you none, but I shore would be proud to carry the 'coon with us."

The 'coon was half-grown and fat and heavy. Mart looked at it wearily. He was already tired.

"You be quare, Florry," he said. "I hates to refuse you, but dogged iffen I kin see ary sense to totin' a half-growed varmint."

"Hit's hard to leave so'thin' behint, ever'time we goes," she said patiently.

As they walked off, she looked back at the 'coon, sitting reared up on the cabin door-sill. As far as she could see behind her, its quizzical masked face was visible.

VII

Dust lay yellow on the palmetto scrub. The rattler coiled in its un-cooling shade was almost invisible. Florry's bare feet padded close to him. He lifted his head, weaving it somnolently. The whirr of his rattle was faint, like a far-off cacophony of dry castor-beans. He was indifferent to her passing, sluggish, an old snake weary in the September heat.

Her lean body was sweaty with carrying a bucket of drinking water from the spring-fed branch two miles away; two miles of hammock, whose undergrowth whipped her face and whose wild bamboo vines left bleeding trails across her arms and legs. Her sun-bleached hair clung wet on her forehead.

She pushed aside the gray curtain of Spanish moss that canopied the live oak beneath which she and Mart had made their camp, waiting for November. The long gray fingers gave such privacy to the clearing that the camp would scarcely be noticed from the clay road a hundred feet away. Three walls of a pine shack were still standing under the oak. The flooring was intact. The shingle roof, drooping like an old hat where the fourth wall was gone, gave a certain shelter. It would do until trapping began. Then they could rent the old cabin in the hammock.

Ordinarily Florry pulsed with vague pleasure whenever she stepped within the cool shade of the oak, but the shade to-day, as for the past weeks, was a dusky delusion. It was more stifling than the open glare of the sun. After putting the bucket of water on the shady side of the camp and laying a palmetto leaf over it, she dropped down on the clean sand carpeted with oak leaves, panting like a dog. The blood beat scalding in her throat and cheeks. It had been hot and dry too long, longer than folks could bear.

The creak of a hand-pump sounded across the road like a sea-gull's cry. If the people in the new house were Crackers, she could get water from their well, but they were Yankees. They made no offer and she did not ask. She was not anxious to remind them of the camp's existence, for she was not sure whether or not they owned the land. Yankees were queer. They put up signs and warned people off.

She peered through the moss. The Yankees' small boy and girl were rolling discarded automobile tires for hoops down the roadway. They were tanned to the golden-brown of ripe pears. They moved with a dancer's grace, lifting their small arms free from the shoulders, like bird wings.

She watched them with a dull hunger. They were tiring in the intense heat. She saw that their faces were crimson. If they were hers, she'd make them lie down while it was so hot. The children trotted in like hot and weary puppies. The boy turned and latched the wooden gate after him.

Florry thought, "Ain't it fine to have a gate an' a house with doors."

The only good house she had ever lived in had been old Jo's cabin in the piney-woods. Her mother's grandfather had built it and her mother's father had put a new shingle roof on it. The front door was soft gray cypress. The kitchen door was pine and it had blown off the hinges the day she went away with Mart. She had been glad to go. She hadn't minded the make-shift camps and cabins since, nor the storms that moved them on to other places. Nobody had anything to say about such things. Mart hadn't been treated right. But you couldn't help other folks' meanness.

She had minded leaving old Sport behind, and the cat and the 'coon, and butchering the pig for rations. She minded the puny baby lying on a Yankee's land, under a Yankee woman's petunias. It came to her that if Mart had stayed on the clearing, in old Jo's cabin that she had a right to, she would still have the hound, and it might be the baby. They had let their fear move them on.

Maybe, she thought, the winter's trapping would be good and they could buy them some land, free and clear; an acre or two from which they could not be driven by wind or circumstance. It would be fine to have Mart own a piece of ground, and a cabin with good doors to it. She lay motionless under the live oak, closing her eyes against the sand gnats. The summer had been so long. It had bothered Mart. She thought uneasily that he was late returning.

He was trading at Cap'n Tack's store in the village, four miles away. He had a string of perch and cat-fish he had caught in the lake. They came to sixty-six cents in trade. The storekeeper gave him a chunk of white bacon, five pounds of grits, a sack of meal and a can of Railroad snuff. Mart hesitated in the hot, dark store, odorous of rancid salt pork, of sour tobacco juice, of fish hummed above by swarms of flies. He wanted to ask some questions but the thick heat dulled his brain.

"This be September, eh?" he asked.

The storekeeper nodded.

"The tenth."

"How long 'twel the season gits opened?"

"End o' November."

Cap'n Tack had gone over to the law since the loss of his fishing equipment. He hoped to be appointed game warden this year.

"Plenty o' ducks flyin' over jest afore dark," he commented slyly. "Fixin' to do a leetle shootin'?"

"No," Mart said, "I done a piece o' trappin' a few miles fum here, afore I fished fer you. I got my trapses yistiddy fum the nigger I left 'em with. Jest fixin' to oil 'em an git 'em ready."

He wanted to reassure Cap'n Tack that he was a man with property and good for his bill.

"I sees. Col' drink afore you goes?"

A thought stirred in the storekeeper's shrewd brain. He lifted the lid of the ice-box. A wave of cold air washed over Mart's face. He was tempted.

"Shore would cool my gullet—"

He hated to get in debt another nickel. Cap'n Tack had already given him more than five dollars' credit. Storekeepers were smart that way. They worked your bill up, when a cold drink would feel so good. You thought, Only a nickel. There flashed across the weariness of his mind old Martha's chant—

> "Fi' cents in my pocket, ten cents on my bill.
> If I don't git no better, I'se boun' fo' Sugar Hill."

He smiled to himself.

"Reckon not to-day," he said.

The ice-box lid dropped down. He thought of asking for a chip of ice to suck, but he hated to. It was a nigger trick. If he was Cap'n Tack, a day like this, he'd lift that lid and just lie in that box, all through the heat of the day. He'd let the ice strike through him until his bones were cold.

When he set out down the road, the sun was at its zenith. It struck through the holes in his broad-brimmed straw hat. It made a golden inferno of the clay road under his calloused feet. It was an effort to keep a grip on the sack of rations and the strip of bear-grass on which he had kept three perch for Florry. His fingers prickled. The four miles were endless. Now and then he stopped by the side of the road to rest. He felt hotter than when he was in motion. Dry heat crawled over his body. He didn't believe he was sweating enough. It was always cooler when you could sweat.

He stepped off the road into the ditch to get out of the way of a truck he had seen gassing up in the village. The driver had been drinking cold pop at the gas station. Mart had noticed him fishing around for his favorite flavor in a great circular tank that held hundreds of pounds of ice and dozens of bottles. As the truck rattled past, the driver finished a final bottle and tossed it into the ditch. It lay at Mart's feet, still frosted, with a few mouthfuls of brown liquid bubbling in the bottom.

He picked it up, wiped the sand from the mouth and drained it thirstily. The last drops trickled down his parched throat in cold pinpoints of ecstasy. Ice made it feel that way. Warm pop was no better than sweetened water. He fondled the frigid glass of the bottle. He passed his dry lips over it. He laid it against his throat. Its coolness passed into him and the bottle became tepid. Only the concave bottom was cold and he slid it inside his shirt and back and forth across his belly. If he could choose between ice and 'shine, he would choose ice. Maybe not in the winter, but certainly now, in September, while it was so hot. He wished he had bought a cold dope of Cap'n Tack.

He remembered the look in the storekeeper's eyes. They had been talking about trapping. Suddenly the sweat started out of him. In a moment he was wet all over. The last thing in the world he should have mentioned was his traps. Cap'n Tack would take them away for his bill. He was always making off with some nigger's shotgun, or even his mule, and white men's too, when he could. He always took something that was worth several times the bill, but when you owed him money, what could you do?

Mart thought maybe he and Florry had better get out right away. The traps were all he had. If he lost those, there was nothing left.

Yet he knew no place to go, no good trapping place, where Cap'n Tack wouldn't hear about it and run him down. He'd heard the storekeeper was thick with the sheriff these days, doing low tricks together. No use having the law after him again. He was worn out now from those thirty days on the gang, road-building in the blistering summer sun. He'd been hot ever since, and tired.

As he turned off the road to the camp, he noticed his neighbor out working. He was painting his new house, slapping bright yellow paint on its fresh pine boarding. Sweat streamed down his face and arms. Now and then a drop spattered into his paint bucket. Mart laughed noiselessly.

"Paint! Yaller paint on fresh pine!"

Nothing was funnier than a Yankee coming down here with his money in the bank and trying to paint fresh pine. His fine paint would be flakes in the sand, this time next year. Nobody but a Yankee could help knowing that. Over his shoulder Mart saw the Yankee woman come out of the screen door with a pitcher of water. He could hear the ice in it clink against the glass. He had never wanted anything that didn't belong to him, but he couldn't help thinking how good it would be to have your old woman bring you ice water in the heat of the day; and when you were through your work, to sleep behind screens away from the sand flies and mosquitoes.

Florry sat up, hands on knees, as his familiar step crackled through the bone-dry under-brush. He placed the sack of groceries in a box nailed to a tree. Bull ants began at once to climb the trunk to wave their feelers about the sack of grits. He took off his hat, drew his faded blue sleeve across his damp face. He lifted the palmetto leaf over the drinking water, already lukewarm, dipped a rusty tin cup and drank again and again, his head thrown back. Drops of water fell crystal on the amber of his throat. He replaced the covering and laid the fish on it. He had cleaned them at the lake, because fish guts around the camp drew flies. He lay down with his head and shoulders against the trunk of the oak tree.

"Florry, I done played me the fool."

"How come?"

"I done let on to Cap'n Tack I had me my trapses here. He'll take 'em shore."

"Cain't you hide 'em gooder?"

"No use, now he know I got 'em."

"He mought not study none on takin' 'em. When kin us trap?"

"Us kin crowd the trappin' a mite. Iffen he don't bother me, 'bout a month fum now I'll set me a few trapses. Us kin hide the skins, like, 'twel I kin sell 'em."

"A month be four weeks, eh?" she mused.

She picked up Mart's pocket knife from the camp table and cut a straight length from the oak limb overhead. She began to cut notches, to make a calendar, so that if the moon wasn't clear, to show them, they could tell when a month had passed.

"Sunday, Monday, Chewsday, We'n'sday, Friday, Satiddy—"

That was one week. She began over again.

"Sunday—"

Mart closed his eyes.

"Hit's powerful hot," Florry said.

"Don't seem like I kin breathe. Don't seem like it's ever been so hot so long. Seems like it's plumb wore me out."

"Mebbe you got the fever," she suggested.

"Mought be. Don't seem like I kin stand it. Seems like the only thing'd cool me'd be lyin' deep down in water, some'eres, with chips o' ice floatin' around in it."

He drew his hat over his face for protection against any rays of the sun that might filter through the leaves as the afternoon wore on. Florry resumed her outstretched position near him. In the fevered coma of mid-afternoon there was no sound, neither of bird nor beast, neither of grass nor pine nor palmetto. The September heat smothered them all against her parched, unbreathing breast.

A car stopping in the road wakened them from their siesta. Two men were pushing their way in to the camp. Mart reared to his feet. Florry stepped behind the oak.

"Hit's them," he said.

Cap'n Tack lifted a hand in greeting.

"Howdy, Mart," he called jovially.

"Howdy."

The storekeeper leaned down casually to pick sandspurs from his pants.

"Mart, meet the sheriff."

The sheriff was a sallow fellow with thin yellow hands always open for chance fees. He did his profitable duty mournfully, as though the expense and trouble fell all upon his hunched shoulders.

"Howdy, Mart."

Mart's eyes moved up and down the man's frame, noting the uneasy gesture of the nervous fingers toward the ponderous revolver in the hip holster. He did not acknowledge the sheriff's greeting. He shifted his weight to lean one shoulder against the oak tree.

As though he were the host, Cap'n Tack waved toward the upturned boxes about the camp.

"Set down, Sheriff."

The officer eased himself to a seat.

"Nice camp you got here."

"Couldn't git you one no sorrier," Mart said.

The sheriff looked about him. He caught sight of Florry's dark head leaning forward around the oak, her bright alarmed eyes on him.

"How do, Ma'am. How you?"

She bobbed her head to him.

Cap'n Tack drew out his plug of tobacco and pared off a shaving. He held it out to the sheriff questioningly.

"Reckon I'll smoke a cigarette."

The officer passed his package. Mart hesitated and took one, lighting it quickly with his own match. Cap'n Tack worked up his chew. The cigarette smoke hung blue and heavy on the thick air. A buzzard wheeled in the hot sky. A hawk screamed from a nearby pine. Mart smoked thoughtfully, as though he were alone. The sheriff cleared his throat.

"Mart," he said, "I'm sorry to crowd you, but I reckon you'd best hand over your traps for your debt to Tack here. He says he's got no other way to collect."

"Thet ain't so. Soon's I kin git to trappin' I kin git ketched up." Mart spoke slowly, watching the end of his cigarette.

"I got no way o' knowin'," interrupted the storekeeper, "he ain't goin' to jest pick up an' go off, traps an' all."

"I ain't fixin' to go off."

"That's what he says." The storekeeper nodded suggestively to the officer, who nodded back.

Mart said flatly, "The trapses is wuth a sight more'n the bill."

"They don't bring nothin' when you sells 'em, Sheriff," Cap'n Tack insisted.

"That's right," the sheriff agreed gravely. He shook out a handkerchief and wiped his face.

"Tell you what I'll do for him," the storekeeper spoke amiably, slapping his knee. "I'll let him take back the loan of his traps come winter and trap for me on shares."

Mart stamped out his cigarette butt angrily.

"You jest a-figgered it out thet-a-way," he raged. "Dogged iffen I'll do it."

"Reckon you will."

The two men glanced at each other and moved in together toward him.

"You two pilferin' pole-cats—" He spat contemptuously.

"Look out how you talk to the law," the sheriff warned him sadly.

Mart kicked at a pile of leaves at the base of the oak.

"Take 'em," he said, "an' git."

He turned his back and walked away.

Cap'n Tack raked out the dozen traps. The sheriff kept an uneasy watch on the contemptuous ragged back.

"I hates to crowd you," the storekeeper remarked cheerfully.

The two men made off smartly, increasing their pace as they approached the road. Mart wheeled.

"Look at 'em scat," he said bitterly.

He reached suddenly for his shotgun leaning against the far side of the tree. He lifted it, trembling. Then he laid it carefully down.

"Hit ain't wuth it," he said.

The sun set molten, beneficence gone mad. The evening was a soft gray velvet suffocation. Sand gnats and mosquitoes hummed and stung. Mart opened his shirt and fanned himself with its tails. Florry was wet with the labor of waving a palmetto leaf for fan. The fish for supper had made them thirsty. Their lips were cracking. Mart set the bucket of water between them. It was the temperature of the air, nauseating on the palate. Its leaf-flavored brackishness tasted slightly rotten. It was good neither to quench thirst nor to cool the throat. Only ice could make it fit to drink. Florry drank, but Mart pushed the bucket aside.

He sat down with his back to the tree and leaned his head despairingly against the gray trunk. He closed and unclosed his broad fists, then his hands relaxed and lay loosely on the ground. Florry moved to the camp table and cleared off the debris of supper.

"Save them cold grits, Florry. Thet sack o' rations is like to be the last you'll git."

She stared at him. In the faint light the sweat glistened on his face. She could see his pulse work desperately in and out from his knotted throat. She crouched beside him and peered at him.

"Mart! You be'n't afeered?"

"I ain't skeert o' nobody," he answered heavily.

"No, I knows thet." She pushed the soft hair impatiently behind her ears. She fixed the bright squirrel eyes earnestly on him. "I means, you ain't afeered o' not gittin' no rations? Not gittin' no place fer us to be? You ain't afeered o' what-all kin happen to folkses?"

He did not answer. He closed his eyes and rubbed the back of his dark head against the roughness of oak-bark.

Florry thought, "Mart's in trouble, shore."

"I knows how you feels," she said comfortingly.

She moved away to build the night's mosquito smudge and sat down in the slow gray drift of smoke. She frowned anxiously, seizing at thoughts that swept by like the wild flight of doves. She had felt secure so long. Now security was slipping away. Mart's despair was quicksand under her feet. In the old days of the cypress swamp her courage had stood like a wind-break against old Jo and the chill brown waters. Since the day she had gone away with Mart, through wind and rain, she had not needed courage.

"—*burden down*—"

She had laid her burden down on his lean, strong knees. She thought, "I've done had me a rest, like." A burden laid down could be picked up again.

"Mart," she said, "likely you're worrit up abouten me. You belong to know I ain't skeert, not one leetle mite."

"You leetle ole froggy thing, you," he said gently, "rabbity, like your daddy said—"

His voice turned harsh.

"You belong to be skeert."

He spat in the smoky fire and swung forward so that he sat on his heels, rocking.

"Hit ain't like I was a sorry thing wouldn't do a man's work nor a day's work, neither," he said passionately. "You knows I've scratched like a hound dog at a gopher hole. Nor I ain't been pertickler what 'twas I done, fishin' or trappin' or 'shinin' or sich. Exscusin' workin' fer a Yankee," he corrected himself.

"I cain't work fer folkses thet-a-way, no-how," he said unhappily. "Does they git biggety, I gits uppity, an' it's trouble shore. An' evvything I done, Florry, has got so messed up there wa'n't no straightenin' to it. Storms an' sich, a-spoilin' the fishin', an' other fellers' meanness a-spoilin' t'other things. Hain't done nary good to kep' a-workin', no more good then squattin' by a creek with a cat-fish line."

He wiped his wet face with his shirt sleeve.

"You belong to be skeert, a'right. There ain't nothin' left to try. There ain't no'eres left to go. Us been a-climbin' ol' Jacob's ladder thouten no end to it."

"Them trapses—" she interrupted.

"Them trapses finished us off, shore," he said. "Did I try to trap on shares fer thet storekeepin' buzzard, I'd owe him twicet the hides, come the yare's end. Him takin' the trapses finished us. An' the heat, Florry." His eyes rested on her appealingly, like those of a dog. "Seems like the heat's plumb wore me out."

His head drooped forward between his knees. Florry brushed away the mosquitoes on his hair. She threw a handful of oak leaves on the smudge.

"He's like to had the chidlin's beat out of him," she thought.

"I don't belong to be skeert," she said doggedly. "You done tole me your very self, hit don't make no difference where we goes nor what we does, not where we squats to eat our rations."

"Iffen we got any—"

"An' thet don't make no difference, neither," she persisted. "Goin' hungry don't matter. Nor a roof to git under don't matter. Nor folks drawin' in their necks an' strikin' like a rattlesnake. Them's all things you cain't he'p."

She wrinkled her forehead and rubbed her thin hands tensely up and down her thighs.

"But you kin he'p bein' afeered!" she said fiercely.

She reached in his pocket for his snuff box and lipped a pinch quickly.

"Folks is wusser'n storms," she pondered. "Git you a place you got a right to, a place you kin drive folks offen, steaden their chunkin' things at you—you ain't so likely to hev trouble."

Mart lifted his head impatiently.

"Florry, you're talkin' wild as a coot."

"Mart," she said, "you knows good I got me a right to Pappy's cabin, yonder in the piney-woods. Would you jest stand up to him one time an' maybe framm him with them big hands o' yourn, us'd be safe-like right on. I got me my rights there."

"An' I done had me my rights, too," he said bitterly, "evvy time I been moved on." He stretched flat, an arm across his face. "Wisht thet bucket o' water was cold an' fitten."

"Our well water had sulphur to it, but it shore were cold an' fine."

"Hit ain't a mite o' use, Florry. I ain't got the strength to leg it thet fur, jest to git th'owed out agin. Hit's goin' to a goat's house fer wool."

"Be you skeert?"

"I ain't skeert o' yer daddy." He was sullen.

She took a deep, slow breath.

"Well, I'm a-headin' fer the cabin, come day. Reckon you'd bes' foller jes' to take keer o' me."

"Florry, leave me be. I cain't hold out. I'm wore out. Damn thet fire! Put it out! I kin stand the skeeters better'n a smudge to-night."

"You got you a tech o' fever. Hit'll do you good to git outen the hammocks. Hit's the last chanct, shore, Mart, headin' fer the piney-woods. Us got to try it. If us cain't stay there—" she did not finish.

"Mart—"

Her small voice was gentle.

"Mart, be you skeert o' what-all kin happen to folkses?"

He did not answer for so long that she thought he had gone to sleep in his weariness. She leaned over him to hear what he was saying.

"I got a right to be—"

VIII

Florry thought that she had moved through such a nightmare before. The trek to Dixie County was like the hot seas of fever in which she had once swum. The air, like that of delirium, was palpable, pressing on her bony shoulders an insupportable weight. Her straight muscular calves ached as though the flat roads wound forever up-hill. Old Jo's blows had never fallen on her head so heavily as the direct rays of the September sun. No cypress log had tugged so ponderously against her as the burden of Mart's heavy spirit. He followed her like a hound unwillingly at heel.

The thought of the clearing drew her ahead, as resistless as the sun. If she could reach it before the storms caught them up, she would willingly lie down on the cabin floor and let old Jo flail about him. She was weak with longing for the piney-woods, where the sun dropped visibly behind the tall trees, and peace lay like a cloak of pine-needles, pierced only by the rhythmic pattern of the hoot-owl's cry.

She felt hurried. The thick heat was a warning of change to come. It had been hot too long. There had been no rain since the torrents of June, and these had long since sunk deep into the soil. The sand was like powder. The clay ridges were burned brick. The flat-woods were brown. The occasional hammocks were dried up except in the lowest swamps and along the edges of lakes and streams. The creeks were withered down to the brown beds, cracking wide with thirst. The frogs, who had sung all spring in the good damp, were silent under the ooze where they had burrowed. Across the roads the moccasins and king snakes moved all day in search of water. Now the winds had stopped, and there was no breath of coolness anywhere. September was so still, so hot, that the very elements could not endure it. In a little while they would explode. They would burst out with wind and rain, tearing the heat to tatters.

In Levy County they passed a gang cutting ties in the flatwoods.

Mart said, "Mus' us stop, an' me git a job, two-three days?"

Florry shook her head.

"Us got to keep goin'. Hit's time fer the high winds. Us'll git ketched shore, do us stop."

They travelled fast on light rations. They were worn down to assemblages of bones that kept moving forward. Florry's feet were blistered under the worn soles of her shoes. Whenever they left the highways and cut through on the dirt roads, she walked barefooted, treading surely with long, spread toes. The high cheek-bones lay across her thin pointed face like sun-baked ridges. Her eyes were sink-holes filled with leaf-brown water. In rough going, her long arm, lean as a crane's wing, held aside thorny vines to spare Mart, shuffling dull-eyed and indifferent behind her.

At night they tried to camp near water, to cool their feet and wash the sweat from their bodies. Florry was clean. They had now no change of clothing, and she washed their shirts by starlight or by moonlight, in running water. She cooked hoe-cake in a palm-leaf in hot ashes and roasted what fish they stopped to catch. They sat each night by their camp-fire, staring wearily at the embers. Mart crouched dazed, until his eyes closed and his shoulders fell back on the moss-pile Florry gathered.

"You got the fever," she repeated again and again.

"Don't seem like I kin stand it," he would answer.

Yet she knew that it was more than fever ailed him. Random fears scampered like young rabbits before her. Old Jo might meet them, first thing, with a load of buckshot. He might have let the house burn down, lying drunk before the fireplace. Violence was reasonable, concerning him. She had promised Mart security. If it was not there to give—

She watched the white, hot skies anxiously. She was sure of her directions, but they had been more than a week on the way without a landmark. A Georgia sweet potato peddler offered them a lift in his truck. Timidly, they accepted. Mart sat talking with the driver, but Florry slept most of the day, joggling snugly on potato sacks fragrant with the smell of Georgia earth. When she roused toward sunset, she recognized a bridge over which she and Mart had passed in their first flight south. They had come far in the one day's travel.

The peddler gave them a few pounds of potatoes. Mart shot a young 'possum as they camped at dusk. That night they feasted. The thick air smothered them, but in the heaviness a restlessness stirred at last, like a quiver of wind across still water.

The next day Mart began to recognize the territory he had once so briefly visited. They were in the open piney-woods, walking over brown pine-needles inches deep. Sparkleberry leaves caught spots of sunlight that filtered through the shadows. Gallberries shone black like small eyes. Quail ran ahead of them down the ruts of the wagon trail. Doves whirred from the tops of the pines in rose-gray flocks. Squirrels chattered shrilly from a safe distance.

Mart's eyes grew wide. He shifted his shotgun from the crook of his elbow to his shoulders, fingering the trigger.

"I mean, this is shore good huntin' woods."

Florry nodded.

"The squirrels is extry thick count o' this bein' seed yare."

That night they talked late by the campfire. The abundant game stirred Mart to interest. She told him what she knew of trapping here; of logging; of cane-growing. Long after she had gone to sleep he sat hunched by the live oak coals. At midnight a shiver passed across the lethargy of the pines. A sudden chill moved through.

When Florry wakened in the first silver daylight, she said, "Us cain't no more'n make it."

The woods creatures were stirring excitedly, the squirrels scampering up and down the trees with a tail-whisking madness.

"They allus acts thet-a-way afore a storm," she told him.

There was a breathless hush in the forest, but overhead gray clouds scudded wildly to the southwest. There was terror in the flight of these imponderable things, as though the forces pounding in behind them were those of a pestilence. The sky blackened moment by moment. Twilight took over the woods; then dark. There was no morning; no day; no longer any time. The mottled bark of the pines spotted the blackness. Mart's face and Florry's floated white, detached from their bodies that were blended with the myrtle bushes and the dark trunks of trees. They were phantoms, hurrying unhappily through the endless piney-woods of space.

Florry said, "Us got a mile to go."

She stared over her shoulder. As she looked, the black sky turned luminous. A green translucence filled the east. A gust of cold wind puffed in from nowhere and was gone. A few drops of rain flicked their throats. Florry pulled her gray cotton blouse together across her slim brown neck. Suddenly the air about them vibrated. There was no perceptible wind, but the pines quivered. Their needles rustled frantically a moment. Something like a shudder stirred in the palmettos. Florry laid a quick hand on Mart's bare forearm.

"Listen!"

Far off a giant sea of wind was pounding on the shingle that was the forest. A roar as of surf beat in, wave on wave, seething and angry. It was coming nearer. A rumble—a boom—as the gale moved close it climbed the scale until its voice was a high-pitched whine. It hung there shrieking, shrill beyond all mortal bagpipes. The sky was black and green glass. The storm was shattering it into uncountable brittle pieces. The sky crashed. Floods of rain fell slantwise. Chaos came in and ripped the piney-woods to pieces. This was the hurricane.

Mart tried to shelter Florry with his body. He pushed his side against the gale, pulling her along in the lee of him. The first rush of the storm deluged them. It drove blinding into their eyes and cascaded down their thin frames. The wind choked off their breath. Sometimes it was a great wall against which there was no moving. They stood balancing, heads lowered, until a hole broke in the wall to let them through. Their clothes were pasted flat against them, so that they were like wet dark statues. With her eyes wide, her soft hair plastered over her ears, her small pointed breasts and slender thighs, Florry had to Mart the look of a child.

He shouted, "Leave me tote you."

She shook her head.

"I kin make out."

Her voice, close against his ear, was a thin sweet flute above the scream of the hurricane.

Her knowledge of the ways of trees kept them safe. When an old pine, rotten of heart, crashed down, her quick eye caught in time the ominous sway. Against falling limbs, palmetto fans driven like spears before the gale, they could only keep their arms over their heads and take the stinging blows as they came. Their sleeves were torn in shreds. The rain washed the blood from their cuts as it ran. They fought ahead, tripping over logs and into holes made invisible by rushing water.

At noon they reached the cabin. Florry stamped the sand from her bare feet and wrung the water from her full skirt. She lifted the latch of the gray cypress door. Together they threw their shoulders against it. It swung violently open and thumped flat against the wall. Florry sprawled headlong into the room. Mart turned his back to tug the door shut again.

He heard old Jo's amazed curse and Florry's cry. He bolted the door and wheeled to see the old man lift a heavy light-wood knot from the clay hearth above the girl's thin shoulders. Fierce, not with anger but with a strange delight, he knocked the stick from old Jo's claw and closed his hands about the leathery neck. He tightened his grip until the blood-shot eyes grew wild and the strong old hands quit their beating upon him. A terrified whimper came from the scrawny throat. Old Jo's body drooped limply. Mart held him up by the jaws. The neck under his fingers seemed suddenly weak and small. He pushed the man from him, tumbling him across the sagging pine bedstead. Old Jo sobbed and gasped. Mart loomed over him.

"Ole feller," he said, "mebbe you'll be a mite more pertickler about yer meanness. Reckon you an' me's goin' to make out over the same pot o' grits."

Old Jo snuffled and wiped his nose.

Florry's blood stirred warm again, where for a moment there had been the old chill of fear. Jo was old; frightened, old and beaten. She stared at the unhappy huddle on the bed. He was mumbling miserably, his old face wrinkled in distress. The ancient terror was gone.

Mart strode about, appraising the bare room with satisfaction. His step, that had shuffled all summer, in spite of his weariness was hard and sure. Something of the shy delight was in him that he had brought to her in this place those several years ago. His wet clothes steamed as he move closer to the hearth fire. The gale drummed fiercely on the shingled roof. The small-paned windows rattled like loose teeth.

"Ole feller," he called to the sniffling heap on the bed, "is they rations in yer kitchen?"

"There be meal an' sich," the old man proffered grudgingly.

"Le's go, Florry."

They dashed through the east door, across the breezeway, Mart pushing Florry ahead of him against the pounding winds. They burst into the kitchen, only to have the full force of the hurricane sweep in upon them through the gaping doorway.

"Thet ole rascal," Mart yelled, "never put back thet door blowed off."

She put out a hand to hold him, but he was already in the storm, freeing the fallen door from a tangle of weeds. He loped across the sand, searching out an implement for his uses. He picked up at last a rusty axe-head, and brought in a pine sapling to use for batten. The wind shrieked over the kitchen, but it was no longer blowing through. Mart had the door in place.

Florry called through the thin pine.

"Kin you make thet sorry door stay shet?"

He thumped confidently with the rusty axe-head.

"Hit'll hold," he said.

LORD BILL OF THE SUWANNEE RIVER

OVER in the Suwannee River country of Florida, men read little history and no mythology. They talk instead of big Bill Boyle. The children listen to stories about him. The stories end:

"He went up and down the Suwannee River in a floatin' palace, straddlin' the stern and shuckin' hisself oysters. He ate them all the way up from the Gulf of Mexico, three or four crocus sacks of oysters."

I first heard of him in Ocala. An old-timer told me about an early railroad man who "looked like Stone Mountain moving," with a voice to match. Big Bill Boyle. He gave a dinner to ten men in the old Ocala hotel with the famous bar. Along toward midnight, to keep his guests from getting drunk, he drank the last round of ten drinks himself.

The old ex-sheriff slapped his leg and chuckled, "He was a great one."

I asked my Cracker friend Tom if he'd ever heard of big Bill Boyle.

"Anybody in these three counties old enough to chaw an' bigger'n a Georgia thumper, knowed thet man—or of him. Them as knowed him done tole abouten him to them as didn't."

So I went over to the Suwannee River to see if I could find anybody left who'd worked or played with him. He was real, all right.

For about thirty miles my road paralleled his railroad. I stopped in the town he built, prosperous and substantial. I saw the rich territory he opened up. I found traces of the keel of the "floating palace" on an east bank of the Suwannee. I saw a picture of him and I found men who'd known him.

He had a big square ruddy face with a jaw like a cow-catcher. He was about the size of two Teddy Roosevelts and looked a lot like him, without the whiskers. He weighed three hundred pounds most of the time. Sometimes he put on an extra twenty-five. He was hard, not fat; an inch or two of fat, perhaps, on his big paunch. His voice was as deep as thunder and as rich as flat-woods honey.

The minute I mentioned his name to men who'd known him, they'd grin. They'd put a finger against their noses and ask me, "What do you know about him?"

We'd sit down, on the stoop of a feed and seed place, in the back of a general merchandise store, or the bank—all the solid businesses he set up when he built his town; or on a pine Cracker porch back in the flat-woods, or leaning on a split-rail fence around a watermelon field; or on cabin steps in the deer and turkey country, where he'd bought his rights-of-way for the railroad; or we'd just stand in the sun in a sandy road, with the dogs and children and mules and automobiles going around us, and we'd talk about big Bill Boyle.

I'd tell them tales I'd heard about him from down-state, such as the one about the ten drinks. I'd tell them about the time at Lakeland, in the pioneer days, when it was only a wide spot in the road, and big Bill was eating his God-awful pile of dinner at the good Cracker boarding house where all the railroad and phosphate and turpentine men stopped. A little Jewish drummer was complaining about the food. He pointed to Bill's plate, heaped with country ham, hominy grits and turnip greens.

"Look what the man is eating! The food's not fit for a dog!"

Bill's arm reached over like a derrick for the stranger's plate. He piled it higher than his own. He drew out his two .44's from his hip-pockets and laid them on either side of his plate. He said in his big voice:

"Now eat your rations, son, or I'll have to work on you a little."

The drummer ate two plates, with an extra helping of ham. When Bill got up from the table and went on, and he saw the size of him, he trembled all over and they had to help him up.

"That's just like him! I'll bet his voice hit that fellow like a freight train! You could hear him a quarter of a mile away. You could hear him just at daybreak, getting his niggers started."

That was the way it went, all up and down the Suwannee River. Anyone who knew him is ready to grin at a stranger and talk about him. They can't get over the delight in him.

It isn't because of what he did, although as a pioneer he is important. He showed up in Florida on foot from Georgia—for all I know he may have followed the Suwannee down from its sources in the big Okefenokee Swamp—a huge fifteen-year-old boy who had never had enough sausage meat to eat, and who wanted to build bridges. He learned bridge-building from a negro contractor in the post-bellum days, and with his first four dollars in wages he went into a frontier cafe and ate it out in sausage.

He timbered and he turpentined. He knew the piney-woods, the flat-woods, the hammocks and the cypress swamps of north-central Florida. From that he came to building railroads for the old Plant system. He built what has become the key to West Coast traffic. He wanted a town, so he built a town in a cornfield. He wanted to see the wilderness under cultivation, so he picked out the fertile soils and had the land turned by the thousands of acres. He went to Kentucky and bought blooded stock to replace the gaunt, tick-bitten, scrub range cattle; pedigreed red Durocs and Poland Chinas to breed with the razor-backed piney-woods rooters.

He became lord of the Suwannee River territory, king of two counties, their industries, their people and their courts. Not because it was his ambition, but because it was his intention. He made fortunes because he wanted to and gave them away for the same reason. All his life he did whatever he wanted to do. And the things he did, tickled men so, that they'll never be done with talking about him.

It just naturally tickles them to hear, and tell, of the time he shook hands with Governor Gilchrist on the porch of the old Thomas House in Gainesville. The governor walked by in his frock coat and silk hat and turned aside, all bows and smiles, to speak with Bill, sitting in a rocking chair in his old boots and breeches and slouch hat. When Bill stood up, and shook hands with the governor, the rocking chair stuck to his rear. Mighty few chairs were big enough for those great thighs. He talked politics as unconcerned as though the furniture on his back was a butterfly, and sat down again without so much as mentioning the chair or putting his hands to it.

When he was ready to go fishing down the Suwannee, and bait was scarce, he wired a bank president up in Georgia to express a can of angleworms. Once the bank president had to go out and dig the worms himself.

He gave a formal game dinner at the camp-house to a big Chicago packer, when he was getting ready to open up the American market to Florida beef and pork, and he walked in to dinner with his dress coat just the way it had been laid away in a trunk—inside out.

That was the way he was. He couldn't be bothered with what didn't matter. He didn't do things the way the rest of us do them. A gray-haired merchant whom Bill took under his wing as a boy, told me that if he wanted to make a short cut across the model farm he ran, to show the section how to make money, he simply made a short cut. He had some of his henchmen who always traveled with him, unstaple the fence. They'd flip out the staples at two or three posts, hold down the fencing with their feet, and Bill drove over. When he got where he was going, he sent men back to staple it up again.

He picked out fields he wanted to hunt in and had grits scattered over them by the hundred-pounds, to bring in the birds. He sent fertilizer to anyone who had pecan trees, so that whenever he was going by, he could stop and eat pecans. When he wanted a personal job done at the railroad camp, he'd say to anybody handy, "Go bring me a bunch of old hats."

Fifteen or twenty negroes from the Quarters would be sent in, grinning and shuffling.

"What you boys doing?"

"Nothin', Lawd Bill. Jes' loafin'."

"All of you go on back—but you. You, Sam, go catch that shoat yonder with the mange and grease him."

When he saw a good man working without proper equipment, he sent him out whatever was needed—mules, cattle, hogs, ploughs, lumber or engines. Old man Janny Williams, overlooking his good acres of peanuts, corn and melons, told me:

"Cap'n Bill said to me one day, 'Hell, you're too good a Cracker not to be workin' for yourself. You take a deed to the Marsh three hundred acres, a pair of mules, some cattle and hogs and tools. I'll send you a carload of lumber. You take what you need to build you a house and keep track of what you use.'

"I said, 'I cain't pay fer it.'

"He said, 'That's no matter.'

"I said, 'I won't do it thet-a-way'."

The old fellow hesitated. His wife spat over the porch railing and said, "Go on, Janny. Tell hit."

"Well, he done th'owed me down side o' his desk, and he helt me thar with one hand, and goed on a-writin' with 'tother. Reckon he helt me a good hour. When I seed 'twa'n't no use to fuss nor squirm, I said, 'Cap'n, I cain't spend my mortal days on yer floor. Leave me hev thet deed.'

"You jest as good to say he done give hit me, I paid so leetle. Thet's the way he done fer most o' this section. He wouldn't let no good worker shy offen takin' up land."

He'd do anything for a man he favored. He had his pets, like every potentate. He kept them in fine clothes; gave them horses and hunting dogs and land. He had, as well, a monarch's fear of treachery. Here and there a man had the chidlings to cross him. When it happened, that man was to be watched; if dangerous enough, to be gotten rid of.

It was true of him, as of Henry the eighth, of whom a historian has written, that "once he thought of himself as deceived, or believed himself menaced, he lost his placidity ****. He who appeared tolerant and smiling and lordly, his eyes twinkling and his heart expanding **** suddenly contracted, hardened, bristled **** so that he seemed like a different man. The moment that he felt himself to be in danger, his robustness passed from large geniality into bitter self-preservation."

At such times, big Bill Boyle rode over men as implacably as he rode over fences.

His wife once called him to kill a mouse trapped in a fruit jar. He walked into the woods and liberated it. He laughed at the absurdity of his—big Bill's—killing a mouse. He didn't laugh at the killing of Thomas Wilkins. That wasn't absurd. Wilkins wouldn't get out of his way. Old Senator Merley told me about it.

"Wilkins was living a shameful life in rooms right on the public square, with a noisy, drunken, painted woman. He dared us all to interfere with him. You can see how Bill felt about it. A decent, honest town he'd built, of respectable people he'd hand-picked to populate it—and this Wilkins throwing bawdiness right in their faces. Bill gave him three days to get out of town. He didn't budge. He laughed. He even dared to threaten Bill. That had never happened before."

The old gentleman tapped the floor with his cane. He ruminated.

"I can see how he felt. Wilkins said that Boyle wanted to be a little tin god. Well—Boyle was. Even the men who hated him had to admit that. He was king around here, absolutely king. And I can see how he'd have a fear of ambush. He sent for me one morning. He pointed out of the window on the camp-house."

" 'Merley, do you see those tracks under my window? They were made last night.'

"I said, 'You haven't asked me, but if you want to know what I'd do, I'd shoot it out, man to man.'

"Well—man to man. That's the way ordinary men do it. But you can see—a man like that does things differently from the rest of us.

"I was hunting outside of town that day. I heard the bombardment. I jumped on my horse and rode in as fast as I could. I could see the flames coming up from the shed Wilkins was hiding in. I ran into the Bank. Bill was walking up and down, sweating.

"He said, 'God, Merley, get out of here. You'll get shot.'

"I said, 'It seems to me you make a good deal better target than I do.'

"I think perhaps I could have stopped things then. At least, when Wilkins came out with his hands up, and they shot him down. I don't know. A mob's an awful thing. That's the only reason I've fought lynching, as maybe you know. To be lost in a mob does something to a man's integrity. That was it. Bill's men, doing his work, that was all right. But they turned into Bill's mob, wild, crazy, killing a man who had surrendered—

"You know, you'll find people who say it showed a streak of cowardice—feet of clay. They're wrong. Bill Boyle wasn't afraid of anything on the face of the earth. Cowardice is negative. This thing was positive. He saw treachery. He knew he was in danger. Life was so fine a thing. That's what it comes down to—

"He loved living so. He didn't propose to give it up."

"Nothing came of the killing?"

"In this county?" He laughed. "Of course not."

He didn't allow any material thing to get in his way. He was driving an old Ford across a bridge, and a negro driving the same kind ran into him, taking a wheel off each car. Bill stopped what he was talking about long enough to say:

"Boy, take that other front wheel off your Ford and put it on mine."

"He drove on in a few minutes," Williams said, "still talkin', and left the nigger sittin' by the road with two wheels gone."

Williams went out to camp once and found him sitting in the end of a flat-car with his .44's crossed in his hands. Two black boys about sixteen years old were digging a deep hole. They were crying and shaking. In the old days, negroes were often imported from Georgia and South Carolina. They had to work out their railroad fare. These boys had turned homesick and been caught running away before their debt was paid.

"What you doin' with them boys, Cap'n Bill?"

"Fixing to shoot 'em as soon as they get their graves dug."

The young blacks sobbed.

After a time Bill said to them, "I can't wait for you to finish right now. You go work on the grade and finish the graves some other time."

Somehow the graves were never finished. When he did things like that, he didn't know how he tickled people, and how they passed on the yarn. Sometimes he really set out to give folks fun. They say you could spot him in town half a mile away, from the swarm around him, listening and laughing. When he was through holding court, he would gather up a crowd and take them home to dinner.

A little lady-wife followed his fortunes in the latter part of his life. She collapsed just once under the strain of his hospitality. The first day of hunting season, he brought home fourteen men and fourteen dogs. The fourteen men stamped and roared and rattled their guns, the fourteen dogs bayed and yelped and tumbled and fought, and Bill's voice boomed like a cannon above the tumult. His wife suddenly went into hysterics. Fourteen men were not unreasonable, but fourteen dogs were too much. Bill bellowed for niggers to kick out the dogs.

His wife was never able to induce him to build a home in keeping with his importance. He made the camp-house his permanent home.

He said, "Any kind of a barn will do for me."

Once he had an assortment of choice woods ready to build a house. He decided his forty-foot power launch on the river wasn't big enough, and used the lumber to build the house-boat known as "the hotel" or "the floating palace." Again, he had Georgia brick shipped in. The night before the contractors were to come to build his mansion, the town cotton-gin burned down. He used the contractors— and the brick—to build the town a new gin.

In Jacksonville he saw a display of French china in a shop window. He walked in, said to the storekeeper, "I've been eating out of my hands all my life and now I'm going to buy me some dishes," and had four hundred dollars' worth sent home. His wife remembered having mentioned that she was short of platters.

That was all money was for; that was all men were for; to help him do what he wanted to, delighting people as he did it.

He loved money and power and men and railroads and food and drink and jesting. Life spread all these things before him on the broad table of the Florida frontier and he bolted them raw. He had some connection with the sources of things. He wanted his vegetables raw. He'd pull pindar vines by the armful and strip off the green peanuts, still mucky with earth. He'd walk through the camp garden and pull up rutabagas as big as his head and munch them, the way other people eat radishes.

He said, "Nothing can hurt me."

It was almost literally true. Once in a while he'd over-reach himself. Old man Henson, who boasts of having hunted with him, told me about the Japanese oil.

"We set out at daybreak in his hunting wagon. It was a foggy morning, with the mist in layers. The air was so full of smells you could almost get bird-scent yourself, and the dogs in the wagon were crazy. We hunted all morning, putting out the dogs two at a time. We got over a hundred birds. His nigger cooked us a fine dinner out in the woods, and Bill ate too much, even for him. Two, three, sometimes four quail are all an ordinary man can eat. It took a dozen to make him a mess. That day he ate sixteen and he got a touch of colic.

"We stopped at the first cabin we came to and Bill called for something for the colic. The man had nothing but some Japanese oil, the kind you use for mules. Everbody knows the stuff's so fiery, a teaspoonful will set a mule to braying.

"Bill says, 'Give me two teaspoons.'

"We drove on for the evening's hunting, and he called up to the nigger to stop the wagon for him to spit.

"I says, 'Why do you need the wagon stopped?'

"He says, 'For you to put out the fires after me, for I'm that burning up, that where I spit I'll set the Florida woods a-fire.'"

No man ever knew him to say he'd had enough to eat or drink. Three pounds of beefsteak were just a light snack. Sometimes he'd get up before dawn and go out to the camp cook-car and eat a kettle of cold boiled cabbage before breakfast.

The whole Suwannee River section tells tales of his strength, with a personal pride in the matter. It seems to give them a primitive right to their pleasure in him.

"If he hit a nigger who didn't fall down, he looked to see what was holding him up."

They laugh and laugh when they tell of the time a crazy black stuck a broken clasp-knife in his stomach. He picked it out as if it were a sandspur.

He said, "Boys, there's nothing in the world like a good thick belly."

Williams said, "You've seed a man pile a passel o' boys, one on 'tother, and keep pullin' the bottom one out an' pilin' him on top, holdin' down the pack with one hand, changin' boys with 'tother? He'd do that with men."

The pilot of his house-boat missed the channel at the mouth of the river, grounding at low tide on a bar. Half a dozen men pushing with poles could not float the boat. When they called quits, Bill stepped out on the bar, put his great shoulder under the bow and heaved her clear.

Most men believe that he never met his match. Henson heard the fight in the box-car and says that for once he was hard pushed. Up the river a negro seven feet tall had murdered and headed south. The Dixie county sheriff sent down his description. When the black walked into the railroad camp, asking for work, Bill saw him and recognized him. He assigned him to a lower bunk in one of the box cars used for sleeping quarters. He gave the man time to be off his guard. The negro lay face downward, resting, his arm over his head.

Bill gripped his head with his left arm in the strangle-lock from which no man before had ever shaken himself loose. The black broke free. Bill cracked his pistol over the hard skull, bending it so that it would never shoot again. The negro got it away from him and found it worthless. In the tussle, the small swinging brass kerosene lamp with open wick was knocked down, so that the men fought in darkness.

Henson said that it was like two hurricanes shut up together in the box-car. No one dared go in. The camp was frightened. Lord Bill was toppling on his throne. The sides of the box-car shook as first one Behemoth and then the other made a throw. At the end, Bill came to the door of the car, kicking the black giant's prone body ahead of him.

His strength didn't tickle the negroes. It scared them. When he knocked them down with the careless back-handed swipe he used on them, they got up running. He had two thousand of them working on the grade. They were the scrappings of the south. He had less trouble in his camps than any man in the state. He didn't care who they were or what devilment they'd done. When a new man showed up with fresh razor-cuts, he didn't ask any questions. He put him to work. He never ran a man off, not even a sorry one.

"Because," he said, "he'll take a good man with him. And I need men."

The law wasn't allowed to fool with his camp. Sometimes Bill took the high sheriff through the Quarters himself.

"If you see anybody you want, take him."

Otherwise, it was hands off. A sheriff's raid Sunday night was likely to mean a deserted camp on Monday morning.

Bill said, "I can't have them flushing my niggers like quail."

He allowed no professional gamblers near the camps, but he allowed the men to gamble among themselves. The gambling sometimes tempted a new deputy who hadn't yet found out that most of the pork and grits in the county came from Boyle. Bill's white men all knew how to handle such occasions.

Williams was playing cards in camp on Sunday night with one of the locomotive engineers. A black beat on the door.

"Boss, deputy jes' raid crap game! Took he-se'f 'bout twenty o' de boys! He walkin' de grade right now, headin' fo' town! Lawd Bill in town an' won' know nothin' 'bout it 'til them niggers be's in de jail-house!"

The engineer and Williams had just come back from a pleasure ride in the locomotive to the Suwannee, and there was still fire in the engine-box and enough steam up to start. They overtook the deputy and the men half a mile from camp. The engine slowed down.

The engineer called out, "Hey, sheriff, where you taking those boys?"

"To the jail-house."

"Cap'n Bill don't want 'em in the jail-house. He'll give you bail for 'em. He's in town now. Come jump on the engine and I'll take you to him."

The deputy and his prisoners flocked into the cab. As he slowed down for a curve, the engineer said carelessly:

"Pretty good time to join the bird-gang."

Williams said, "Them twenty niggers flopped offen thet engine like buzzards."

The engineer put on speed and the deputy was afraid to jump off after them. When they reached Bill, the engineer said:

"Deputy here wants bail for twenty men."

"Where are the men?"

The deputy said, "They jumped off the cab a ways back."

"What are their names?"

"I didn't have time to get their names."

Once in a while Bill opened his throat and let out his voice, like a bull romping out of a pen.

He roared, "God-damdest craziest thing I ever heard of! Deputy come for bail with no names and no niggers!"

The man was glad to get back to the river on foot. The locomotive went back without him. As it pulled up the grade it whistled derisively. Williams said in the Quarters the men laughed all night long.

"You knows how niggers laughs—cacklin'."

I found an old negro by the name of Tobe who was Bill's own man for twenty-five years. He is white-headed, lean with age. He came from his cornpatch to talk with me of Bill Boyle. It was the Quarters, he said, that began calling him "Lord Bill." They stuck to it, even when he laughed at them.

Tobe said, "We tole him, 'You Lawd to us'."

The negroes feared Bill's strength. They worshiped his person and his power. They loved him because he took care of them. Money never did matter much to a nigger, but he likes to be taken care of. And nothing on earth will love a man the way a black can, unless it's a pointer dog. He would send fifty miles for a doctor and spend a hundred dollars to save the life of the most worthless black.

When the camp became permanent, and the negroes took wives, the women sometimes went along on the hand-cars in summer and picked blackberries while the men worked. Once when one of the women did not return, Bill sent a car up the grade in the morning to look for her. They found her in a berrypatch, dead, snake-bitten in the lip—and clutched tight in her cold black fist, just back of its head, the rattler, as dead as she. Nobody but Lord Bill would have bothered even to send back for her.

He looked out for them. They were his men, and he needed them on the railroad; to open up new country. But they had to behave.

He kept out liquor, dope, camp women and all the shysters that infest a frontier. There were no "cuttings" in the Quarters. Fights were stopped as soon as they began. I asked Tobe if Cap'n Bill came out and stopped them himself.

"No need. He jes' send out the Big Word."

Bill laid off his men from Friday night to Tuesday morning. That was the time he played, himself. Besides, he knew they were no good on pay-roll, or rations, day, on Sunday and on the day after. Wages were high. The pay-roll ran to the tens of thousands of dollars each week. He said that a man who would work hard four days, could work for him.

Friday evening at dusk the week was over. Even the swarms of dogs Bill kept at camp got extra rations. Tobe said Big Un fed the dogs. Big Un would come out under the oak trees at twilight and he'd call them:

"Hi-yah! Come git yo' rations! Hi-yah, all you bird-dogs, houn' dogs, 'coon dogs, rabbit dogs, ketch dogs an' jes' dogs!"

After supper, the gaming and "skinning" began. Every sort of card game and skin-game was allowed among the men. Sometimes, especially when he had week-end guests—senators, bank officials, university presidents, industrial executives and Cracker cronies—Lord Bill would come out at dark and call for wrestling. Those were the big nights. They'd build up a lighter'd knot bonfire so high its flames could be seen from the Suwannee River. Any man who wanted to, could wrestle for the money Lord Bill threw down. The rest watched, and heaped fat-wood on the bonfire, and joked, and laid their bets, and tussled on the side-lines. They brought out their guitars and banjos and sang under the mossy live-oaks in the firelight.

After a while Bill would call for Mengo, the dwarf. Tobe called him "Lawd Bill's rasslin' boy." The dwarf was "built like a stump, and nobody couldn't get down to him." Powerful shoulders over stumpy legs gave the little black ape the ability to throw bucks two and three times his weight. Once he threw a two-hundred-pound man clear over his shoulder and landed him like a ball against Bill's chest. It didn't even throw Bill off his balance.

Tobe said, "You jes' as good to try to shake a hill."

Lord Bill loved the big nights himself. He liked to see his boys having a good time, hundreds of them at once, gaming and wrestling and laughing and singing, all night long. He liked to see his wrestling boy fool them all, and scoop up the money from the sand with his long black monkey-fingers. Bill laughed and shouted with them, encouraged them, made fun of them. His big face shone ruddy in the firelight like a full moon. Everybody, blacks and white company and Lord Bill, had such a good time the camp was in a delirium all night. Big nights.

At daybreak they let the fire die down. The owls quit "Whoo-o-o-ing" and the bob-whites began to call. The long-leafed yellow pines came to life, glittering, as the sun touched their needles. Mengo bowed and scraped to his master and scampered off to his bunk to count his money. The camp settled down to sleep until pay-roll at noon. Bill and his party went to the camp-house to eat gallons of batter baked into corn cakes, home-made sausage and thick Florida cane syrup. The men yawned.

Bill ate another twelve-inch stack of cakes and another quart of syrup, thumped his chest and was ready to begin the day. He wore men out that tried to keep up with him, working or playing. He'd work all day and run wild-cats all night. He hunted twenty-four hours at a time. On the house-boat on the river, he kept men up in relays, fishing all day with him, playing cards or telling stories all night.

He had for everything an insatiable appetite. Best of all he loved the Suwannee River. He spent weeks at a time upon it, up and down the swift, red-gold waters bordered with live oaks and sweet gum and cypresses.

Those are some of the true stories I heard over in the Suwannee River section about big Bill Boyle. His death was consistent. Who but Bill would have eaten pecans for six consecutive hours? Half an hour's eating, and most men are done. Bill ate them on the train all the way from the river to Clearwater. Crack and eat, crack and eat, crack and eat, for six steady hours. Everybody I met told me what killed him. For the first time, the great mechanism balked. The intestines locked. The Atlantic Coast Line backed one of its fast trains from Tampa to Clearwater to rush him to the hospital.

The invisible sources from which he drew his strength hid their faces from him. Death made a momentary interruption to the general belief that he and his great belly were beyond mortal harm.

I heard some other things that startled me when I realized what they meant. The first few times it happened, I dismissed it, thinking, "This man is lying." Because every now and again someone told me something so preposterous that I knew it could not be true. Suddenly I understood.

They are not lying. They are creating. While he lived, Bill Boyle delighted them. When he died, their imaginations took up where he left off. They can't give him up.

They are making a legend of him.

Sometimes they don't have very far to go. The truth about the pecans is stretched, not broken, when they name the fatal quantity, as I heard it named, as two full bushels. The story of the ten drinks needed only a little furbishing to come out again as twenty. The kettle of boiled cabbage is often a five-gallon wash-pot. When I asked one man how much liquor it took for Boyle to know he'd had a drink, I was told, "About a gallon." The devil himself couldn't hold a gallon of Florida 'shine.

Old man Henson told me blandly, "The quail are scarce now hereabouts because Bill ate the woods clean."

It is pure fiction for old Williams to say:

"Heap o' men when they died, didn't think they goed to God. They figgered they jes' goed over to the Suwannee River to Bill Boyle."

The blacks? I couldn't pin Tobe down to an explanation of what he meant by the "Big Word" Lord Bill sent out. I believe that he meant the very mention of his name. "I am the Word."

He had prodigious physical strength. That is unquestionable. It is something else to be told by those who knew him only by hearsay, of the giant—A Hercules of the Suwannee—who picked up his boat and his ponderous early Cadillac sedan in his hands, the way a boy picks up his toys. That is the kind of tale I mean.

Perhaps the Suwannee River has touched him with its magic. Broad and deep between dark, untenanted banks, the river of the song will always stir the mind. It will be a long day before men in that territory forget the picture of Lord Bill going up and down its waters in a floating palace, straddling the stern and shucking oysters.

How far the legend will go, it is impossible to tell. I only know that it is happening. It was an exciting thing, fifteen years after a man's death, to have other men re-create him so vividly that when I saw the photograph of him, I recognized him.

It is uncanny to see, nebulous beyond the jovial, powerful figure, another, like ghostly protoplasm taking shape—a myth in the making—a Bill Boyle ten times the size, stuffing pecans and quail and men down a Gargantuan maw.

A PLUMB CLARE CONSCIENCE

'SHINER Tim was missing.

He had left his cabin in the piney woods, without food, without money, without a gun, and he had not returned.

Fifteen years of 'shining have scraped his Cracker ribs through tight places. Revenue agents have found and destroyed his still time and again. But a few hours after, he is usually home, personally un-damaged, ready to set another mash when the horizon shall be clear of the federal storm. This he attributes to his far ancestry of Carolina Irish. He is "mostly Irish," he says.

"Like a bird-dog. Times, he's brown and white; times, he's black and white, or mixed-like; times, he's got a leetle collie in him, or a leetle hound. But that's what he is, mostly bird-dog."

He has clung zestfully to his 'shining. It is his destiny to make low-bush corn liquor. His removal, by death or incarceration, would be a loss to the county, for his liquor is as sound as the best Kentucky Bourbon. It is made of pure running branch water, corn, and cane-sugar. He has a fierce contempt for 'shiners who cut the mash with lye, color the liquor with tobacco-juice, or hurry the fermentation with stable manure. Ocklawaha River 'shine ranks next after Tim's, but it is vitriol in comparison.

During the forty-eight hours of his disappearance it seemed that he must have made his last run. He was trapped in the swamp. His new partner, a Georgia boy, showed up at the cabin at the end of the first twenty-four hours to report the catastrophe to Tim's wife. They had mixed the mash by moonlight the previous night, and had been trailed to the still early that morning. Two agents had taken them by surprise, had smashed the still and seized Tim's battered old car. The Georgia boy escaped. Tim was hemmed in.

"Cooter" in person must have been tipped off to the still's location. The federal agent has the long, leathery brown neck, the beaked nose, and glittering pop-eyes of that variety of turtle, and it was only logical that the Florida 'shiners should give him its name. "Cooter" surely, said the Georgian, had shot Tim, if he did not soon bring him in.

The morning of the second day Tim had not been brought in. He must therefore be lying in the swamp, dead or mortally wounded. He could not be there alive, voluntarily. We drove over to his cabin. Tim's wife was there, the Georgia boy, and two Cracker friends who, like us, had received word of his plight. The Georgian described the lay of the country where Tim was caught.

The still, against Tim's better judgment, was located in black-jack. Black-jack, for Florida, is open country. Scraggly black-jack oaks, an inch or two in thickness, are scattered loosely. The sandy soil is spotted with scrub palmettos, sweet myrtle, and low-bush huckle-berries. The still lay here, in a thicket. The land sloped down to a leaf-brown branch which widened into something of a pond. Be-yond the branch was a loathsome stretch of marsh, mucky of water, a-stink with decaying lily-pads, swarming with frogs, mosquitoes, and moccasins. Next came a fringe of impenetrably dense palmetto scrub, and then the lush jungle of virgin hammock.

Proximity to running water is the first requisite for 'shining, but the need of good cover runs it a close second. It was in hammock that Tim was most at home and there he would have preferred to locate the still. He had yielded to his partner's dislike of crossing the swamp to get to water. The Georgian admitted they had been on the right side for comfort but the wrong for safety. He had last seen Tim at the edge of the swamp, about to cross, with Cooter close on his heels and Cooter's henchman heading him off from the safe refuge of the hammock.

"He's shore drownded or shot, one," the boy lamented.

A Plumb Clare Conscience 125

Tim's wife said: "Give him 'til late evenin' afore you raises up a fuss, lookin' fer him."

At two o'clock in the afternoon Tim walked in.

He was scarcely recognizable. His face and hands were swollen out of shape. The Mongolian cast of his heavy-lidded eyes was accentuated, and he looked like a puffy scarlet Chinaman. He was soaked with sweat from his long walk. The front of his blue shirt and blue pin-check pants was stained with dark muck.

"Hi-yah!" he said and went to the water-bucket.

He drained the gourd dipper several times. He looked at the last empty bottom.

"I drinkt more water then," he remarked, "then I've drinkt ary week."

He picked up a slab of corn bread and a piece of white bacon from the remains on the table and sat down in a cowhide-bottomed chair by the clay fireplace. He looked around with interest to see who was present. He ignored all questions and remarks as he ate, concentratedly but without greed. When he had finished he opened the snuff-box on the pine mantel and rolled a generous pinch inside his lips. He leaned forward, his hands on his knees. The two Cracker friends hitched closer and spat in the fireplace.

Tim nodded at us severally.

"I orter allus let my conscience be my guide," he announced solemnly.

The Georgia boy fidgeted, scuffling his feet on the deerskin rug.

"Didn't I say I was oneasy, yistiddy mornin' afore we sets out fer the still?"

The boy nodded.

"Thet was my conscience a-tellin' me to lay low!

"We'd done set the mash thet night and gone back to git us a piece o' sleep," he explained for the general benefit. "When I waked up at crack o' day I felt kind o' froggy. Not scairt, jest froggy. And I says to myself, iffen I still feels thet-a-way when we gits there, I ain't goin' to turn into no still.

"My conscience had tole me 'twa'n't no place fer a still. No trees around the water, jest a plumb naked pond." He frowned sternly at his partner. "I've had me a ground-hog still like thet one, in open country, but I've had me some watchment."

"I should of give in to you," agreed the Georgia boy. "I thought you was kilt daid. Last time I seed you, you was shore surrounded. What the devil did you do with Cooter?"

Tim pondered. Then he slapped his knees and broke into cat-sneezes of laughter.

"Well, I cain't say I've outrunned Cooter. I cain't exactly say I've outsmarted him. But I shore kin say I've done outwaited him!"

"Tim!" said his wife. "Where at?"

He ignored her and addressed the boy.

"Remember jest afore we turns in to the dirt road yistiddy mornin'? A car passes us, a Chivvolay? A couple o' quare-lookin' sap-suckers in it?"

"I shore remember thet thing."

"And recolleck, I says my conscience done tole me to keep right on a-goin'? Well, I shore orter allus foller my conscience. That was Cooter hisself, a-trackin' us. And we pottered around a piece, and was fixin' to take out, when we heerd a pistol shoot? Well, right then we'd orter done been gone!

"But we stops to look, like dogged cur'us deer—and into the black-jack comes the Chivvolay. And I says to you, 'Yonder's them scoundrels now!'"

The Georgian shivered. Tim jerked a thumb in his direction.

"He's a noble-timid boy," he remarked to the rest of us. "So I tells him, 'You walk down to the branch and squat. I'll see kin I mislead 'em into the hammock.'"

"But when I sees one o' them fellers nosin' along behind me," interrupted the Georgian, "I lights out fer the hard road and I'm long gone. I looks back and sees you headed fer the swamp."

Tim nodded.

"I seed you had a fair chanct," he said, "so I thew over the ole barrel thumper, and the whole works took after me.

"Well," he chuckled, "hit's a pore set o' heels cain't save a scairt body. I reckon I could outrun ary one o' them rascals myself, jest runnin'. Me and Cooter done some runnin', too.

"And while we was runnin', I had about half a mile to study in. We was crowdin' on toward the swamp, not makin' as much time as we was at first, when I looks back and notices hit's jest only Cooter after me. The other of them catbirds, the one thet took after you, had done cut in the short way from the side, like, and was makin' the hammock ahead o' me.

"We splashed thu the swamp and hit the palmeeters.

"If I'd had thirty more yards, I'd done been safe in the hammock. I'd done been in the clare. I'd been home yistiddy fer a hot dinner."

He nodded to his wife.

"But I couldn't make the hammock."

He lipped snuff again and lowered his voice confidentially.

"So I plays the rabbit on them. I jumps into the palmeeters. I gits down hog-style and crawls off. I plumb snaked into those palmeeter clumps and takes me a palmeeter root fer a pillow.

"That was yistiddy mornin'," he said, "and I ain't so much as moved my jawbones until this mornin'."

The Georgian puzzled. "Cain't them fellers foller ary track?" he asked.

"Cooter's a prime bloodhound." Tim winked broadly. "But I was hittin' the ground too fur apart!

"Well," he went on, "they was shore I hadn't made the hammock without they'd of seed me. So they beats around and tracks here and yonder, and pokes in the palmeeters, scairt as chickens they'd fall on snakeses, and they sits down to wait fer me.

"I says to myself, 'I hope you scoundrels does squat there.'

"I could hear them talkin' plain as this room. Cooter says: 'I know thet feller in the blue pants squatted in here in the palmeeters, but say, thet son of a bitch in the striped shirt that runned to the hard road, he didn't even go around the stumps, he jest tossed over 'em!'

"We was jest out of the swamp, like, and I was all buried up in the mud. Hit shore was cold, wet muck, black as a nigger's gizzard. When the sun gits high and beats down thu those palmeeter fans, one side o' me was a-freezin' and the other was a-burnin' up.

"Along toward noon I was so half froze and half scorched I thinks I've been there long enough. And then I studies, and I says, 'Hit'll be a heap longer thirty days in the county jail.' So I settles down to enjoy myself. There's times a palmeeter root's shore a soft pillow. If my wife was to put me a thing like thet in the bed, I'd shore chunk it at her, but me and thet palmeeter root got real fondlike.

"The antses got to me and got a-stingin', but Cooter must a plumb set in some, fer I heerd him a-slappin' and a-cussin'. I begins to get thirsty and my tongue shore swole up when the other catbird goes back to the Chivvolay and brings 'em a jar o' water. But I thinks: 'Let 'em drink.'

"Cooter sends his man back to smash up the still, but he done a mighty sorry job. I can git it together again in no great whiles.

"Then I hears 'em crank up the Chivvolay and my ole flivver and go off. I studies some and I figgers they mought not o' gone no further than the hard road, a trap, like. So I lays quiet a piece longer.

" 'Long in the evenin' 'bout three o'clock I could smell my shirt smokin' in the heat. I heerd the mosquitoes makin' thet fuss they makes when they's so full o' blood they cain't fly. I says to 'em, 'Git yer rations, you scoundrels. I'll git mine to-morrer.' I don't even slap 'em. You kin hear a feller slappin'.

"I thought of liftin' my head to look. But I've done turkey-hunted. You know, when you're sittin' quiet, waitin' fer a gobbler to fly in? And a squirrel comes down a tree and comes on you sudden-like? Thet squirrel is goin' to run up and chatter. And over yonder in the black-jack I heerd a squirrel run up and chatter. So I knowed Cooter was there right on.

" 'Long about good-dark he starts hisself a skeeter smudge and I could smell hit a-smokin'. I says: 'Well, you rascal, hit's a question who fust gits a bait o' waitin', you or me, one.' The mosquitoes was crowdin' so on me they was fightin' fer standin'-room. A big ole moccasin slides by so clost I could o' spit on him, but I figgers 'twa'n't no use to budge. I could smell rattlesnake musk along in the night. Lyin' there in the dark, dogged iffen hit didn't make me kind o' faintified. I says: 'Go give Cooter a smell of you.' "

Tim chuckled deeply.

"I don't reckon Cooter nor me would study none on spendin' another day and another night in jest thet pertickler fashion. But anyways, I shore outwaited him.

"Come crack o' day, the other feller comes back. They comes to the edge o' the palmeeters.

" 'They ain't nary mortal in there,' says the other.

" 'I reckon not,' says Cooter. 'If they is, hit ain't no human being. Hit's half rabbit or half snake or half wildcat, but hit ain't human.'

"And then they goes off. I mean, they's good gone."

Tim yawned sleepily.

"Well, hit serves me dogged right," he admitted. "I shore knowed better. It proves I orter allus let my conscience be my guide."

"I mean!" agreed the Georgia boy. "You kin put thet ole still on top of a alligator and I ain't got ary word to say. How soon kin we fix to git to work again?"

"To-morrer. Them scoundrels done the carelessest smashin'."

"Reckon they'll be traipsin' back again?"

Tim shook his head.

"No. We ain't in ary danger a whiles yet. Cooter'll be crowdin' on to Marion County. I reckon—"

He arose and stretched.

"I reckon fer about thirty days I'd orter have a plumb clare conscience."

A CROP OF BEANS

A Story

ATILLIE-HAWK swooped into the top of a dead cypress. The mocking-birds and red-birds that had scurried like wind-buffeted leaves ahead of him, stirred uneasily in the live oaks and palmettos, where they had concealed themselves. The sky had emptied itself for him of living things. Against the blinding blue of the Florida afternoon hung indolent masses of white cloud. The hawk shifted from one claw to the other, hitching his shoulders like a cripple. There ran a road—a fat chicken snake— a man—

The young Cracker swung his shotgun from his waist to his shoulder in a quick semicircle. The tillie-hawk exploded into a mass of buff feathers and tumbled to the edge of the road. The Cracker girl caught her breath.

"Lige!" she reproached him. "You hadn't orter wasted a shell on a ol' tillie-hawk."

A horn sounded behind them and a truck loaded with bean hampers lurched by in the deep ruts of the sand road. Old man Tainter and his Negro driver passed without the customary "Hey!" or lift of the hand. The young woman crowded back into the dry dog-fennel. The man no more than stepped aside, unbreaching his gun. He kicked a cloud of sand after the truck.

"His beans ain't a mite better'n mine. Parts of 'em is plumb sorry-lookin'."

"They're earlier, ain't they?"

"Jest a week. He ain't no more likely to miss frost than me. Ary time, now it's a'most November, we're like to git us one o' them piddlin' leetle ol' frosts don't mean nothin'. To-night, mebbe."

They turned between chinaberries into the Widow Sellers' gate. Her sharp tongue clicked at them from the porch.

"You Lige Gentry, you, how'll I ever git my cane cut? I ain't payin' you by the week reg'lar to traipse around with your wife."

He rose to the familiar bait.

"Dog take it, ol' woman, Drenna's been a-cuttin' cane with me all evenin'. An' who'll pay fer it? Not you. I'll be hornswoggled if you ain't the meanest white woman in the county."

He stamped across the porch. Drenna dropped down on the top step, draping her gray percale skirt across her worn shoes. The widow hunched herself on the cowhide seat of her hickory rocker, drawing her shawl around her shoulders against the chill air from the northwest.

"Ain't you sick o' keepin' Drenna hangin' around where you kin look at her all the day? I ain't done laughin', the way you begun a-courtin' her, like you was huntin' a squirrel goin' acrost a oak thicket an' you tryin' to keep sight of it. How many yares ago was it? Two, three? Anyways, long enough to git you a couple o' young uns. An' you ain't sick o' lookin' at her yit!"

The young Cracker towered over her. He shook back the curly sun-bleached hair from his sweaty forehead like an infuriated bull. He plunged roaring into her trap.

"Dog take you! You ain't fitten to fish the same creek 'longside of her! Drenna, move offen the stoop away from her! You'd orter study on sayin', is she sick o' lookin' at me! A pore sorry thing like me, to git a woman—"

The Widow Sellers rocked violently in sheer delight. Her little black chinquapin eyes danced. She scratched her white head excitedly with a piece of the okra she was cutting. She shrilled above him.

"Now you said it! Now you and me agrees for onct, Mister Gentry! A pore sorry thing like you! Now you're talkin'!"

He stopped short.

"Oh, go to the devil," he said good-naturedly.

Drenna smiled uneasily. The ribald quarrelling of this pair still disturbed her. It was scandalous for two people so dependent on each other to talk so. No other man, black or white, would work so hard for the old woman, at the low wages of six dollars a week. Certainly no other employer would allow Lige time off every afternoon to work his own few acres. They threw these facts at each other at every encounter.

The Widow Sellers was admitting now, "Shore you works hard. Bless Katy, all you know is to work. You don't know nothin' else. You got you no sense."

"You wait 'til my beans gits top price next week. You'll say I got sense."

"You got Davis wax, eh? Them new-fangled ones. They're pretty, but they ain't got the good flavor. Sellers always planted Wardwell's. You won't never make you no crop," she said comfortably. "Here," she reached behind her rocker and pushed a pair of worn child's shoes in his hands. "I had me a box from Janey, in Alabamy. Git along to yer sorry bean-patch."

He hurled the shoes past her head.

"Give yer dogged shoes to a nigger young un."

He spat over the edge of the porch and strode off fiercely.

"Fust crop o' beans I make," he called back over his shoulder, "you've seed the last o' me, ol' woman."

"You'll be white-headed as me," she mocked after him, "an' still proud to be takin' my rations money!"

"No need to holler," he soothed from the gate. "You got you a voice like a limpkin."

"A limpkin?" she puzzled. "Thet brownified crane screeches like a wild-cat?"

"Now you said it!" he whooped.

His teeth flashed in his tanned face. He was off at a violent trot for his two acres of beans. The old woman grinned.

"Ain't he the biggety thing!"

"Hain't biggety," the young woman said gently. "Jest turrible prideful. . . . He shot him a tillie-hawk a ways back, jest account o' ol' man Tainter was drivin' up behind us. He figgers he's as good as ary man to shoot his shells reckless."

The old woman nodded and chuckled. She put down her pan of okra and picked up the child shoes, dusting them with her apron. Drenna put them under her arm.

"Thank you, ma'am. They'll fit one o' the chappies, shore."

They walked together to the road. The widow shivered.

"That scamp knows as good as I do we'll git heavy frost to-night. We cain't skip it. The whole State o' Texas is a-breathin' cold in on us. Floridy don't make none o' her own troubles," she grumbled. "They all comes in from some'eres else. Wind from the south an' cold from Texas. He better say good-by to them beans to-day whilst they're pretty."

She laid a hand on the girl's arm.

"I was jest a-baitin' Lige about you. Leave me tell you, when he got you, he got him a saint."

The chinaberry cast a lacelike shadow across the translucence of the young sharp-chiselled face.

"There's no harm to neither one of you," the girl said quietly. "I don't pay no mind when either one or t'other of you gits to rarin'."

* * *

The three-room rough-pine dwelling a mile from the village was bare and shabby. Drenna's father, prospering one year in hogs, had given her a small melodeon. It was the sole ornament of the main room. When Lige was not so tired that he tumbled, sometimes in his underwear, sometimes fully dressed, into their bed in the adjoining room, he coaxed her at night to play on it. She sat stiffly upright on the seat and picked out awkward, quavering hymns.

To-night he sat teetering in his pine-slab chair, smoking his pipe, his blue eyes staring into space. His shaggy hair curled unnoticed into them. Drenna put the drowsy children, the baby and the boy of two, between clean unbleached muslin sheets over a corn-shucks mattress on the hand-made bed opposite the fireplace. When Lige did not make the usual sign, she went hesitantly to the melodeon. He relaxed a little as the notes of "Rock of Ages" wheezed sweetly from it.

"Dog take it, Drenna, thet's pretty."

His voice, with her, was gentle. Men who had grown up with him, gone their few scattered seasons with him to the village school, were still astonished at the taming of his exuberance. Passing the small house at night, they reported, through fire-lit windows, the sight of wild Lige smoking peacefully by the hearth, his eyes wide and hungry on the woman pedalling and playing. To-night the spell did not hold. Suddenly he stood up and knocked out his pipe into the lighter'd knot fire.

"I cain't set here an' let my beans freeze," he burst out. "Tainter's firin'. He's got him smudges all over his field. I don't figger it'll do a mite o' good to burn wood, but I got to try it."

"What wood you got to use, Lige?"

He ran his big hand across her head.

"I aim to give yer winter woodpile the devil, ma'am."

He went whistling to the field. The full moon had risen, coldly silver, on a night so still he heard the gray fox in the hammock on dry magnolia leaves. The young beans hung thickly on the bushes, slim and faintly yellow in the moonlight. The dark, tangled hammock pressed in on three sides of the clearing. The field was ordered and beautiful. He cursed out loud.

"Jesus! Only three days more'd o' made them beans—"

He had no hope of his fatwood fires, but building them, he felt better. A line of them blazed along the westerly, higher end. Thick black smoke drifted across the patch to settle in the lower corner. Drenna joined him toward midnight with a paper of cornbread. The cold was tangible. In the stillness it moved in perceptibly, a chill white ghost from Texas. Under the ineffectual blanket of smoke, it closed stiff hands tight about the succulent plants.

At daybreak, a breeze stirred from the southeast. The day, and the days following, would be warm. There would perhaps not be frost again until the next full moon. The frosted leaves were curling. White spots appeared on the beans. Then they turned translucent, like pale yellow icicles. By night they would be mush; the leaves black and shrivelled.

Walking around the wilting field, Lige saw that he had saved the lower end. The smudge had lain across the last few rows. The east line of the hammock protected them from the sun, as deadly on the injured plants as the frost itself. He made a quick estimate. Fifteen or twenty hampers saved—

He was late at the Widow Sellers', shivering in his thin blue shirt and pin-check pants. She greeted him amiably. Her own crops of okra, squash, peanuts, corn and sweet potatoes were safely harvested.

"Thermometer went to forty at day," she told him.

"No need to tell me," he answered wearily. "I been settin' up nussin' them forty degrees. I fired. I figger I jest about saved my seed an' fertilizer. I'm clearin' more o' the hammock. Next time I plant late, I'm goin' to have four acres instid o' two, all at the lower end. Then if frost ketches me, I got more'll come thu."

She stared at him.

"The bigger fool, you. You'd do best to leave off beans an' work fer me full time. I could mebbe pay ten dollars a week," she said slyly.

"You mind yer own business, ol' woman. I'll make me a crop o' beans'll git me shet o' you an' yer ten dollars, an' yer six."

She eyed him dubiously.

"What did you fire with?"

He walked away carelessly.

"A damn good wood-pile an' a damn good woman."

II

When a stranger—a Georgia truck driver or a platform buyer—asked Lige his business, he answered with a mustered defiance:

"I'm a bean man!"

It was true. The long hours he gave to the Widow Sellers' rich farms had no meaning beyond their moment. In mid-afternoon he hurried off to his own field, sweaty and excited, to turn furrows, to plant, to cultivate, to hoe, to harvest.

The quick growth of the crop stirred him. One week, the sandy loam lay golden, its expanse passive for the reception of the seed. The next week, the clearing in the hammock was covered with cotyledons, pale-green and pushing, like twin sails dotting a tawny sea. In forty-eight days the first crop was ready for picking. The emerald bushes crowded one another in the straight rows. The long beans hung like pendants, butter-yellow if they were wax, jade-green if Giant Stringless or Red Valentine.

The earth responded to him. When he and the soil were not interfered with, they made beans as fine as old man Tainter, who kept a wagon-load of niggers and bought fertilizer by the carload.

He was betrayed constantly by elements beyond his control. He fared no worse than the other growers, but the common misfortunes struck more implacably. Men who could borrow money for seed and fertilizer and rations, who were free to do other farming or stock-raising, made out more or less comfortably until the inevitable time when a good crop sold on a high market. There was a finality about his loss of a crop.

He lost beans from cold or rain or blight three seasons in succession. The fourth season, the second autumn, he made a fair crop. The market dropped so low it scarcely paid to ship. In October he quarrelled violently with the Widow Sellers. The old woman, in a growing security that he would never shake free of her, taunted him.

"You jest as good to say yer done. You jest as good to say you got no sense fer bean-makin'. Drenna's like to go naked, and you piddlin' away with beans. Yer young uns'd be stark if 'twa'n't fer Janey's things from Alabamy. You know it. You take me up on steady work at ten dollars, afore I studies you ain't wuth nothin'."

If Drenna had been with him, he would not have touched her. He shook the old woman by the shoulders until she screeched for her neighbors. He shouted her down.

"Damn your gizzard! If I figgered like the niggers, I'd say you'd put a cunjur on my bean-fields! 'Twon't be too long 'til you sees the last o' me. Dogged if I wouldn't ruther do without rations than take yer talk."

They sputtered fiercely at each other. It did not occur to her to fire him, nor to him to quit.

He was excited when he came home to supper that night. He had forgotten his anger at the widow. He had forgotten his unprofitable season. He was eager with his plans for spring beans. His lunch bucket had contained the usual meal of soda biscuits and syrup, but he sat at the table, scarcely eating. Drenna listened with her grave smile.

"We got to make out on four dollars a week this winter an' save two. I kin make me a crop o' beans on thet hammock land and I know it. I aim to have six acres ready, come spring. Does the rains come on to drownd 'em, I'll ditch. Does frost come, I'll lay me a smudge. And dog take it, Drenna, if they ain't no rain at all, and them beans goes to swivvellin', I kin water 'em a gourdful at a time."

The four-year-old nodded gravely.

"I kin water 'em."

Drenna smiled at him.

"Tell yer Daddy the whole lot of us kin tote water fer him."

"Tainter don't always make a crop," he went on, "and I cain't always lose it."

"Shore cain't," she agreed placidly.

Lige and Drenna planted when the red-bud came in bloom. All the signs were of warmth. Robins and blue-birds were moving north. The cautious chinaberry had put out young leaves. The last of the jasmine perfumed the roadside. Lige strode steadily up and down the long furrows, seeing nothing but the white seed dropping against the golden earth. Drenna stopped now and then to staighten her back. Her gray eyes rested on the rosy flush across the hammock. They picked out the swaying palms, precise and formal against a turquoise sky. When she bent to her work again, the half-smile habitual to her was brighter.

Lige sent her to the house when the end of the planting was in sight.

"Go git me my rations, woman," he told her. He turned her away from the field. "Git!" He took his hands from her shoulders. "Now shame to me. My hands has smuttied yer clean dress."

"Soap an' water's plenteeful."

His eyes followed her across the clearing and into the house.

The March night was chilly. When supper was eaten, he piled the fireplace with blocks of magnolia. The cream-colored wood gave out a sweet odor, like a mild thin spice. As the fire dulled, he threw on pine. He took off his high boots and stretched his bare sandy toes to the fire.

"Wisht I'd takened my boots off in the dark. Look at them feet. Now I got to git up an' wash 'em afore I goes to bed."

From the kitchen Drenna brought him a basin of warm water and a towel of flour sacking.

"Whooey, ain't thet fine!"

He dabbled luxuriously, drying his feet with the warm towel.

"Now you been a-waitin' on me, leave me do somethin' fer you. Leave me play fer you."

They both laughed. His playing was limited to two tunes on the mouth-organ.

"I'll blow 'The Tall Pine Tree.'"

She sat on a three-legged stool by the fireplace, her smooth head resting against the gray clay, her eyes closed. Lige played his tunes over and over, patting his bare right foot on the pine floor. The children stirred in their low bed, sighing in deep sleep. The magnolia burned into soft gray checks. Drenna nodded.

"Go on to bed, Sugar. I'll set up a whiles. I've wore you out, plantin' them beans. But Drenna—I got no question. We'll make us a crop, shore as dogs runs rabbits."

"Shore will," she agreed sleepily.

He sat by the fire an hour after she had gone, blowing softly into the harmonica, patting his foot.

Lige saved his beans two weeks later by a scanty margin. He had planted dangerously early, and as the crooks came through, it was plain that heavy frost was moving in. Two nights in succession were increasingly colder. All the beans in the region were slightly nipped. The third night would bring real damage. A smudge would be useless over the young juicy plants. In the crisp morning he said to Drenna:

"Ain't a reason in the world why I cain't cover them leetle bean plants with dirt to-day."

But when he drove the mule and cultivator between the rows, the earth he turned did not quite cover them.

Drenna, come out to watch him, said, "Kin do it by hand, Lige."

"Six acres?"

"Well, what we kin git covered is better'n nothin'."

The work went surprisingly fast. Except for the increasing ache of their backs, it was satisfying to move rapidly down the straight lines, swinging and stooping, ape-fashion, and cup the soft yellow dirt over the tops of the plants with their two hands. The four-year-old was fascinated. He followed like a young monkey, and in his clumsy way, throwing the sand with too-great enthusiasm, imitated them on adjacent rows.

"I kin rest to-morrer," she thought, and after dinner went at it again.

They worked until the night blended plants and earth and hammock and sky into a nothingness as deep and black as a 'gator cave. Drenna brought out kerosene lanterns. They were toiling slowly. The extra labor of moving the lights seemed insupportable. The beans were covered down to a last half-acre at the lower end. They went, stooped, for they could not quite straighten their backs, to their cold bed. They could do nothing more.

The night's frost wiped out the entire section, including Tainter. Those who had the money were planting again. Those who did not were done for the season. Lige waited two days for the cold to pass. Under a benign March sun, with a neighbor boy hired in the light of his hopes, he carefully fingered the sandy loam away from his beans. The plants emerged a little yellowed, wilted and leathery, but none the worse for their warm burying.

The town was aghast at news of the saving. The Widow Sellers said to Lige:

"Nobody but you'd be fool enough to scratch dirt over six acres o' beans—and then scratch 'em out again!"

He was generous in his good fortune. He pinched her wrinkled cheek and jumped away before her quick hand fell.

"Ol' woman, don't you wisht you'd had you a rale man like me, to make you crops when nobody else couldn't make 'em?"

* * *

It became apparent that Lige would have almost the earliest beans in the State. Other sections had been drowned out on the first planting, and he would come in at least two weeks ahead of his neighbors. He ordered fancy hampers, with green and red bands. The small crate factory trusted him for them. His beans were perfection. The bushes were loaded.

His first picking was small. He and Drenna and the neighbor boy managed it without help. The beans ripened rapidly, inexorably. The storekeeper, interested, loaned him money to hire pickers. He brought in a truck-load of hands for the second picking. Drenna culled, sorted and packed. The Widow Sellers came over. Other neighbor women dropped in to look at the big crop, and stayed to help with the packing. Drenna cooked a generous dinner of ham and grits and cornbread; made a great kettle of coffee and chicory; opened Mason jars of the past summer's blueberries and peaches and figs.

In the field, white and Negro pickers worked alternate rows. The white children squatted on their haunches, sliding along from bush to bush. The Negroes for the most part bent to their picking, their black arms gathering the beans like swift sickles. The six acres were alive.

Lige worked desperately in and out of the field. The sorting and packing proceeded steadily under Drenna's quiet authority. The volunteer neighbor help chattered and gossiped, but the work was familiar, and they did it carefully. A Negro asked "Captain Gentry" for buckets of drinking water to take to the pickers. The Widow Sellers' tongue flashed like hail across the work. Her small black eyes watched uneasily the growing spread of finished hampers, stacked up to go to the express office. The picking totalled a hundred and thirty hampers. The neighbors divided up the cull beans and went home.

The third picking ran to nearly two hundred crates. It was the most ample yield the section had produced in seasons. The checks began to arrive. A telegram from the New York commission house preceded the first. Lige's initial shipment had brought the record price of nine dollars a hamper.

The market price dropped rapidly as other sections came in. Yet his returns were consistently good. The last three checks reached him on one mail. His net for the crop was over fifteen hundred dollars.

He went a little crazy.

III

Lige began his celebration at four o'clock in the afternoon. He hurled himself into the house; changed into Sunday clothes without washing or shaving. He slapped into Drenna's hands the accumulation of bean checks, keeping out one for fifty dollars. His stiff store collar was already wet with sweat. Tousled hair hung damp in his eyes.

"Drenna, if I ain't fitten to-morrer, you git the ice-truck to take you to Pondland and go to the bank and put these in it. It's what they calls openin' a account."

"You don't want I should git the cash-money an' fetch it back an' hide it?"

"Now, Drenna, you do like I tell you. Thet's the ol'-timey way. Don't nobody hide their money these days."

He was bounding down the low steps.

"Lige, what you fixin' to do?"

"Sugar, I'm fixin' to git so drunk you'll be 'shamed fer me all year, but I got it to do an' you got it to put up with."

He waved a long arm and was gone at his loping trot down the road toward the village, where the Brinley boys waited in their old Ford. The earth swayed from under her. She dropped trembling on the rickety stoop. She wanted to run after him, to call him back, but numbness held her. Lige had been so good; with her, so gentle. Year after year, with his bean-crops failing him, he had been patient. Yet violence simmered in him. He had been always like a great kettle of cane juice, ready, at a little too much heat, to boil over.

With her, he had been like a wild thing tamed; a 'coon or 'possum or young panther that had come to enjoy captivity. Now, in his prosperity, he had broken out of the cage and was gone, dangling his ropes behind him. For a moment, he did not seem to belong to her. It was as though a stranger had gone galloping down the road to meet the Brinley boys and get drunk.

She rose from the stoop, told the children to stay in the house, and went to the Widow Sellers.

"Yes," the old woman said before she could speak, "the grand rascal's been here an' gone. Th'owed over his job an' gone to raise him some hell."

Drenna stiffened. She lifted her chin.

"If he's took the notion to git drunk, I reckon he's got the right to do it."

The widow gaped. When the young woman turned defiantly for home again, she scurried through town telling that Drenna didn't give a rap whether Lige got drunk or no. The town buzzed with it.

"I ain't surprised at Lige, but who'd a-figgered Drenna'd turn out plumb shameless!"

No one came near her that evening. The village was busy waiting for news of Lige's hilarity to come in piece by piece. Drenna sat in her low rocker, holding the baby. The older child played in and out of the house and at last gave up asking questions. Twilight came, and still she sat, rocking and staring. She put the children to bed and went back to her rocker. The kerosene lamps went unlit. She was chilly and wrapped a patchwork quilt around her. A hoot owl startled her in the pine tree by the window. In the hammock, the first whip-poor-will gave his yearning cry.

"When the whip-poor-will calls, it's time for the corn to be in the ground."

Would Lige bother to plant corn this spring? Would he get drunk every once and again, now he had money? They had planned to repair the leaking shingled roof; to buy hogs and raise peanuts and chufas; there was money in stock, if you could get a start; to have a real mattress for the bed, some more chairs and a new cook-stove; to take a trip to Alabama to visit Drenna's folks; to be done once and for all with the Widow Sellers; and of course, to lay by money for an increasing acreage of beans.

She listened intently at every sound. A car went by; a nigger riding a mule and singing. A pair of hounds bayed past, trailing 'coon. She was drowsing in her chair when a clatter sounded on the porch and Lige was home.

" 'Lo, Sugar. I shore done the job."

She was trembling again. To keep from looking at him, she did not light a lamp. He was knocking into everything. She took his arm and led him into the bedroom.

"Lay down, Lige, an' leave me take off your shoes an' breeches."

He was asleep, puffing and moaning, before she could undress him. She got off his shoes and threw a cover over him. Lying between the babies, she dozed the two or three hours until daylight.

She roused him at breakfast-time to offer a cup of coffee. He took a few swallows and was suddenly sick. He turned over on his side, groaning, and went to sleep again. She shut the door of the room when she saw two women coming up the walk.

People came all morning; women to bring her juicy bits about the drunken night, with Lige and the Brinleys and the Twillers and Tom Parker driving all over the county shouting and treating everybody. Men came to ask, grinning, if she needed any help with Lige; curious, to see how she was taking it; and men and women grabbing for the bean money.

The owner of the crate factory came for his pay. She gave him one of the checks endorsed in Lige's uneven hand. The storekeeper came for the picking money. The Widow Lykes came whining to borrow whatever she could get. Drenna was bewildered; then resentful.

* * *

She was dressed to go to Pondland to the bank when the preacher arrived. It startled her. He had never been in the house before, although she had slipped in and out of church almost every preaching Sunday. He spoke severely on the sin of drunkenness. She braced herself to it. He spoke at last of the desirability, under the shocking circumstances, of tithing the fortune they were squandering, and giving to the Lord. She caught her breath. The parson was after the bean money, too.

Fury took possession of her, like a moccasin swallowing a small gray rabbit. She hated everybody; Lige, crying out now and then behind the closed door in his drunken sickness; the town, with its intruding eyes and waggling tongues; the Widow Sellers; the parson; above everything else, the bean money. She stamped her foot.

"What's a-goin' on ain't nobody's business. I'll settle with God when I git straightened out. I got no money fer you now, nor maybe never. I've give what I could fer missions, an' I always will. But I need what we got now fer the chappies an' things you know nothin' about. You go on now."

She drove him from the house, locked the door and plodded furiously down the road to hail the ice-truck. In Pondland, she opened the account at the bank with a boldness foreign to her.

"I want fifty dollars o' thet back in cash money," she said belligerently.

Her lips moved.

"Jest what Lige takened," she said to herself.

On the streets of the city again, she found herself dazed. The bills were clutched in her fist. She knew only that she intended to spend them, recklessly, foolishly, wickedly. In the shop windows were dresses for summer; hats and shoes. She smoothed back her soft hair. She had come off without any hat at all. A red chiffon dress caught her eye. She walked in a dream into the shop and pointed out the frock. The saleswomen lifted their eyebrows at one another. They helped her take off her calico dress and put on the red chiffon over her white muslin slip.

"Of course now, with a silk slip, and nice shoes—"

In the long mirror were reflected a white frightened face with gray eyes, pale tight lips, and bare arms and throat above a flaming pile of soft fabric. She nodded. The saleswoman folded the dress in tissue paper and laid it carefully in a box.

"Forty-five dollars."

She held out the bills.

Bean money. Lige's fine crop of beans. She saw the six acres, green with gold pendants hung over them. She remembered the pickers moving in with the tall hampers on their shoulders, swaying and singing. The field was empty now, waiting for fall beans. The new bills crackled in her fingers. This was all they had to show for the crop. The rest was in Lige's tormented belly; and in the strange, impersonal bank, dropped from sight like a stone in a pond.

The bean money had been queer stuff. Checks in writing, that everybody scrambled to get at. . . . Lige acting scandalously. . . . Her impudence to the preacher. . . . Now a red dress tempting her to go about like a lewd woman. She shivered.

"I cain't do it."

She put the money behind her back.

"I cain't do it."

Outside the shop she stuffed the bills inside her blouse. She rode home on the loaded ice-truck.

She walked from the heart of the village out to the house, running the last of the way. The children were playing with chicken feathers in the sandy yard. Lige was lying awake in bed, smoking his pipe. He put his arm over his face in mock shame.

"Say it, Drenna," he grinned. "I got it comin'. Yore ol' man's disgraced ye, like I tol' you. But dog take it"—she sat on the bed, and he reached out his arms for her—"it was fine! Jest to turn thet ol' quart bottle topside down an' let 'er drip!"

She had to laugh at him. They wouldn't say any more about it. She had very nearly done as wrong as he. She had been wilder, crazier.

She was cooking dinner when the ice-truck lumbered up to the gate. Tim ran up the walk and into the house.

"Drenna! The Pondland bank's closed down! No more'n a good hour after you-all put yore money in. Tainter jest brought the word. Ev'ybody's caught."

He mopped his face and started away again.

"I got to go out back o' the Creek an' tell the Philbins."

At the gate he waved his hand to her and called:

"Tell Lige ev'ybody says they bet he'll wish he'd got twicet as drunk!"

He rattled off.

She watched the truck out of sight. She was not astonished. She had not been brought up to consider a bank the place for money. Her father had always said:

"Nothin' ain't safe ner sartin exscusin' a iron pot o' gold or siller, put deep in a place where nobody else cain't find hit."

She went into the bedroom to Lige. He was getting his wracked body into clean clothes.

"I heard him! Oh my God, Drenna!"

Sweat rolled into his blood-shot eyes.

"I'll kill somebody fer this—"

He was unsteady on his feet. He picked up his shotgun from behind the head of the bed.

"Philbin's 'll go. Buckshot's too good fer thet bank preseedent."

"Lige," she said gently.

He stopped. His eyes softened.

"No need to take on so. Banks closes and you cain't blame nobody special."

She drew out the fifty dollars from her blouse. The stiff paper was warm from the skin of her breast. He stared. The money was real and tangible.

"Reckon I was jest led to keep it out in cash-money. It'll git us seed fer fall."

"But, Drenna—all thet other gone like as if 'twas stole—"

Don't study that-a-way. I figger, we jest lost another bean-crop."

He replaced the shotgun slowly. He sat down on the side of the bed, his muscular hands closing and unclosing. He pondered. At last he nodded gravely.

"Jest done lost us another crop o' beans."

GAL YOUNG UN

A Story in Two Parts

T

HE house was invisible from the road which wound, almost untraveled, through the flat-woods. Once every five days a turpentine wagon creaked down the ruts, and negroes moved like shadows among the pines. A few hunters in season came upon them chipping boxes, scraping aromatic gum from red pots into encrusted buckets; inquired the way and whether quail or squirrel or turkey had been seen. Then hunters and turpentiners moved again along the road, stepping on violets and yellow pitcher-plants that rimmed the edges.

The negroes were aware of the house. It stood a few hundred yards away, hidden behind two live oaks, isolated and remote in a patch of hammock. It was a tall square two-stories. The woman who gave them water from her well when the nearby branch was dry looked to them like the house, tall and bare and lonely, weathered gray, like its unpainted cypress. She seemed forgotten.

The two white men, hunting lazily down the road, did not remember—if they had ever known—that a dwelling stood here. Flushing a covey of quail that flung themselves like feathered bronze discs at the cover of the hammock, their first shots flicked through the twin oaks. They followed their pointer dog on the trail of single birds and stopped short in amazement. Entering the north fringe of the hammock, they had come out on a sandy open yard. A woman was

148

watching them from the back stoop of an old house.

"Shootin' mighty close, men," she called.

Her voice sounded unused, like a rusty iron hinge.

The older man whistled in the dog, ranging feverishly in the low palmettos. The younger swaggered to the porch. He pushed back the black slouch hat from his brazen eyes.

"Never knowed nobody lived in six miles o' here."

His tone was insolent. He drew a flattened package of cigarettes from his corduroy hunting jacket, lighted one, and waited for her to begin scolding. Women always quarreled with him. Middle-aged women, like this one, quarreled earnestly; young ones snapped at him playfully.

"It's a long ways from anybody, ain't it?" she agreed.

He stared at her between puffs.

"Jesus, yes."

"I don't keer about you shootin'," she said. "It's purely sociable, hearin' men-folks acrost the woods. A shot come thu a winder jest now, that's all the reason I spoke."

The intruders shifted their shotguns uneasily. The older man touched his finger to his cap.

"That's all right, ma'am."

His companion strolled to the stone curbing of an open well. He peered into its depths, shimmering where the sun of high noon struck vertically.

"Good water?"

"The finest ever. Leave me fetch you a clean cup."

She turned into the house for a white china coffee cup. The men wound up a bucket of water on creaking ropes. The older man drank politely from the proffered cup. The other guzzled directly from the bucket. He reared back his head like a satisfied hound, dripping a stream of crystal drops from his red mouth.

"Ain't your dog thirsty? Here—reckon my ol' cat won't fuss if he drinks outen his dish." The woman stroked the animal's flanks as he lapped. "Ain't he a fine feller."

The hunters began to edge away.

"Men, I jest got common rations, bacon an' biscuit an' coffee, but you're plumb welcome to set down with me."

"No, thank you, ma'am." They looked at the sun. "Got to be moseyin' home."

The younger man was already on his way, sucking a straw. The other fumbled in his game-pocket.

"Sorry we come so clost up on you, lady. How 'bout a bird fer your dinner?"

She reached out a large hand for the quail.

"I'd shore thank you fer it. I'm a good shot on squirrel, an' turkeys when I git 'em roosted. Birds is hard without no dog to point 'em. I gits hungry fer quail . . ."

Her voice trailed off as the hunters walked through the pines toward the road. She waved her hand in case they should turn around. They did not look back.

The man was hunting alone because he had been laughed at. His cronies in the Florida village, to which he had returned after a few years' wandering, knew that he detested solitude. It was alien to him, a silent void into which he sank as into quicksand. He had stopped at the general store to pick up a hunting partner. The men lounging there hours at a time were usually willing to go with him. This time none was ready.

"Come go with me, Willy," he insisted. "I cain't go by myself."

The storekeeper called over his shoulder, weighing out a quarter's worth of water-ground meal for a negro.

"You'll git ketched out alone in the woods sometime, Trax, an' nobody won't know who 'tis."

The men guffawed.

"Trax always got to git him a buddy."

His smoldering eyes flared at them. He spat furiously across the rough pine floor of the store.

"I ain't got to git me none o' these sorry catbirds."

He had clattered down the wooden steps, spitting angrily every few feet. They were jealous, he thought, because he had been over on the east coast. He had turned instinctively down the south road out of the village. Old man Blaine had brought him this way last week. He hunted carelessly for two or three hours, taking pot shots at several coveys that rose under his feet. His anger made him miss the birds widely. It was poor sport without a companion and a dog.

Now he realized that he was lost. As a boy he had hunted these woods, but always with other boys and men. He had gone through them unseeing, stretching his young muscles luxuriously, absorbing lazily the rich Florida sun, cooling his face at every running branch. His shooting had been careless, avid. He liked to see the brown birds tumble in midair. He liked to hunt with the pack, to gorge on the game dinners they cooked by lake shores under oak trees. When the group turned homeward, he followed, thinking of supper; of the 'shine his old man kept hidden in the smokehouse; of the girls he knew. Someone else knew north and south, and the cross patterns of the piney-woods roads. The lonely region was now as unfamiliar as though he had been a stranger.

It was an hour or two past noon. He leaned his 12-gauge shotgun against a pine and looked about him nervously. He knew by the sun that he had come continuously south. He had crossed and recrossed the road, and could not decide whether it now lay to the right or left. If he missed it to the right, he would come to cypress swamp. He licked his lips. If he picked the wrong road to the left, it would bring him out a couple of miles above the village. That would be better. He could always get a lift back. He picked up his gun and began to walk.

In a few minutes a flat gray surface flashed suddenly from a patch of hammock. He stopped short. Pleasure swept over him, cooling his hot irritation. He recognized the house where he and Blaine had drawn water. He had cursed Blaine for giving a quail to the woman. He wiped the sweat from his face. The woman would feed him and direct him out of the flat-woods. Instinctively he changed his gait from a shuffling drag to his customary swagger.

He rapped loudly on the smooth cypress front door. It had a half-moon fanlight over it. The house was old but it was capacious and good. There was, for all its bareness, an air of prosperity. Clean white curtains hung at the windows. A striped cat startled him by rearing against his legs. He kicked it away. The woman must be gone. A twig cracked in the yard beyond the high piazza. He turned. The woman was stalking around the side of the house to see before she was seen.

Her gray face lightened as she recognized him. She laughed.

"Mister, if you knowed how long it's been since I heerd a rap. Don't nobody knock on my front door. The turpentine niggers calls so's I won't shoot, and the hunters comes a-talkin' to the well."

She climbed the front steps with the awkwardness of middle age. She dried a hand on her flour-sacking apron and held it out to him. He took it limply, interrupting the talk that began to flow from her. He was ugly with hunger and fatigue and boredom.

"How 'bout a mess o' them rations you was offerin' me last week?"

His impatience was tempered with the tone of casual intimacy in which he spoke to all women. It bridged time and space. The woman flushed.

"I'd be mighty well pleased—"

She opened the front door. It stuck at the sill, and she threw a strong body against it. He did not offer to help. He strolled in ahead of her. As she apologized for the moments it would take to fry bacon and make coffee, he was already staring about him at the large room. When she came to him from the kitchen half an hour later, her face red with her hurry, the room had made an impress on his mind, as roads and forests could not do. The size of the room, of the clay fireplace, the adequacy of chairs and tables of a frontier period, the luxury of a Brussels carpet, although ancient, over wood, the plenitude of polished, unused kerosene lamps—the details lay snugly in his mind like hoarded money.

Hungry, with the smell of hot food filling his breath, he took time to smooth his sleek black hair at a walnut-framed mirror on the varnished matchboard wall. He made his toilet boldly in front of the woman. A close watching of his dark face, of the quickness of his hands moving over his affectation of clipped side-burns, could only show her that he was good to look at. He walked to the kitchen with a roll, sprawling his long legs under the table.

With the first few mouthfuls of food good humor returned to him. He indulged himself in graciousness. The woman served him lavishly with fried cornbread and syrup, coffee, white bacon in thick slices, and fruits and vegetables of her own canning. His gluttony delighted her. His mouth was full, bent low over his heaped plate.

"You live fine, ma'am, for anyone lives plumb alone."

She sat down opposite him, wiping back the wet gray hair from her forehead, and poured herself a convivial cup of coffee.

"Jim—that was my husband—an' Pa always did say if they was good rations in the house they'd orter be on the table. I ain't got over the habit."

"You been livin' alone quite some time?"

"Jim's fifteen year dead. Pa 'bout six."

"Don't you never go nowheres?"

"I got no way to go. I kep' up stock fer two-three year after Pa died, but 'twa'n't wuth the worry. They's a family lives two mile closer to town than me, has a horse an' wagon. I take 'em my list o' things 'bout oncet a month. Seems like . . ."

He scarcely listened.

A change of atmosphere in her narrative indicated suddenly to him that she was asking him about himself.

"You a stranger?"

She was eager, leaning on the table waiting for his answer.

He finished a saucer of preserved figs, scraping at the rich syrup with relish. He tilted back in his chair luxuriously and threw the match from his cigarette in the general direction of the wood stove. He was entirely at home. His belly well filled with good food, his spirit touched with the unfailing intoxication to him of a woman's interest, he teetered and smoked and talked of his life, of his deeds, his dangers.

"You ever heard the name o' Trax Colton?"

She shook her head. He tapped his chest significantly, nodding at her.

"That's me. You've heard tell, if you on'y remembered, o' me leavin' here a few years back on account of a little cuttin' fuss. I been on the east coast—Daytona, Melbourne, all them places. The fuss blowed over an' I come back. Fixin' to take up business here."

He frowned importantly. He tapped a fresh cigarette on the table, as he had learned to do from his companions of the past years. He thought with pleasure of all that he had learned, of the sophistication that lay over his Cracker speech and ways like a cheap bright coat.

"I'm an A-1 bootlegger, ma'am."

For the time being he was a big operator from the east coast. He told her of small sturdy boats from Cuba, of signal flares on the St. Augustine beach at midnight, of the stream of swift automobiles moving in and out just before high tide. Her eyes shone. She plucked at the throat of her brown-checked gingham dress, breathing quickly. It was fitting that this dark glamorous young man should belong to the rocket-lit world of danger. It was ecstasy painful in its sharpness, that he should be tilted back at her table, flicking his fragrant ashes on her clean, lonely floor.

He was entirely amiable as he left her. Pleased with himself, he was for a moment pleased with her. She was a good woman. He laid his hand patronizingly on her shoulder. He stroked the striped cat on his way down the steps. This time he turned to lift his hand to her. She waved heartily as long as his lithe body moved in sight among the pines.

An impulse took her to the mirror where he had smoothed his hair, as though it would bring him within her vision again. She saw herself completely for the first time in many years. Isolation had taken the meaning from age. She had forgotten until this moment that she was no longer young. She turned from the mirror and washed the dishes soberly. It occurred to her that the young man had not even asked her name.

The hammock that had been always a friendly curtain about the old house was suddenly a wall. The flat-woods that had been sunny and open, populous with birds and the voice of winds, grew dense and dark. She had been solitary. She had grieved for Jim and for the old man her father. But solitude had kept her company in a warm natural way, sitting cozily at her hearth, like the cat. Now loneliness washed intolerably over her, as though she were drowning in a cold black pond.

The young man's complacency lasted a mile or two. As his feet began to drag, fact intruded on the fiction with which he had enraptured the gray-haired woman. Memories seeped back into him like a poison: memories of the lean years as ignorant hanger-on of the prosperous bootleggers; of his peddling to small garages of lye-cut 'shine in ignominious pints. The world for which he considered himself fitted had evaded him. His condition was desperate. He thought of the woman who had fed him, whom he had entranced with his story. Distaste for her flooded him, as though it was her fault the story was a lie. He lifted his shotgun and blew the head from a redbird trilling in a wild plum tree.

The storekeeper in the village was the only person who recognized Mattie Syles. The store was packed with the Saturday-night buyers of rations. A layer of whites milled in front of the meat counter; a layer of blacks shifted behind them. At the far grocery counter along a side wall a wedge of negroes had worked in toward the meal and sugar barrels, where helpers weighed out the dimes' and quarters' worth with deliberately inaccurate haste. Two white women were buying percale of the storekeeper's wife at the dry-goods counter.

The woman came in defiantly, as though the store was a shameful place where she had no business. She looked searchingly from side to side. The storekeeper's wife called, "Evenin', ma'am," and the two white women wheeled to stare and whisper after her. She advanced toward the meat counter. The negroes parted to let her in. The storekeeper poised his knife over a pork backbone to look at her. He laid it down, wiped his hands with a flourish on his front, and shook hands across the counter.

"If this ain't a surprise! Must be four-five years since you been to town! Meat I been sendin' you by Lantrys been all right? What kin I do fer you? Butchered this mornin'—got fresh beef. How 'bout a nice thin steak?"

She made her purchases slowly and moved to the staples counter. She insisted on being left until the last.

"I ain't in no hurry."

The store was almost empty and ready to close when she gathered her sacks together and climbed into the Lantrys' wagon, waiting outside the door. As Lantry clicked to his horse and they moved off she did not notice that the man she had hoped desperately to see was just strolling into the store.

"Gimme a couple o' packs o' Camels to tide me over Sunday."

"Fifteen cents straight now, Trax."

"Jest one, then."

The storekeeper spoke across the vacant store to his wife, rolling up the bolts of cloth.

"Edna, you have better manners with the customers, or we'll be losing 'em. Why'n't you take up some time with Mis' Syles?"

"Who?"

"Mis' Syles—Jim Syles' widder—ol' man Terry's daughter—lives four-five mile south, out beyond Lantry's. You know her, Edna. Lantry's been buyin' fer her."

"I never knowed her. How'd I know her now? Why'n't you call her by name, so's I'd of knowed?"

"Well, you keep better track of her if she's goin' to take to comin' to town agin. She's rich."

Trax turned in the doorway.

"You talkin' about that gank-gutted woman left jest now?"

He had avoided going into the store until she left. He had not intended to bring her volubility upon him in public, have her refer to their meal together. He had half-guessed she had come looking for him. Women did.

"She live alone in a two-story house you cain't see from the road?"

"That's her," the storekeeper agreed. "That's Mis' Syles, a'right."

"She's rich?"

"I mean rich. Got her five dollars a week steady rent-money from turpentine, an' three thousand dollars insurance in the bank her daddy left her. An' then lives 'tother end o' nowhere. Won't leave the old house."

" 'Bout time somebody was fixin' to marry all that, goin' to waste."

"She wouldn't suit you, Trax. You didn't git a good look at her. You been used to 'em younger an' purtier."

The man Colton was excited. He walked out of the store without the customary "Well, evenin' " of departure. He hurried to Blaine's, where he was boarding, but did not go in. It was necessary to sit alone on the bench outside and think. His luck had not deserted him. As he leaned his dark head back against the wall, the tropical stars glittering over him were the bright lights of city streets. Here and there a fat star flickered. These were the burnished kerosene lamps of the widow Syles. The big room—the fireplace that would heat it on the coolest nights—one by one he drew out the remembered details and tucked them into his plans.

The man courted the woman with the careless impatience of his quail hunting. He intended to be done with it as quickly as possible. There was, astonishingly, a certain pleasure in her infatuation. He responded to any woman's warmth as a hound does to a grate fire, stretching comfortably before it. The maternal lavishness of her emotion for him was satisfying. Younger women, pretty women, expected something of him, coaxed and coquetted.

On his several visits to the widow before he condescended to be married to her, he sprawled in the early spring nights before the big fireplace. He made it plain that he was not one to sit around the kitchen stove. His fastidiousness charmed her. She staggered into the room with her generous arms heaped with wood: live oak and hickory, and some cedar chips, because Trax liked the smell. From his chair he directed the placing of the heavy logs. A fire must crackle constantly to please him. She learned to roll cigarettes for him, bringing them to him to lick flickeringly, like a snake, with his quick tongue. The process stirred her. When she placed the finished cigarette between his lips and lighted it with a blazing lighter'd splinter; when he puffed languidly on it and half-closed his eyes, and laid his fingers perhaps on her large-boned hand, she shivered.

The courting was needlessly protracted because she could not believe that he would have her. It was miracle enough that he should be here at all in these remote flat-woods. It was unbelievable that he should be willing to prolong the favor, to stay with her in this place forever.

She said, "Cain't be you raly wants me."

Yet she drank in his casual insistence.

"Why not? Ain't a thing the matter with you."

She understood sometimes—when she wakened with a clear mind in the middle of the night—that something strange had happened to her. She was moving in a delirium, like the haze of malaria when the fever was on. She solaced herself by thinking that Trax too might be submerged in such a delicious fog.

When he left her one night in the Blaine Ford he had borrowed, the retreating explosions of the car left behind a silence that terrified her. She ran to the beginning of the pines to listen. There was no sound but the breath of the south wind in the needles. There was no light but the endless flickering of stars. She knew that if the man did not come back again she would have to follow him. Solitude she had endured. She could not endure desolation.

When he came the next day she was ready to go to the village with him to the preacher. He laughed easily at her hurry and climbed ahead of her into the borrowed car. He drove zestfully, with abandon, bouncing the woman's big frame over the ruts of the dirt road.

As they approached the village he said casually, "I keep my money in Clark City. We'd orter do our business together. Where's yours?"

"Mine's there too. Some's in the post office an' some in the bank."

"Supposin' we go git married there. An' reckon you kin lend me a hundred till I add up my account?"

She nodded an assent to both questions.

"Don't you go spendin' no money on me, Trax, if you ain't got it real free to spend." She was alarmed for his interests. "You leave me pay fer things a while."

He drew a deep breath of relief. He was tempted for a moment to get her cash and head for the east coast at once. But he had made his plans to stay. He needed the old house in the safe flat-woods to make his start. He could even use the woman.

When they came back through the village from the city she stopped at the store for supplies. The storekeeper leaned across the fresh sausage to whisper confidentially:

"Tain't my business, Mis' Syles, but folks is sayin' Trax Colton is sort o' courtin' you. You come of good stock, an' you'd orter step easy. Trax is purely trash, Mis' Syles."

She looked at him without comprehension.

She said, "Me and Trax is married."

The gray of the house was overlaid with the tenderness of the April sun. The walls were washed with its thin gold. The ferns and lichens of the shingled roof were shot through with light, and the wren's nest under the eaves was luminous. The striped cat sprawled flattened on the rear stoop, exposing his belly to the soft warmth. The woman moved quietly at her work, for fear of awakening the man. She was washing. When she drew a bucket of water from the well she steadied it with one hand as it swung to the coping, so that there should be no sound.

Near the well stood bamboo and oleander. She left her bucket to draw her fingers along the satin stoutness of the fresh green bamboo shoots, to press apart the new buds of the oleander in search of the pale pinkness of the first blossoms. The sun lay like a friendly arm across her square shoulders. It seemed to her that she had been chilled, year on year, and that now for the first time she was warmed through to her marrow. Spring after the snapping viciousness of February; Trax sleeping in the bed after her solitude. . . . When she finished her washing she slipped in to look at him. A boyish quiet wiped out the nervous shiftiness of his waking expression. She wanted to gather him up, sleeping, in her strong arms and hold him against her capacious breast.

When his breakfast was almost ready, she made a light clatter in the kitchen. It irritated him to be called. He liked to get up of his own accord and find breakfast smoking, waiting for him. He came out gaping, washed his face and hands in the granite basin on the water-shelf, combed his hair leisurely at the kitchen mirror, turning his face this way and that. Matt stood watching him, twisting her apron. When he was quite through, she came to him and laid her cheek against his.

"Mornin', Trax-honey."

Her voice was vibrant.

"Mornin'."

He yawned again as he dropped into his chair. He beat lightly on his down-turned plate with his knife and surveyed the table. He scowled.

"Where's the bacon?"

"Honey, I didn't think you'd want none with the squirrel an' eggs an' fish."

"My God, I cain't eat breakfast without bacon."

"I'm sorry, Trax. 'Twon't take me but a minute now."

She was miserable because she had not fried bacon and he wanted it.

He slid eggs and meat and biscuits to his plate, poured coffee with an angry jerk, so that it spilled on the table, shoveled the food in, chewing with his mouth open. When Matt put the crisp thick slices of white bacon before him, he did not touch them. He lighted a cigarette and strolled to the stoop, pushing off the cat so that he might sit down. He leaned back and absorbed the sun. This was fine.

He had deliberately allowed himself these few idle weeks. He had gone long without comfort. His body needed it. His swaggering spirit needed it. The woman's adoration fed him. He could have had no greater sense of well-being, of affluence if she had been a nigger servant. Now he was ready for business. His weasel mind was gnawing its hole into the world he longed for.

"Matt!"

She left her dishes and came to stand over him.

"Matt, you're goin' in business with me. I want you should git me three hundred dollars. I want to set up a eight-barrel still back o' the house, down by the branch."

Trax had crashed like a meteor into the flat-woods. It had not occurred to her that his world must follow him. That was detached from him, only a strange story that he had told. She had a sensation of dismay that any thing, any person, must intrude on her ecstasy.

She said anxiously, "I got enough to make out on, Trax. You don't need to go startin' up nothin' like that."

"All right—if you want I should put my outfit some'eres else—"

"No, no. Don't you do that. Don't you go 'way. I didn't know you was studyin' on nothin' like that—you jest go ahead an' put it clost as you like."

"Down by the branch, like I said."

He visioned the lay-out for her. She listened, distraught. The platform here, for the barrels of mash. There, the wood-pile for the slow fire. Here again, the copper still itself. The cover was dense, utterly concealing. The location was remote.

"The idee, Matt," he was hunched forward, glowing, "is to sell yer own stuff what they call retail, see? It costs you fifty, seventy-five cents a gallon to make. You sell by the five-gallon jug fer seven dollars, like they're doin' now, you don't make nothin'. That's nigger pay. But what do you git fer it by the drink? A quarter. A quarter a drink an' a dollar a pint. You let people know they kin git 'em a drink out here any time to Trax Colton's, you got 'em comin' in from two-three counties fer it. You git twenty gallons ahead an' color some up, cook it a whiles underground to darken it, an' you take it to places like Jacksonville an' Miami—you got you real money."

It was as though thunder and lightning threatened over the flat-woods. The darkness of impending violence filled them. She stared at him.

" 'Course, if you don't want to invest in my business with me, I got to be gittin' back where I come from."

The smoke from his cigarette drifted across her.

"No, no! It's all right!"

His glamorousness enfolded her like the April sun.

"Honey, anything you want to do's all right."

Setting up the still was a week's work. Men began to come and go. Where there had been, once in five days, the silent turpentiners, once in a while the winter hunters, there were now negroes bringing in cut wood; a local mason putting together brick and mortar; a hack carpenter building a platform with a roof; men in trucks bringing in sacks of meal and sugar, glass demijohns and oak kegs.

The storekeeper brought five hundred pounds of sugar.

"Howdy, Mis' Colton. Reckon you never figgered you'd be 'shinin'."

"No."

"But you couldn't git you no better place fer it."

Her square face brightened.

"That's jest what Trax says."

That night she approached him.

"Trax, all these here men knowin' what you're doin'—reckon it's safe?"

"They got no reason to say nothin'. The only reason anybody'd turn anybody else up was if he'd done somethin' to him. Then they'd git at him that-a-way. Git his still, see? Git him tore up. That way they'd git him."

She made no further comment. Her silence made its way through the wall of his egotism.

"You don't talk as much as you did, Matt. Else I got used to it."

"I was alone so long, honey. Seemed like I had to git caught up."

But the spring warmth was no longer so loosening to the tongue.

The alien life the man was bringing in chilled the exuberance that had made her voluble.

"I'm fixin' to learn you to make the whiskey, Matt."

She stared at him.

"Less help we have, knowin' how much I got an' where 'tis, better it suits me, see?"

She said finally, "I kin learn."

The work seemed strange, when all her folk had farmed and timbered. But her closest contact with Trax was over the sour, seething mash. When they walked together back of the house, down to the running branch, their bodies pushing side by side through the low palmettos, they were a unit. Except to curse her briefly when she was clumsy, he was good-natured at his work. Crouching by the fire burning under the copper drum, the slow dripping from the coils, of the distillate, the only sound except for small woods life, she felt themselves man and wife. At other times his lovely body and unlovely spirit both evaded her.

He was ready to sell his wares. He drove to the village and to neighboring towns and cities, inviting friends and acquaintances to have a drink from one of the gallon jugs under the rear seat of the borrowed car. They pronounced it good 'shine. To the favored few financially able to indulge themselves he gave a drink of the "aged" liquor. Accustomed to the water-clear, scalding rawness of fresh 'shine, they agreed gravely that no better whiskey ever came in from Cuba. He let it be known that both brands would be available at any time, day or night, at the old Terry house four miles south of the village. He made a profound impression. Most bootleggers sold stuff whose origin and maker were unknown. Most 'shiners had always made it, or drifted into it aimlessly. Trax brought a pomp and ceremony to the local business.

Men found their way out the deep-rutted road. They left their cars among the pines and stumbled through the hammock to the house. They gathered in the big room Trax had recognized as suitable for his purposes. The long trenchered table old man Terry had sliced from red bay, held the china pitcher of "corn" and the jelly glasses from which they drank. Their bird-dogs and hounds padded across the piazza and lay before the fire. Trax drank with them, keying their gatherings to hilarity. He was a convivial host. Sometimes Blaine brought along his guitar, and Trax clapped his hands and beat his feet on the floor as the old man picked the strings. But he was uneasy when a quarrel developed. Then he moved, white-faced among the men, urging someone else to stop it.

At first the woman tried to meet them hospitably. When, deep in the hammock at the still, she heard the vibration of a motor, she hurried up to the house to greet the guests. She smoothed back the gray hair from her worn face and presented her middle-aged bulk in a clean apron. If there was one man alone, Trax introduced her casually, insolently:

"This is my old woman."

When a group of men came together, he ignored her. She stood in the doorway, smiling vaguely. He continued his talk as though she were not there. Sometimes one of the group, embarrassed, acknowledged her presence.

"How do, ma'am."

For the most part they took their cue from Trax and did not see her. Once, on her withdrawal to the kitchen, a stranger had followed for a match.

"Don't you mind workin' way out here in the woods?"

But she decided that Trax was too delicate to want his wife mixing with men who came to drink. At night he sometimes invited her into the big room with conspicuous courtesy. That was when one or two women had come with the men. Her dignity established the place as one where they might safely come. She sat miserably in their midst while they made banal jokes and drank from the thick glasses. They were intruders. Their laughter was alien among the pine trees. She stayed at the still most of the time. The labor was heavy and exacting. The run must be made when the mash was ready, whether it was day or night. It was better for Trax to stay at the house to take care of the customers.

In the early fall he was ready to expand. Matt was alone, scrubbing the floors between runs of whiskey. She heard a powerful car throbbing down the dirt road. It blew a horn constantly in a minor key. Men usually came into this place silently. She went to the piazza, wet brush in hand. With the autumnal drying of foliage, the road was discernible. The scent of wild vanilla filled the flat-woods. She drew in the sweetness, craning her neck to see.

A large blue sedan of expensive make swerved and rounded into the tracks other cars had made to the house. Trax was driving. He swung past the twin live oaks and into the sandy yard. He slammed the door behind him as he stepped out. He had bought the car with the remainder of Matt's three thousand and most of the summer's profits. He was ready to flash across his old haunts, a big operator from the interior.

"I kin sell that hundred gallons of aged stuff now fer what it's worth."

He nodded wisely. He sauntered into the house, humming under his breath.

"Hi-diddy-um-tum—" He was vibrant with an expectancy in which she had no part.

She heard him curse because the floor was wet. The cat crossed his path. He lifted it by the tail and slid it along the slippery boards. The animal came to her on the piazza. She drew it into her lap and sat on her haunches a long time, stroking the smooth hard head.

Life was a bad dream. Trax was away a week at a time. He hired the two Lantry boys to take his place. Matt worked with them, for the boys unwatched would let the mash ferment too long. Trax returned to the flat-woods only for fresh supplies of liquor and of clean clothes. It pleased him to dress in blues that harmonized not too subtly with the blue sedan. He wore light-blue shirts and a red necktie that was a challenging fire under the dark insolent face. Matt spent hours each week washing and ironing the blue shirts. She protested his increasing absences.

"Trax, you jest ain't here at all. I hardly got the heart fer makin' the runs, an' you gone."

He smiled.

"Any time it don't suit you, I kin move my outfit to the east coast."

He laid the threat across her like a whip.

The young Lantrys too saw Trax glamorously. They talked of him to Matt as they mixed the mash, fired, and kept their vigils. This seemed all she had these days of the man: talk of him with the boys beside the still. She was frustrated, filled, not with resentment, but with despair. Yet she could not put her finger on the injustice. She flailed herself with his words, "Any time you don't like it, I kin move."

She waited on Trax' old customers as best she could, running up the slight incline from the still-site to the house when she heard a car. Her strong body was exhausted at the end of the week. Yet when she had finished her elaborate baking on Saturday night she built up a roaring fire in the front room, hung the hot water kettle close to it for his bath, and sat down to wait for him.

Sometimes she sat by the fire almost all night. Sometimes he did not come at all. Men learned they could get a drink at Colton's any hour of the night on Saturday. When the square dance at Trimtree's was done, they came out to the flat-woods at two or three o'clock in the morning. The woman was always awake. They stepped up on the piazza and saw her through the window. She sat brooding by the fire, the striped cat curled in her lap. Around her bony shoulders she hugged the corduroy hunting jacket Trax had worn when he came to her.

She existed for the Saturday nights when the throb of the blue sedan came close; the Sunday mornings when he slept late and arose, sulky, for a lavish breakfast and dinner. Then he was gone again, and she was waving after him down the road. She thought that her love and knowledge of him had been always nothing but this watching through the pine trees as he went away.

The village saw more of him. Occasionally he loitered there a day to show off before he headed for the coast. At times he returned in the middle of the week and picked up fifteen or twenty gallons cached at Blaine's and did not go out to the flat-woods at all. On these occasions he had invariably a girl or woman with him; cheap pretty things whose lightness brought them no more than their shoddy clothes. The storekeeper, delivering meal and sugar to Matt, lingered one day. The still needed her, but she could not with courtesy dismiss him. At last he drew courage.

"Mis' Matt, dogged if I don't hate to complain on Trax to you, but folks thinks you don't know how he's a-doin' you. You're workin' like a dog, an' he ain't never home."

"I know."

"You work at 'shinin', somethin' you nor your folks never done—not that it ain't all right— An' Trax off in that big fine car spendin' the money fast as he turns it over."

"I know."

"The Klan talks some o' givin' him down the country fer it."

" 'Tain't nobody's business but his an' mine."

"Mis' Matt"—he scuffled in the sand—"I promised I'd speak of it. D'you know Trax has got him women goin' round with him?"

"No. I didn't know that."

"Ev'ybody figgered you didn't know that." He mopped his forehead. "The day you an' Trax was married, I was fixin' to tell you 'twa'n't nothin' but your money an' place he wanted to git him set up."

"That's my business, too," she said stonily.

He dropped his eyes before the cold face and moved to his truck. She called after him defiantly:

"What else did I have he'd want anyway!"

She went into the house. She understood the quality of her betrayal. The injustice was clear. It was only this: Trax had taken what he had not wanted. If he had said, "Give me the money and for the time, the house," it would have been pleasant to give, solely because he wanted. This was the humiliation: that she had been thrown in on the deal, like an old mare traded in with a farm.

The Lantry boys called unanswered from the palmettos.

She had known. There was no need of pretense. There was no difference between to-day and yesterday. There was only the dissipation of a haze, as though a sheet had been lifted from a dead body, so that, instead of knowing, she saw.

The man came home late Saturday afternoon. Startled, Matt heard the purr of the motor and hurried to the house from the still. She thought the woman with him had come for liquor. She came to meet them, wiping her hands on her brown gingham apron. Trax walked ahead of his companion, carrying his own shiny patent leather bag and a smaller shabby one. As they came into the house, she saw that it was not a woman, but a girl.

The girl was close on his heels, like a dog. She was painted crudely, as with a haphazard conception of how it should be done. Stiff blond curls were bunched under a tilted hat. A flimsy silk dress hung loosely on an immature frame. Cheap silk stockings bagged on thin legs. She rocked, rather than walked, on incredibly spiked heels. Her shoes absorbed Matt's attention. They were pumps of blue kid, the precise blue of the sedan.

"I mean, things got hot fer me on the east coast." Trax was voluble. "Used that coastal highway oncet too often. First thing I knowed, down below New Smyrna, I seed a feller at a garage give the high sign, an' I'm lookin' into the end of a .45." He flushed. "I jest did git away. It'll pay me to work this territory a whiles, till they git where they don't pay me no mind over there agin."

The girl was watching Matt with solemn blue eyes. Beside the gray bulk of the older woman, she was like a small gaudy doll. Trax indicated her to Matt with his thumb.

"Elly here'll be stayin' at the house a while."

He picked up the shabby bag and started up the stairs.

"Long as you an' me is usin' the downstairs, Matt, she kin sleep upstairs in that back room got a bed in it."

She pushed past the girl and caught him by the sleeve.

"Trax! What's this gal?"

"Ain't no harm to her." He laughed comfortably. He tweaked a wisp of her gray hair.

"She's jest a little gal young un," he said blandly, " 's got no place to go."

He drew the girl after him. The woman stared at the high-heeled blue slippers clicking on every step.

PART II

A warm winter rain thrummed on the roof. The light rush of water sank muffled into the moss that padded the shingles. The sharpest sound was a gurgling in the gutter over the rain-barrel. There had been no visible rising of the sun. Only the gray daylight had protracted itself, so that it was no longer dawn, but day. Matt sat close to the kitchen stove, her bulk shadowy in the dimness. Now and then she opened the door of the fire-box to push in a stick of pine, and the light of the flames flickered over her drawn face.

She could not tell how much of the night she had sat crouched by the range. She had lain long hours unsleeping, while Trax breathed regularly beside her. When the rain began, she left the bed and dressed by the fresh-kindled fire. The heat did not warm her. Her mouth was dry; yet every few minutes an uncontrollable chill shook her body. It would be easy to walk up the unused stairs, down the dusty hall to the back room with the rough pine bed in it, to open the door and look in, to see if anyone was there. Yet if she continued to sit by the fire, moving back the coffee pot when it boiled, surely Trax would come to the kitchen alone, and she would know that yesterday no woman had come home with him. Through the long days her distraught mind had been busy with imaginings. They might easily have materialized, for a moment, in a painted girl, small and very young, in blue kid slippers.

Trax was moving about. She put the frying pan on the stove, sliced bacon into it, stirred up cornmeal into a pone with soda and salt and water. Trax called someone. He came into the kitchen, warmed his hands at the stove. He poured water into the wash basin and soused his face in it. Matt set the coffee pot on the table. The girl pushed open the door a little way and came through. She came to the table uncertainly as though she expected to be ordered away. Matt did not speak.

Trax said, "How's my gal?"

The girl brought her wide eyes to him and took a few steps to his chair.

"Where your shoes, honey?"

She looked down at her stockinged feet.

"I gotta be keerful of 'em."

He laughed indulgently.

"You kin have more when them's gone. Matt, give the young un somethin' to eat."

The thought struck the woman like the warning whir of a rattler that if she looked at the girl in this moment she would be compelled to lift her in her hands and drop her like a scorpion on the hot stove.

She thought, "I cain't do sich as that." She kept her back turned until the impulse passed and she could control her trembling. Her body was of metal and wood. It moved of itself, in jerks. A stiff wooden head creaked above a frame so heavy it seemed immovable. Her stomach weighed her down. Her ample breasts hurt her ribs, as though they were of lead. She thought, "I got to settle this now."

She said aloud slowly, "I'll not wait on her, nor no other woman."

The girl twisted one foot over the other.

She said, "I ain't hungry."

Trax stood up. His mouth was thin. He said to Matt, "You'll wait on her, old lady, or you'll git along without my comp'ny."

She thought, "I got to settle it. I got to say it."

But she could not speak.

The girl repeated eagerly, "I ain't a bit hungry."

Trax picked up a plate from the table. He held it out to his wife.

She thought, "Anyway, cornbread an' bacon's got nothin' to do with it."

She dished out meat and bread. Trax held out a cup. She filled it with coffee. The man sat down complacently. The girl sat beside him and pecked at the food. Her eyes were lowered. Between mouthfuls, she twisted her fingers in her lap or leaned over to inspect her unshod feet.

Matt thought, "Remindin' me."

The paint had been rubbed from the round face. The hair was yellow, like allamanda blooms. The artificial curls that had protruded from the pert hat had flattened out during the damp night, and hung in loose waves on the slim neck. She wore the blue silk dress in which she had arrived.

Trax said, "You eat up good, Elly. May be night 'fore we git back to eat agin." He turned to Matt. "Lantry boys been doin' all right?"

"They been doin' all right. Them's good boys. I heerd 'em come in a hour back. But they needs watchin' right on. They'll let the mash go too long, spite of everything, if I ain't right on top of 'em."

She hardened herself.

"You jest as good to stay home an' do the work yourself. I ain't goin' near the outfit."

"They kin make out by theirselves," he said easily.

He rose from the table, picking his teeth.

"Come on, Elly."

The girl turned her large eyes to the older woman, as though she were the logical recipient of her confession.

"I forgot to wash my hands an' face," she said.

Trax spoke curtly.

"Well, do it now, an' be quick."

He poured warm water in the basin for her and stood behind her, waiting. She washed slowly, with neat, small motions, like a cat. Trax handed her the clean end of the towel. They went upstairs together. Trax' voice was low and muffled. It dripped through the ceiling like thick syrup. Suddenly Matt heard the girl laugh.

She thought, "I figgered all thet owl-face didn't let on no more'n she meant it to."

In a few minutes they came down again. Trax called from the front room.

"Best to cook dinner to-night, Matt. We're like not to git back at noon."

They ran from the porch through the rain.

She walked after them. She was in time to see them step in the blue sedan. The high-heeled slippers flickered across the running-board. The car roared through the live oaks, down the tracks among the pines. Matt closed her eyes against the sight of it.

She thought, "Maybe she takened her satchel an' I jest didn't see it. Maybe she ain't comin' back."

She forced herself to go to the upstairs bedroom. The drumming on the roof sounded close and louder. The bed was awkwardly made. The shabby handbag stood open in a hickory rocker, exposing its sparse contents. A sound startled her. The cat had followed, and was sniffing the unfamiliar garments in the chair. The woman gathered the animal in her arms. They were alone together in the house, desolate and lonely in the rain-drenched flat-woods.

She thought of the Lantry boys under the palmettos. They were careless when they were cold and wet. They might not put the last five hundred pounds of sugar under cover. Shivering in the drizzle, they might use muddy water from the bank of the branch, instead of going a few yards upstream where it ran deep and clear. She threw Trax' corduroy jacket about her and went down the incline behind the house to oversee the work.

She had decided not to cook anything for the evening. But when the mist lifted in late afternoon, and the sun struck slantwise through the wet dark trees, she left the Lantry boys to finish and went to the house. She fried ham and baked soda biscuits and sweet potatoes. The meal was ready and waiting and she stirred up a quick ginger cake and put it in the oven.

She said aloud, desperately, "Might be he'll be back alone."

Yet when the dark gathered the bare house into its loneliness, as she had gathered the cat, and she lighted kerosene lamps in the long front room and a fire, the man and girl came together as she had known they would. Where she had felt only despair, suddenly she was able to hate. She picked up her anger like a stone and hurled it after the blue heels.

"Go eat your dinner."

She spoke to them as she would to negro field hands. Trax stared at her. He herded Elly nervously ahead of him, as though to protect her from an obscure violence. Matt watched them, standing solidly on big feet. She had not been whole. She had charred herself against the man's youth and beauty. Her hate was healthful. It waked her from a drugged sleep, and she stirred faculties hurt and long unused.

She sat by the clay fireplace in the front room while the pair ate. They spoke in whispers, shot through by the sudden laugh of the girl. It was a single high sound, like the one note of the thrush. Hearing it, Matt twisted her mouth. When the casual clatter of plates subsided, she went to the kitchen and began scraping the dishes to wash them. Trax sat warily in his place. The girl made an effort to hand Matt odds and ends from the table. The woman ignored her.

Trax said to Elly, "Le's go by the fire."

Matt cleaned up the kitchen and fed the cat. She stroked its arching back as it chewed sideways on scraps of meat and potato. She took off her apron, listened at the open door for sounds from the Lantrys, bolted the door, and walked to the front room to sit stiff and defiant by the blazing pine fire. The girl sat with thin legs tucked under her chair. She looked from the man to the woman and back again. Trax stretched and yawned.

He said, "Guess I'll go down back an' give the boys a hand. I ain't any too sure they run one batch soon enough. I got to keep up my stuff. I got high-class trade. Ain't I, Elly?" He touched her face with his finger as he passed her.

The woman and the girl sat silently after his going. The cat padded in and sat between them.

The girl called timidly. "Kitty!"

Matt turned savagely.

"Keep your hands off him."

The girl laced her fingers and studied the animal.

"Do he scratch?"

Matt did not answer. She loosened her gray hair and combed it by the fire with a side-comb, plaiting it into two thin braids over her shoulders. Inside the childish hairdressing her face was bony and haggard. She went into the adjoining bedroom, undressed and got into bed. She lay reared up on one elbow, straining for every sound. The fire popped and crackled. Once the juice oozed from a pine log faster than it could burn. It made a sizzling, like boiling fat. A chair scraped and Elly went up to the back bedroom. Her high heels clicked overhead. Matt thought with satisfaction that the girl had no light. She was floundering around in the dark in the unfamiliar house.

In a little while the front door opened and closed softly. Matt heard Trax creak cautiously up the stairs to the back room.

Trax was sleeping away the bright March morning. Matt made no effort to be silent about her washing. She dipped noisily into the rain barrel. When the soft water was gone she drew from the well, rattling galvanized buckets. Elly sat on the bottom step of the rear stoop, scuffling her bare toes in the sand. She wore the blue silk dress. Beside her was a handful of her own garments in need of washing, a pair of silk stockings and two or three pieces of underwear. Matt passed in front of her to go to the clothes line.

Elly said, "Trax give me this dress."

The woman did not seem to hear her.

Elly continued. "Reckon it'll wash? It's spotted."

Matt did not answer. She hung flour-sacking towels on the line. The girl picked up her small pile, looked uncertainly at the tub of soapsuds, laid down the clothes. She went to the tub and began rubbing on the first garment she drew from the suds. It was one of Matt's gingham aprons. She rubbed with energy, and Matt towered over her before she noticed that the woman had left the line.

"Take your dirty hands out o' my tub."

The girl drew back, dripping suds from her thin arms. She turned her hands back and forth.

"They ain't dirty," she protested.

Matt laughed shortly. "Mighty simple, ain't you?"

An obscure doubt brushed her, like a dove that wavers to a perch and is gone again without lighting.

"Who do you figger I am?"

The girl faced her across the wash-tub. She said gravely, "The lady lives in Trax' house."

"Trax' house? Well, he lives in mine. Never heerd tell o' no sich thing as his wife, eh?"

The girl hesitated. "Trax jest said the old woman."

Matt breathed heavily. The girl took her silence and her questions for a mark of interest.

"Trax said you'd romp on me," she offered confidentially, "but you ain't." She wrapped one bare leg around the other. "I been romped on," she went on brightly. "Pa romped on me reg'lar."

"You got you folks then!"

"Yessum, but I don't know where he is. He run a blacksmith shop an' garage offen the hard road, but he closed up an' goed to Georgia with a lady. Then I lived with another lady down the road a piece. Trax sold her liquor, that's how come him to know me. She moved off, an' he takened me with him from there. Now I'm gonna live with him," she finished, adding with studied tact "—and you."

Trax came yawning to the rear stoop in time to see Matt walk toward the girl. Elly stared uncomprehending. He jumped to the sand and caught the woman's muscular arms from behind.

"Don't you touch her." He cracked his familiar whip over her. "You hurt that gal young un an' you've seed the last o' me."

The woman shook free from him in the strength of her rage.

"You git out o' here before I hurts her an' you, too. You take yer gal young un an' git."

He adjusted his mind slowly. Inconceivably, he had gone too far. Bringing the girl to the flat-woods had been dangerously brazen. It was done now. He understood that his hold on this place had become suddenly precarious. He had the car and he could move the still. Yet the lay-out suited his needs too exactly to be relinquished. He could not give it up. If the gray-headed woman was done with her infatuation, he was in trouble.

He said boldly, "I got no idee o' goin'. Me an' Elly'll be here right on."

She said, "I kin break ary one o' you in two with my hands."

"Not me, you cain't. Leave me tell you, ol' woman, I'm too quick fer you. An' if you hurt Elly"—his dark face nodded at her—"if you crack down on her—with them big hands o' yourn—if you got any notion o' knifin'"—he paused for emphasis—"I'll git you sent to the chair, or up fer life—an' I'll be here in these flat-woods—in this house—right on."

He pushed the girl ahead of him and walked into the house, lighting a cigarette. He said over his shoulder, thickly between puffs, "An' that'd suit me jest fine."

She turned blindly to the wash-tub. She soaped the blue shirts without seeing them, rubbing them up and down automatically. Her life that had run like the flat-woods road, straight and untraveled, was now a maze, doubling back on itself darkly, twisted with confusion. The man stood with his neat trap at the end of every path; the girl with her yellow hair and big eyes, at the beginning.

She thought, "I got to settle it."

Trax and Elly came and went like a pair of bright birds. The blue kid slippers, scuffed by the sand, flashed in and out of the old house. Matt watched the comings and goings heavily, standing solidly on the hand-hewn pine-board floors.

She did not go near the still. Her absence did not make the difference she had imagined. The Lantrys had the work well in hand. Trax paid their wages, and their product was satisfactory. Often she did not hear them come to their work through the pines and past the hammock. A northwest wind sometimes brought the scent of the mash to her nose. The storekeeper brought in sugar and meal by a lower trail, and she seldom saw him. Trax was selling all his liquor at a high urban price, and local patronage dwindled away. The woods were quiet day and night.

Then Trax and Elly were back again, talking of hotels and highways, of new business, the talk pierced through now and again by the girl's single-noted laughter. She eyed Matt gravely, but the woman felt that the girl, oddly, had no fear. Trax was insolent, as always, his eyes narrow and his ways wary. Matt cut down on the table. She cooked scarcely enough for the three to eat. Elly ate with her catlike slowness, taking twice as long at her meager plate as the others. Matt took to rising and clearing the table as soon as she and Trax had finished. She picked up the plates casually, as though unaware that the third one still showed half its food uneaten. Trax did not seem to notice. The girl sometimes looked hungrily after the vanishing portion. She made no protest. Once Matt found her in the kitchen between meals, eating cold cornbread. Trax backed her up in her curt order to Elly to keep out.

It enraged Matt to see Elly feed the cat. Elly saved bits from her sparse helpings and held them under the table when she thought herself unobserved. Occasionally when the girl held the animal in her lap, and Matt ignored it, Trax stroked him too, because it was Elly who held him. Matt knew they sometimes had food in Elly's room at night. She began to hear a soft padding up the stairs and on the bare floor overhead, and knew the cat went up to join them. In the morning he was smug, washing his whiskers enigmatically. His desertion was intolerable. She shut him out at night. He wailed for hours at the door, accustomed to sleeping snugly inside the house.

Suddenly Trax was not taking Elly with him any more. The village had become accustomed to the grave childish face beside him when it disappeared. Casually he left her behind with Matt in the flat-woods. He drove away one morning and did not come back that night or the next.

Matt took it for a taunt. It seemed to her that he was daring her to trap herself. Elly watched the road anxiously the first day. She accepted, hours before Matt, his solitary departure. At their first breakfast alone together, she said hesitantly:

"I had a idee Trax was fixin' to go off alone."

Matt thought, "The fool don't know enough to keep quiet about it."

After the second day, Elly devoted herself to exploring outside the house. Trax had kept her close to him, and the hammock had been only a cluster of shrubs and great trees through which they came and went. The Spanish moss was hazed with green by the early spring, and she discovered that the gray strands were alive with infinitesimal rosy blossoms. Matt saw her sitting at the far edge of the hammock, pulling the stuff apart.

The woman thought, "She better git herself out o' my sight."

Elly roamed through the pines as far as the road, staring up and down its silent winding, then scampered back toward the house like an alarmed squirrel. She walked stealthily to the palmettos where the Lantrys worked the still, and watched them for hours, unseen. Except when Matt stared directly at her, her round-eyed gravity lifted into a certain lightness, as though she felt newly free to move about in the sunlight. She seemed content.

On a rainy afternoon Matt, ironing in the kitchen, heard a steady snipping from the front room. She stole to the door and peered through a crack. Elly was cutting pictures from an old magazine and making an arrangement of rooms and figures of men and women and children. She was talking to herself and occasionally to them. The cat was curled in her lap, shifting lazily as she moved forward or back.

Their meals together were silent. Matt became aware at dinner one day that the pink oleanders in a jelly glass were not of her picking and placing. She had always a spray of flowers or greenery on the table. Because Elly had brought in the blooms, she snatched them from the water and stuffed them in the stove.

She allowed the girl a minimum of food. Once when she took

away the plates before Elly had fairly begun, the girl reached after her desperately and said "Matt!" Again, when Matt moved from the table, leaving a plate of biscuits behind, Elly pounced on the largest and crammed it into her mouth. She began to laugh, poking in the crumbs.

She said, "You ain't romped on me yet."

Matt decided that Trax had put Elly up to goading her. She spoke for the first time in days.

"Don't you let Trax put no notions in yore head. I got no idee o' rompin' on you. That ain't what I'm fixin' to do."

For the most part, the girl was uncomplaining and strangely satisfied. The immature body, however, was becoming rapidly emaciated.

Trax was gone two weeks. He came in for an afternoon and loaded up with twenty gallon-jugs concealed under the large rear seat, and went hurriedly away. He called to the two women who stood watching on the piazza.

"Got a order."

Matt nodded grimly after him. She thought, "You got you one more chance, too, if you on'y knowed it." She turned to observe the girl beside her. There was apparent on the young face a faint wistfulness and no surprise. Matt thought, "She's got her orders jest to set tight."

Trax came home for the following week-end. He slept most of the time and was sulky. He paid no more attention to Elly than to the older woman. At no time in the two days or nights did he go to the upstairs room. When he was about, Elly followed him a few steps. Then, as he continued to ignore her, she dropped behind and took up her own simple affairs. Matt told herself that if he left this time without the girl, she was ready. On Monday morning, after loading, he went alone to the car.

She said carelessly, "I might take a notion to go some'eres or do somethin'. When you comin' back this time?"

He laughed insolently. "Steppin' out, Matt?" He was sure of himself. He was too quick for her. Whatever futilities she was planning, it would surprise her most to return on the day he named.

"Be back Sat'day."

He drove off smiling.

Matt was nervous all week. On Saturday morning she surprised the Lantry boys by appearing at the still. They had come and gone without contact with her for some weeks.

She said, "Boys, I jest got word the Pro-hi's is comin' lookin' fer Trax' outfit. Now I ain't quick as you-all, an' I want each one o' you should go down the road a good piece an' stay there all day, watchin', one to the north an' 'tother to the south. I'll tend the outfit, an' if I hears a whistle I'll know what it means an' it'll give me time to smash the jugs an' git to the house."

The boys were in instant alarm.

"Must be somebody's turned Trax up," they said.

Matt said, "Mighty likely. Somebody's likely got it in fer him. Trax hisself done tole me a long ways back, if anybody had it in fer a man, that was the way they'd git at him."

They nodded in agreement.

"That's about it, Mis' Matt. Git him tore up an' git at him that-a-way."

They hid several demijohns in near-by cover and hurried anxiously the two ways of the road. They reported later in the village that they heard no sound for an hour or so. Toward noon their straining ears caught the crash of an axe on metal. There was the high thin splintering of glass. The isolated crashes settled into a steady shattering of wood and iron and copper. A column of smoke began to rise from the vicinity of the still. The Lantry to the south skirted the road through the pines and joined his brother. They cut through the woods to the village and announced that the Pro-hi's had come in from the west and were tearing up Colton's outfit. The word went out to avoid the flat-woods road.

The Lantrys were waiting for Trax when he came through in late afternoon. They flagged him down. They drove with him as far as their own place, telling him what they knew.

"When we lit out we could hear 'em maulin' on the barrels an' purely see the smoke. Things is tore up an' burnt up all right."

They conjectured who, of his numerous enemies, might have betrayed him. He drove at a spring-breaking clip over the root-filled ruts of the sand road. His face was black and frightened. When he let the boys out of the car he had said nothing about the week's wages. They looked at each other.

One said, "How 'bout us gittin' ten dollars, anyway, Trax?"

"That's it. I ain't got it. I on'y got five myself. I was fixin' to turn over this lot quick."

"We hid out 'bout twenty gallons, if they ain't found it," they informed him eagerly. He listened tensely to a description of the location and was gone.

He drove into the yard and stopped the car in gear with a jerk. No one was in sight. He ran back of the house to the palmettos. A ring of fire had blackened palms and oaks and myrtle for a hundred feet around. A smoldering pile of bricks and barrel hoops and twisted metal in the center marked the site of the still. He began a frenzied search for the hidden jugs.

Matt peered from a window in the front room. She ordered Elly upstairs.

"You stay there till I tell you different."

The woman hurried into the yard with a jug of kerosene and a handful of papers. The sedan was twenty-five feet from the house, but the direction of the wind was safe. She soaked the hood and seats of the car with oil and piled papers on the floor. She tied a bundle of oil-soaked paper on the end of her longest clothes prop; touched a match to it. She lowered the pole to the machine. The oil caught fire. When the blaze reached the gas tank, the explosion disintegrated an already charring mass.

Trax heard the muffled roar up the incline behind him. The demi-johns were where the Lantry boys had indicated. They were broken. He left the stench of over-turned mash and spilled alcohol and ran to the house. He could not for a moment comprehend that the twisting mass of metal and flame was the blue sedan.

Matt stood on the rear stoop. He looked at her in bewilderment. His stare dropped from her straggling gray hair down the length of her frame. Her apron was smudged and torn. Her hands were black and raw. He came back to her implacable cold eyes. He choked.

"You done it yourself!"

He burst into spasmodic curses, then broke off, overcome by their futility. The sweat ran into his eyes. He wiped it out and gaped about him in loose-mouthed confusion. He shuffled a few feet to the stoop and sank down on the bottom step. The woman looked down at him.

"Better git goin'."

He rose, swaying.

"You ol' . . ."

His obscenities fell away from her as rain washed from the weathered shingles of the old house. She towered over him. The tall house towered over him. He was as alien as on the bright day when he had first come hunting here.

He plunged up the steps toward her, his head low between his shoulders.

"Better git back."

His outstretched fists dropped at his sides. The fingers fell open. The woman lifted the shotgun.

"Better git—"

He shook his head, unbelieving. His eyes clung to the dark cavities of the pitted steel. He moved one foot slowly to the next step.

The woman aimed carefully at the shoe, as though it were some strange reptile creeping into the house. She fired a trifle to the left, so that the pattern of the double-ought buckshot shell sprayed in a close mass into the sand. One pellet clipped through the leather, and a drop of blood sank placidly into the pine step. The man stared fascinated. His hand jerked to his mouth, like a wooden toy moved by strings. He stifled a sound, or tried to make one. The woman could not tell. He lifted a face dry with fear and backed down the steps.

It was necessary to walk widely to the side to avoid the heat of the burned car. He threw out his hands hopelessly and hesitated. The sun slanted orange and gold through the hammock. Beyond, there were already shadows among the dark pines. It would be twilight before he could be out of the flat-woods. He found voice.

"Matt," he whined, "how'll I git to town?"

The woman wiped her streaked face with a corner of her apron.

"Reckon you'll have to git there on foot, Mister—the way you come in the first place."

She turned her back and went into the house. The girl had come down the stairs and was flattened against a wall. Her face was brushed with a desperate knowledge. Matt jerked her head at the open front door.

"All right. I'm thu. You kin go on with him now."

"Matt—"

"Go on. Git."

The girl did not move. Matt pushed her headlong to the door. Elly took hold of the big arm with both hands, drawing back, and Matt struck her away. She went confusedly down the steps. Trax was leaving the hammock. He struck wildly through the pines. The girl took a few steps after him, then turned toward the woman watching from the doorway. Matt called loudly:

"Go on. Git."

The man had reached the road and was plunging along it to the north. The girl ran three or four paces in his direction, then stopped again, like a stray dog or cat that would not be driven away. She hesitated at the edge of the hammock. The small uncertain figure was visible between the twin oaks beyond the high porch. Matt turned into the house and closed the door.

She was strong and whole. She was fixed, deep-rooted as the pine trees. They leaned a little, bent by an ancient storm. Nothing more could move them.

The car in the yard had settled into a smoking heap. The acrid smell of burned rubber and paint filled the house. Matt closed the north window to keep out the stench. The glass rattled in its frame. The air was gusty and the spring night would be cold. There were swift movements and rattlings among the oak boughs above the roof, as though small creatures were pattering across the floor of the wind.

Matt shivered and kindled a fire in the front room. She looked about for the cat. The noise and disorder of the day had driven him to distant hunting grounds and he had not yet ventured to return. She drew close to the fire in her rocker and held her smudged hands to the blaze.

She thought, "I've lit a bait o' fires to-day."

That was over and done with. There would be no more 'shining among the palmettos; no more coming and going of folk; no more Trax and his owl-faced girl. She was very tired. Her square frame relaxed in its exhaustion. She leaned back her head and drowsed deeply in her chair.

When she wakened, the fire had burned to ashes. The moon rode high over the flat-woods, with clouds scurrying underneath. The room was silver, then black, as the moonlight came and went. The chill wind sucked through the pines. There was another sound; the sobbing of a lighter breath. Suddenly Matt knew the girl was still there.

She rose in a plunge from the rocker. She wasn't done with them yet. . . . She opened the door a few inches and listened. The muffled sound was unmistakable. It was the choked gasping of a child that has cried itself breathless. It came from the edge of the hammock. Where the pines began she could distinguish a huddle on the ground that was neither stump nor bushes. She closed the door.

Trax was gone—and Elly was here.

He had flung away and left her behind. She was discarded, as Matt had been long discarded. He was through with Elly, too. For the first time the woman was able to conceive of them separately. And the one was gone, and the other was here. She groped her way stupefied to the kitchen, lighted a kerosene lamp, and made a fire in the range. She wanted a scalding pot of tea to stop her shivering. She split a cold biscuit and fried it and sat down with her plate and tea-cup. She breathed hard, and ate and drank mechanically.

"He was done with her a long ways back."

He had driven off alone in the blue sedan, not to infuriate, but because there was nothing else to do with the girl. Matt chewed her biscuit slowly. She laughed grimly.

"I give him too much credit fer smartness."

A flash of anger stirred her, like a spurt of flame from an old fire, that Elly should be now at the edge of the hammock.

"Trax wa'n't man enough to take off his mess with him."

She sipped her cooling tea.

She remembered grudgingly the girl's contentment. The shadow of the man, passing away, left clear the picture of a child, pulling moss apart and cutting paper dolls. Rage at Trax possessed her.

"I'd orter hided him fer takin' sech a young un along his low-down way."

In a burst of fury she conceded the girl's youth. Elly was too young . . .

"I'd orter been hided. Me an' Trax together."

Matt rose from the table and gathered up the few dishes. She stopped in the act. She looked at her hands as though their knotty strength were strange to her.

"Snatchin' off a young un's rations . . ."

She leaned heavily on the table, pondering. Emptiness filled the house—a living presence—appalling—still.

She strode abruptly out the door and through the hammock to the pines. The moon had swung toward its setting and the rays lay long under the trees. The girl lay crouched against a broad mottled trunk.

Matt said, "You kin come on back."

The emaciated figure wavered from the ground on spindling legs. It tried to crowd close to the warmth of the woman's body. As they moved toward the house, the girl stumbled in the run-over slippers.

Matt said, "Here. Gimme them crazy shoes."

Elly stooped and took them from her bare feet. The woman put them in her apron pockets. She went ahead of the girl into the front room and bent down to kindle a fire.

ALLIGATORS

LESS Katy, I don't know nothing about alligators. You belong to talk to some of them real old-timey Florida 'gator hunters that has messed up with 'em deliberate. I don't never mess up with no alligator. If so chance me and one meets, it's just because he comes up with me—I don't never try to come up with him. There ain't never been but once when me and a alligator met more than accidental.

'Gators is a mess. And a pain. I run over one last night. I'd been out to Lobkirk's for a snort, and coming back by Gopher Creek I saw the knocker climbing out of the ditch to cross the road to water. I shot the juice to the Model-T and I hit him just the time he got his head over the rut. When he rared up, he carried the front wheels of the car plumb over in the ditch. The Model-T shook loose, but before it got shut of him, he had me going in the creek. I don't fancy 'em.

Special Delivery for Br'er Cresey

I don't much mind handling a small un. Partickler if it's to torment somebody is worse scairt of 'em than me. Like Br'er Cresey. He hates a varmint or a snake or a 'gator the most of any man I know. I don't never get my hands on a little alligator but I goes to studying: Where can I put him so's Br'er Cresey will get the most good of him?

184

Cresey'll holler like a woman if you catch him just right. A while ago, me and Raymond caught him just right in the post office.

Br'er Cresey was standing back of the delivery window, sorting mail from the 2:10 train. We eases in at the back door and lays a three-foot 'gator just back of his heels and eases out again. Directly the 'gator goes to blowing. A 'gator's the blowingest thing I know of. 'Tain't rightly a blowing, nor yet a sighing, nor even a groaning— you know the way it sounds. It's a damn peculiar sound—partickler in a post office. Cresey looks around and sees nothing. Directly the 'gator heaves another. Cresey looks down between his legs and there's the alligator bopping his lips and blowing.

Now, Cresey come out from behind that delivery window like a man with ants in his breeches. He squealed and whinnied like a Maud mule, and when he sees me and Raymond, he goes to cussing. It's a pure treat to hear Br'er Cresey cussing. He calms down when we takes the 'gator off. He don't know we'd only moved it to the back of the express wagon. The rest ain't so funny. He was so mad, and scairt, too, when he steps on the 'gator in the express wagon, he just picks it up by the tail and pitches it. I happens to be the first thing in the way, and when Br'er Cresey pitches the alligator, bless Katy if it don't land on me and get all wropped around my neck. And I don't enjoy that much more'n Cresey.

When I was a young un, I fooled with alligators a little. I used to go with Rance Deese when he'd go hunting 'em. A little old shirt-tail boy, here I'd go barefooted across the flat woods with Rance. You didn't never know there was alligators in the flat woods? Why, sure, there's alligator caves there. Ain't you noticed there's always cypress ponds in a flat woods? The 'gators travels in from the lakes and creeks to them and builds theirselves caves. Like a gopher hole, only bigger. They dig 'em in the pond bank, under the water. A 'gator cave's about three feet across and anywhere from six to fifteen feet deep, according to the 'gator's size and notions. He generally likes to holler it out so he can roll over in it. A 'gator's the very devil for rolling.

You take down around Fort McCoy in the pine. Look and you'll see a little piece of water. It'll lead off some way. You'll see in the mud where the 'gator comes up and suns hisself. In a dry time, them cypress ponds in the flat woods goes dry, all excepting the 'gator caves. They're easy found. If you're aiming to catch the big 'gator, you take a hook on a pole and job it down. The 'gator'll bite it. You pull him out and kill him and skin him. 'Gator hides is worth about two-eighty-five right now for seven-foot or better. I've seen 'em go to four and a half.

The first time I come up with alligators personal-like was on one of them ja'nts with Rance Deese. Rance was grunting the little 'gators out of the caves. Calling 'em—grunting the way they grunt. Here they come, little 'gators, swarming to the top of the pond. Some of 'em comes out of the pond and goes to running ever' which-a-way. Rance was chooging 'em in a crocus sack. I was grabbing 'em here and yon. I had both hands full. I tried to get 'em all in one hand so I could grab and choog with t'other. Directly here one of them little scapers gets me by the finger and rips it clear open to the bone. I slung him here to yonder. He makes it up across the hill. I was eleven years old, but I had chitlin's enough to follow him and fall on him and catch him.

Rance hisself learned to be right respectful of alligators before he was done with 'em. I was with him one time at the Big Cypress slough—you know where 'tis. 'Gators like to get where there's a bunch of cypresses. They dig caves under the roots. Rance was kneeling down by a cave and fishing out little baby alligators about twelve inches long. He wasn't paying no mind, and directly the old mammy 'gator come to the top of the water and caught Rance across the neck with her tail like it was a cow whip.

You see, a alligator don't generally set out to bite you. He'll flip his tail toward his head, and whatever his tail brings in to him, he'll catch a-holt of. Rance ducked back out of range and the old 'gator sunk.

Rance jammed his hook down, but he couldn't find her. He said, "She'll turn up again."

Rance Changes His Notions

He eased over into the water and went to wading. The water in the slough caught him just above his waist. There was little 'gators milling around in the water and he went on scooping 'em in. He'd stuff 'em in his shirt. Rance always wore his pants tight, and his shirt stayed down good, and when he waded in amongst 'em thataway, he'd get a shirt full before he come out.

Rance said, "Joog the hook down again, Freddy; see can you find the old un."

I jooged the hook down.

I said, "I can't find her, Rance."

He had his shirt full of little 'gators and he had both hands full.

He said, "I'll find her."

He waded around some more, feeling with his foot. Now, I wouldn't say Rance found the alligator. It's more like it to say she found him. She heaved up out of the water, and before he could get out of the way she was right on top of him, flipping her tail. She smacked him square across the face with it, and next thing I knowed, Rance had lost his little alligators out of both his hands, and his footing to boot. The old mammy was right in behind him. He slipped and sprawled and made mighty poor headway, and I could see him changing his notions about alligators.

Just as he scrambled out, she caught the heel of his shoe in her teeth and commenced to drop back into the water. As soon as a 'gator catches anything, it'll go backward. Rance hollered to me to hand him something to bop her. I handed him a hatchet we had with us—had about a two-and-a-half-foot handle. Rance bopped her in the head with it—and you know that alligator let go of his heel and caught the handle of that hatchet in her mouth. Rance hated to lose the hatchet and he rassled with her. He finally got the hatchet, but he never got the alligator. Now, that learned Rance Deese to be right respectful of 'em. He kept that shoe with the heel bit for several years and he showed it to several people. That broke him from getting right in with a alligator. Now, me—I ain't never been unbroke.

You understand, it don't do to be too timid with a alligator. It just don't do. You got to know their ways, like them old 'gator hunters do, and you got to be bold according. If a 'gator faces you in close quarters, you got to watch your chance to shut his mouth for him, and when the chance comes, you got to take it or the 'gator'll take his. Like the night me and Raymond was gigging frogs in Black Sink Prairie. Raymond shined his light in a 'gator's eyes and shot him. He was about nine feet long and we dragged him in the boat. I was paddling the boat and Raymond was gigging in the bow. Now, it turned out Raymond had shot the alligator too far down the nose— not backwards to where his brains was. The 'gator wasn't dead—he was only addled.

I hollered to Raymond, "Shine you light back here!"

He shined his light back for me, and here was the 'gator with his mouth wide open. Right there is where a feller'd be in trouble if he was too timid. Raymond held the light steady. The minute the 'gator closed his mouth, I caught him by the lips and held them shut while Raymond finished him with a knife. You can hold a 'gator's lips together with one hand if you catch him with his mouth shut. But once he's got his jaws open, you can't get the purchase to close them again.

Riding a Roller

Alligators is mighty strong. They're that strong to where they can fool you. Like John Milliken at Salt Springs last week. We was gigging mullet. I seen a right small 'gator rise and sink. I whammed the gig into him. When I grabbed the gig handle he commenced a-rolling.

I says, "Here, John, hold him."

John takes the gig handle and says, "What is it?"

The 'gator was rolling to beat the devil. I like to fell in the spring, laughing.

I says, "Hold him, John—hold him."

The gig was purely playing a tune. It blistered John's hands and like to beat his brains out. How come it wabbling so, the 'gator had done grabbed the gig handle in his mouth. So, with him rolling, it made right hard holding. If a 'gator once shuts down on you, that's his trick—he goes to rolling. If he grabs your arm in the water, say, he goes to rolling. It's like to twist your arm right out of the shoulder.

Now, a 'gator will bite. Don't never let nobody tell you a alligator won't bite. I've knowed several fellers to get bit to hurt 'em. Nub-footed Turner—a twenty-foot 'gator bit his foot off. But generally speaking, a 'gator'll go his way if you'll go yours. But he don't like to be fooled up with. He most particklerly don't like nobody monkeying around his cave.

I remember one time there was three of us white men and a nigger working on the grove on the south side of Orange Lake. We knocks off for dinner and we goes in swimming, the way God made us. Gundy White, that was the nigger. Old Gundy.

The nigger says, "White men, what about lettin' me come in where you-all's at? Does you keer? If I was to go in and come out east a ways, I'd get powerful muddied."

'Twasn't muddy where we was. You know the current in Orange Lake is always going east.

We says, "You wait for us to come out."

So, when we comes out, Gundy goes in. He was just fixing to come out, about fifteen feet from shore. Bless Katy, if a big old alligator don't come up to him and catch him by the shoulder. Nothing serious—just turned him around and led him out about a hundred yards and turned him loose.

Gundy starts swimming back for shore, his eyes a-popping. He knowed good and well a 'gator'll pass up a dog any day to catch a nigger. The alligator swims back with him, head for head. When he gets to the same place, the 'gator catches him and leads him out again. He done it three-four times. It come to me we'd done been swimming over a 'gator cave. Three big white bodies was too much for the 'gator to bother. But let the one dark body go in alone, and the 'gator was man enough to turn him.

So I calls to Gundy, "Don't try to come out there! Come on out east a ways!"

He changes his course—and you know the alligator don't bother him a mite? Just sticks his head out and watches him. Just as good as to say, "You go do your landing somewheres else. You got you no business here."

That old nigger has 'gator sign on his shoulder to this day. It looks just like buckshot had tore out some little pieces.

A Nose for 'Gators

We should of knowed we was over a cave by the smell. You remember the time me and you was fishing on Lochloosy and we couldn't find the bream on the bed? And we both smells something sweet and marshified? And I backs the boat up and says, "Wait a minute. It's a bream bed or a 'gator cave, one"? And we fished and fished and never did find no bream? It was a 'gator cave, sure. Ain't no mistaking it, unless it's bream. Peculiar—that's it. A 'gator cave just naturally smells peculiar.

I tell you who you belong to talk to about alligators, and that's Endy Wilkers. He really knows 'em. He's still making a living 'gatoring and catching frog legs. He'd rather 'gator hunt than work. If 'twasn't for the alligators and the bullfrogs, Endy and his family would of gone hungry several times. I was with Endy one time when a fifteen-foot 'gator took us to ride. Me and Endy was on the dock when we seen the 'gator yonder in the lake. He was so big he looked like a rowboat drifting. We jumped in my fishing launch and heads for him. That was Endy—take right out after 'em.

The 'gator sunk. Then he pops up over yonder. Then he sinks again. He done it three times and don't come up no more. Endy knows then he's on the bottom. Bottom there was about nine feet. Directly we sees a row of blubbers. That was the 'gator breathing. The blubbers stop, and Endy lets him have the harpoon. Ka-whow! Just back of his hind legs. Endy knowed right where to feel for him.

Then bless Katy, here we go across the lake. We played out all our rope. I starts up the engine. You know we couldn't catch up with him? That 'gator was going better'n twelve miles a hour. He had to be, to keep the harpoon rope taut with the engine going. I threw it in reverse. It didn't no more'n slow him down a little. That 'gator was just naturally carrying us off. Sometimes it looked like he didn't have no more'n three feet of tail in the water. The rest of him was scrambling along on top. I never heard such a fuss. It sounded like fifteen oxen a-wallering in the water.

He finally headed for a tussock to get shut of whatever 'twas he had, and Endy got the chance to shoot him. Whooey! When I'm riding on the water, I want to know where I'm going and can I stop what's carrying me.

I don't know but what I'd rather be behind an alligator than in front of one, come to think of it. I've seen one outrun a horse through the palmettos and across a flat woods. Like Uncle Breck. He'd of give a pretty to of been behind the alligator the time it run him. That was over in Gulf Hammock, not far from the Gulf of Mexico. Me and Uncle Breck was to a pond, shooting ducks. The ducks'd circle overhead and we'd shoot 'em so's they'd fall in the woods behind us, and us not have to wade in the pond amongst the alligators. I'll swear, I never seen so many alligators. I reckon there was three hundred heads in sight, all sticking up out of the water. 'Gators just ain't plentiful in Florida now, the way they was then in Gulf Hammock.

Uncle Breck's Get-Away

I was watching for ducks—shooting and watching. Directly I hears Uncle Breck say, "Oo-o-ee-e!" Then he says, kind of faintified, "Shoot him, Fred—shoot him!" I looks around. Now, what he'd done to him first—if he shot him or what—I don't know, but it was Uncle Breck and the alligator across the woods.

Chasing him? The alligator was really chasing Uncle Breck.

I reckon there's been men has traveled faster than Uncle Breck. I don't reckon there's ever been a man has tried to travel faster. I mean, he was selling out. The 'gator was this high off the ground. . . . They made a turn around a bay tree. They was coming mighty near straight to me.

Uncle Breck calls in a weak voice, "Shoot him, Fred—shoot him!"

The devil of it was, I couldn't shoot the alligator for shooting Uncle Breck.

Directly they hits a log two-three feet high. Uncle Breck jumps it—he hurdled fast and pretty—and the alligator has to take a minute to waddle over it. It didn't stop him—a 'gator'll go right over a five-foot fence—but he couldn't take it as fast as Uncle Breck. The 'gator slowing down for the log give me the first chance, what with laughing and not craving to shoot Uncle Breck, to get a shot at him.

And then, bless Katy, Uncle Breck was fixing to tear me down for not shooting sooner!

You wouldn't think it, but a 'gator's the hardest thing there is to kill, to his size. That is, to kill so he's dead good. Must be because his brain's so small he ain't got the sense to know when he belongs to be dead. One fooled me thataway just a while back when I was out with Endy Wilkers, and him 'gator hunting. We was in Indian Prairie, and it about dry. Endy was working the marsh edge and catching little old bitty ones, and he steps in a 'gator cave. The old mammy takened out after him. I shot one time and I figured I'd killed her dead.

Trying a New Seine

We got her over in the boat and sets out. And bless Katy, all of a sudden that pebble-hided knocker comes crawling up between my legs, a-bellering. Her tail was going bam-bam. I looked for her to crawl out of the boat and I was fixing to shoot the rest of her head off. She just kept that tail a-going and didn't make no move to crawl out, and I couldn't shoot for putting holes in the boat. There wasn't nothing for me to do but get down there and straddle her. I sets down on her, one hand back of the eyes, and I popped my knife where her head joins together. I must of hit it plumb, for she ain't moved since.

But that un died easy, compared to some. Now, take the one I caught in my seine—that 'gator was really hard to kill. It was the spring I had me a seine on Lake Lochloosy. I owned a four-hundred-and-fifty-yard seine and two hundred and eighty fish traps and a fish house. Nub-footed Turner pulled the seine for me on shares. The same feller I told you about—a alligator had bit his foot off.

Now all I knowed about a seine at that time was, you put it in the water and drawed it together. I knowed it had a pocket, but that was all. I used to use it, nice moonlight nights, to catch me six-eight bream and fry 'em on shore.

One night me and Nub-footed Turner was at the fish house on Lochloosy. Oh, my, it was a fine night, just as still and pretty. It wasn't too cold, it wasn't too hot. It was just a fine, calm night in the spring of the year. The lake was as still as a glass candle.

Nub says, "I'd just naturally love to go fishing tonight."

I says, "I ain't never really pulled the net since I've owned it, but I'll pull one end of it."

We goes out in the launch and throws the seine, and we takes about two hundred pounds of bream on the first haul. Now, Nub-footed Turner liked to fish on the moon.

He says, "I'd love to make a moon haul. I'd love to pull this seine just at moonrise."

Didn't neither one of us happen to know the time of moonrise.

I says, "We just as good to go on shore and eat."

We goes on back to shore and lights us a oak fire and cooks fish and coffee. Nub-footed Turner, he lays down and goes to sleep. I sets a while watching the east for the moon to rise. I commenced getting cold. Our clothes was wet and I couldn't never sleep right in wet clothes. So I totes up logs and limbs and builds up a big fire. I dried first one side and then t'other. Directly I lays down by the fire and goes to sleep. Now and again I'd raise up and look out east. By then I didn't want to go fishing.

I says, "I hope the moon don't never rise."

I lays down and goes to sleep again. Directly I wakes up, and here the east was done turned red, the moon a half hour high, and day a-breaking.

"Wake up, Nub," I says. "Here 'tis daylight and the moon done rose."

He says, "We'll pull a haul regardless."

We sets out in the launch close to shore in shallow water.

I says, "You jump off; I'll hold the land stake."

We lays the seine.

Now, how come the alligator in the pocket, it was thisaway. When one of them fishermen made a haul he'd do it easy and a alliga-tor'd swim out of the net and sell out through them cypress timbers. Them as knowed this partickler 'gator told me he'd of swum out if he'd had the chance. But I didn't know no better and we worked too fast for him. He didn't get off at the right place.

I ties up the haul, and when the time comes, here I am, pulling away. We had the fish, all right, but directly the net commenced a-banging.

A Right Tough 'Gator

I says, "Nub, I'm tearing all the webbing loose from the lead line. The net's hung up on a log."

He says, "Next time it hangs, leave me see it."

"All right. It's hung."

He looks.

" 'Tain't nothing."

I says, "Listen, Nub, there's a alligator in this net."

He says, "Yeah, but he's a little one. He won't hurt you."

I says, "Are you sure he's a little one?"

I was inside the circle and I had to pull it my way. I had to hold fast on the lead line to keep from losing the fish. The circle got right small.

Directly Nub says, "Wait, Fred."

I says, "Nub, you ain't lied to me?"

Now, we'd done had a couple of snorts, but not enough to where I wanted to catch no alligator.

I says, "Nub, I'm as close to what's in that net as I aim to be. Now, if that 'gator catches you, don't never say a alligator caught you and I goed off and left you. I'm just telling you ahead of time—I'm gone now. I hate to leave you, but I'm gone."

He says, "Come back here with your pistol."

I says, "I'll come a foot closer."

I untied the launch from a cypress tree. I pulls up on the lead line. I shot the .38 where I figured the 'gator belonged to be.

Nub says, "You got him."

All right. I pulls up the seine. I knowed I'd killed him. You ever fished a seine? Well, you have to fish the pocket out. We fished out the pocket.

I says, "Where'd that alligator go?"

About that time something comes up between us.

I says, "Nub, the first man moves is the first man caught!"

That alligator's head was three feet long. He was bopping his lips, and when they was wide open you could of put a yardstick between 'em. His mouth come together. Nub catches his lips.

He says, "Gimme your pistol."

"Here 'tis."

Nub shot him in one eye, one ear and the neck. The 'gator lays quiet. We goes on fishing the net. Then we piled the net on board the boat. We like to turned it over, loading the alligator. We finally got him in, facing to the rear. He had his front legs laying on a seat. Nub, he climbs in the bow of the boat by the 'gator's tail. I got back in the stern on the pile of webbing, me and the 'gator face to face. I reloaded my pistol and picked up one of the twelve-foot oars and Nub takened the other.

Here we go, a-paddling. That alligator commences raising up on his toes on that seat.

I says, "Nub, I'm going to shoot him."

He says, "Fred, don't shoot him! You'll kill me. He'll settle down right where he is."

Sure enough, he did. He settled down. Then he begun winking that good eye at me. He raised up again that high to where I had to look up at him. He settles down and goes to winking. I ain't never objected to nothing much more'n that alligator setting there winking that red eye at me. I shot him in the good eye and in t'other ear, and that quieted him down for a little while. Directly he rared up and give a flounce. He hit that pile of webbing just about the time I left it. Now, if he'd hit where I'd done been, there'd of been no funeral— just a water burial.

The Fourth at Lochloosy

We makes it on in to shore. We had about three hundred pounds of fish. Nub takes a fish scoop and goes to shoveling fish.

I says, "Nub, never mind the fish. Let's get this alligator out of this boat."

When I said that, the daggone alligator rared up and knocked that fish scoop out of Nub's hands to where it ain't never been found.

Nub says, "Hand me another scoop."

About then the alligator takened a notion it was time to leave the boat. I want to tell you, the only way we kept him from going out was Nub lost his patience and takened a ax and chopped him through the backbone. He was thirteen feet and nine inches—and he was really hard to kill.

Now, that's just the way it's always been with me and alligators. I don't never mess up with 'em on purpose. No, no; the one time I fooled with one deliberate don't count. No use scarcely telling about it. 'Twasn't nothing in the world but the banana brandy. If 'twasn't for that, hell nor high water couldn't of got me to ride no alligator. And even then, now mind you, even then I didn't, so to speak, figure on doing it. It was old man Crocky aimed to do it. Old man Crocky had done set the Fourth of July to catch the alligator that had been bothering people swimming at Lochloosy Station.

He was a big old 'gator, and by bothering, I mean that when people was swimming he'd come in close enough that they'd come out. Fourth of July used to be a big time at Lochloosy. I've seen five hundred niggers come down for the frolicking and fighting. The first train that come in would unload right peaceable. Then, as t'other trains come in, there was fights all ready, waiting for 'em. I was deputy sheriff at Lochloosy, but 'twasn't no use for one deputy to go in to 'em. It would of takened fifteen or twenty.

This partickler Fourth of July the word had done gone out that old man Crocky was fixing to ride the alligator out of Lake Lochloosy. What with the niggers swarming, and the white folks congregating, there was a crowd on shore like a Baptist baptizing. And you know, old man Crocky never did show up?

Potable and Potent

Now, I figured, long as there wasn't nothing one deputy could do to stop a crowd from quarreling, I had the same right as them to enjoy myself on the Fourth of July. And the way I was enjoying myself was drinking banana brandy. You ain't never been high on banana brandy? There ain't nothing more I can say about banana brandy than this: It put me to where I got the idea it was my duty, as deputy sheriff, to take the place of old man Crocky and ride the alligator.

The word went out I was fixing to substitute for old man Crocky. Folks goes to clustering along the shore. I pushes in amongst 'em and I hollers, "Get out of the way! I'm fixing to ride the alligator!"

I remember somebody yelling, "You fixing to ride the alligator or is he fixing to ride you?"

And I can just remember me saying, "You go eat your rations and drink your 'shine, and leave me 'tend to the alligator."

I walks out into the water and goes to swimming. I have the stick in my fist old man Crocky had aimed to use and had left at the fish house. It was big around as my fist, and whittled to a point at both ends. I swims out a ways more. Directly here comes the alligator, starting in to meet me. He's got his jaws open. I swims up to him and feeds him the stick. I jobbed it straight up and down in his mouth to where he couldn't close it. The alligator commences rolling and I stayed with him, rolling too. Him with his mouth held open, it didn't pleasure him, rolling, no more than me. When he quits, I slings one leg over the back of his neck, and here we go, me riding the alligator.

I give him plenty of room. I knowed he wouldn't sink with me, for a 'gator's got sense, and he knowed he'd drown hisself with his mouth open. I put my hands over his eyes so he couldn't see where he was going. I guided him thisaway and that just as good as if I'd been riding a halter-broke mule. The way I turned him, I'd job my thumb in one of his eyes. He'd swing t'other way to try and break his eye loose.

I can just remember, dimlike, the crowd a-cheering and the niggers screaming. I rode the daggone alligator out of Lake Lochloosy and plumb up on shore.

You can see how come it to happen. 'Twasn't nothing in the world but the banana brandy. I didn't have no intention of riding no alligator. I ain't the man you belong to talk to at all. You go talk to some of them fellers that has hunted alligators. I just naturally don't know nothing about 'em.

BENNY AND THE BIRD DOGS

YOU can't change a man, no-ways. By the time his mammy turns him loose and he takes up with some innocent woman and marries her, he's what he is. If it's his nature to set by the hearth-fire and scratch hisself, you just as good to let him set and scratch. If it's his nature, like Will Dover, my man, to go to the garage in his Sunday clothes and lay down under some backwoods Cracker's old greasy Ford and tinker with it, you just as good to let him lay and tinker. And if it's his nature, like Uncle Benny, to prowl; if it's his nature to cut the fool; why, it's interfering in the ways of Providence even to stop to quarrel with him about it. Some women is born knowing that. Sometimes a woman, like the Old Hen (Uncle Benny's wife, poor soul!), has to quarrel a lifetime before she learns it. Then when it does come to her, she's like a cow has tried to jump a high fence and has got hung up on it—she's hornswoggled.

The Old Hen's a mighty fine woman—one of the finest I know. She looks just the way she did when she married Uncle Benny Mathers thirty years ago, except her hair has turned gray, like the feathers on a Gray Hackle game hen. She's plump and pretty and kind of pale from thirty years' fretting about Uncle Benny. She has a disposition, by nature, as sweet as new cane syrup. When she settled down for a lifetime's quarrelling at him, it was for the same reason syrup sours—the heat had just been put to her too long.

I can't remember a time when the Old Hen wasn't quarrelling at Uncle Benny. It begun a week after they was married. He went off prowling by hisself, to a frolic or such as that, and didn't come home until four o'clock in the morning. She was setting up waiting for him. When she crawled him about it, he said, "Bless Katy, wife, let's sleep now and quarrel in the morning." So she quarrelled in the morning and just kept it up. For thirty years. Not for meanness— she just kept hoping she could change him.

Change him? When he takened notice of the way she was fussing and clucking and ruffing her feathers, he quit calling her by her given name and begun calling her the Old Hen. That's all I could ever see she changed him.

Uncle Benny's a sight. He's been constable here at Oak Bluff, Florida, for twenty years. We figure it keeps him out of worse trouble to let him be constable. He's the quickest shot in three counties and the colored folks is all as superstitious of him as if he was the devil hisself. He's a comical-appearing somebody. He's small and quick and he don't move—he prances. He has a little bald sun-tanned head with a rim of white hair around the back of it. Where the hair ends at the sides of his head, it sticks straight up over his ears in two little white tufts like goat-horns. He's got bright blue eyes that look at you quick and wicked, the way a goat looks. That's exactly what he looks and acts like—a mischievous little old billy-goat. And he's been popping up under folks' noses and playing tricks on them as long as Oak Bluff has knowed him. Doc in particular. He loved to torment Doc.

And stay home? Uncle Benny don't know what it is to stay home. The Old Hen'll cook hot dinner for him and he won't come. She'll start another fire in the range and warm it up for him about dusk-dark and he won't come. She'll set up till midnight, times till daybreak, and maybe just about the time the east lightens and the birds gets to whistling good, he'll come home. Where's he been? He's been with somebody 'gatoring, or with somebody catching crabs to Salt Springs; he's been to a square-dance twenty miles away in the flat-woods; he's been on the highway in that Ford car, just rambling as long as his gas held out—and them seven pieded bird-dogs setting up in the back keeping him company.

It was seven years ago, during the Boom, that he bought the Model-T and begun collecting bird-dogs. Everybody in Florida was rich for a whiles, selling gopher holes to the Yankees. Now putting an automobile under Uncle Benny was like putting wings on a wild-cat—it just opened up new territory. Instead of rambling over one county, he could ramble over ten. And the way he drove—like a bat out of Torment. He's one of them men just loves to cover the ground. And that car and all them bird-dogs worked on the Old Hen like a quart of gasoline on a camp-fire. She really went to raring. I tried to tell her then 'twasn't no use to pay him no mind, but she wouldn't listen.

I said, "It's just his nature. You can't do a thing about it but take it for your share and go on. You and Uncle Benny is just made dif-ferent. You want him home and he don't want to be home. You're a barn-yard fowl and he's a wild fowl."

"Mis' Dover," she said, "it's easy for you to talk. Your man runs a garage and comes home nights. You don't know how terrible it is to have a man that prowls."

I said, "Leave him prowl."

She said, "Yes, but when he's on the prowl, I don't no more know where to look for him than somebody's tom-cat."

I said, "If 'twas me, I wouldn't look for him."

She said, "Moonlight nights he's the worst. Just like the varmints."

I said, "Don't that tell you nothing?"

She said, "If he'd content hisself with prowling— But he ain't content until he cuts the fool. He takes that Ford car and them seven bird-dogs and maybe a pint of moonshine, and maybe picks up Doc to prowl with him, and he don't rest until he's done something crazy. What I keep figuring is, he'll kill hisself in that Ford car, cutting the fool."

I said, "You don't need to fret about him and that Ford. What's unnatural for one man is plumb natural for another. And cutting the fool is so natural for Uncle Benny, it's like a bird in the air or a fish in water—there won't no harm come to him from it."

She said, "Mis' Dover, what the devil throws over his back has got to come down under his belly."

I said, "Uncle Benny Mathers is beyond rules and sayings. I know men-folks, and if you'll listen to me, you'll settle down and quit quarrelling and leave him go his way in quiet."

I happened to be in on it this spring, the last time the Old Hen ever quarrelled at Uncle Benny. Me and Doc was both in on it. It was the day of old lady Weller's burying. Doc carried me in his car to the cemetery. My Will couldn't leave the garage, because the trucks hauling the Florida oranges north was bringing in pretty good business. Doc felt obliged to go to the burying. He's a patent-medicine salesman—a big fat fellow with a red face and yellow hair. He sells the Little Giant line of remedies. Old lady Weller had been one of his best customers. She'd taken no nourishment the last week of her life except them remedies, and Doc figured he ought to pay her the proper respect and show everybody he was a man was always grateful to his customers.

Uncle Benny and the Old Hen went to the burying in the Model-T. And the seven bird-dogs went, setting up in the back seat. They always went to the buryings.

Uncle Benny said, "Walls nor chains won't hold 'em. Better to have 'em go along riding decent and quiet, than to bust loose and foller the Model-T like a daggone pack of bloodhounds."

That was true enough. Those bird-dogs could hear that old Ford crank up and go off in low gear, clear across the town. They'd always hope it was time to go bird-hunting again, and here they'd come, trailing it. So there were the bird-dogs riding along to old lady Weller's burying, with their ears flopping and their noses in the air for quail. As constable, Uncle Benny sort of represented the town, and he was right in behind the hearse. I mean, that car was a pain, to be part of a funeral procession. In the seven years he'd had it, he'd all but drove it to pieces, and it looked like a rusty, mangy razor-back hog. The hood was thin and narrow, like a shoat's nose—you remember the way all Model-T Fords were built. It had no top to it, nor no doors to the front seat, and the back seat rose up in a hump where the bird-dogs had squeezed the excelsior chitlin's out of it.

The Old Hen sat up stiff and proud, not letting on she minded. Doc and I figured she'd been quarrelling at Uncle Benny about the bird-dogs, because when one of them put his paws on her shoulders and begun licking around her ears, she turned and smacked the breath out of him.

The funeral procession had just left the Oak Bluff dirt road and turned onto No. 9 Highway, when the garage keeper at the bend ran out.

He hollered, "I just got a 'phone call for Uncle Benny Mathers from the high sheriff!"

So Uncle Benny cut out of the procession and drove over to the pay station by the kerosene tank to take the message. He caught up again in a minute and called to Doc, "A drunken nigger is headed this way in a Chevrolet and the sheriff wants I should stop him."

About that time here come the Chevrolet and started to pass the procession, wobbling back and forth as if it had the blind staggers. You may well know the nigger was drunk or he wouldn't have passed a funeral. Uncle Benny cut out of line and took out after him. When he saw who was chasing him, the nigger turned around and headed back the way he'd come from. Uncle Benny was gaining on him when they passed the hearse. The bird-dogs begun to take an interest and rared up, barking. What does Uncle Benny do but go to the side of the Chevrolet so the nigger turns around—and then Uncle Benny crowded him so all he could do was to shoot into line in the funeral procession. Uncle Benny cut right in after him and the nigger shot out of line and Uncle Benny crowded him in again.

I'll declare, I was glad old lady Weller wasn't alive to see it. She'd had no use for Uncle Benny, she'd hated a nigger, and she'd despised dogs so to where she kept a shotgun by her door to shoot at them if one so much as crossed her cornfield. And here on the way to her burying, where you'd figure she was entitled to have things the way she liked them, here was Uncle Benny chasing a nigger in and out of line, and seven bird-dogs were going *Ki-yippity-yi! Ki-yippity-yi! Ki-yippity-yi!* I was mighty proud the corpse was no kin to me.

The Old Hen was plumb mortified. She put her hands over her face and when the Ford would swerve by or cut in ahead of us, Doc and me could see her swaying back and forth and suffering. I don't scarcely need to say Uncle Benny was enjoying hisself. If he'd looked sorrowful-like, as if he was just doing his duty, you could of forgive him. Near a filling-station the Chevrolet shot ahead and stopped and the nigger jumped out and started to run. Uncle Benny stopped and climbed out of the Ford and drew his pistol and called "Stop!" The nigger kept on going.

Now Uncle Benny claims that shooting at niggers in the line of duty is what keeps him in practice for bird-shooting. He dropped a ball to the right of the nigger's heel and he dropped a ball to the left of it. He called "Stop!" and the nigger kept on going. Then Uncle Benny took his pistol in both hands and took a slow aim and he laid the third ball against the nigger's shin-bone. He dropped like a string-haltered mule.

Uncle Benny said to the man that ran the filling-station, "Get your gun. That there nigger is under arrest and I deputize you to keep him that-a-way. The sheriff'll be along to pick him up direckly."

He cut back into the funeral procession between us and the hearse, and we could tell by them wicked blue eyes he didn't know when he'd enjoyed a burying like old lady Weller's. When we got back from the burying, he stopped by Will's garage. The Old Hen was giving him down-the-country.

She said, "That was the most scandalous thing I've ever knowed you to do, chasing that nigger in and out of Mis' Weller's funeral."

Uncle Benny's eyes begun to dance and he said, "I know it, wife, but I couldn't help it. 'Twasn't me done the chasing—it was the Model-T."

Doc got in to it then and sided with the Old Hen. He gets excited, the way fat men do, and he swelled up like a spreading adder.

"Benny," he said, "you shock my modesty. This ain't no occasion for laughing nor lying."

Uncle Benny said, "I know it, Doc. I wouldn't think of laughing nor lying. You didn't know I've got that Ford trained? I've got it trained to where it'll do two things. It's helped me chase so many niggers, I've got it to where it just natually takes out after 'em by itself."

Doc got red in the face and asked, real sarcastic, "And what's the other piece of training?"

Uncle Benny said, "Doc, that Ford has carried me home drunk so many times, I've got it trained to where it'll take care of me and carry me home safe when I ain't fitten."

Doc spit half-way across the road and he said, "You lying old jay-bird."

Uncle Benny said, "Doc, I've got a pint of moonshine, and if you'll come go camping with me to Salt Springs this evening, I'll prove it."

The Old Hen spoke up and she said, "Benny, Heaven forgive you for I won't, if you go on the prowl again before you've cleared the weeds out of my old pindar field. I'm a month late now, getting it planted."

Doc loves Salt Springs crab and mullet as good as Uncle Benny does, and I could see he was tempted.

But he said, "Benny, you go along home and do what your wife wants, and when you're done—when she says you're done—then we'll go to Salt Springs."

So Uncle Benny and the Old Hen drove off. Doc watched after them.

He said, "Anyways, cutting the fool at a burying had ought to last Benny quite a while."

I said, "You don't know him. Cutting the fool don't last him no time at all."

I was right. I ain't so special wise a woman, but if I once know a man, I can come right close to telling you what he'll do. Uncle Benny hadn't been gone hardly no time, when somebody come by the garage hollering that he'd done set the Old Hen's pindar field on fire.

I said to Doc, "What did I tell you? The last thing in the world was safe for that woman to do, was to turn him loose on them weeds. He figured firing was the quickest way to get shut of them."

Doc said, "Let's go see."

We got in his car and drove out to Uncle Benny's place. Here was smoke rolling up back of the house, and the big live oak in the yard was black with soldier blackbirds the grass fire had drove out of the pindar field. The field hadn't had peanuts in it since fall, but bless Katy, it was full of something else. Uncle Benny's wife had it plumb full of setting guinea-hens. She hadn't told him, because he didn't like guineas.

Far off to the west corner of the field was the Old Hen, trying to run the guineas into a coop. They were flying every which-a-way and hollering *Pod-rac! Pod-rac!* the way guineas holler. All the young uns in the neighborhood were in the middle of the field, beating out the grass fire with palmettos. And setting up on top of the east gate, just as unconcerned, was Uncle Benny, with them two little horns of white hair curling in the heat. Now what do you reckon he was doing? He had all seven of them bird-dogs running back and forth retrieving guinea eggs. He'd say now and again, "Dead— fetch!" and they'd wag their tails and go hunt up another nest and here they'd come, with guinea eggs carried gentle in their mouths. He was putting the eggs in a basket.

When the commotion was over, and the fire out, and everybody gone on but Doc and me, we went to the front porch to set down and rest. The Old Hen was wore out. She admitted it was her fault not letting Uncle Benny know about the setting guinea-hens. She was about to forgive him setting the field a-fire, because him and the bird-dogs had saved the guinea eggs. But when we got to the porch, here lay the bird-dogs in the rocking chairs. There was one to every chair, rocking away and cutting their eyes at her. Their coats and paws were smuttied from the burnt grass—and the Old Hen had put clean sugar-sacking covers on every blessed chair that morning. That settled it. She was stirred up anyway about the way he'd cut the fool at the burying, and she really set in to quarrel at Uncle Benny. And like I say, it turned out to be the last piece of quarrelling she ever done.

She said to him, "You taught them bird-dogs to rock in a rocking-chair just to torment me. Ever' beast or varmint you've brought home, you've learned to cut the fool as bad as you do."

"Now wife, what beast or varmint did I ever learn to cut the fool?"

"You learned the 'coon to screw the tops off my syrup cans. You learned the 'possum to hang upside down in my cupboards, and I'd go for a jar of maybe pepper relish and put my hand on him. . . . There's been plenty of such as that. I've raised ever'thing in the world for you but a stallion horse."

Doc said, "Give him time, he'll have one of them stabled in the kitchen."

"Bird-dogs is natural to have around," she said, "I was raised to bird-dogs. But it ain't natural for 'em to rock in a rocking-chair.

There's so terrible many of them, and when they put in the night on the porch laying in the rocking chairs and rocking, I don't close my eyes for the fuss."

Uncle Benny said, "You see, Doc? You see, Mis' Dover? She's always quarrelling that me and the dogs ain't never home at night. Then when we do come in, she ain't willing we should all be comf'table.

"We just as good to go on to Salt Springs, Doc. Wait while I go in the house and get my camping oufit and we'll set out."

He went in the house and came out with his camping stuff. She knowed he was gone for nobody knew how long.

We walked on down to the gate and the Old Hen followed, sniffling a little and twisting the corner of her apron.

"Benny," she said, "please don't go to Salt Springs. You always lose your teeth in the Boil."

"I ain't lost 'em but three times," he said, and he cranked up the Model-T and climbed in. "I couldn't help losing 'em the first time. That was when I was laughing at the Yankee casting for bass, and his plug caught me in the open mouth and lifted my teeth out. Nor I couldn't help it the second time, when Doc and me was rassling in the rowboat and he pushed me in."

"Yes," she said, "and how'd you lose 'em the third time?"

His eyes twinkled and he shoved the Ford in low. "Cuttin' the fool," he said.

"That's just it," she said, and the tears begun to roll out of her eyes. "Anybody with false teeth hadn't ought to cut the fool!"

Now I always thought it was right cute, the way Uncle Benny fooled Doc about the trained Ford. You know how the old-timey Fords get the gas—it feeds from the hand-throttle on the wheel. Well, Uncle Benny had spent the day before old lady Weller's funeral at Will's garage, putting in a foot accelerator. He didn't say a word to anybody, and Will and me was the only ones knowed he had it. Doc and Uncle Benny stayed three-four days camping at Salt Springs. Now the night they decided to come home, they'd both had something to drink, but Uncle Benny let on like he was in worse shape than he was.

Doc said, "Benny, you better leave me drive."

Uncle Benny pretended to rock on his feet and roll his head and he said, "I've got that Model-T trained to carry me home, drunk or sober."

Doc said, "Never mind that lie again. You get up there in the seat and whistle in the dogs. I'm fixing to drive us home."

Well, I'd of give a pretty to of been in the back seat with them bird-dogs that night when Doc drove the Ford back to Oak Bluff. It's a treat, anyways, to see a fat man get excited. The first thing Doc knowed, the Ford was running away with him. The Ford lights were none too good, and Doc just did clear a stump by the road-side, and he run clean over a black-jack sapling. He looked at the hand throttle on the wheel and here it was where the car had ought to be going about twenty miles an hour and it was going forty-five. That rascal of an Uncle Benny had his foot on the foot accelerator.

Doc shut off the gas altogether and the Ford kept right on going.

He said, "Something's the matter."

Uncle Benny seemed to be dozing and didn't pay no mind. The Ford whipped back and forth in the sand road like a 'gator's tail. Directly they got on to the hard road and the Model-T put on speed. They begun to get near a curve. It was a dark night and the car-lights wobbling, but Doc could see it coming. He took a tight holt of the wheel and begun to sweat. He felt for the brakes, but Uncle Benny never did have any.

He said, "We'll all be kilt."

When they started to take the curve, the Model-T was going nearly fifty-five—and then just as they got there, all of a sudden it slowed down as if it knowed what it was doing, and went around the curve as gentle as a day-old kitten. Uncle Benny had eased his foot off the accelerator. Doc drawed a breath again.

It's a wonder to me that trip didn't make Doc a nervous wreck. On every straightaway the Ford would rare back on its haunches and stretch out like a grayhound. Every curve they come to, it would go to it like a jack-rabbit. Then just as the sweat would pour down Doc's face and the drops would splash on the wheel, and he'd gather hisself together ready to jump, the Ford would slow down. It was a hot spring night, but Uncle Benny says Doc's teeth were chattering. The Model-T made the last mile lickety-brindle with the gas at the hand-throttle shut off entirely—and it coasted down in front of Will's garage and of its own free will come to a dead stop.

It was nine o'clock at night. Will was just closing up and I had locked the candy and cigarette counter and was waiting for him. There was a whole bunch of the men and boys around, like always, because the garage is the last place in Oak Bluff to put the lights out. Doc climbed out of the Ford trembling like a dish of custard. Uncle Benny eased out after him and I looked at him and right away I knowed he'd been up to mischief.

Doc said, "I don't know how he done it—but dogged if he wasn't telling the truth when he said he had that blankety-blank Model-T trained to carry him home when he ain't fitten."

Will asked, "How come?" and Doc told us. Will looked at me and begun to chuckle and we knowed what Uncle Benny had done to him. I think maybe I would of let Uncle Benny get away with it, but Will couldn't keep it.

"Come here, Doc," he said. "Here's your training."

I thought the bunch would laugh Doc out of town. He swelled up like a toad-fish and he got in his car without a word and drove away.

It's a wonderful thing just to set down and figure out how many different ways there are to be crazy. We never thought of Uncle Benny as being really crazy. We'd say, "Uncle Benny's cutting the fool again," and we'd mean he was just messing around some sort of foolishness like a daggone young un. We figured his was what you might call the bottom kind of craziness. The next would be the half-witted. The next would be the senseless. The next would be what the colored folks call "mindless." And clear up at the top would be what you'd call cold-out crazy. With all his foolishness, we never figured Uncle Benny was cold-out crazy.

Well, we missed Uncle Benny from Oak Bluff a day or two. When I came to ask questions, I found he'd gone on a long prowl and was over on the Withlacoochie River camping with some oyster fisher-men. I didn't think much about it, because he was liable to stay off that-a-way. But time rocked on and he didn't show up. I dropped by his house to ask the Old Hen about him. She didn't know a blessed thing.

She said, "Ain't it God's mercy we've got no young uns? The pore things would be as good as fatherless."

And then a few days later Doc came driving up to the garage. He got out and blew his nose and we could see his eyes were red.

He said, "Ain't it awful! I can't hardly bear to think about it."

Will said, "Doc, if you know bad news, you must be carrying it. Ain't nothing sorrowful I know of, except the Prohi's have found Philbin's still."

Doc said, "Don't talk about such little accidents at a time like this. You don't mean you ain't heard about Benny?"

The bunch was there and they all perked up, interested. They knowed if it was Uncle Benny, they could expect 'most any news.

I said, "We ain't heard a word since he went off to the west coast."

"You ain't heard about him going crazy?"

I said, "Doc, you mean being crazy. He's always been that-a-way."

"I mean being crazy and going crazy. Pore ol' Benny Mathers has gone really cold-out crazy."

Well, we all just looked at him and we looked at one another. And it came over the whole bunch of us that we weren't surprised. A nigger setting by the free air hose said, "Do, Jesus!" and eased away to tell the others.

Doc blew his nose and wiped his eyes and he said, "I'm sure we all forgive the pore ol' feller all the things he done. He wasn't responsible. I feel mighty bad, to think the hard way I've often spoke to him."

Will asked, "How come it to finally happen?"

Doc said, "He'd been up to some foolishness all night, raring through some of them Gulf coast flat-woods. Him and the fellers he was camping with was setting on the steps of the camp-house after breakfast. All of a sudden Uncle Benny goes to whistling, loud and shrill like a jay-bird. Then he says, 'I'm Sampson,' and he begun to tear down the camp-house."

Will asked, "What'd they do with him?"

Doc said, "You really ain't heard? I declare, I can't believe the news has come so slow. They had a terrible time holding him and tying him. They got in the doctors and the sheriff and they takened pore ol' Uncle Benny to the lunatic asylum at Chattahoochie."

Doc wiped his eyes and we all begun to sniffle and our eyes to burn. I declare, it was just as if Uncle Benny Mathers had died on us.

I said, "Oh, his pore wife——."

Will said, "We'll have to be good to him and go see him and take him cigarettes and maybe slip him a pint of 'shine now and again."

I said, "The way he loved his freedom—shutting him up in a crazy-house will be like putting a wild-cat in a crocus sack."

Doc said, "Oh, he ain't in the asylum right now. He's broke loose. That's what makes me feel so bad. He's headed this way, and no telling the harm he'll do before he's ketched again."

Everybody jumped up and begun feeling in their hip pockets for their guns.

Doc said, "No use to try to put no guns on him. He's got his'n and they say he's shooting just as accurate as ever."

That was enough for me. I ran back of the counter at the garage and begun locking up.

I said, "Doc, you're a sight. 'Tain't no time to go to feeling sorry for Uncle Benny and our lives and property in danger."

Doc said, "I know, but I knowed him so long and I knowed him so good. I can't help feeling bad about it."

I said, "Do something about it. Don't just set there, and him liable to come shooting his way in any minute."

Doc said, "I know, but what can anybody do to stop him? Pore man, with all them deputies after him."

Will said, "Deputies?"

Doc said, "Why, yes. The sheriff at Ocala asked me would I stop along the road and leave word for all the deputies to try and ketch him. Pore ol' Benny, I'll swear. I hated doing it the worst way."

I scooped the money out of the cash register and I told them, "Now, men, I'm leaving. I've put up with Uncle Benny Mathers when he was drunk and I've put up with him when he was cutting the fool. But the reckless way he drives that Ford and the way he shoots a pistol, I ain't studying on messing up around him and him gone cold-out crazy."

Doc said, "Ain't a thing in the world would stop him when he goes by, and all them deputies after him, but a barricade acrost the road."

I said, "Then for goodness' sake, you sorry, low-down, no-account, varminty white men tear down the wire fence around my chicken yard and fix Uncle Benny a barricade."

Doc said, "I just hated to suggest it."

Will said, "He'd slow down for the barricade and we could come in from behind and hem him in."

Doc said, "It'll be an awful thing to hem him in and have to see him sent back to Chattahoochie."

Will said, "I'll commence pulling out the posts and you-all can wind up the fencing."

They worked fast and I went out and looked up the road now and again to see if Uncle Benny was coming. Doc had stopped at the Standard filling-station on his way, to leave the news, and we could see the people there stirring around and going out to look, the same as we were doing. When we dragged the roll of wire fencing out into the road we hollered to them so they could see what we were doing and they all cheered and waved their hats. The word had spread, and the young uns begun traipsing bare-footed down to the road, until some of their mammies ran down and cuffed them and hurried them back home out of the way of Uncle Benny. The men strung the fencing tight across the road between the garage on one side and our smoke-house on the other. They nailed it firm at both ends.

Doc said, "Leave me drive the last nail, men—it may be the last thing I can do for Benny this side of Chattahoochie."

I talked the men into unloading their guns.

"He'll have to stop when he sees the barricade," I said, "and then you can all go in on him with your guns drawed and capture him. I just can't hear to a loaded gun being drawed on him, for fear of somebody getting excited and shooting him."

Doc wiped the sweat off his forehead and he said, "Men, this is a mighty serious occasion. I'd be mighty proud if you'd all have a little snort on me," and he passed the bottle.

"Here's to Uncle Benny, the way we all knowed him before he went cold-out crazy," he said.

And then we heard a shouting up the dirt road and young uns

whistling and women and girls screaming and chickens scattering.

"Yonder comes Uncle Benny!"

And yonder he came.

The Model-T was swooping down like a bull-bat after a mosquito. The water was boiling up out of the radiator in a foot-high stream. The seven pieded bird-dogs were hanging out of the back seat and trembling as if they craved to tell the things they'd seen. And behind Uncle Benny was a string of deputy sheriffs in Fords and Chevrolets and motor-cycles that had gathered together from every town between Oak Bluff and Ocala. And Uncle Benny was hunched over the steering wheel with them two tufts of goat-horn hair sticking up in the breeze—and the minute I laid eyes on him I knowed he wasn't one mite crazier than he ever had been. I knowed right then Doc had laid out to get even with him and had lied on him all the way down the road.

It was too late then. I knowed, whatever happened, there'd be people to the end of his life would always believe it. I knowed there'd be young uns running from him and niggers hiding. And I knowed there wasn't a thing in the world now could keep him out of Chattahoochie for the time being. I knowed he'd fight when he was taken, and all them mad and hot and dusty deputies would get him to the lunatic asylum quicker than a black snake can cross hot ashes. And once a man that has cut the fool all his life, like Uncle Benny, is in the crazy-house, there'll be plenty of folks to say to keep him there.

It was too late. Uncle Benny was bearing down toward the garage and right in front of him was the barricade.

Doc hollered, "Be ready to jump on him when he stops!"

Stop? Uncle Benny stop? He kept right on coming. The sight of that chicken-wire barricade was no more to him than an aggravation. Uncle Benny and the Model-T dived into the barricade like a water-turkey into a pool. The barricade held. And the next thing we knowed, the Ford had somersaulted over the fencing and crumpled up like a paper shoe-box and scattered bird-dogs over ten acres and laid Uncle Benny in a heap over against the wall of the smoke-house. I was raised to use the language of a lady, but I couldn't hold in.

"Doc," I said, "you low-down son of a—."

He said, "Mis' Dover, the name's too good. I've killed my friend."

Killed him? Killed Uncle Benny? It can't be done until the Almighty Hisself hollers "Sooey!" Uncle Benny was messed up considerable, but him nor none of the bird-dogs was dead.

The doctor took a few stitches in him at the garage before he come to, and tied up his head right pretty in a white bandage. We left Will to quiet the deputies and we put Uncle Benny in Doc's car and carried him home to the Old Hen. Naturally, I figured it would set her to quarrelling. Instead, it just brought out all her sweetness. I can guess a man, but I can't guess another woman.

"The pore ol' feller," she said. "I knowed he had it coming to him. What the devil throws over his back—. I knowed he'd kill hisself in that Ford car, cutting the fool and prowling. The biggest load is off my mind. Now," she said, "now, by God's mercy, when it did come to him, he got out alive."

She began fanning him with a palmetto fan where he lay on the bed, and Doc poured out a drink of 'shine to have ready for him when he come to. Doc's hand was trembling. Uncle Benny opened his eyes. He eased one hand up to the bandage across his head and he groaned and grunted. He looked at Doc as if he couldn't make up his mind whether or not to reach for his pistol. Doc put the 'shine to his mouth and Uncle Benny swallowed. Them wicked blue eyes begun to dance.

"Doc," he said, "how will I get home when I'm drunk, now you've tore up my trained Ford?"

Doc broke down and cried like a little baby.

"I ain't got the money to replace it," he said, "but I'll give you my car. I'll carry the Little Giant line of remedies on foot."

Uncle Benny said, "I don't want your car. It ain't trained."

Doc said, "Then I'll tote you on my back, anywheres you say."

The Old Hen let in the bird-dogs, some of them limping a little, and they climbed on the bed and beat their tails on the counterpane and licked Uncle Benny. We felt mighty relieved things had come out that way.

Uncle Benny was up and around in a few days, with his head bandaged, and him as pert as a woodpecker. He just about owned Oak Bluff—all except the people that did like I figured, never did get over the idea he'd gone really crazy. Most people figured he'd had a mighty good lesson and it would learn him not to cut the fool. The Old Hen was as happy as a bride. She was so proud to have the Ford torn up, and no money to get another, that she'd even now and again pet one of the bird-dogs. She waited on Uncle Benny hand and foot and couldn't do enough to please him.

She said to me, "The pore ol' feller sure stays home nights now."

Stay home? Uncle Benny stay home? Two weeks after the accident the wreck of the Model-T disappeared from behind the garage where Will had dragged it. The next day the seven bird-dogs disappeared. The day after that Doc and Uncle Benny went to Ocala in Doc's car. Will wouldn't answer me when I asked him questions. The Old Hen stopped by the garage and got a Coco-Cola and she didn't know any more than I did. Then Will pointed down the road.

He said, "Yonder he comes."

And yonder he came. You could tell him way off by the white bandage with the tufts of hair sticking up over it. He was scrooched down behind the wheel of what looked like a brand-new automobile. Doc was following behind him. They swooped into the garage.

Will said, "It's a new second-hand body put on the chassis and around the engine of the old Ford."

Uncle Benny got out and he greeted us.

He said, "Will, it's just possible it was the motor of the Model-T that had takened the training. The motor ain't hurt, and me and Doc are real hopeful."

The Old Hen said, "Benny, where'd you get the money to pay for it?"

He said, "Why, a daggone bootlegger in a truck going from Miami to New York bought the bird-dogs for twenty-five dollars apiece. The low-down rascal knowed good and well they was worth seventy-five."

She brightened some. Getting shut of the bird-dogs was a little progress. She walked over to the car and began looking around it.

"Benny," she said, and her voice come kind of faintified, "if you sold the bird-dogs, what's this place back here looks like it was fixed for 'em?"

We all looked, and here was a open compartment-like in the back, fixed up with seven crocus sacks stuffed with corn-shucks. About that time here come a cloud of dust down the road. It was the seven bird-dogs. They were about give out. Their tongues were hanging out and their feet looked blistered.

Uncle Benny said, "I knowed they'd jump out of that bootlegger's truck. I told him so."

I tell you, what's in a man's nature you can't change. It takened the Old Hen thirty years and all them goings-on to learn it. She went and climbed in the front seat of the car and just sat there waiting for Uncle Benny to drive home for his dinner. He lifted the bird-dogs up and set them down to rest on the corn-shucks cushions, and he brought them a pan of water.

He said, "I figure they busted loose just about Lawtey."

The Old Hen never opened her mouth. She hasn't quarrelled at him from that day to this. She was hornswoggled.

THE PARDON

A DRIFT of small hard leaves clicked from the live oak at the main gate of the penitentiary. The man Adams looked at the sky and turned up the collar of his misfit coat. Then he turned it down again, with the uncertainty of a man for whom decisions have been made too long. The sky was gray, mottled with the harsh blue of November.

A guard at the gate said, "Don't forget anything. It's unlucky to turn back."

The trusties clustered at the gatehouse made a clatter of thin laughter.

A man serving a life sentence said, "It's more unlucky, turning in—" and they laughed again, with the sound of men applauding from a distance.

Adams put his hand inside his coat and touched the sharp edge of parchment paper that was the pardon. He wanted to show it. His fumbling was ignored and he let his hand drop at his side.

He said, "Well, so long."

The guard answered indifferently, "So long," and spat into the sand. The group was silent; immobile; understanding the futility of speech or movement.

Adams shuffled into the roadway and searched the line of parked cars of visitors. A woman fluttered toward him and retreated to the

216

protection of an open Ford. She lifted a hand, entrenched on the far side of the high hood.

He called "Emma!" and moved his feet faster, his pulse thick in his throat.

He saw that it was Joe Porter at the wheel of the Ford.

He said, "Hey, Joe."

Joe said, "Hey," and absorbed himself with the gears.

Adams turned to the woman.

He said, "Hey, wife."

She looked at him. He thought that he had never before noticed how much she looked like a rabbit. When he had worked on the penitentiary farm they had killed dozens of rabbits. They sat staring with frightened eyes and trembling noses, pretending not to be seen.

He asked, "Where's the two young uns?"

She said, belligerently, "I didn't see fitten to carry 'em. I ain't never yet carried 'em here."

"No," he said.

He hesitated between the front seat and the back, and climbed stiffly into the back. The woman licked her lips.

She said, "I reckon you'll be glad of the room," and stepped into the front seat beside Joe Porter.

Joe said, "First chance in seven years to spread hisself, eh, Emma?"

Adams stared at the back of his wife's neck. It was plump, with the hair dark and low-growing.

The Ford lurched in the deep ruts of the sand road leading away from the penitentiary. Adams bounced on the worn springs, holding his black felt hat with one hand against the wind that whipped through the rear of the car. It seemed to him that he was moving with incredible speed. The prison farm trailed out of sight; the nursery telescoping into the dairy farm; the dairy farm into the hog pasture; the hog pasture into the open fields; the fields, at last, beyond the bridge, into pine woods.

Nine miles beyond the penitentiary the Ford left the dirt road and ran smoothly along a paved highway. The pine forest appeared to march, closing its ranks, filling in its shadowy spaces with its own dark members. He abandoned himself to the motion. He felt as he had once done under the influence of gas in the prison hospital. He was conscious of a rush of blood in his body, of wind in his ears, of an increasing numbness; conscious of a darkness on either side of him through which he passed, hour after hour, without effort or volition of his own.

Joe said to Emma, "It'll be dusk dark, time we get him home."

Adams stirred uneasily. He felt like a sack of mule feed, or a hog's carcass. He wanted to call to Joe above the wind, to apologize, to transform himself into a sentient being. He hunched forward, gripping the front seat with his fingers. No one noticed him and he could not think of anything to say. He leaned back and the pardon creaked inside his pocket. His heart jumped with relief, as though he were a child, forgetting its recitation on the school platform, who had been prompted.

He shouted, "I didn't some way never figure I'd get a pardon."

There was no answer. He thought he had not been heard. Then he wondered in a panic whether he had actually spoken. He may only, as he had so often, have imagined his voice in loud clear speech.

Joe said, "Didn't nobody else figure so, neither."

The car began to pass through towns he knew. Near Busby marsh, turtle doves in a flock hurled themselves toward the night's watering place. Their under-bodies were rosy, facing the west. Then they passed into the sunset and were at once black, as though charred to a crisp by its heatless fire. The doves wheeled and could be seen plunging to the marsh edge.

Adams called out, "We been having them things by the hundreds in the chufa fields. You got chufas this year, Emma?"

She turned her head half-way across her shoulder and shook it briefly.

Joe said, "She can't raise nothing hardly, for other folks' hogs. Rooting and rambling. Them fences you left wasn't none too good when you left 'em. I've mended parts of 'em."

She added, "Joe put new brick to the old chimney for me. I couldn't scarcely have managed."

The Ford left the highway for the sand road that led through Busby flat woods to the farm. The wind was high. It lashed the flexible boughs of the pine trees and they flailed the car top. Adams recognized landmarks; an abandoned cattle pen; a sink-hole; the pond where his hogs had always watered. Yet the house moved unexpectedly into sight around the familiar bend, standing suddenly small and smoke-gray in the November twilight.

The Ford stopped outside the gate. The chinaberry tree in the yard had grown higher than the house, and in the silence of the car's halting, its gaunt branches scraped the bricks of the chimney. Adams passed through the gate and took a few steps up the path. The place seemed uninhabited; not his home, but merely a place he had remembered. He waited for Joe and Emma, lagging behind when the woman lifted the shoestring latch and pushed open the door.

At first the large kitchen appeared empty. He blinked. An oak fire glowed dull in the range. He searched the darkness. There was a stirring in the dusk in the far corner. The faces of two children took shape, their eyes wide and glinting.

Adams called across the room, "It ain't Quincie and Lila, is it?"

Joe said, "Ain't either of you girls big enough to get the lamp going without somebody should come home and light it for you?"

Emma said, "Hush up, Joe. I'll light it. Go fetch me an armful of wood. You girls come speak to your father."

The girls moved woodenly into the light of the swinging kerosene lamp. They too, he thought, looked like rabbits, small-mouthed and frightened. They had grown tall and thin.

He questioned, "Quincie, that you with them longest legs? Let's see—I been away seven years—you must be thirteen. Lila? You about ten—"

He held out one hand toward them. They did not move.

Emma called, "Start the bacon, Quincie. We'll never be done."

Adams stood in the middle of the floor. The bustle of supper-making stirred about him. Joe returned by the back door, dropping wood in the box with a clatter. He washed his hands in the basin on the water shelf and combed his thick hair with a comb he took from behind the mirror.

He called to Adams, "Set down, man."

Emma said sharply, "Let him come wash first. He's got that jail house smell."

Adams flushed.

"We all kept mighty clean up there," he said. "We had running water. My clothes is all clean."

Joe dilated his nostrils, testing the air with relish.

"It's the disinfectant they use in them places," he said.

Adams moved to the water shelf and washed his face and hands carefully. He dampened an end of the towel and rubbed it inside his collar. He smoothed his hair with his hands and edged into a chair at the long table against the wall. His wife leaned over him to place a plate of cold biscuits. He caught at a fold of her skirt as she moved away.

He said playfully, "Don't make company of me in my own house, Emma."

The thin girls gaped at him. He was uncomfortable, as though he had tried to make a joke in church. Emma brought hot dishes from the stove. She stood looking at the table, and pushed back a fore-lock of hair. The gesture made her in an instant his wife again. He remembered teasing her about it, telling her she would wear herself baldheaded. He had seen her lie in bed beside him, her hair braided neatly for the night, and lift her hand to brush back that very soft dark forelock. A sharp sweetness struck through him.

A rap sounded on the door. Voices lifted, and the near neighbors, Mr. and Mrs. Mobbley, came noisily into the kitchen. Adams jerked from his chair to shake hands. He was pleased and proud that they had come to see him on his first night at home.

Emma said in a low voice, "Fetch Jackie," and in the confusion the older girl went out of the room, returning with a child of four, rubbing his eyes from sleep. Adams glanced at him vaguely, turning back to Mobbley with delight in the visit. The Mobbleys were obese and florid. Insisting that they had already eaten, they sat at table and joined heartily in the food.

Mobbley said between mouthfuls, "I ain't one to hold his trouble against a man. I've always said, you didn't do no more than ary other man in a quarrel, and the argument going against him. If you hadn't of pushed that sorry Wilbur out of the rowboat into the lake, he'd of pitched you out and it would of been you drowned and him in the penitentiary."

Adams said eagerly, "That's what the new superintendent said, getting me the pardon. He said it was self-defense, like, and I shouldn't never of been allowed to plead guilty to second-degree murder. It was manslaughter at the very worst, he said, and that ain't serious. Not twenty years sentence, no-how."

Mobbley frowned.

He said, "Course, it ain't every neighbor would come to you right off, like me. There's folks figure the jail is the jail."

Adams said humbly, "It's mighty good of you, coming." He hitched himself about on his chair. He asked eagerly, "You want to see the pardon?"

They leaned forward in their chairs.

"I've always wanted to see one," Mrs. Mobbley said.

The kitchen became vitalized with the pardon. He drew it out slowly from his inside coat pocket and unrolled it. The large seal shone in the lamp-light. The parchment paper was thick and white, like a magnolia petal. Mrs. Mobbley trailed her fingers over its smoothness.

Mobbley asked, "Do the governor hisself sign them?"

Adams pointed to the scrawled name.

"I'll be blest." Mobbley studied the signature. "He don't write no better than no other man."

Adams apologized, "I reckon he gets to writing careless, with all them state documents to sign."

The four-year-old boy whimpered.

The girl Quincie whispered, "Lila, give him some gravy for his grits. You know he don't like 'em dry."

Mrs. Mobbley said, "I reckon home cooking tastes mighty good after jail-house rations."

He brought himself back with a start from the pardon to the table. The food was inferior to the penitentiary fare.

He said reluctantly, "Well, we had mighty good rations. Not much change— If you got tired of beans, why, nobody felt bad about it— you had to eat beans, or go hungry, right on."

Mobbley and Joe Porter laughed with him. His numbness dissolved. He was aware of the warmth of the room and the crackling of wood in the stove. He stretched his legs under the table, feeling the pine boards of the floor rough under his feet.

He said, "Dogged if the floor don't feel peculiar. The floor up yonder was cement."

The penitentiary loomed before his sight; immensely white; modern and bright and handsome. It was a cross between heaven and hell, he thought hazily, a fabulous place where doomed men moved in a silent torment in the midst of electric-lit, immaculate surroundings. The gray unpainted room about him, fire-lit and intimate in the November darkness, was the world, and he had come back to it. His toes and fingers tingled, as though life had begun to prick through a disembodied spirit.

The two girls and the small boy sat stiffly in the pain of young sleepiness, their eyelids fluttering. The Mobbleys took up the talk and chattered of county news, correcting each other. Emma said, "I'd ought to clear up the table," but she sat still, moving only her hands, now along the edge of the oilcloth tablecover, now up and back across her hair. Joe Porter filled his pipe and teetered in his chair. The Mobbleys rose to take their leave. Mrs. Mobbley looked quickly from Emma to Adams, and then to Joe.

She asked with an excited sucking of breath, "Joe, you coming with us tonight?"

He teetered a moment. He moved slowly to the stove and knocked out his pipe against it.

"I reckon," he said and joined the Mobbleys at the door.

Emma called after him, "You studying on digging the sweet potatoes tomorrow?"

He hesitated.

"I'll let you know about it."

Adams left them talking in the doorway and walked to the larger of the two bedrooms. On the bed was a quilt he recognized. His heart raced. The door closed after Joe and the Mobbleys and the front gate clicked. Emma walked past him into the bedroom and knelt down to draw extra quilts from a box under the double bed. He followed her and crouched beside her. He put an arm around her waist. It felt rounder than he had remembered it. Her flesh was soft and pliable.

"Emma—"

She did not answer. Her eyes focused without attention on the box of quilts.

"No need to be so rabbity with me, Honey," he said.

She dropped a quilt on the floor, handling it absently.

"I been thinking the past hour," he said, "about sleeping with you."

She said desperately, "You got the right. The law gives you the right."

He stood up.

"I hate you should talk about the law for such as that." He pondered, "I reckon I feel strange to you."

She straightened, standing with her back to the wall, the quilt bundled in front of her. Her mouth quivered. Her eyes were like a mare's in panic. He looked out into the kitchen. The two girls were putting away the last of the dishes. The four-year-old boy lay curled on the floor in front of the stove, sleeping like a puppy. Adams stared at him. A sick fear paralyzed him.

"Emma—" He seemed to hear his own voice coming from a great distance. "Who's the little feller?" The woman did not speak. He faltered, "I figured he come with Mobbleys—"

The older girl bent protectively over the child, arranging his clothes.

The younger girl called shrilly, "He's ours."

His head thickened. He shook it to lighten the weight. His mouth jumped at one corner. He turned toward the woman. She stood with the back of her head pressed hard against the wall, rolling it from side to side. Her eyes were closed. The quilt slid from her arms and she lifted one hand and crammed it against her mouth. She opened her eyes and looked at him.

She cried out in a loud voice, "I had to have help on the place. A woman can't farm it alone. The fences was near about rotted to the ground."

He opened and closed his fingers. Fire moved in tongues across his numbness, as though life and death competed for his body.

The woman whimpered, "Nobody didn't never figure on no pardon."

The wind in the chinaberry was blowing from an alien world and passing to another. The room lay inside it, lost in stillness. The fire died away through his limbs and the numbness possessed him. He moved to the door of the smaller bedroom.

"Where must I sleep?" he asked.

"I just don't know—"

He looked from one bedroom toward the other.

She offered hurriedly, "The girls is mighty big to be sleeping in the bed with a man—but the little bed is awful small."

The girl Quincie carried the child toward them. She looked questioningly from the man to the woman.

Emma said, moistening her lips, "You'll have to let your father say, about the sleeping."

He said dully, "You and the two girls keep the big bed."

The girl went into the smaller room with the child; fumbled with its garments and left it and went away. The door of the large bedroom closed behind her.

The man felt chilled. He undressed by the kitchen range, hanging his clothes on wooden pegs on the wall. He turned out the kerosene lamp. Darkness closed in on him. Where he had been cold, he was suffocated. He shuffled across the boards in his bare feet, careless of splinters, and threw open the front door. The wind bit like cold teeth into his body. He shivered and closed the door, standing uncertainly with his hands against it.

It seemed to him that he had forgotten something. He rubbed his forehead. He had forgotten the pardon. He had left it lying on the table, where something might happen to it in the night. A gust of wind might blow it near the stove and a spark ignite it. He groped his way across the kitchen and laid his hands on the parchment. An ember glowed in the range and the seal shone briefly in the blackness. He rolled up the paper and went to his bedroom.

The boy lay sleeping. Adams could not bring himself to lie down beside him. He sat on the edge of the narrow bed, warming his feet one with the other. He twisted the roll of parchment aimlessly in his hands. The room was a black box over him. He crossed his arms over his stomach, bending his upper body, swaying. A ghost must feel so, he thought, homeless between two worlds.

He pictured the penitentiary at this moment. It would be not quite dark, for a light would be glinting at the far end of the corridor. It would be not quite silent, for the guard would walk along the cement floor. It would be not quite lonely, for every man had a cell-mate. A wave of desolation washed over him, so that he thought he should never swim to the top of it.

Beside him, the child mumbled. Adams drew a deep breath. He reached out his hand and touched the fine hair of the head. He trembled. He moved his hand slowly over the small hump of body under the quilt.

"Pore little bastard," he said, "I reckon you wasn't much wanted."

The boy cried out sharply in a nightmare. His legs convulsed. Adams drew the quilt closer about the thin neck.

"Running from the booger-man, sonny?" he asked. "Don't you fret—I've got a-holt of you."

He slipped under the covers and pushed the pardon carefully beneath his pillow.

VARMINTS

Oak Bluff had three pet varmints—
Luty and Jim and Snort

HERE'S no woman in the State of Florida
has got more patience with the varmint in a man than me. It's in
his blood, just like a woman has got a little snake and a mite of
cat. A man's borned varminty and he dies varminty, and when the
preacher asks do we believe our great-great-granddaddies was monkeys, I can't scarcely keep from standing up and saying, "Brother,
a good ways back, I figure things was a heap worse mixed up than
monkeys."

I ain't throwing off on my Will. Will Dover's a good man and
a gentle. It ain't Will. It's Jim Lee and Luty Higgenbotham. That
pair . . . I understand them. I've done been understanding them since
we was young uns, and I've had patience with them.

My Will said yesterday, "Quincey, you been making the peace between them two all your lives. Nobody can't see how come you now
to be so hard on them."

That's it. That's just it. They plumb wore out my patience. Men-
folks had ought to know such things. A man'll seem like a person to
a woman, year in, year out. She'll put up and she'll put up. Then one
day he'll do something maybe no worse than what he's been a-doing
all his life. She'll look at him. And without no warning he'll look like
a varmint. That day come to me with Jim and Luty. It come on account of that blasted mule they owned together. And I say they got
no good right to crawl me for what I wrote and the *Bugle* printed it.

Jim Lee and Luty Higgenbotham—Why, them two had never ought to have begun to own no mule together. Let alone no such mule as that un, that'd raise aggravation amongst the angels. Jim and Luty always was like pure game-cocks for mixing it. They begun it forty year gone, when they was two little old shirt-tail boys going to the Oak Bluff school together, and me a little old gal young un with a red knitted petticoat.

I remember oncet the three of us eased off from school and went fishing in Cross Creek. In them days the bream in the Creek was right smart plentiful. Jim looked over at Luty's string of bream and he said, "You putting my bream on your string."

Luty's easy-going, most ways, as a hound dog at noon in August. He's a little round feller with brown eyes, looked just the same then as now, mild and puppyfied. And hard-headed, too, like them gentle dogs can be.

He said, "No, I ain't putting your bream on my string."

Jim had one of his ornery fits on. Jim ain't changed none, neither. Shingle-butted and holler-chested and a mouth like a sewed-up buttonhole, and light blue eyes as mean as the Book of Job.

He said, "I ain't going to go fishing with nobody that puts my fish on his string."

Now if Luty had of spoke humble one more time, Jim would likely have shut up. But that's it. Neither one ain't never waited for t'other to speak humble one more time. So what did Luty do? He takened Jim's string of bream and he takened hissen and he turned them both upside down over the side of the rowboat, and the bream all swum off to where they'd come from. Luty rolled up his little old raggedy breeches and he stepped outen the rowboat, waist-deep amongst the lily-pads and the water-moccasins, and he waded back to shore. And that's the pair that growed up to try to own a mule together.

Oak Bluff don't entirely agree on just exactly how Jim and Luty did grow up. Jim's daddy owned the General Store and a nigger jook and a row of shanties in the Quarters. Jim growed up mean and close-fisted and now he owns the Store and two nigger jooks and the whole mess of shanties and ain't nary son of Ham in the county ain't always in debt to him, on account of him keeping the books hisself. When he got to be buggy-riding size, he got hisself married.

His daddy was still alive and holding tight to what he had, so Jim seed to it he married him a gal had a nice little farm. And that's how come him to grow up to need a mule along about when he was twenty-one.

Now the way Luty growed up, some say the Lord done a pore job of raising him, for there wasn't nobody else to blame. He was an orphan and all he ever had to his name was his daddy's rowboat and a dozen fish-traps and a wore-out seine. Until he was a growed man, he never had no more shoes than a yard-dog. He fished along a little and he ketched alligators. He made a good haul of fish one time and he bought ten acres of land that joined up behind me and Will. He planted it to sugar-cane and he rigged up a piece of a mill and set up a syrup-kettle. And that's how come him to need a mule for the cane-grinding.

I was passing Perry's sink-hole the very October day, twenty-eight year ago, when they traded. Old Man Perry had a small kind of a mule on a halter. Jim and Luty was standing thoughtful, just looking at the mule, the way men do when they're trading. Right then, it was only Jim was trading. Luty wasn't into it.

Old Man Perry called out to me, "Quincey, what'd you say to a feller won't offer but thirty dollars for a fine young mule?"

Jim said, "What'd you say to a feller asks fifty, and the mule not much more'n a colt, has never been broke nor worked?"

In them days I hadn't learned to keep my mouth shut. I said, "I reckon fifty ain't too much for him."

Jim spit one way and Old Man Perry t'other, and Luty grinned.

Jim said, "I'll raise me my own mule."

Luty said, "Jackasses is always the daddies, ain't they?"

Jim wheeled around, but Luty was scuffling the sand. Jim watched him, and I could see him catch a-holt of an idea.

"Looky here, Luty," he said. "You got you a fine stand of cane, and frost due on it, and no horse nor mule to grind it. Now my crops is all spring crops. You and me good friends, the way we always been, what say we buy this mule together?"

"Well," said Luty, "the way we always been friends, I don't know as buying no mule together has got too much sense to it."

I said, "You mighty right. You can't throw a mule in the Creek when you get put out at each other."

"Quincey," said Jim, "if you don't shut your mouth—"

About that time the mule hoisted up his ears and wrinkled his nose. He pulled loose from Old Man Perry and walked over to Luty. Luty had him a plug of tobaccy and he just shaved hisself off a nice thin sliver. The mule reached out his tongue and wrapped it around the sliver. He stepped back, closed his eyes, and went to chewing.

"Well, I'll be dogged," said Luty. "I'll just be dogged."

Old Man Perry begun to jump up and down.

"That don't mean nothing," he said, "he's normal."

"He ain't normal," I said. "I'll bet he's a stump-sucker."

"He's a May mule and he'll waller in the water," Old Man Perry said, "but if he's a stump-sucker, all I got to say is I ain't never seed him suck no stumps nor postes."

"I'll bet you're obliged to turn your back in mighty big of a hurry," I said.

Luty walked on over to the mule and pared him off another shaving of tobaccy. The mule takened it and kind of nuzzled him and went to chewing again.

"I'll be dogged," Luty said.

"I'll take thirty dollars," Old Man Perry said, getting nervous.

"Don't you trade, fellers," I said to Jim and Luty. "The mule's peculiar, and you-all are peculiar. Don't go adding no fat to no bonfire."

They paid me no more mind than the wind a-blowing.

"I got fifteen dollars cash-money," Luty said.

"I got fifteen," Jim said.

All two of them fished it outen their pants pockets. Old Man Perry takened it like a bream taking a earthworm. He dropped the halter over a myrtle bush and he headed it for home before they could change their minds. Jim and Luty stood a minute, looking pleased with theirselves.

"Well, you're bogged up now," I said.

"I expect you to feed him till spring," Jim said to Luty.

"I'll feed him," Luty said. "I sort of aim to enjoy his company as much as his work."

"What's that fuss?" I said.

It was the mule. He had a grip with his teeth on a lighter'd stump and he was sucking at it until you'd think he'd pop the breath outen his body.

"The blasted thing's a stump-sucker, all right," I said.

II

Nothing ever takened to a new life the way that no-account mule takened to cane-grinding. All the week I could hear the rusty gears in Luty's cane-mill creaking like a whooping-crane. Right from the beginning the grinding just suited that mule. Walking slowlike around and around, nothing to do, no plow to pull, just walking in a easy circle like a buzzard wheeling. Now and again snatching hisself a stalk of sugar-cane to chew on. Figuring, "Ain't life pleasant."

I went on over to Luty's one day when he was setting on his stoop, giving his rum a fair try-out. The gyp was sleeping, and the mule was scratching hisself against a post, and I set down amongst them.

"Luty," I said, "what on earth's different about that blasted mule?"

"He's a mite sway-backed," Luty said.

I said, "A mort of mules is sway-backed. Look at him," I said. "Look at him droop his ears. He droops his ears more'n most mules droops them. He don't seem to want to hear much."

"He's just smart," Luty said. "He knows there's nothing much in the world wuth listening to."

"Look at him," I said. "Look at that trick he's got. Resting on three legs and tucking t'other leg under him. Like as if he used that leg the most. The left front un."

"He do use it the most," Luty said, and the mule went to pawing the sand. "He craves tobaccy. He uses that leg to paw the sand when he wants a chew." Luty got up from the stoop and pared off a shaving, and the mule went to chewing. "Or," said Luty, "a pinch of snuff will do him if no tobaccy ain't handy."

"Luty," I said, "the creetur ain't natural."

The mule looked at me then. Iffen you'll notice, most animals don't look much at persons. But this mule looked at me, and I knowed I was done looked at. Then he looked off again, chewing vigorous.

He'd done forgot me, studying on whatever 'tis mules studies on. Then it come to me. He was knowing. That was it. He was knowing. He had a human kind of a look, blest if he didn't. And it was Luty hisself he looked like. He looked like Luty more'n most persons could of done. Pot-bellied and low-coupled and big-eyed and easygoing, and biggety, too. And chewing his tobaccy and looking at you sideways. I'll swear.

"Luty," I said, "it'll be like a sandspur under Jim's tail just to see the two of you together."

"Why so? Looking at us won't cost him nothing."

"Get rid of the creetur. I'd not give him lot-room."

"I would," he said, "and Jim Lee'll not trade me outen him, neither."

That night at dead midnight I was laying sleeping and trusting beside my Will. In my dreams, like, I heard a sound like a person choking to death. It come to me my Will was strangling, and I lep outen the bed, me not plumb used to him being in it. 'Twa'n't Will at all. He was snoring, but not no such sound as that un. It chilled my backbone. It come from the yard, and I knowed somebody was out there getting murdered. The sound quit, and I heard steps in the sand. I called out, "Will!" and I leaned out the window. I wasn't prepared. I just wasn't prepared. I run my face smack into that blasted mule's nose, and him standing there in the moonlight, peeking in the window.

And in the morning, there was my gate-post chewed to splinters where that on-natural mule had been sucking on it in the darkness. And that wasn't all. There was my fresh-set petunia plants—I've always been a fool for petunias—mashed to nothing. I followed the tracks, and there was my sweet-potato beds trampled something astonishing. Most creeturs'll walk in a low place, like the ruts of a road. But this mule had done rambled right down the tops of my potato beds. He'd walked down one row and up t'other, like a young un walking a fence, and ary place he'd set them big feet down, he'd cut a peck of sweet potatoes to where they wasn't only fit for the hogs.

You know what I done? I done nothing. I didn't want to lose all chancet of talking give-and-take between Luty and Jim.

III

Spring come. The yellow jessamine had done quit blooming. I'd done cut back my petunia plants. Jim come to the house, and it about dusk-dark.

"I'm on my way to Luty's," he said, "to carry home my mule for my spring planting."

"I'll walk on over with you," I said, "and carry him a mess of greens and bacon for his breakfast."

So me and Jim walked on over to Luty's.

"Well," Jim said, "I've done come to carry home my mule."

"*My* mule ain't to home right now," Luty said, "iffen that's the mule you're speaking about."

"Well, *our* mule," Jim said. Then he rared up and hollered, "Why ain't he to home? Iffen you've done gone and rented him out—"

"He ain't rented," Luty said. "He's restless."

"Well," Jim said to Luty, "go ketch him."

"I wouldn't know where to go to," Luty said.

"It's four good mile to my place, Luty Higgenbotham. You should of had him in the lot. I can't traipse back and to, waiting and waiting all the time for no mule to get on-restless."

"Spend the night, Jim," Luty offered. "I got a extry bed in the south room off the blow-way. Snort'll ease in during the night, I'm satisfied."

"Well," Jim said, reluctant, "my wife'll quarrel, but I'd liefer hear her quarrel tomorrow than walk eight mile tonight. 'Snort'?" he asked. "How come you to call him 'Snort'?"

"He answers to it."

"It's a queer name." Jim said.

IV

The next thing I knowed, it was day. I was in the kitchen cooking breakfast. I heard the gate click, and there was Jim leading the mule into the yard.

I called, "Come get you some breakfast, Jim, afore you rides away."

He come into the kitchen, and where the light from the lamp

fell on his face, I seed he had him a lump on his forehead like a turkey egg.

"You see that?" he said, pointing to the lump. "Luty and that mule between them nigh onto kilt me, along toward day."

"Have some grits while you're talking," I said. "They're soft and soothing."

"Quincey," he told me, swallowing grits, "I should of knowed better than to stay the night. I goes to sleep in the room on the south side of the blow-way, just as trusting as a baby. I had me the door shut, but I was sleeping a mite light, it being Luty's house. Along about after midnight I hears a 'Pip-pip!' on the floor of the blow-way and then, 'Bam!' and my door flies open. I gets up and strikes a match and looks down the blow-way, and there's nary thing in sight. I figures I was maybe dreaming and I shuts the door—it don't latch too good—and I goes back to sleep. Two-three hours later, I hears 'Pip-pip!' on the blow-way and, 'Bam!' the door comes open again.

"I says to myself, 'Luty's maybe pranking.' But nobody ain't going to Bam my door open in the middle of the night without me objecting. So I gets up and I draws a chair up close to the door and shuts it and I sets there. I must of drowsed off, just at daybreak. The next thing I knows, that blasted door Bams open and knocks me that dead to where I couldn't of told a house-cat from my grandmammy. I staggers out when I comes to my senses, and there's Luty setting on the stoop feeding that tormented mule plug tobaccy.

"'Who done Bammed my door open and knocked me senseless?' I said.

"I'll swear, Quincey, I don't know how come me to keep from laying out the pair of them.

"'Must of been Snort,' Luty says, 'kicking the door open. Don't he trot acrost the blow-way delicate? I forgot to tell you last night, he don't like no doors left closed agin him.'"

I thought, "The Lord'll settle this thing, after all."

"You pore feller," I said. "Of course you can't be bothered owning no such creetur along with Luty—you just buy Luty's share offen him."

"Quincey," he said, "not at no price—not at none—Luty won't sell."

"Then sell Luty your share," I said. "Be done with the torment."

Jim narrered his eyes and he scrooched his mouth.

"He won't offer but ten dollars, and I'll not take less than the mule's wuth, not if I'm tormented until Kingdom Come."

"Merciful jaybird!" I said. "If all two of you aim to be more mulified than the mule, it's birds of a feather."

"Go back on me," he said, bristling up. "You always did favor Luty."

"I'd like to crack his head open," I said, "and agin yours'd be the finest place I can think of."

Then I seed things was getting worse by the minute.

"Don't pay me no mind, Jim," I said. "I'm just all fretted up by the creetur myself. You go home and shame Luty. You go learn the mule just the opposite. Learn him real nice and Christian ways."

"I'll do it, Quincey," he said. "I'll sure do that thing."

And you know what happened that fine Spring morning? This is what done happened. Jim put the mule to the plow. He lined up his first furrow. He said, "Giddap, Snort!" And what did Snort do? He set off as brisk as a gal in her first silk petticoat. But instead of going straight ahead, the way a plow mule belongs to go, he curved to the right and he made him a sweep and he curved to the left and dogged if he didn't make the purtiest circle in Jim's cornfield you'd hope to make for the circle pattern in a patch-work quilt. Jim's wife said he like to lost his salvation, cussing, he was that put out about it.

It takened Jim a month to get Snort to where he'd plow a furrow without sashaying like a square dancer. And when he got him to where he'd plow straight, he'd stop anywheres and paw the sand with his left front hoof, wanting tobaccy. I didn't blame Jim one mite for being short of patience. I sided with Jim all that summer. For the blasted mule'd get lonesome for Luty and he'd get lonesome for a chew and he'd leave out from Jim's farm t'other side of town and he'd hit it through Oak Bluff and he'd come cutting acrost my yard and my petunias and Bam open my back gate and head through my sweet potatoes and into Luty's cane-field and up to the stoop where Luty was generally sitting, expecting him.

And you know what happened that sure enough fixed things? This is what done happened. I seed it and I'll bear witness, for I went with Jim when he follered Snort to Luty's.

There set Luty on the stoop, and there set his rum jug. And there stood Snort, so wobbly on them short legs he couldn't scarcely stand. His eyes was closed. Swinging above his nose on a wire hung from the porch roof was a baby's nursing bottle. It was upside down and it was empty. Snort opened one eye. He looked at Jim and he looked at me, purely cock-eyed. Then he closed that eye again. Jim run and snatched down the bottle and he smelt of it. And him voting Temperance—

"It's rum!" he hollered. "You been giving him rum!"

"He'd ruther of had cane-skimmings," Luty said, "but I was out."

Merciful jaybird! I never seed a man go as wild as Jim Lee.

"That's why the creetur leaves Christian surroundings and slips off!" he squalled. "That's why he don't act like a decent mule belongs to act! You've done corrupted him! You've takened a pore beast along your evil way!"

"Don't think hard of me, Jim," Luty said. "I just found out the pore old feller's tastes by accident. The first fall we takened up together, I ketched him with his head in the barrel of buck. He was some kind of enjoying hisself. I drove him off, but he'd hang around and he'd hang around. 'Wait,' I tells him. 'Wait till I runs the skimmings through the still.' I no more dreamed he'd care for the rum— But I don't break no promises, not even to a creetur. So when I'd done run the buck through the still, I give him a snort, and Jim, I'll swear, his gratitude was pitiful."

"You heathen mule-corrupter, that's how come you to call him 'Snort.' How dast you even admit to it!"

"Now Jim," Luty said, mild as a May day, and Snort drooped his ears, not wishing to hear the conversation. "I'm surprised to hear you talk so harsh and all, you with a loving wife and family. Jim, ain't it never occurred to you I'm doing this pore feller a kindness? Iffen you'll just study on it a mite, Jim, it'll come to you, there ain't too much in life a mule can enjoy."

V

Then come the cow business. Things was getting springified again, and I was setting on the porch, rocking and resting.

I heard a scraping and a clomping. Snort was sailing down my fence-row. I hollered and I run at him. He done a buck-and-wing and put his head on one side and give me that knowing look and brayed the most impudent a mule could bray. He kicked up his heels and jumped the fence and lit out for Jim Lee's. That's where we found him. My Will drove Luty and me out to Jim's in his first Model-T.

Luty said, riding along, "I can't believe Snort's gone off and left me."

"Luty," I said, "I do believe you're getting to where you put too much store by that on-natural animal."

"No, Quincey, you're wrong. Snort's faithful to me, and he's loyal. He don't only go to Jim when he's obliged to. I'd take it hard if Snort found ary piece of pleasure, going to Jim's."

"Well, he's found it," I said. "Looky there."

There was Snort. There he was, the sly somebody. Jim's two cows was in the lot, and there was Snort hanging his head over the lot-fence. And them two cows was licking his nose. Now Luty always kept a salt-brick for Snort, and Jim didn't never keep none for his stock, and them two cows was getting theirselves a lick of salt. But Snort takened it for affection. His eyes was half-closed and he had him the silliest look I've ever seed on a mule. He inched up closer to the lot and he rested his chin on the top of the fence, bob-wire and all. No mistake about it, he'd come all them miles on account of figuring them cows was fond of him.

Luty set dazed-like in the Model-T.

"I'd not of thought it," he said.

"Perk up, Luty," I said. "A blasted mule's a blasted mule, right on."

"I know," he said, "but I've done nussed that mule. He'd have the colic, and I'd put hot towels to his stummick. He'd be bound, and I'd drench him with lard and syrup. He'd come to me from Jim's plow-ing, hongry, and I'd feed him till he couldn't hold another mouthful. He'd want his tobaccy, and iffen so be I was a mite short, I'd give him mine and go without. And when it come to the cane-skimmings and the rum, I'd share and share alike."

"You don't expect gratitude from that creetur, do you?"

"Well, no," he said. "And well, yes. You don't understand a lonely man, Quincey. When a man's lonely, he'll set his heart on most ary thing that be companionable."

And Luty looked so cheerless that all the rest of the time him and Jim was having it, ary quarrel where I seed the chancet, I put in to take up for Luty.

VI

It don't make sense for no two men to quarrel twenty-eight year over no mule. If 'twas over a woman, that'd make little sense enough. But that Snort—that droop-eared, sway-backed, wise-looking, tobaccy-chewing, rum-drinking, trompling son of a donkey—that just don't make sense. I'll not admit to one scrap of dishonor for what I done. It was a month ago, come Monday. And what I done, come about like this.

Luty had him a fine stand of sugar-cane this fall. He was the last person in the county to grind. He invited all Oak Bluff to come to his last night of cane-grinding and syrup-boiling and make a frolic of it.

"It's a pity to leave out Jim Lee," I said to him, feeling mighty smart. "Ain't it about time you two was neighboring, more'n just to fetch that old mule back and to?"

"I can bear his snout in my cane-juice if he can," Luty said.

So I said to Jim, "Luty's takened the greatest notion you should come to syrup-boiling. You-all ain't getting no younger, and that mule that's stood between you ain't getting no younger. Somebody's due to feel shame too late."

"That's right, Quincey," he said, "but it wasn't me has been on-reasonable."

"Merciful jaybird!" I said. "Can it be I've listened to that for forty year? Come go with me and make Luty to feel good."

"I'll come," he said. "Can't be his cane-juice is poison."

Luty was pouring the last bucket of cane-juice into the syrup kettle when we got there.

"Look who's here," he said, "old Quincey, light as thistledown. And pore little old Will—"

"Oh, I make out," Will said, laughing.

"And here's Jim," I said, and I laid my hands on both their shoulders.

Luty hesitated and swallered. Then he put out his hand, and Jim takened it.

"Proud to see you, Jim," he said. "Welcome to syrup-boiling."

"I'm in pore shape for it," Jim said, "full of Quincey's rations. But I ain't never seed the day when I couldn't tuck cane-skimmings in around whatever else I'd ate, like wrapping a baby in a blanket. That right, Will Dover?"

"I got sickened of cane-skimmings," Will said, "on account of me being a puny young un and oncet gorging myself."

"You and me never was puny, was we, Quincey?" Luty said.

"Only you quit where you was, Luty," Jim said, "and old Quincey kept on growing sideways."

"You can't shock my modesty that-a-way," I said. "I can out-eat ary one of you and get enjoyment ten to your one," and we all laughed, sociable and nice as could be. I felt mighty pleased with myself.

Nigh onto all of Oak Bluff must of been there. The full moon rose, and I say there's nothing finer than full moon on a cool October night of cane-grinding. It raised up over the tall pine trees beyond Luty's house and it filled the night better'n kerosene or candles. The light from the brick cane-furnace glowed red and flamified ary time Luty opened the door to push in fat-wood.

"You plumb finished grinding?" I asked him. "I'd be proud to have me a drink of cane-juice, afore I gets down to serious business."

"I helt out a wagon-load of cane, just so folks could do that thing. Snort," he hollered, "wake up and wait on Quincey."

Off in the shadows that blasted old mule was standing hitched to the cane-mill. When he heard Luty holler, he put one ear up and t'other down. He cut his eyes at me.

"I'd as lief do my own grinding," I said, "as have that sway-backed son of Satan do it for me."

"Now Quincey," Luty said, "Snort's just about thirty year old. And look at him go."

The old mule was sure strutting hisself. You'd of thought he was dancing, the way he takened the curves, going around the cane-mill.

"Let's not waste his movements," Jim said to me. "He's like to stop and go to pawing."

So Jim and me went on over to the mill and we fed stalks of cane into the gears and dipped into the bucket that hung on the spout. The old mule passed us, making the curve.

"Quincey," Jim said, "what's that I smells? Smells like rum to me."

Blest if it wasn't. No mistaking the breath on that mule.

" 'Tain't nothing in the world but the cane-juice boiling in the kettle," I said. "Let's get on back to the company."

I edged Jim away and dogged if that old mule didn't near about wink at me, his eyes was that knowing.

The syrup begun to cook down good in the kettle, and Luty begun skimming. After a while the syrup begun to hiss, and the rank smell of the cane was gone. Me and Jim slipped up to the kettle and raked some of the thickest goody from around the edge. Then the syrup begun to cook with a Plop! like frogs a-jumping, and Luty's long-handled skimmer sailed over it like a swallow darting.

Folks hollered, "Luty's fixing to pour!"

All the young uns come a-running to watch. Luty sure is clever with his pouring.

"Stand back for the spattering!" he called.

He dipped his ladling bucket back and to so fast you couldn't foller it. He kept a steady stream, like a gold creek, running down the little cooling trough. The syrup around the edge of the kettle cooked down into candy, and the young uns went for it something comical to see.

Then Luty said, "Well, reckon nobody won't be craving no more cane-juice. I'll turn old Snort a-loose now, to rest and graze."

He on-loosed the mule from the cane-mill. And what did the creetur do? What did he do? He stood a minute, studying, and he lit out. That's what he done. He lit out acrost Luty's stubbly cane-field, heading for Jim's place t'other side of town, the way I'd seed him do it a hundred times. But there was something on-natural about the way he lit out, and Jim and Luty and Will and me takened out after him.

He cut into my sweet-potato field. And what did he do there? He stopped stock-still in the middle of it. And then what did he do?

He begun to go in circles. Right in the middle of my sweet-potato patch, he went around and around in circles.

"He's gone crazy," Will said.

"He's drunk," Jim said. "That's what's the matter. Luty's been corrupting him again."

"He's more'n drunk or crazy," I said. "His time has come."

Sure enough, he come to a stop as sudden as if the Angel Gabriel had hollered, "Whoa!" He teetered on his legs, like the underpinnings of a house wavering in a storm. He sunk down to the ground and heaved a relieved kind of a sigh and he didn't move no more. Wherever 'twas he'd had it in his mind to go, he'd done got there.

"He's dead," Will called. "Snort's dead."

All the Oak Bluff folks come running, men and women and young uns. It was like a person had died. A annoying kind of a person, but you can't be annoyed for nearly thirty year without feeling sober-like when the hand of Death ends it.

"Well, men," I said to Jim and Luty, "I reckon now you're proud you made up your quarrel, and the old feller on his last legs."

They nodded. Then something come to me like a lightning bolt. It come to me the creetur'd been as ornery dying as he was a-living. He'd done died right smack in the middle of my sweet potatoes.

I held in a while, not wishing not to show no respect.

Then I said, "I reckon you'll be hauling the pore feller off together to bury him. You, Jim, and Luty, together."

"Well," Jim said, hesitant, "I hadn't yet takened possession of him. He was yet working for Luty. And drunk to boot. But if it don't come too high, I reckon I'd as lief bear my share."

Luty didn't say nothing. Jim couldn't think of nothing but the expense, but Luty was deep-grieved. Then Jim brightened. He was fixing to get his money's worth in meanness.

"Anyway," he said, "it's a satisfaction to know he was on his way home to me. Old Snort sure lit out for my place when his last hour come."

Luty looked up then. He faced Jim and he studied him. I could see his look plain in the moonlight. It was the same look he'd had when he throwed the bream in the Creek.

"Well, Jim," he said, and his voice was slow and easy and cold as ice, "seeing as how you say he was on his way to you and them sneaking cows, I don't figure it's my responsibility. He's your mule, Snort is. You been wanting him for yours all his life. Now you take him."

And he turned and walked off home, and his hound behind him.

"Indeed, you'll not get out of it that-a-way, Luty Higgenbotham," Jim hollered. "I might of knowed you'd try to get out of paying your just due. I'll not lift a hand to bury him."

A desperate kind of a feeling come over me.

"But Jim!" I called. "But Luty! The creetur's in my sweet potatoes!"

I got no answer. And now this is the rest of it.

Every day I'd beg Luty and every second day I'd have Will carry me out to beg Jim. Then my Will was obliged to drive to Georgia where his folks was sick. I ain't never felt so alone in my life as the day he drove off. That left me with no way to get to Jim's place. So I set in to work double on Luty.

"Jim don't surprise me," I said, "but you do. I should think you'd feel shame."

There wasn't no more shame to him than to a jack-rabbit. Then we had a long hot spell and no rain, and it was hot the way it can get hot in Florida in a dry November.

"I should think you'd mind it as much as me," I said.

"The wind's been westerly," he said. "I ain't noticed a thing." Just as stubborn as the day he walked to shore from the rowboat. "Snort went back on me at the end, so Jim says. I got no more interest."

And there was my sweet potatoes waiting to be dug. I give up.

"I'll pay for hauling him off and burying him, myself," I said.

So I set hunting me a man. And merciful jaybird, I had the luck, the pure bad luck, to run into the first of orange-picking and bean-picking. There wasn't a man, black or white, I could get to come bury that mule. And my Will gone to Georgia.

It all happened the tenth of November. I reckon there ain't never been no tenth of November as hot as that un. It was midday, and the dry sand was throwing out the heat like a cook-stove. I went out into my sweet-potato patch and I buried that mule myself. I digged a hole deep and wide. Now I weigh a sight more'n two hundred and I ain't modest about it. But ary person who thinks digging a hole deep enough to bury a mule, on a hot day in the blazing sun, is fairy's work for a woman weighs more'n two hundred, had ought to get in the same fix.

I got to burning so there wasn't no place left for the heat to come out, excusing my tongue. I begun to talk out loud. I used all the language I'd oncet heard my old granddaddy use, the one that died without salvation. I rolled that mule in that hole and I kivered him and I tromped the earth down over him.

"Anyway," I said, "you'll not romp on no more of my petunias."

I straightened my back. The sweat run down in my eyes so I couldn't see.

And all of a sudden my patience was wore out.

I walked down to Will's garage. I stopped a fruit-truck to carry me into Trayville and up to the office of the *Trayville Bugle*. The man at the desk looked at me sharp, me all red and wet and dirty.

"Fetch me paper and pencil," I said. "I got a little news item will be of interest to all your Oak Bluff subscribers."

And this is what I wrote, and the *Bugle* printed:

OAK BLUFF'S VARMINTS

Oak Bluff has lost by death one of its three pet varmints. The one that died was named Snort. He was the best of the three. The ones left are named Jim and Luty. These remaining varmints have had the advantage of human contact and have a few of the ways of persons. Visitors passing through Oak Bluff are invited to stop and take a look at these clever creatures that Providence chose to make varmints and denied them being men.

And when Jim and Luty come back from where they been hiding out until folks quits coming and laughing, I ain't taking nothing back. And them that claim I had no right to make a fun-box outen the pair, for them I say:

They ain't never had no two, ornery, long-eared, butt-headed, quarreling men to leave no dead mule in their sweet-potato patch.

A MOTHER IN MANNVILLE

THE orphanage is high in the Carolina mountains. Sometimes in winter the snow-drifts are so deep that the institution is cut off from the village below, from all the world. Fog hides the mountain peaks, the snow swirls down the valleys, and wind blows so bitterly that the orphanage boys who take the milk twice daily to the baby cottage reach the door with fingers stiff in an agony of numbness.

"Or when we carry trays from the cookhouse for the ones that are sick," Jerry said, "we get our faces frostbit, because we can't put our hands over them. I have gloves," he added. "Some of the boys don't have any."

He liked the late spring, he said. The rhododendron was in bloom, a carpet of color, across the mountainsides, soft as the May winds that stirred the hemlocks. He called it laurel.

"It's pretty when the laurel blooms," he said. "Some of it's pink and some of it's white."

I was there in the autumn. I wanted quiet, isolation, to do some troublesome writing. I wanted mountain air to blow out the malaria from too long a time in the subtropics. I was homesick, too, for the flaming of maples in October, and for corn shocks and pumpkins and black-walnut trees and the lift of hills. I found them all, living in a cabin that belonged to the orphanage, half a mile beyond the orphanage farm. When I took the cabin, I asked for a boy or man to come and chop wood for the fireplace. The first few days were warm, I found what wood I needed about the cabin, no one came, and I forgot the order.

I looked up from my typewriter one late afternoon, a little startled. A boy stood at the door, and my pointer dog, my companion, was at his side and had not barked to warn me. The boy was probably twelve years old, but undersized. He wore overalls and a torn shirt, and was barefooted.

He said, "I can chop some wood today."

I said, "But I have a boy coming from the orphanage."

"I'm the boy."

"You? But you're small."

"Size don't matter, chopping wood," he said. "Some of the big boys don't chop good. I've been chopping wood at the orphanage a long time."

I visualized mangled and inadequate branches for my fires. I was well into my work and not inclined to conversation. I was a little blunt.

"Very well. There's the ax. Go ahead and see what you can do."

I went back to work, closing the door. At first the sound of the boy dragging brush annoyed me. Then he began to chop. The blows were rhythmic and steady, and shortly I had forgotten him, the sound no more of an interruption than a consistent rain. I suppose an hour and a half passed, for when I stopped and stretched, and heard the boy's steps on the cabin stoop, the sun was dropping behind the farthest mountain, and the valleys were purple with something deeper than the asters.

The boy said, "I have to go to supper now. I can come again tomorrow evening."

I said, "I'll pay you now for what you've done," thinking I should probably have to insist on an older boy. "Ten cents an hour?"

"Anything is all right."

We went together back of the cabin. An astonishing amount of solid wood had been cut. There were cherry logs and heavy roots of rhododendron, and blocks from the waste pine and oak left from the building of the cabin.

"But you've done as much as a man," I said. "This is a splendid pile."

I looked at him, actually, for the first time. His hair was the color of the corn shocks and his eyes, very direct, were like the mountain sky when rain is pending—gray, with a shadowing of that miraculous blue. As I spoke, a light came over him, as though the setting sun had touched him with the same suffused glory with which it touched the mountains. I gave him a quarter.

"You may come tomorrow," I said, "and thank you very much."

He looked at me, and at the coin, and seemed to want to speak, but could not, and turned away.

"I'll split kindling tomorrow," he said over his thin ragged shoulder. "You'll need kindling and medium wood and logs and backlogs."

At daylight I was half wakened by the sound of chopping. Again it was so even in texture that I went back to sleep. When I left my bed in the cool morning, the boy had come and gone, and a stack of kindling was neat against the cabin wall. He came again after school in the afternoon and worked until time to return to the orphanage. His name was Jerry; he was twelve years old, and he had been at the orphanage since he was four. I could picture him at four, with the same grave gray-blue eyes and the same—independence? No, the word that comes to me is "integrity."

The word means something very special to me, and the quality for which I use it is a rare one. My father had it—there is another of whom I am almost sure—but almost no man of my acquaintance possesses it with the clarity, the purity, the simplicity of a mountain stream. But the boy Jerry had it. It is bedded on courage, but it is more than brave. It is honest, but it is more than honesty. The ax handle broke one day. Jerry said the woodshop at the orphanage would repair it. I brought money to pay for the job and he refused it.

"I'll pay for it," he said. "I broke it. I brought the ax down careless."

"But no one hits accurately every time," I told him. "The fault was in the wood of the handle. I'll see the man from whom I bought it."

It was only then that he would take the money. He was standing back of his own carelessness. He was a free-will agent and he chose to do careful work, and if he failed, he took the responsibility without subterfuge.

And he did for me the unnecessary thing, the gracious thing, that we find done only by the great of heart. Things no training can teach, for they are done on the instant, with no predicated experience. He found a cubbyhole beside the fireplace that I had not noticed. There, of his own accord, he put kindling and "medium" wood, so that I might always have dry fire material ready in case of sudden wet weather. A stone was loose in the rough walk to the cabin. He dug a deeper hole and steadied it, although he came, himself, by a short cut over the bank. I found that when I tried to return his thoughtfulness with such things as candy and apples, he was wordless. "Thank you" was, perhaps, an expression for which he had had no use, for his courtesy was instinctive. He only looked at the gift and at me, and a curtain lifted, so that I saw deep into the clear well of his eyes, and gratitude was there, and affection, soft over the firm granite of his character.

He made simple excuses to come and sit with me. I could no more have turned him away than if he had been physically hungry. I suggested once that the best time for us to visit was just before supper, when I left off my writing. After that, he waited always until my typewriter had been some time quiet. One day I worked until nearly dark. I went outside the cabin, having forgotten him. I saw him going up over the hill in the twilight toward the orphanage. When I sat down on my stoop, a place was warm from his body where he had been sitting.

He became intimate, of course, with my pointer, Pat. There is a strange communion between a boy and a dog. Perhaps they possess the same singleness of spirit, the same kind of wisdom. It is difficult to explain, but it exists. When I went across the state for a week end, I left the dog in Jerry's charge. I gave him the dog whistle and the key to the cabin, and left sufficient food. He was to come two or three times a day and let out the dog, and feed and exercise him. I should return Sunday night, and Jerry would take out the dog for the last time Sunday afternoon and then leave the key under an agreed hiding place.

My return was belated and fog filled the mountain passes so treacherously that I dared not drive at night. The fog held the next morning, and it was Monday noon before I reached the cabin. The dog had been fed and cared for that morning. Jerry came early in the afternoon, anxious.

"The superintendent said nobody would drive in the fog," he said. "I came just before bedtime last night and you hadn't come. So I brought Pat some of my breakfast this morning. I wouldn't have let anything happen to him."

"I was sure of that. I didn't worry."

"When I heard about the fog, I thought you'd know."

He was needed for work at the orphanage and he had to return at once. I gave him a dollar in payment, and he looked at it and went away. But that night he came in the darkness and knocked at the door.

"Come in, Jerry," I said, "if you're allowed to be away this late."

"I told maybe a story," he said. "I told them I thought you would want to see me."

"That's true," I assured him, and I saw his relief. "I want to hear about how you managed with the dog."

He sat by the fire with me, with no other light, and told me of their two days together. The dog lay close to him, and found a comfort there that I did not have for him. And it seemed to me that being with my dog, and caring for him, had brought the boy and me, too, together, so that he felt that he belonged to me as well as to the animal.

"He stayed right with me," he told me, "except when he ran in the laurel. He likes the laurel. I took him up over the hill and we both ran fast. There was a place where the grass was high and I lay down in it and hid. I could hear Pat hunting for me. He found my trail and he barked. When he found me, he acted crazy, and he ran around and around me, in circles."

We watched the flames.

"That's an apple log," he said. "It burns the prettiest of any wood."

We were very close.

He was suddenly impelled to speak of things he had not spoken of before, nor had I cared to ask him.

"You look a little bit like my mother," he said. "Especially in the dark, by the fire."

"But you were only four, Jerry, when you came here. You have remembered how she looked, all these years?"

"My mother lives in Mannville," he said.

For a moment, finding that he had a mother shocked me as greatly as anything in my life has ever done, and I did not know why it disturbed me. Then I understood my distress. I was filled with a passionate resentment that any woman should go away and leave her son. A fresh anger added itself. A son like this one— The orphanage was a wholesome place, the executives were kind, good people, the food was more than adequate, the boys were healthy, a ragged shirt was no hardship, nor the doing of clean labor. Granted, perhaps, that the boy felt no lack, what blood fed the bowels of a woman who did not yearn over this child's lean body that had come in parturition out of her own? At four he would have looked the same as now. Nothing, I thought, nothing in life could change those eyes. His quality must be apparent to an idiot, a fool. I burned with questions I could not ask. In any, I was afraid, there would be pain.

"Have you seen her, Jerry—lately?"

"I see her every summer. She sends for me."

I wanted to cry out, "Why are you not with her? How can she let you go away again?"

He said, "She comes up here from Mannville whenever she can. She doesn't have a job now."

His face shone in the firelight.

"She wanted to give me a puppy, but they can't let any one boy keep a puppy. You remember the suit I had on last Sunday?" He was plainly proud. "She sent me that for Christmas. The Christmas before that"—he drew a long breath, savoring the memory—"she sent me a pair of skates."

"Roller skates?"

My mind was busy, making pictures of her, trying to understand her. She had not, then, entirely deserted or forgotten him. But why, then— I thought, "I must not condemn her without knowing."

"Roller skates. I let the other boys use them. They're always borrowing them. But they're careful of them."

What circumstance other than poverty—

"I'm going to take the dollar you gave me for taking care of Pat," he said, "and buy her a pair of gloves."

I could only say, "That will be nice. Do you know her size?"

"I think it's 8½," he said.

He looked at my hands.

"Do you wear 8½?" he asked.

"No. I wear a smaller size, a 6."

"Oh! Then I guess her hands are bigger than yours."

I hated her. Poverty or no, there was other food than bread, and the soul could starve as quickly as the body. He was taking his dollar to buy gloves for her big stupid hands, and she lived away from him, in Mannville, and contented herself with sending him skates.

"She likes white gloves," he said. "Do you think I can get them for a dollar?"

"I think so," I said.

I decided that I should not leave the mountains without seeing her and knowing for myself why she had done this thing.

The human mind scatters its interests as though made of thistle-down, and every wind stirs and moves it. I finished my work. It did not please me, and I gave my thoughts to another field. I should need some Mexican material.

I made arrangements to close my Florida place. Mexico immediately, and doing the writing there, if conditions were favorable. Then, Alaska with my brother. After that, heaven knew what or where.

I did not take time to go to Mannville to see Jerry's mother, nor even to talk with the orphanage officials about her. I was a trifle abstracted about the boy, because of my work and plans. And after my first fury at her—we did not speak of her again—his having a mother, any sort at all, not far away, in Mannville, relieved me of the ache I had had about him. He did not question the anomalous relation. He was not lonely. It was none of my concern.

He came every day and cut my wood and did small helpful favors and stayed to talk. The days had become cold, and often I let him come inside the cabin. He would lie on the floor in front of the fire, with one arm across the pointer, and they would both doze and wait quietly for me. Other days they ran with a common ecstasy through the laurel, and since the asters were now gone, he brought me back vermilion maple leaves, and chestnut boughs dripping with imperial yellow. I was ready to go.

I said to him, "You have been my good friend, Jerry. I shall often think of you and miss you. Pat will miss you too. I am leaving to-morrow."

He did not answer. When he went away, I remember that a new moon hung over the mountains, and I watched him go in silence up the hill. I expected him the next day, but he did not come. The details of packing my personal belongings, loading my car, arranging the bed over the seat, where the dog would ride, occupied me until late in the day. I closed the cabin and started the car, noticing that the sun was in the west and I should do well to be out of the mountains by nightfall. I stopped by the orphanage and left the cabin key and money for my light bill with Miss Clark.

"And will you call Jerry for me to say good-by to him?"

"I don't know where he is," she said. "I'm afraid he's not well. He didn't eat his dinner this noon. One of the other boys saw him going over the hill into the laurel. He was supposed to fire the boiler this afternoon. It's not like him; he's unusually reliable."

I was almost relieved, for I knew I should never see him again, and it would be easier not to say good-by to him.

I said, "I wanted to talk with you about his mother—why he's here—but I'm in more of a hurry than I expected to be. It's out of the question for me to see her now too. But here's some money I'd like to leave with you to buy things for him at Christmas and on his birthday. It will be better than for me to try to send him things. I could so easily duplicate—skates, for instance."

She blinked her honest spinster's eyes.

"There's not much use for skates here," she said.

Her stupidity annoyed me.

"What I mean," I said, "is that I don't want to duplicate things his mother sends him. I might have chosen skates if I didn't know she had already given them to him."

She stared at me.

"I don't understand," she said. "He has no mother. He has no skates."

COCKS MUST CROW

I GOT nothing particular against time. Time's a natural thing. Folks is a kind of accident on the face of the earth, but time was here before us. And when we've done finished messing ourselves up, and when the last man turns over to die, saying, "Now how come us to make such a loblolly of living?"—why, time'll rock right on.

It's pure impudence to complain about much of ary thing, excusing human nature, and we all got a just complaint against that. Seems like we could of got borned without so much meanness in us. But just as sure as cooters crawls before a rain, why, we got no right to holler about such things as getting old and dying.

But now what I do hold against time is this: Time be so all-fired slick. It's slick as a otter slide. And how come me to object to that, don't be on account of you slip down it so fast, but you slip down without noticing what time's a-doing to you. That's what I object to. If time's fixing to change you, why, it can't be holpen. But the road's greasy as a darky's cook pot, and what does a feller do? He goes kiyoodling along it, and him changing, like a man getting drunk and not knowing it. And here comes a turn in the road, or a ditch you ain't looking for. And what do you do? You think you got all your senses, and you ain't, and you do the wrong thing and maybe knock your brains out. And if you only had some sign, something to tell you you was drunk instead of sober, something to tell you you was changed, why, you might make it.

Now that happened to me with my Will. I come so clost to losing the only man a woman like me could ever hope to get a-holt of, and a good man to boot, that I can still feel the danger whistling past me like a rattlesnake striking and just missing. And that's it. Time ain't got the decency of a rattlesnake. A rattler most times'll give warning. I almost lost my Will, and me a big fat somebody no man'd look at twicet lessen he was used to me. I almost lost him on account of I had changed and didn't know it, and time never give me the first sign to warn me. Merciful jay bird! No, sir, time's a low-down, sneaking, cottonmouth moccasin, drops its fangs without you knowing it's even in the grass, and was there ary thing I could do about it, I'd do it. Excusing that, I got nothing against time.

My Will married me—some say I married him—when I was a big feather-bolster kind of a gal, pink-cheeked and laughing and easy-going and heavy-eating. I will say, I always did have a tongue in my head, and loved to use it, just like a man with a keen knife loves to keep it sharp. But I used it fair and open. Some said I was lucky to get Will Dover, and some said he was lucky to get me. Will and me was both satisfied. I'd had men was more to look at, come courting me out at Pa's place in the flatwoods, and I'd had men come was nothing but breath and breeches. Will had a gold tooth in the front of his mouth, and I always was a fool for a gold tooth. I takened to the little feller first time I seed him. I was a heap bigger'n him even then.

Third time he come out of a Sunday evening, Pa tipped back in his chair on the porch and said to Will, "Better look out, young feller, Quincey don't take you for a play-dolly."

Will looked him square in the eye.

"You ever tried to holt a hawk in your bare hand?" Will said.

"Why, no," Pa said, "I'd know better."

"Well, a hawk's a heap littler'n you, ain't he? But 'tain't his size or your size makes you leave him be. It's his nature. Now the gal ain't growed so big in these flatwoods, could take me for a play-dolly. I ain't got the size to hold Quincey, here, on my lap. But she shore as hell ain't going to hold me on hers."

Pa laughed and slapped hisself.

"Will Dover," he said, "if you want her and she don't take you, I'll lick her with my own hands."

"Ain't nobody going to lick Quincey but me," Will said, "and I aim just to reason with her."

"Ain't he something?" Pa said to me. "Quincey, I've always told you, you can't judge no man by the length of his suspenders. You got to judge him by the spirit in him."

And I done so. I takened Will first time he offered. The business he was in was just a mite in his favor. He run a livery stable in Oak Bluff, and he come courting in a light trap with a pair of black horses drove tandem. It kind of melted me. I hadn't never see a pair of horses drove tandem.

Me and Will hit it off fine right from the start. He was little and he acted gentle, but couldn't nobody press him no farther than he was o' mind to be pressed. And that was one thing I disremembered as the years went by.

When we was fresh-married I said to him, "You're soft-acting, Will Dover, but you got a will as hard as a gopher shell."

"You ain't fooling me none, neither," he said. "You got a tongue as sharp as a new cane knife, but your heart's as big as your behind, and soft as summer butter." He looked at me with his head on one side, and them blue eyes as bright and quick as a mockingbird's. "And that's why I love you, Quincey Dover," he said.

Ary woman could get along with a man like that. I know now I don't deserve too much credit for us living so nice and friendly. But in them days I takened a mort of credit, on account of I was full of idees about handling men. They was good idees. I still got them. They was mostly this: Man-nature is man-nature, and a woman's a fool to interfere. A man worth his salt can't be helt to heel like a bird dog. Give him his head. Leave him run. If he knows he ain't running under a checkrein, the devil hisself can't get him to run more'n about so far away from his regular rations. Men is the most regular creatures on earth. All they need is to know they can run if they want to. That satisfies them. And that's what I had to go and forget.

Some things about me didn't never change. My tongue didn't

never change and, truth to tell, I'd not want it to, for the times I need it I want to know I can count on it. What Will called my big heart, I don't believe didn't never change; for I can't help being tormented when ary living thing, man, woman or dog, be hungry. I can't help feeling all tore up when another grieves. And when a old tabby cat has got no place to birth her kittens, or some poor soul in the woods is fool enough to be bringing another young'un into the world, and not a piece of cloth to wrap it in, and a blessing if it was stillborn, why, I got to light in and fix a bed for that tabby cat or that fool woman.

What did change about me was my size. I had a mighty good start, and seems like a piece of corn bread with a slab of white bacon on top of it has a sweeter taste in my mouth than it do to one of them puny little old scrawny women. And seems like ary piece of rations I've ever ate has just wrapped itself around my middle and stayed there. The last time I weighed myself was a ways back on the scales in the express office, and it balanced two hundred and twenty, and I quit weighing.

"Don't let it fret you," Will said. "You was a big gal when I got you, and I'd purely hate to turn you back to your Maker without I had added something to the good thing was give me."

My Will has been a heap of comfort. Can ary one figure how I could be mean to a man like that? Seems to me, times, like growing into the biggest woman in the county had something to do with it. I growed so big, I reckon I got biggety too. Here was my Will, little and gentle, and here was me, big as Timmons' pond, and used to all Oak Bluff saying, "Go ask Quincey. See what Quincey think."

I can't no-ways recollect when the change in me begun. First time I remember cold-out bearing down on Will was about two years ago. I remember that.

He said to me one evening after supper, "The boys is having a cockfight down to the garage. Reckon I'll ease on down and watch it."

I said, "You'll do no such of a thing. Cockfighting is a low-down nasty business. Men that's got nothing better to do than watch a pair of roosters kill theirselves, isn't fitten company."

Will looked at me slantwise and he said, "Don't you reckon I can judge my company, Quincey?"

I said, "Judge all you please, but you'll go to no cockfight."

He filled up his pipe and he tamped the tobacco down and he lit it and he said, "Since when you been telling me where I could go?"

I said, "You heered me the first time."

Now I felt mighty righteous about it. That's the trouble with changing, you still feel right about it. I'd never seed a cockfight, but I'd heered tell they was cruel and bloody, and besides, it's agin the law.

Will rocked a while and he smoked a while and he said, "Nothing ain't worth quarreling about. I'll just go on down to the station and wait-see do them automobile parts come in on Number Three."

I said, "All right, but don't you go near no cockfight."

He give me a look I hadn't never seed before, and he said, "No, ma'am," in a funny way, and he went on off.

Now I got to put this together the best way I can. I ain't like them story writers can make a tale come out as even as a first-prize patchwork quilt. Life ain't slick like a story, no-ways. I got to remember this, and remember that, and when I'm done it'll make sense. The Widow Tippett moving to Oak Bluff don't seem to have a thing to do with me and time mixing it. When she come, I sure as all get-out didn't figure she'd make no marks on my piecrust. But move to Oak Bluff she did, and get messed up in my and Will's business, she done so. And that was about a year and a half ago.

First thing I knowed, I heered a strange widow had bought the old Archer farm at the edge of town. I give her time to get nested down, and one afternoon I went out to welcome her. I takened a basket of my guava preserves and my sour-orange marmalade, and a bundle of cuttings from my porch plants. Minute she come to the door to greet me, I seed she had a chip on her shoulder. She was a quiet kind of a looking woman, right pretty if you like skimmed-milk eyes and sand-colored hair with a permanent wave put to it, and a tippy-tippy way of walking.

"Mis' Tippett?" I said. "I'm Mis' Will Dover. Quincey Dover. I come to welcome you."

"Pleased to meet you," she said. "I figured that was who 'twas."

I takened a quick look around. I never seed a place kept so care-less. The front room looked as if a truck had just backed up to the door and dumped everything out together, and she hadn't never straightened it out and didn't aim to. She hadn't washed her dishes and a big old tomcat was asleep in the dishpan. There was cats and kittens and dogs and puppies strowed all over the house and yard. A Dominick hen was on the table, pecking at the butter.

"Set down," she said. "I hear tell Oak Bluff just couldn't make out without you."

There was something about her voice I mistrusted right off.

"When I see my duty, I do it," I said.

"That works good when ever'one sees it the same," she said. "You're the lady don't let her husband go to no cockfight, ain't you?"

"You mighty right," I said.

"Ain't it nice to have a man does just like you tell him?" she said.

I looked at her quick to read her mind, for there was pure sand-spurs under that easy voice.

"I find it so," I said. "You're a widow, they tell me. Sod?"

"Water. Water and whiskey."

"I never heered tell of a water widow."

"He was drunk as ten coots and fell in the water and never did come up. A lake's as good a burying place as any."

"I'm mighty sorry about your loss."

"Don't mention it. I didn't lose much."

I said, "That's a right hard way to speak of the dead."

"So it be," she said, "and the dead was about as hard as they come."

I knowed from then on I didn't like the Widow Tippett and didn't mean to have no truck with her. I got up to go and I gave her the preserves and the cuttings. She didn't offer me my basket back.

I said, "Pleased to of met you. Call on me if a need come," and I walked down the path. I turned at the gate.

"I hope you ain't fixing to farm this land," I said. "It's plumb wore out."

"I thank you," she said. "Just to keep folks from fretting theirselves to death, you can tell Oak Bluff I got steady insurance and aim to raise chickens."

I said to myself, "I'll tell Oak Bluff you're the biggetiest woman I know, to look like a curly-headed mouse."

What she thought of me, she told me when the time come.

Now if I'd of takened to her, I'd of give her settings of my eggs. I have game chickens, on account of they near about feed theirselves, ranging. They lays good, and they grows to fryer size the quickest of ary chicken. The breed is the Roundhead, and the roosters is some kind of handsome bronze and red, and now and again a long white feather mixed in with the shiny green tail. I have to eat them before they get much size to them, for I can't bear to kill them oncet they show up that reddy-bronze and grow them long tail feathers. 'Tain't everybody wants game chickens, on account of the hens'll steal their nests. Could be, I figured, the Widow Tippett'd not crave to raise Roundheads. I felt a mite mean, just the same, not offering. Then I put it out of my mind.

The next thing I can put my finger on was Will asking me for a couple of my frying-size roosters. A year ago past spring I hatched me an early batch of biddies. They growed off big and fine.

"Quincey," Will said, "can I have a couple of them young roosters to give to a friend?"

"I raised them chickens to put in our own bellies," I said. "Anybody you want to invite to set down and eat fried chicken with us, that's another thing."

"I want to give them away," he said.

"Go catch a mess of fish to give away, if you want to feed the county," I said.

A day-two later he said, "Quincey, can I have a setting of them Roundhead eggs to give away?"

I said, "Now who in tarnation are you so fretted about them having chicken to eat?"

"A customer come to the garage."

"No," I said.

"I do pay for the chicken feed, Quincey."

"No."

"Nothing ain't worth quarreling about," he said.

A week later one morning there wasn't an egg in the nests, and two of them frying-size roosters never come up for their feed. I like to had a fit.

"A varmint likely went with them," Will said. "You'd of done better to of give them to me."

"Will," I said, "you reckon that varmint could of had two legs instead of four?" and I looked him in the eye.

He laid a dollar on the table. "Things has come to a pretty pass when a man has to buy eggs and chickens off his own wife," he said.

"Who's this friend you'd steal for?"

"Just a poor soul that don't have much pleasure in life."

"Well, you rob my nests and roosts one more time, and you'll get the living daylights displeasured outen you."

"Yes, ma'am," and he give me that funny look.

A year rocked on. Twice he give me a quarter for a setting of eggs and fifty cents for two more roosters. I knowed there was a preacher he kind of looked out for when times was hard, and I figured it was him he was feeding. Then late this spring, the truth come out. The truth was a red chicken feather in a basket, and ary one thinks a chicken feather in a basket can't boil up hell in a woman, just don't know hell nor women.

I went out to the chicken house on a bright June morning to gather the eggs. I can't see the ground right under my stomach, and my foot catched in something. I backed off so's I could see, and it was a basket. I hadn't left no basket in the chicken house. I looked at it, and I picked it up and I turned it over. It was my basket. It was the basket I'd taken preserves in, and cuttings, to the Widow Tippett. She hadn't never come near me nor returned it. The first thing come to me was, she'd got ashamed of herself for not carrying it back to me, and she'd come and slipped it in my chicken house. But I hadn't seed no woman's tracks in the yard, and me raised in the woods, why, there ain't a polecat, animal or human, can make tracks in the sand of my yard and me not notice it. I looked at the basket again, and there was a bronzy-red chicken feather stuck to the inside of it. It was a tail feather off a Roundhead rooster.

I seed it plain. That slow-speaking, permanent-headed, butter-milk-faced widow with cats in her dishpan had done tolled my Will into her clutches. He'd done stole eggs and chickens from me, his loving and faithful wife, to take and put in her wicked hands. I set right down on the ground of the chicken house, and when I set down on the ground it's serious, for it near about takes a yoke of oxen to get me up again. I didn't even study about getting up again, for it seemed to me life had done gone so black I just as lief lay there and die and be shut of it. It's an awful thing when a woman has done builded her life on a man and she finds his legs is made of sand.

I thought about all the years me and Will had stuck it out together, him losing money on the livery stable, and cars coming in instead of horses, and finally him building the garage on credit, and learning a new trade, and me making a sack of grits last a fortnight. That were the only time in my life I come speaking-close to getting thin. Then things got good, and we prospered, and I fleshed up again, and seemed to me like man and wife couldn't of got along better together lessen they was a pair of angels, and if what they say about heaven be true, married angels couldn't of had near the nice time we had. My Will was always mighty good company.

I set on the ground of the chicken house and I studied. What had I done to deserve such as this? I'd been faithful. 'Course, there'd be them to say a woman as big as me had no choice but being faithful. But I'd been faithful in my mind, and 'tain't every woman goes to the movies can say the same. I'd worked, and I'd saved, and Will Dover hadn't never oncet come in from the garage, no matter how late, and the fruit trucks keeping him busy way into the night, but I had hot rations on the stove. I reckon a woman can put too much store by hot rations. A warm heart'll freshen a man a heap quicker'n hot rations, but all the hot rations in the world can't warm up a cold female tongue.

I set there. I boiled up inside like a sirup kettle filled too full. I boiled up hotter and higher than the fire in a sinners' hell, and I purely boiled over. That cooled the fire a mite, and I panted and fanned myself with my apron and I commenced to study. I laid me a trap for Will. I decided to watch-see when he done ary thing was different from what he generally done, and when I caught him at it I aimed to follow him. I got a-holt of a wall beam for a lever and I finally got myself up off the ground. If Will had of come home then, I like as not wouldn't of held my tongue. When he come in that evening, I was quieted down and I set myself to watching, like an alligator watching for a shote he knows comes to water.

Now the things a suspicioning woman can imagine different about a man would make a new man of him. That evening Will didn't stir from his rocker, just set and smoked. I thought, "Uh-huh, you know I'm watching you." The next evening he put on a clean shirt when he come in from the garage. I thought, "Uh-huh, dressing up for the widow." He didn't have much to say, and it come to me he hadn't been saying much to me for quite some time. I thought, "Uh-huh, saving up them cute things you used to say, for the widow." After supper he eased on out of the house, and I thought, "Uh-huh, I got you now." I followed along a half hour behind him and, bless Katy, there he was setting on the bench in front of the grocery store, visiting with Doc and Uncle Benny.

I said, "I forgot I was out of shortening," and I got me a pound of lard at the store.

Will said, "I'll go on home with you. I come down to hear the fight on the radio, but it's put off."

I thought, "Uh-huh, I just come too soon."

Sunday morning he takened me by surprise. He didn't shave, and he put on the same shirt he'd wore the day before. But he did get out of bed extra early and he acted like he had ants in his pants. I didn't think a thing about it, for he do that, times, of a Sunday. He's a man is restless when he ain't at his work. I never studied on a thing, until I seed him slip off to the fireplace and pull out the loose brick and take out all the money we keep there. Banks is all right, and we got a account in Tray City, but there's nothing feels as safe as a pile of dollar bills under a loose brick in the fireplace. I seed him stuff them in his pocket and look around as sly as a 'possum.

He come to me and he said, "I'm going on down to town. Don't look for me back to dinner."

My heart leapt like a mullet jumping. I thought, "Merciful jay bird, now's the time."

I said, "You're missing some mighty good black-eyed peas," and he went on off.

I give him about forty minutes' start and I lit out. I walked the two miles to the Widow Tippett's like a road-runner snake on its way home. I was puffing and blowing when I got to her gate, and I was just as blowed up inside as out.

I thought, "In a minute now I'll see Will Dover setting beside her and holding her hand, and he ain't held mine since spring."

I stopped to figure what I'd do; would I just crack their heads together, or would I say, proud and stiff, "So! This be the end."

While I was panting and studying, the Widow Tippett come out with her hat on.

She said, "Why, Mis' Dover! You look powerful warm."

I said, "I be warm. Tell me the truth, or you'll figure you never knowed what heat was. My Will here?"

"No," she said, "he ain't here."

I looked down in the sand by the gate, and there was his tracks. "He been here?"

She looked me up and down like a woman trying to make up her mind to step on a cockroach. She throwed back her head.

"Yes," she said. "He's been here."

Now folks talk about seeing red when they're mad. 'Tain't so. Nobody on earth couldn't of been madder'n I was, and what I seed wasn't red. It was white. I seed a white light like looking into the sun, and it was whirling around, and in the middle of it was the Widow Tippett. I closed my eyes against the light.

I said to myself, "O Lord, give my tongue a long reach."

I looked at her. I takened my tongue and I flicked it, like a man flicking a fishing rod. I takened it like a casting line and I laid it down right where I wanted it.

I said, "You figure I aim to leave a man-snatcher like you stay in Oak Bluff? You figure I aim to leave you go from home to home stealing husbands, like a stripety polecat going from nest to nest, stealing eggs? You takened my husband and never returned my preserve basket, and that's how come me to catch up with you, on account of a red chicken feather in that preserve basket. And what I aim to do to Will Dover is my business and not yours, but I ain't aiming to let you clean Oak Bluff out of husbands, for could be they's one or two of them worth keeping."

She tipped back her head and begun to laugh.

I takened my tongue and I drawed it back and I laid it down again. I said, "Devils laughs. Devils with buttermilk faces is the ones laughs. They laughs right on through damnation and brimstone, and that's what'll be your portion."

She said, "You should of been a lady preacher."

I takened my tongue and I purely throwed it.

I said, "I comes to you with a basket of preserves and a bundle of cuttings, and what do you do? You don't even send back a empty basket. Not you. What you sends back is a empty husband. You figure I aim to leave the sun go down on you in Oak Bluff one more time? The sun ain't rose, will set on you in Oak Bluff."

She quit laughing. She licked her lips. I could see her drawing back her tongue like I'd done mine. And when she let it loose, seemed to me like I'd been casting mine full of backlashes, and not coming within ten yards of putting it where I aimed to. For she takened her tongue and she laid it down so accurate I had to stand and admire a expert.

"You was likely a good woman oncet," she said. "You know what you are now? You're nothing but a big old fat hoot-nanny."

I like to of crumpled in the sand. She stepped down off her porch and she walked up to me, and there was nothing between her and me but the gate, and nothing between our souls at all.

She said, "I aim to give you credit for what you was oncet. I come to Oak Bluff, hearing the first day I come that you was a woman wouldn't leave her husband go to no cockfight. I thought, a husband leaves his wife tell him what to do and what not to do, ain't a man no-ways. And then folks begun telling me about you. They told me you was a woman with a tongue sharp enough to slice soft bacon, and a heart like gold. They told me all the good things you done. And they told me you was always a great one for leaving a man go his man's way, and seemed like you bearing down on yours was something had slipped up on you."

I said, "Go on."

She said, "Who be I, a stranger, to tell you to give a man his freedom? Who be I to tell you a man that has his freedom is the man don't particular want it? And the man drove with a short rein, do he be a man, is the one just ain't going to be drove?"

I said, "Tell me."

She said, "I'll tell you this. I got a man of my own. We're marrying soon as he sells out the stock in his store and crates up his fighting chickens and moves down here. I don't want your man nor no other woman's man. Now you quit your hassling and pull up your petticoat that's showing in the back, and I'll carry you where you can see just what your husband's been a-doing behind your big fat back."

She stalked out the gate and I followed her.

"Where you carrying me?" I said.

"To the cockfight."

Now if ary one had ever of said, "I seed Quincey Dover going to the cockfight on a Sunday morning," I'd of figured what they seed come out of the bottle. And if ary one had ever of told me I'd be walking along humble behind another woman, feeling scairt and as mixed up inside as a Brunswick stew, I'd of figured they was cold-out headed for the insane asylum.

But that's what I was doing. The Widow Tippett was purely stepping it off. It was all I could do to keep up with her.

I said to her back, "I ain't of no mind to follow you, without you tell me what to expect."

She never answered.

I puffed and I blowed and I said, "You could tell me how far we got to go."

She kept right on going. The sun beat down and I begun to sweat. The Widow Tippett was about ten yards ahead of me.

I called out after her, "If you aim to carry me to the cockfight, you got to wait a minute, else I'll be toted in as dead as one of them poor roosters."

She stopped then and we set down under a live-oak tree to rest.

I said, "I be blessed if I see how I can go to no cockfight. I've stood out against them things all my life. I can't go setting up to one of them now."

She said, "Can you climb a tree?"

I said, "Can a elephant fly?"

She said, "Then you'll have to let folks see you there," and she got up and give me a boost to get me up and she set off again.

The place where she takened me was out in Wilson's Woods. We come up on it from the south, and here was a clearing in the woods, and a cockpit in the sand, with a wooden ring around it. On the north side was some men standing, and the trees was between us and them.

The Widow Tippett said to me, "Now how come me to ask you could you climb a tree, is on account of that big camphor tree has a flat bough leans right out over the cockpit, and could you oncet make that first crotch, you could get you a ringside seat and watch the show, and nobody ever know you was near if you set quiet. I aim for you to see the show. Then oncet you've seed it, what you do is your business, for I'm done with you."

I said, "If you was to push me a mite, could be I'd make the crotch."

She said, "You ain't asking much, be you?" but she put her shoulder under me and pushed with a will, and I got myself up into the camphor tree. Like she said, it was easy going oncet I was off the ground, and I pulled up a ways and found me a fine seat part-ways out the bough, with another bough right over me to hang onto.

"Now keep your big mouth shut," she said, "and with that green dress you got on, nobody won't no more notice you than if you was a owl. A mighty big owl," and she went on over to where the men was standing.

I hadn't no more than made it, for directly men begun coming in from all over. Most of them had gamecocks tucked under their arms. Some was Roundheads, like mine, and some was White Hackles and Irish Grays, and some was Carolina Blues. They had their combs trimmed and their spurs was cut off to a nub about a half-inch long. Their tail feathers was shaved off till the poor things' butts was naked.

I thought, "Merciful jay bird, them fine roosters throwed to the slaughter."

After I'd looked at the cocks, I begun craning my neck careful to look at the men. Heap of them was strange to me, men had come in from other counties to fight their chickens. And after I'd watched their faces it come to me there was two kinds of men there. One kind had the fighting mark on them. They was men with cold hard eyes and I knowed they'd fight theirselves or their chickens merciless. They had a easy kind of way of moving, a gambler's way. I knowed this kind of man would move slow and talk quiet, and fight until he couldn't get up. And he'd bet his last dollar and his last farm, did the notion take him. He was a kind of man loved to give a licking and could take one, and it was a hard kind of a man, but you had to give him your respect.

Then there was another kind of man there. This kind of man was little, and his eyes was gentle. And I thought to myself, "Now what's that kind of man doing at a cockfight?"

I inched around on my limb so I got a better peephole through the branches. The men milled around, not talking much, just cutting their eyes sideways at t'other feller's chickens. I seed money change hands. The men that was getting their cocks ready was as nervous as brides sewing on their wedding clothes. I could see one man good. He was wrapping little thin strips of leather around the nubs of his rooster's spurs. Then he takened a pair of sharp shiny pointed steel things I knowed must be the gaffs, and he fastened them on, and wrapped them like they was a baby's bandage.

I thought, "Why, them things ain't as cruel as the natural spurs."

I could see they'd go in quick and clean, and if they didn't reach no vital spot they'd not be much more'n a pin prick. It was like a boxer's gloves; they look terrible, but they don't do the harm of a knuckled fist.

A gray-looking feller with his hat on the back of his head stepped into the pit. He drawed three lines acrost the sand with his foot.

He said, "Let's go."

Two men come ambling into the pit with their chickens. They turned their backs one on t'other. Each man on his side of the pit set his cock down on the sand, keeping holt of its wings, and let it run up and down. The cocks lifted their legs high. Their eyes was bright. They was raring to go.

The referee said, "Bill your cocks."

Seemed like electricity goed through all the men. All the easygoing limpness was done gone. They was all stiff and sharp and that high-charged to where you could of lit a match on ary one of them. The two handlers goed up to each other with the cocks cradled in their arms. They poked the cocks' bills together and one cock made him a pass at t'other.

Somebody hollered, "Two to one on the Blue!"

The cocks pecked at each other. Their hackles rose.

The referee said, "Pit your cocks."

The handlers set the birds down, each one on his own line.

The referee said, "Pit!"

The cocks flew at each other. They met in the air. When they come down, one just naturally didn't get up again. The men all relaxed, like a starched napkin had got wet. The handlers picked up the birds and went out. Money passed here and yon.

I thought, "Now nobody much got their money's worth outen that."

The next fight were a dandy. Right off, I picked a big Carolina Blue to win. I never did see such a fight. I'd seed men box and I'd seed men wrestle. I'd seed dogfights and catfights. I'd seed a pair of old male 'coons having it. I thought I'd seed fighting. But them game roosters was the fightingest things I ever laid eyes on. They knowed what they was doing. One'd lay quiet for t'other, and he'd flick up his feet, and whip his wings, and pass a lick with them gaffs.

I thought, "Now them fool roosters is following their nature. They're having them some kind of a good time."

I begun to get uneasy about the Blue I'd picked. Seemed to me he was dodging. He lay still oncet when he had him a fine chancet to hit a lick, and I almost hollered, "Get him now!" Then he kind of shuffled around, and next thing I knowed he laid out the enemy plumb cold. I come near shouting, I was so proud I'd picked the winner. There was three more fights and I picked two of them. I was breathing hard. I leaned back a mite on the camphor bough.

I said to myself, "Quincey Dover, take shame. You're purely enjoying yourself."

'Twas way too late to feel shame. I couldn't scarcely wait for the next fight to begin. I didn't even mind the camphor bough cutting into me. But there was a delay. I could see men look at their watches.

I heered one say, "He knowed he was to fight the Main."

The Widow Tippett called out, "Yonder he comes."

And who come walking in to the cockfight? Who come walking in with a big red Roundhead rooster tucked under his arm? My Will come in, that's who come.

Now I can't say I was plumb surprised to see him. I'd figured, the way the Widow Tippett talked, I could look to see him here. I'd a'ready figured that's what she meant about what-all he'd been a-doing behind my back. But I sure didn't look to see him walk in with no fighting cock. I cut my eye at that chicken. And I recognized it. It was one of my prime young roosters, growed up into the biggest, finest, proudest gamecock I ever did see, and the marks of battle was on him. Seemed to me if a rooster had the choice, he'd a heap rather grow up to fight than perish in the cook pot.

Right off I knowed two things. I knowed the Widow Tippett hadn't done a thing but leave Will raise his chickens, and train them, at that sloppy, easygoing place of hers. And I knowed another thing. I knowed my Will was one of them second kind of men come to the cockfight; the little gentle fellers I couldn't make out why they was there. Well, you'd of thought 'twas the Lord of the Jay Birds had come in to the cockfight, 'stead of Will Dover. The men parted a way for him to go into the pit. They closed in after him, talking and joking and asking questions about his rooster.

Will called out, "I got a hundred dollars says this is my day."

I like to shook the camphor tree to pieces. I near about climbed down to say, "Will Dover, don't you go betting that money from under the fireplace on no cockfight." But I didn't dast give my-self away. And truth to tell, I kind of hankered to see could that chicken fight.

Didn't take long to know. The fight was the big fight of the day. Seemed like Will's rooster was a old winner, and the men figured it were his turn to take a licking. Odds was mostly two to one against him. T'other cock was a Carolina Blue, and directly I seed him my heart sank.

"Bill your cocks," said the referee, and Will and t'other feller billed their cocks. They like to of fought right then and there.

"Pit!"

Nobody didn't have to give his rooster no shove. That pair was mixing it time they hit the ground. Will's Roundhead got hung in the Blue.

"Handle!"

The Blue's owner got him a-loose. "Anyways," I thought, "our chicken got in the first lick." Then they was at it again. Now if I hadn't of seed them other fights first, I'd not of appreciated this one. It was a pair of champions, and they both knowed it. They was both shufflers, and it was as neat as a pair of boxers that knowed their footwork. Didn't neither one waste no energy, but when the moment come one seed him a chancet, he was whipping his wings and striking. Now and again they'd both fly up off the ground and pass their licks a foot in the air.

"Handle!"

I wanted to holler so bad I had to put my hand over my mouth. If our Roundhead takened a licking, that Blue was going to wear me out doing it. Both chickens was breathing hard. Will picked his up and run his mouth down along his feathers, from the top of his head on down his back, cooling him and soothing him. He blowed on him and he dipped his bill in a pan of water.

"Pit!"

I mean, anybody that ain't seed a champion cockfight ain't seed a thing.

All of a sudden the Blue begun to take the fight. He got in a lick to the head and while the Roundhead lay hurt and dazed, the Blue followed through with another.

"Time!"

I takened my first breath in about two minutes. I'd of popped directly.

"Pit!"

This time it looked like it was all over. The Blue come in like a whirlwind and he done a heap of damage. He got hung in the Roundhead's back.

"Handle!"

This time when Will turned him a-loose he talked to him. He made queer little sounds, and one of them sounded like a hen a-clucking, like as if he knowed the cock'd fight better if he figured a faithful wife was encouraging him.

"Pit!"

He set him down, and the light of battle was in the Roundhead's eyes. He fought hard and game, but next thing I knowed the Blue had him out cold, with one wing broke. "He's dead," I said, for he lay on his side just scarcely breathing. I could of cried. Seemed like a thing that noble and that fearless had ought to live to be husband to a hundred hens and daddy to a thousand biddies. The referee begun to count. The Blue give the Roundhead an extra lick as he laid there, and everybody figured that finished him. The men that had bet against the Blue reached in their pockets for their money. I begun to sniffle. I didn't someway even mind Will losing the money. I just couldn't bear to see that Roundhead take a licking. Well, I reckon he figured the same. He opened his eyes and he drawed a breath and where he lay he reached up and he put them gaffs in that big Blue standing over him, and the Blue dropped like he'd been shot.

A grunt come outen the men like as if it was them had been hit. And you know that Roundhead wavered up to his feet, dragging that broke wing, and he climbed up on that Blue, and his head wobbled, and he lifted it up, and he flopped his one good wing, and he crowed! He'd won, and he knowed it, and he crowed.

My Will picked him up and stroked him, and wiped the sweat off his own forehead. He kind of lifted up his face and I could see the look on it. And that look made me feel the funniest I've near about ever felt. It was a deep kind of a male satisfaction. And I knowed that without that look a man just ain't a man. And with it, why, he's cock of the walk, no matter how little and runty and put-upon he be. And I knowed why Will loved a cockfight, and I knowed why all them other little gentle-looking fellers loved it. They was men didn't have no other way to be men.

A shame come over me. Times, it's life'll do that to a man. Mostly, it's his woman. And I'd done that to my Will. I'd tried to take his manhood from him, so he didn't have no way to strut but fighting a rooster. Now he'd won, and he was a man again. And I knowed that cocks must crow.

And about that time you know what happened? I reckon I'd been doing a heap of jiggling around in that camphor tree, and a camphor tree's right limber, but there's a limit to what it can stand.

I heered a creak and then I heered a crack, and the limb I was setting on busted off as neat as if you'd put a ax to it, and I slid down it, and I catched holt of the limb below, and I slid down that, and I plunked off down outen the camphor tree right smack in the middle of the cockpit.

I reckon everybody thought it was the end of the world. Nobody couldn't do nothing but gape at me.

"Well, git me up off the ground," I said. "You sure can't fight no chickens with me in the middle of the pit."

Will run to me then, and two-three others, and they hoisted me up. I brushed off my skirt and the Widow Tippett tidied me up. I looked her in the eye.

"I'd be proud to call you my friend," I said to her.

"All you got to do is call it," she said.

I turned to my Will. His face was in knots. The Lord Hisself couldn't of told what he was thinking.

"Well, Will," I said, "we sure got us some kind of a fighting rooster. Now I'd like a mite softer seat for the next fight."

He drawed a long slow breath.

"We ain't staying for the next," he said. "You're like to be hurt. I'm carrying you home."

The men that had lost to him paid him off. He crammed the bills in his pocket and he tucked up the Roundhead under his arm and he led me off to the car. He cranked up and headed out.

The Roundhead kind of nested down on the seat between us. Directly Will reached in his pocket and he hauled out the money and he dropped it in my lap. I counted out the hundred he'd started with and I put it back in his pocket. Then I divided the rest in two piles, and I put one down inside my blouse and put the other in his pocket. He didn't say the first word.

"Will," I said, "I figured you'd been on-faithful to me with the Widow Tippett."

He shook his head.

"I should of knowed better. You ain't that kind of a man. But something in you had drawed off from me."

He nodded.

"I know why you drawed off," I said. "I'd done drove you to it. And I knowed better than to treat a man the way I'd got to treating you."

He never answered.

"Will," I said, "I hope it's in your heart to forgive me. I didn't use to be thataway. Time changed me, Will, and I didn't never notice it.

I'd be proud if you'd blame time for it, and spare me."

He kind of blinked his eyes, like he was fixing to cry.

"Will," I said, "you ain't got to go raising no chickens behind my back. I'll raise them for you."

"No, Quincey," he said, slowlike. "No. I reckon I'll quit cockfighting. It's a foolish business, for a man can lose his shirt at it. And you didn't happen to see one of them long, bloody, ugly fights, makes a man sick to watch it. No, Quincey, I'm done." He looked at me. "Seems like something inside me is satisfied."

Well, I busted out crying. The excitement and the camphor limb cracking, and finding I hadn't plumb lost him, and all, I couldn't stand it. I blubbered like a baby.

"Oh, Will," I said, "I wisht I was young again. An awful thing has done happened to me. You know what I be? I be nothing but a big old fat hoot-nanny."

"Why, Quincey," he said. "Why, Quincey. Don't you dast say such as that. You're my good, sweet Quincey, and I love every hundred pounds of you."

And we busted out laughing.

"Quincey," he said, "you remember when I come courting you and I told you I aimed to fatten you up, for a man couldn't have too much of a good thing?"

I blowed my nose and he put his arm around me.

"Will," I said, "we're on a public highway."

"It's a free road," he said, and he kissed me.

"Will," I said, "home's the place for such as that."

"Ain't I headed for home fast as I can go?" he said, and we laughed like a pair of young'uns.

My Will ain't much to look at, but he's mighty good company.

FISH FRY AND FIREWORKS

I ain't in me to fail a friend. Uncle Benny
Mathers come to me in his hour of need and I done more'n mortal woman should ever be called on to do. But the next time Uncle Benny runs for constable of Oak Bluff, he can run by hisself. If my own Will was to run for Governor, I'd run like a rabbit in 'tother direction. Well, that ain't too good a way to put it, me being the size I be. Run like a elephant is more like it, I hear tell the speed of a elephant astonished them few as has seed it.

It ain't that I figure women-folks belong to do nothing but keep the fire a-going in the kitchen range with rations hot in it, and scratch around in the flower garden and mebbe get a hour-two to set on the porch and rock and leave the world to men. The world is looking over the shoulder of any woman who stirs a stew or wipes her younguns' noses. The world ain't a separate place at all. It's in ever' kitchen and garden and front porch from Turkey Creek to Timbuctoo, and if ever' woman rared back on her dew-claws and hollered, "Don't you men go a-messing up my kitchen and my garden and my porch no more," all them fellers studying on armies and navies and oil leases and when to act polite and when to act biggety, would go to the woods to hide like a batch of boys their mammy had caught tracking mud on her clean floor.

Women don't pay enough attention. It ain't that. It's just that I got to feeling smart, like I do, times, and drug a thing into politics that had no business there. Trying to help Uncle Benny Mathers. I like to kilt both of us. It cured me of meddling without I'm certain the Lord's on my side, and if the Lord was around when I was being so all-fired clever, it was only to spare me to learn me a lesson. I've done learned it. I aim to vote the best I know how, and when I've voted I aim to go on home and punish myself with darning socks. And if another political rally, with fish fry and fireworks, was to show up in my own back yard, I'd take to the out-house 'til 'twas over.

It was natural, Uncle Benny coming to me when he lost his reputation. Me and him has been friends long as I can remember. Many's the time I've talked the Old Hen, his wife, into leaving him come home again, when he'd cut the fool oncet too often. Uncle Benny has a high opinion of the turn of my tongue. I reckon it flattered me. When a woman's flattered, particular a big fat elephant one like me, has got nothing else but her cooking to take for a compliment, they's no telling how far she'll go to get into trouble. It begun with the new state and county elections coming up, and Uncle Benny losing his good name when he got bird-shot in his backside.

Now we always vote Uncle Benny Mathers to be constable at Oak Bluff just as regular and automatic as rain in June. He makes a good constable, and besides, if we didn't keep him busy with the law, we're afeared the law'd keep busy with him. His nature makes him prowl and ramble and cut the fool and get hisself into hot water, and it's a fine thing when a man can do such as that in the line of duty. This year, looked like nothing on earth could keep Uncle Benny from being throwed out as constable in the voting and him innocent as a baby yellowhammer in the nest. 'Twas all a matter of trying to stop the meanness of old man Crapson.

Old man Crapson is so mean that when a poor old colored woman was dying on his rural free delivery mail route, he wouldn't trust her old husband for the three cents to mail a letter to their only son in Jacksonville, to come for the dying. All the mailmen ahead of him would of paid the three cents out of their own pockets if the son hadn't not of come to pay them back. That's how mean old man Crapson be. And ary time he can put his bill in 'tother feller's business, he's happy as a dead hog in the sunshine. When Uncle Benny crawled him he was fixing to be just as mean. It was this-a-way.

Old man Crapson finishes his rural free delivery about two o'clock, and has plenty of time to set and study meanness the rest of the day. He makes out like he's religious, and whilst he passes the collection plate in church, it gives him a fine chance for nobody not to notice that he doesn't put nothing in it hisself. He's done more damage in the Lord's name than the devil could figure in a month of Sundays. He got to studying how to get a good girl sent to the reformatory.

Now when I say a good girl, she had made her one little slip, so to speak. She had give more than the law of man allows to her childhood sweetheart afore he goed to the war. If he'd of come home, they'd of been wed, and nobody the worse for wear. He was kilt a far piece from home, and her love was made public in the shape of a illegitimate young un. She was heart-broke to lose her true-love, but she takened a job waiting table at Lowden's Cafe and Short Orders, and aimed to raise the child decent. Old man Crapson set out secret to get her sent to the reformatory to protect Oak Bluff's morals. The times Oak Bluff's morals has tottered and fell, is not for me to mention.

Uncle Benny and me was standing on the post-office steps waiting for the mail train and passing the time of day. Old man Crapson came out from turning in his receipts on his run. He looked like a cottonmouth moccasin has just swallered a fish.

He says, "Well, nobody can't say I don't do the Lord's work. I aim to clear sin outen all of Oak Bluff."

I says, "You'll sure need to live a long life, Mr. Crapson."

He says, "A lifetime ain't too long for it. I've done made me a good start. I been writing to the Welfare Board, and they've just wrote back, is it true this Morley gal has her a young un and is working in a public place with lipstick on her mouth and her skirts short, they'll sure put her in the reformatory and the young un in a orphanage."

Uncle Benny gazed at him. I was fixing to say my mind, when Uncle Benny spoke.

"Brother Crapson," he said, "I'm fixing to give you the beating of your ugly old life, a-persecuting of that poor girl that only loved her soldier fancy. I'll give you a head start, and then I aim to catch you and whop you."

Old man Crapson turned white as the belly of a dead fish. He drawed a long breath and he lit out for home. Uncle Benny give him ten yards' start and takened out after him. I follered after, a-huffing and a-puffing, not to miss the fun. Now old man Crapson is near about my size and shape, and Uncle Benny is a little-bitty man, lean and wiry, and the three of us must of looked like a pair of feather beds with a flea in the middle. Uncle Benny begun a-gaining. They rounded the fence into Crapson's yard.

Crapson bellered like a bull.

"Sis! Sis! Sis! Save me!"

Sis is old lady Crapson. She ain't mean, like him. She's a good woman, but what you might call hasty. She takened one look outen the door and picked up her shotgun. She keeps it handy, with a load of No. 10 bird-shot in it. She says when she takes a impulse she don't like to waste time loading. Old Crapson made the front steps and collapsed acrost them. That give Uncle Benny his first view of Sis. She clicked back the hammer on the gun. Uncle Benny called, "Wait a minute, Mis' Crapson. Like as not you'll agree with me." Him and me both seed there wasn't no minute to wait. Old lady Crapson lifted the gun and got the sights on him.

Now women is not as afeered of women as men is, but I knowed Mis' Crapson was fixing to pull that trigger in about seconds more. I heaved myself around in 'tother direction and begun getting away.

I yelled, "Run, Benny, run! She'll shoot your eyes out!"

If Uncle Benny had of stood his ground, she might just possibly not never have shot. But he turned tail to run, and Mis' Crapson couldn't no more of resisted than I can resist another piece of syrup pie. She pulled the trigger and the gun bammed and I could hear the shot hitting Uncle Benny like big drops of rain hitting dry sand. He yelped like a running hound dog that has tripped over a tree stump. We met at the post-office.

It was plain bad luck that the mail train was just in, and half of Oak Bluff was there, coming out looking over their catalogues and advertisements for fertilizer and fence-wire and patent medicines. Uncle Benny was clutching at the back of his breeches. If we'd of been alone, we could of covered ever'thing up, and nobody the wiser. It was too late. We didn't have no time.

Joe Turnbuck said, "Why, Mr. Mathers, what-all has happened to you?"

Uncle Benny groaned and he busted right out with it.

"Old lady Crapson takened a pot shot after me. I'm ruined."

All the folks around the post-office fell into a hush.

Joe said, "Takened a pot shot after you? You mean you was running away?"

I knowed then Uncle Benny was ruined, and the elections coming up, and the ruin was ahead of him like the sting behind him. I spoke up quick.

I said, "He'd of been a fool not to of run away. You all know Mis' Crapson shoots first and re-loads second."

There was another hush, like the quiet before a big wind. Then ever'body around busted out laughing, and they laughed 'til they fell against one another. The preacher's wife was leaning against one of the fishermen, the president of the Ladies' Missionary Circle laid her head on the shoulder of the half-witted snake hunter, Mr. Baskerville, and all the social classes of Oak Bluff was mixed up together, laughing their heads off. They finally quit and wiped their eyes and the preacher's wife and the president of the Ladies' Missionary Circle become haughty again.

Joe Turnbuck said, "I'd not never have thought it. Uncle Benny Mathers, the fearless constable, shot by a woman from the rear."

Ever'body had to laugh some more. Joe was feeling proud of his-self.

"Reckon it's time we had a new constable," he said. "Mebbe Mis' Crapson might take the job."

Folks kind of sobered up. Our elections is always hot and heavy, but nobody hadn't never questioned Uncle Benny Mathers before. Now they done so. Uncle Benny and me watched them drift away, studying.

We was left alone on the post-office steps.

I said, "Benny, I'd lay my soul against old man Crapson's soul, that woman would of shot your eyes out if you'd faced her."

He said, "That's the way I figures. What's a-bothering me right now, is the shot in my seat."

I said, "Well, come on to my Will's garage. He'll pick it out for you."

"It'll be like picking out a thousand hornet stings," he said.

When we laid Uncle Benny acrost my Will's tool bench by the grease pit, his breeches looked like a sieve. It takened Will four hours to pick the bird-shot outen Uncle Benny's back-side. Will Dover is the kindest man in the world, but he had him a time, keeping from laughing, too. What Uncle Benny told the Old Hen when he had to sleep on his stummick, I'd not know. He stayed a-bed a day-two and I didn't go by. When he showed up in town again, the snow-ball had got to rolling so's it seemed to me 'twould take all the fires of hell to stop it. For ever'body in Oak Bluff had done decided Uncle Benny Mathers, after all these years, was a coward.

It was Joe Turnbuck who come out as candidate for constable against Uncle Benny. I was to my Will's garage when Joe walked in with a stack of posters under his arm. He was humming to hisself.

He said, "Howdy, Will Dover. Howdy, Mis' Quincy. Reckon you got no objections do I set some pretty pictures around your place."

Will takened a look at one of the posters.

He said, "Well, you ain't no uglier'n the rest of 'em. I'm for Benny Mathers, but go ahead and put up your picture."

Joe set a poster in the office window and another over the Coca-Cola machine and tacked another to the telephone pole. They was pictures of him with his hand stuck inside his coat like Napoleon. Underneath it read:

JOE TURNBUCK FOR CONSTABLE
Vote for a Man that DON'T RUN!

I said, "Look here, Joe. That ain't fair. You know good and well Uncle Benny has many a time walked into a jook and takened a razor right outen the hand of a wild-drunk colored boy. He walked between Big John and Long Massey when they was fighting. He hauled off Mr. Simpson when he was beating his wife. He's the bravest constable in four counties."

"He run from old lady Crapson," Joe said. "That's all I need to put me in office," and he goed off whistling to put up more posters.

Posters for candidates for the state and county offices blossomed all over like the may-haw bush in April. School commissioners, state legislature representatives, road commissioners, sheriffs, constables and dog-catchers, they was all out to get elected. Good men, sorry men, old men and young veterans, smart men and crazy men. And among all the posters they was nary one of Uncle Benny.

"Just no use me advertising," he said. "All I can do is depend on my friends."

Then the county candidates got together and agreed to have a big doings the day before elections. They settled on it to have the biggest fish fry ever heard tell of. Following the fish fry, when folks 'd be too full to move away, all the candidates would make speeches. To make certain nobody slipped off, the speeches was to be followed by a hour of fire-works. The posters went up for that, too.

FISH-FRY and FIRE-WORKS
Everybody Welcome
Everything Free

Nothing was said about the speeches, but folks knowed that was the price they'd be obliged to pay, listening. The candidates was all so pleased with theirselves that each feller figured his speech'd put him in office.

Time rocked on to the very day before the doings and the elections. Ever' place I turned, Oak Bluff was saying, "Well, it's sure a pity about Uncle Benny Mathers. He made a good constable in his day."

Then Uncle Benny come to the house to see me. I ain't never seed him so beat down. The Old Hen herself had never romped on him to where he got so low, for she usually had the right of it and he knowed it. What laid heavy on him now was the injustice. I tried to cheer him up with a quarter of sweet potato pie, but he only nibbled at it and give the rest to his bird-dogs that come with him.

I said, "I got something mighty good for the gullet, made from cane skimmings. I'd take a snort with you."

He shook his head.

"It'd freeze my stummick and my heart," he said. "I got a cold stone where my heart belongs to be. Don't reckon I'll even go to the fish-fry."

I said, "It just ain't right, Benny. I been reminding folks of all the brave things you've did as constable."

He brightened a mite.

"That's what I come to talk about. Now you got more influence in Oak Bluff than the preacher. If it ain't asking too much, how about you taking the evening and calling on ever' family in town? If you was to explain to the ladies just exactly how come me to run from old lady Crapson, seems like they'd have sympathy and work on their men-folks. You could do it, Quincy Dover. You got a tongue could turn sour milk sweet."

"Or 'tother way around," I said, and he did laugh. "I hate to tell you, Benny, but them as I've already talked to, I ain't no more converted than Lucifer converted Satan."

"But you're so smart, Quincy," he said, plaintive-like. "You can think up somehow to save me." He stood up to go. "You just study on it. I'm desperate."

I did feel mighty flattered. But I didn't see no hope, and I said so. He takened his farewell, and I went in the house and cut me another quarter of the sweet potato pie, for I cain't think good when I'm empty. And whilst I was finishing it, I heard a car draw up to the gate. Somebody walked in the house and called "Hey, Quincy Dover." It were my friend Ross Allen, him as fools around with snakes and varmints.

I said, "Why, hey there, you old snake-loving son of a possum. You alone?"

"No," he said, "I got a couple of Indians with me."

Now you know how folks joking say a thing like that, meaning they got sort of rough friends along.

I said, "Bring 'em in. I still got half a sweet potato pie."

Ross goed to the door and called something peculiar, and bless Katy, a couple of Indians got outen his snake-hunting truck and come in. They was real Seminole Indians. They had crocus sacks in their hands. I like to swooned, for I'd never seed a Indian that close to, before. Now I'd not know how I looked to the Indians, but they was more scared than me. They backed theirselves into a corner and was plumb miserable. Ross laughed.

"They brought their snakes with them," he said. A thing must of stirred in my mind right then. "I don't speak Seminole very well, and I guess they thought you wanted to buy a rattlesnake."

The thing in my mind turned over like mush a-boiling. I felt faintified.

"You all set down," I said, "Indians and all. I'll bring out the pie."

"No, thank you," Ross said. "We've got to be getting back to Silver Springs. I was supposed to meet one of my snake-hunters up the road, but he wasn't there. I was just passing by and thought I'd say Hello."

The thing in my mind plopped like cane syrup when it's ready to pour.

I said, "Come to think of it, I'd be mighty proud to buy a rattlesnake. But I'd want the teeth drawed out."

Ross laughed and said, "Come to see me at the Springs. I've got some new raccoons."

The thing in my mind come to full birth. I laid my hand on his arm.

I said, "I ain't funning. I want a rattlesnake, with its teeth drawed."

Ross stared at me.

He said, "Mrs. Dover, I couldn't let you have a rattler for any reason. The teeth, as you call them, grow back in a very short time."

I said, "I'll get the good of it before the teeth grows back. I want you should sell me the biggest rattler you got."

"You have a reputation for playing jokes," Ross said, "but I can't be a party to a joke that concerns a rattlesnake. If you're planning to scare your husband, you'd better just refuse to feed him."

And him and the Indians went off to Silver Springs, in the snake truck. I set down on my front porch and rocked and studied. For the idea that had come to me seemed the way to save Uncle Benny. Uncle Benny had turned to me for help, he'd claimed I was the smartest person in all of Oak Bluff, and I'd figured out a thing, and Ross Allen had paid me no mind. I rocked some more. Then I sat up straight. The half-witted snake-hunter Ross had missed at the crossroads, was passing by along my south fence line, with a crocus sack in his hand.

"Blessed day," I said to myself, "I can yet do it."

I hollered.

"Mister Baskerville, what you got in your crocus sack? Come here."

Now Mr. Baskerville hasn't been around Oak Bluff but about a year, and we was all sure he was half-witted on account of he lived like a hermit in a little old hut in the hammock, and catched snakes and varmints to make a living. He never had nothing to say to nobody, and that made us more certain, for if a man's civilized, he's obliged to talk and mix with people. Leastwise, that's the way we all figured. He come over to my porch.

"I have a rattlesnake in my crocus sack," he said politely, "since you ask me. An extremely large rattlesnake."

I drawed a long breath.

"That's what I hoped," I said. "I aim to buy it."

He dropped the sack on the porch.

"The most interesting things happen in life," he said. "May I inquire what possible use you might make of a rattlesnake?"

It seemed to me he was talking mighty fancy and high-faluting, and while I'd take a turn-down from Ross Allen, I'd not take it from a half-wit.

I said, "Mister Baskerville, I understand you sells snakes for a living. I aim to buy me a nice fresh large live rattler, and no questions asked. I'll pay above the going price, but I want its teeth drawed."

"Well, now," he said.

"I got no pliers here," I said, "but my Will, Mr. Dover at the garage, has pliers, if so be you has none, and tomorrow early of the morning, kindly fetch me that there large rattlesnake with its teeth drawed. What price do you put on a rattler?"

"Mr. Allen," he said mild-like, "pays me three dollars for one this size."

"I'll pay six," I said. "Without no teeth."

"Very well. I shall deliver the snake tomorrow. It will have no teeth."

I felt so good I ate the rest of the sweet potato pie. I hustled on over to Uncle Benny Mathers. He was setting on a stump in the yard, and he was lower'n a doodle-bug.

I said, "Well, it'll seem mighty nice and natural when you're elected constable again."

He said, "Don't torment me, Quincy."

"I ain't tormenting you. I got a plan. Leave me set down."

He give me the stump to set on and he squatted on his heels in the sand and we puttened our heads together and I told him what I'd figured out to save him. His eyes got bigger and bigger and his face lit up and when I was done, he slapped his leg and he beat me on the back.

"Quincy Dover," he said, "you ain't the smartest woman in Oak Bluff. You're the smartest woman in the whole state of Florida. I knowed you could save me if you put your mind to it."

I did feel real pleased with myself.

" 'Tis a right nice little idee, ain't it?" I said.

"Only thing I begrudge, is I wasn't the one to think it up." His face kind of wrinkled. "Quincy, you sure that half-witted Baskerville understood you good? You certain that rattlesnake's teeth'll be drawed?"

"He understood," I said. "Last thing he said was 'It'll have no teeth.' In fact, I don't know's the man is half-witted. I hadn't never talked to him before, nobody hasn't, but bless Katy if he didn't talk like a professor."

"I hear tell they're most of 'em crazy," he said, "but they do understand good."

I couldn't hardly sleep all night. I kept tossing and turning. I longed to wake up my Will and tell him how I was fixing to save Uncle Benny. But my Will, times, don't see things the way Benny and me does, and I was afeered he'd try to talk me out of it. Day broke bright and fair for the fish-fry. Will went to the garage early, for he looked for a big day in trade. I'd promised a basket of syrup pies, and I set to work and made them extra sweet and rich. I was just taking the last batch outen the oven when Mr. Baskerville come to the back door with his crocus sack. It kind of moved when he set it down.

"See you got my snake," I said real loud. I don't know why 'tis you want to holler at the feeble-minded.

"I am not deaf, Mrs. Dover," he said.

"Proud to know it," I said. "Reckon you heard me good, then, when I told you to draw its teeth. You guarantee it's got no teeth to it?"

"The rattler has no teeth," he said.

"That's fine."

"Now I got a basket here I'd crave to have you ease the snake into it. I don't want it a-rattling, neither. Reckon you'd best cut off the rattles?"

"There will not be space for the snake to rattle, I assure you. But the basket will make a fine conveyance. A rattlesnake is a most delicate creature, you know," and whilst I turned my head, he slipped the snake in my covered wicker basket.

I looked at him sharp. "You and me had ought to have a talk some day. You sound kind of educated to me."

"Education is such a relative matter, Mrs. Dover, I am an ignorant man."

"Well, you just stay ignorant enough not to open your mouth about all this. Understand?"

"I understand."

I paid him his six dollars and he bowed as polite as anybody and goed on off.

"Poor old feller," I thought, "I had ought to of give him a syrup pie."

Now I won't say I didn't have the all-overs, toting that rattlesnake to the doings. Mis' Poppers carried me in her Ford. I set in the back seat with my basket of pies on one side of me and the basket of snake on 'tother side. I sweat free and edged so clost to the pies I mashed part of one of them. When we got to Huckleberry Pond, the fires was going for to fry the fish in the Dutch ovens, and the long tables was set up, and all the ladies was laying out their victuals. There was boiled ham and baked ham, pork roasts and fried chicken, potato salad and deviled eggs, biscuits and corn-pone and cakes and cookies, and I must say, I didn't have to hang my head for my syrup pies.

Mis' Poppers said, "You want I should help empty that other basket, Mis' Dover?"

I trembled like a dish of jelly, but I said, cool-like, "This ain't rations."

I was obliged to holt to that basket for dear life. I ain't never so dis-enjoyed a doings in all my days. The beer flowed free, and I do purely love a bottle of cold beer on a hot afternoon, but I didn't dast have one. The candidates circulated and made jokes and told lies about how handsome the young uns was, folks got hungrier and hungrier, and the ladies begun frying the fish. I usually help with the frying, and I'm counted on to make the hush-puppies, but I begged off. I was double anxious, what with the snake in the basket, and not having seed Uncle Benny yet. The dinner bell was rung, and ever'body come running from all over the grounds, and fell to. I couldn't swaller a mouthful. When I cain't eat, you may know I'm fretted. I could smell that rattlesnake, and seemed to me ever'body else was obliged to smell him, too.

Like the candidates figured, folks was so full they just dropped on the ground to listen to the speeches. They was a big wooden platform built, about three foot off the ground, where the candidates was sitting in funeral chairs. I eased over the back of it, behind the setting candidates. I rested my basket in front of me on the platform. The speeches begun. Them as was running for the county offices talked first. Folks nodded and drowsed. Then the Oak Bluff local candidates begun a-talking. I looked around nervous, and I seed Uncle Benny, just slipping in to set down at one end of the front row of speakers. He nodded, and I tapped one finger on the top of my basket. I felt easier, and I drawed a breath and looked around. Bless Katy, it was a crowd. The whole county was there. And then I noticed, leaning right over the front of the platform, that poor half-witted Mr. Baskerville. He was looking around, too, and seemed like he tried to catch my eye, but I acted like I'd never seed him in all my life before. I was still afeered he'd say something, like crazy people does. And then Joe Turnbuck got up from his seat to urge hisself for constable of Oak Bluff.

"You good people," he said, pompous-like, "is going to have to listen to a awful lot of reasons for voting for this man or 'tother. You all have seed my posters. I say this one thing: vote for a man that don't run!"

They was cheers and stompings and laughings. Uncle Benny eased hisself out of his seat real slow and walked to the front of the platform. They was a silence, for folks had loved and admired him so long, they didn't feel like cold-out shaming him now he was ruined.

"My friends—" he said.

That was the signal we'd done agreed on. I was quivering like a mess of frog-eggs. I opened the lid of my wicker basket, and I tilted the basket, and that big old five-foot rattlesnake slithered out. What with one thing and another, my heart fair stood still. We hadn't figured on which way the rattler'd move. He laid there a minute, then slow, slow, he begun crawling towards the front of the platform. He crawled right past the legs of the candidates. He crawled to the middle of the platform. He crawled right to the feet of Uncle Benny Mathers. One of the candidates seed him then, and he let out a sound like a cat being strangled.

"Yee-ow-w-w-!"

Uncle Benny looked down and around. There was the rattlesnake in front of him, crawling toward the edge of the platform. The other candidates seed it, and the sounds they made was like one of them jitter-bug orchestras. And Uncle Benny swooped down, and he picked up that rattlesnake back of its head, and he held it up high in the air.

"I got it!" he hollered. "I got it!"

The candidates was turning over their funeral chairs, getting away, and Joe Turnbuck was the first to leap offen the platform and head for the piney-woods. The voters was confused, for only them in front had seed what was a-happening, and them in front begun climbing over the ones behind.

"A rattler! A rattler on the platform! Benny Mathers has got it!"

Uncle Benny held up his other hand like Joshua commanding the sun and the moon.

"Take it easy, folks! They's no more danger! I'm a-pertecting you all!"

Well, about that time, the fire-works begun to go off. One of them politicians had dropped his cigar, and it had done lighted a Roman candle, and the Roman candle had done set off a flower-spray, and before you could say "Scat," all the fire-works was a-blazing like the end of the world. The pin-wheels joined with the rockets, and the rockets was lost amongst the set pieces, and the last set piece I recall was the attack on Fort Sumter. They was never such a display of fire-works in the world, on account of them all going off at oncet.

All through it, Uncle Benny stood at the front of the platform, holding the rattlesnake back of its head.

Folks begun to cheer. The fire-works was mighty exciting, and the sight of Uncle Benny, to boot, standing there waving a rattler, put them to where they was near about crazy with pleasure.

"Hooray for Benny Mathers!" they yelled. "Hooray for our good old fearless constable! Hooray! Hooray! Hooray!"

That was all fine, and just the way me and Uncle Benny had fig-ured 'twould work out, but there was Uncle Benny still a-holding the rattlesnake. And then that poor old Mr. Baskerville stepped forward, and he said, mild-like, "May I have the snake?"

Uncle Benny leaned down to him and said, "Proud to let you have it, I'm certain you can make good use of it."

Mr. Baskerville said, "Just drop the snake."

So Uncle Benny dropped it, and Mr. Baskerville laid a forked stick acrost the back of its head, and picked it up. And whilst Uncle Benny and me watched, and whilst the crowds was cheering, and whilst the candidates was a-sneaking back again, Mr. Baskerville kind of squeezed down on the rattler's neck, and it opened its mouth, and bless Katy, there was its wicked teeth a-shining in the evening sun.

I looked at Uncle Benny and he looked at me. I still say he's a brave man. He turned the color of hardwood ashes, but he kept his feet. I swoonded dead away.

When I come to, Uncle Benny was pouring a snort of 'shine down my throat, and Fort Sumter was dying away in the sunset. Six can-didates finally got me lifted up. I got my wits together.

I said, "Ain't speeches bad enough, without a rattlesnake on the platform, too? Somebody carry me home."

Uncle Benny said, "I'll carry you, Quincy."

Having near about kilt him, seemed to me I'd ought to do the right thing now.

"Oh no," I said. "You never got to finish your speech. You got your duty."

"The doings is done," he said. "Folks is full of fish and speeches and the fire-works is over and that rattler had made 'em oneasy. A candidate for president couldn't hold attention."

I tottered to his old Ford and sunk into the front seat beside him. Uncle Benny cranked her up and we set off for home. He took a back road to get away from the traffic. He never reproached me nor said a word. In the middle of that back road we seed old Baskerville, moseying along with his crocus sack with the rattlesnake into it. Uncle Benny was of the same mind as me, for he stopped the car. I spoke.

"Mr. Baskerville, you mought not deem a rattlesnake dangerous, but you yet got to reckon with me. You guaranteed that snake would not have no teeth. It had teeth."

"Mrs. Dover," he said, "I still insist the reptile had and has, no teeth. A rattlesnake has *fangs*. I deplore any ignorant inaccuracy, and felt obliged to make my point. Just as, I gather, you made yours."

I stared.

"You'd of kilt mebbe half a dozen human beings to make a point?"

"Oh, no. Do not forget that I stood close to the platform all the time, ready to take charge if Mr. Mathers had not proved so brave and capable. I followed you all afternoon, to take precautions in the event that your plan went astray."

I stared again.

"How come you to figure I had me a plan?"

"It was obvious. I did believe that your scheme was merely to frighten Mr. Mathers' political opponent. The denouement surprised me."

Uncle Benny said, "Get in the car, and I'll carry you home. Long as you got that snake to where it's safe."

I said, "Mr. Baskerville, I'd be proud did you tell us how come you got the reputation of being half-witted? You're a smart feller."

"Mrs. Dover, that is the first intelligent question asked me since I came to reside in Oak Bluff. I am a herpetologist, a student of reptiles, and I am writing a monograph on the Florida varieties. My means are modest, and when once I have established the data on a particular reptile, I sell that reptile to Mr. Allen."

I said, "Do, Jesus."

Mr. Baskerville said, "But I must congratulate you on the idea of having Mr. Mathers retrieve the rattler. That, Mrs. Dover, was a stroke of genius."

"Genius or no," I said, "I am through with politics all the rest of my born days."

"Halt the automobile just a moment," said Mr. Baskerville. "I notice in the bushes a specimen related to the coral snake, but surely a distant cousin."

THE PELICAN'S SHADOW

THE lemon-colored awning over the terrace swelled in the south-easterly breeze from the ocean. Dr. Tifton had chosen lemon so that when the hungry Florida sun had fed on the canvas the color would still be approximately the same.

"Being practical on one's honeymoon," he had said to Elsa, "stabilizes one's future."

At the moment she had thought it would have been nicer to say "our" honeymoon and "our" future, but she had dismissed it as another indication of her gift for critical analysis, which her husband considered unfortunate.

"I am the scientist of the family, my mouse," he said often. "Let me do the analyzing. I want you to develop all your latent femininity."

Being called "my mouse" was probably part of the development. It had seemed quite sweet at the beginning, but repetition had made the mouse feel somehow as though the fur were being worn off in patches.

Elsa leaned back in the long beach chair and let the magazine containing her husband's new article drop to the rough coquina paving of the terrace. Howard did express himself with an exquisite precision. The article was a gem, just scientific enough, just humorous, just human enough to give the impression of a choice mind back of it. It was his semi-scientific writings that had brought them together.

Fresh from college, she had tumbled, butter side up, into a job as assistant to the feature editor of *Home Life*. Because of her enthusiasm for the Tifton series of articles, she had been allowed to handle the magazine's correspondence with him. He had written her, on her letter of acceptance of "Algae and Their Human Brothers":

MY DEAR MISS WHITTINGTON:

Fancy a woman's editor being appealed to by my algae! Will you have tea with me, so that my eyes, accustomed to the microscope, may feast themselves on a *femme du monde* who recognizes not only that science is important but that in the proper hands it may be made important even to those little fire-lit circles of domesticity for which your publication is the *raison d'être*!

She had had tea with him, and he had proved as distinguished as his articles. He was not handsome. He was, in fact, definitely tubby. His hair was steel-gray and he wore gray tweed suits, so that, for all his squattiness, the effect was smoothly sharp. His age, forty-odd, was a part of his distinction. He had marriage, it appeared, in the back of his mind. He informed her with engaging frankness that his wife must be young and therefore malleable. His charm, his prestige, were irresistible. The "union," as he called it, had followed quickly, and of course she had dropped her meaningless career to give a feminine backing to his endeavors, scientific and literary.

"It is not enough," he said, "to be a scientist. One must also be articulate."

He was immensely articulate. No problem, from the simple ones of a fresh matrimony to the involved matters of his studies and his writings, found him without an expression.

"Howard intellectualizes about everything," she wrote her former editor, May Morrow, from her honeymoon. She felt a vague disloyalty as she wrote it, for it did not convey his terrific humanity.

"A man is a man first," he said, "and *then* a scientist."

His science took care of itself, in his capable hands. It was his manhood that occupied her energies. Not his male potency—which again took care of itself, with no particular concern for her own needs—but all the elaborate mechanism that, to him, made up the substance of a man's life. Hollandaise sauce, for instance. He had a passion for hollandaise, and like his microscopic studies, like his essays, it must be perfect. She looked at her wristwatch. It was his wedding gift. She would have liked something delicate and diamond-studded and feminine, something suitable for "the mouse," but he had chosen a large, plain-faced gold Hamilton of railroad accuracy. It was six o'clock. It was not time for the hollandaise, but it was time to check up on Jones, the man-servant and cook. Jones had a trick of boiling the vegetables too early, so that they lay limply under the hollandaise instead of standing up firm and decisive. She stirred in the beach chair and picked up the magazine. It would seem as though she were careless, indifferent to his achievements, if he found it sprawled on the coquina instead of arranged on top of the copies of *Fortune* on the red velvet fire seat.

She gave a start. A shadow passed between the terrace and the ocean. It flapped along on the sand with a reality greater than what-ever cast the shadow. She looked out from under the awning. One of those obnoxious pelicans was flapping slowly down the coast. She felt an unreasonable irritation at sight of the thick, hunched shoul-ders, and out-of-proportion wings, the peculiar contour of the head, lifting at the back to something of a peak. She could not understand why she so disliked the birds. They were hungry, they searched out their food, they moved and mated like every living thing. They were basically drab, like most human beings, but all that was no reason for giving a slight shudder when one passed over the lemon-colored awning and winged its self-satisfied way down the Florida coastline.

She rose from the beach chair, controlling her annoyance. Howard was not sensitive to her moods, for which she was grateful, but she had found that the inexplicable crossness which sometimes seized her made her unduly sensitive to his. As she feared, Jones had started the cauliflower ahead of time. It was only just in the boiling water, so she snatched it out and plunged it in ice water.

"Put the cauliflower in the boiling water at exactly six-thirty," she said to Jones.

As Howard so wisely pointed out, most of the trouble with ser-vants lay in not giving exact orders.

"If servants knew as much as you do," he said, "they would not be working for you. Their minds are vague. That is why they are servants."

Whenever she caught herself being vague, she had a moment's unhappy feeling that she should probably have been a lady's maid. It would at least have been a preparation for matrimony. Turning now from the cauliflower, she wondered if marriage always laid these necessities for exactness on a woman. Perhaps all men were not concerned with domestic precision. She shook off the thought, with the sense of disloyalty that always stabbed her when she was critical. As Howard said, a household either ran smoothly, with the mechanism hidden, or it clanked and jangled. No one wanted clanking and jangling.

She went to her room to comb her hair and powder her face and freshen her lipstick. Howard liked her careful grooming. He was himself immaculate. His gray hair smoothed back over his scientist's head that lifted to a little peak in the back, his gray suits, even his gray pajamas were incredibly neat, as smooth and trim as feathers.

She heard the car on the shell drive and went to meet him. He had brought the mail from the adjacent city, where he had the use of a laboratory.

"A ghost from the past," he said sententiously, and handed her a letter from *Home Life*.

He kissed her with a longer clinging than usual, so that she checked the date in her mind. Two weeks ago—yes, this was his evening to make love to her. Their months of marriage were marked off into two-week periods as definitely as though the / line on the typewriter cut through them. He drew off from her with disapproval if she showed fondness between a / and a /. She went to the living room to read her letter from May Morrow.

DEAR ELSA:

Your beach house sounds altogether too idyllic. What previous incarnated suffering has licenced you to drop into an idyll? And so young in life. Well, maybe I'll get mine next time.

As you can imagine, there have been a hundred people after your job. The Collins girl that I rushed into it temporarily didn't work out at all, and I was beginning to despair when Jane Maxe, from *Woman's Outlook*, gave me a ring and said she was fed up with their politics and would come to us if the job was permanent. I assured her that it was hers until she had to be carried out on her shield. You see, I know your young type. You've burned your bridges and set out to be A Good Wife, and hell will freeze before you quit anything you tackle.

Glad the Distinguished Spouse proves as clever in daily conversation as in print. Have you had time to notice that trick writers have of saying something neat, recognizing it at once as a precious nut to be stored, then bringing it out later in the long hard winter of literary composition? You will. Drop me a line. I wonder about things sometimes.

MAY

She wanted to sit down at the portable at once, but Dr. Tifton came into the room.

"I'll have my shower later," he said, and rolled his round gray eyes with meaning.

His mouth, she noticed, made a long, thin line that gave the impression of a perpetual half-smile. She mixed the Martinis and he sipped his with appreciation. He had a smug expectancy that she recognized from her brief dealings with established authors. He was waiting for her favorable comment on his article.

"Your article was grand," she said. "If I were still an editor, I'd have grabbed it."

He lifted his eyebrows. "Of course," he said, "editors were grabbing my articles before I knew you." He added complacently, "And after."

"I mean," she said uncomfortably, "that an editor can only judge things by her own acceptance."

"An editor?" He looked sideways at her. His eye seemed to have the ability to focus backward. "And what does a wife think of my article?"

She laughed. "Oh, a wife thinks that anything you do is perfect." She added, "Isn't that what wives are for?"

She regretted the comment immediately, but he was bland.

294　*Marjorie Kinnan Rawlings*

"I really think I gave the effect I wanted," he said. "Science is of no use to the layman unless it's humanized."

They sipped the Martinis.

"I'd like to have you read it aloud," he said, studying his glass casually. "One learns things from another's reading."

She picked up the magazine gratefully. The reading would fill nicely the time between cocktails and dinner.

"It really gives the effect, doesn't it?" he said when she had finished. "I think anyone would get the connection, of which I am always conscious, between the lower forms of life and the human."

"It's a swell job," she said.

Dinner began successfully. The donac broth was strong enough. She had gone out in her bathing suit to gather the tiny clams just before high tide. The broiled pompano was delicately brown and flaky. The cauliflower was all right, after all. The hollandaise, unfortunately, was thin. She had so frightened Jones about the heinousness of cooking it too long that he had taken it off the fire before it had quite thickened.

"My dear," Dr. Tifton said, laying down his fork, "surely it is not too much to ask of an intelligent woman to teach a servant to make a simple sauce."

She felt a little hysterical. "Maybe I'm not intelligent," she said.

"Of course you are," he said soothingly. "Don't misunderstand me. I am not questioning your intelligence. You just do not realize the importance of being exact with an inferior."

He took a large mouthful of the cauliflower and hollandaise. The flavor was beyond reproach, and he weakened.

"I know," he said, swallowing and scooping generously again, "I know that I am a perfectionist. It's a bit of a bother sometimes, but of course it is the quality that makes me a scientist. A literary—shall I say literate?—no, articulate scientist."

He helped himself to a large pat of curled butter for his roll. The salad, the pineapple mousse, the after-dinner coffee and liqueur went off acceptably. He smacked his lips ever so faintly.

"Excuse me a moment, my mouse," he said. His digestion was rapid and perfect.

Now that he was in the bathroom, it had evidently occurred to him to take his shower and get into his dressing gown. She heard the water running and the satisfied humming he emitted when all was well. She would have time, for he was meticulous with his fort-nightly special toilet, to begin a letter to May Morrow. She took the portable typewriter out to a glass-covered table on the terrace. The setting sun reached benignly under the awning. She drew a deep breath. It was a little difficult to begin. May had almost sounded as though she did not put full credence in the idyll. She wanted to write enthusiastically but judiciously, so May would understand that she, Elsa, was indeed a fortunate young woman, wed irrevocably, by her own deliberate, intelligent choice, to a brilliant man—a real man, second only in scientific and literary rating to Dr. Beebe.

DEAR MAY:

It was grand to hear from you. I'm thrilled about Jane Maxe. What a scoop! I could almost be jealous of both of you if my lines hadn't fallen into such gloriously pleasant places.

I am, of course, supremely happy—

She leaned back. She was writing gushily. Married women had the damnedest way, she had always noticed, of gushing. Perhaps the true feminine nature was sloppy, after all. She deleted "gloriously," crossed out "supremely," and inserted "tremendously." She would have to copy the letter.

A shadow passed between the terrace and the ocean. She looked up. One of those beastly pelicans was flapping down the coast over the sand dunes. He had already fed, or he would be flapping, in that same sure way of finding what he wanted, over the surf. It was ridicu-lous to be disturbed by him. Yet somewhere she suspected there must be an association of thoughts that had its base in an unrecog-nized antipathy. Something about the pelican's shadow, darkening her heart and mind with that absurd desperation, must be connected with some profound and secret dread, but she could not seem to put her finger on it.

She looked out from under the lemon-colored awning. The peli-can had turned and was flapping back again. She had a good look at him. He was neatly gray, objectionably neat for a creature with such greedy habits. His round head, lifted to a peak, was sunk against his heavy shoulders. His round gray eye looked down below him, a little behind him, with a cold, pleased, superior expression. His long, thin mouth was unbearably smug, with the expression of a partial smile.

"Oh, go on about your business!" she shouted at him.

THE ENEMY

AMOCKINGBIRD chirped from the rooftree of the Milford cabin. His note was as dry as the weather. A basin of water was emptied from a rear window and the bird flew instantly to the puddle. He splashed hurriedly in the few seconds before the water sank into the hot sand.

Doney Milford called to him from the window, "'Twon't do you no more good than me. I'm hot again a'ready."

The room in his father's house used by young Tom Milford and his wife was a low lean-to. The August heat lay trapped inside it. Tom had a brief sense of being trapped, too, like a dog in too small a kennel. The front room would make a fine bedroom, but his father kept it piled with such things as tanned cowhides, saddles and sweet feed for the horses, and would not allow them to be disturbed.

Tom drew a clean shirt over his head and left the room to Doney. The girl mopped a towel over her bare arms and neck, but they were wet again at once. She put on her one good dress, left from the courting days before her marriage. The thin red silk stuck to her skin. She combed back her soft hair in front of the dime-store mirror. It was hard to see exactly how she looked against the distortion of its rippling. She was too thin, she knew, and her eyes—damn calf eyes, her father-in-law said—were too big in her small pointed face. But Tom thought she was as pretty as a play-dolly, and there was no reality beyond his opinion. The harshness of old man Milford played like harmless heat lightning outside her contentment. She heard him now, grumbling in the yard, and hurried to the porch, not to stir his anger by delaying him.

He was trying to mount his horse. He put a wrinkled boot into the stirrup and heaved his obese bulk up toward the saddle. Each time that he heaved, his paunch reached as high as the horse's backbone, but there was no muscle in arm or thigh to lift him higher.

The horse stood patiently. Milford's broad-brimmed straw hat slipped from his bald head to the sand, and the horse shied. The old man jerked the reins and gave a wordless bellow.

Young Tom said, "Go get up on the porch. You've got too heavy to mount from the ground."

He took the reins from his father and led the horse to the edge of the open porch. Milford panted up the steps. He flung his leg violently across the saddle, not to be done out of the appearance of capacity. Doney ran to the yard and handed up his hat to him. He slapped it on his head. He stared down at her.

He said, "What's my daughter-in-law doin', wearin' her red silk dress to the unloadin'?"

The girl dropped her eyes and stroked the tight, short skirt.

"Since when you gettin' dressed up to go look at a mess of cattle?"

She said, "I figured there'd be people there."

"Fixin' to catch the eye of that Yankee, eh? Fixin' to go gape at that thief. Don't neither of you get no idee we're goin' to look at no outlander. I aim to get me one look of that Barnum bull, and then we're shut of the whole damned unloadin'."

Doney looked at her husband.

He said gently, "Best go change it, honey. It's too tight to ride in, anyhow."

She darted into the house and changed the red silk for a percale house dress. Tom was on the mare. She put one foot in the stirrup left free for her, and he pulled her up behind him. Old Milford rode ahead. His buttocks shook back and forth like a vast bowl of clabber. Doney tightened her arms around Tom's thin waist and leaned one cheek against his back. It was almost as good as being close beside him in the bed, to ride so with him.

He said, "Pa wants to see that stranger bad as aryone. Whatever he looks like, he'll go right on despisin' him."

She accepted the comfort of their closeness, and gave her thoughts to the newcomer in the cattle section. His name was Dixon. He had appeared from nowhere and had bought four thousand acres of land for taxes. The land lay along the river, and over it the cattle belonging to Milford, the Wilsons, the Dibbles, and others, had for years ranged free. Dixon had sent in a big crew, who built a fine log lodge. Then, in the space of a few days, it seemed, before anyone quite understood what was happening, the crew had fenced in the whole four thousand acres, and now the local cattle must feed over the poorer land to the west. Doney agreed with her father-in-law that it was not right for a rich man to snap up, for next to nothing, land that poor men had been unable to hold. Dixon was bringing in his own herd of cattle, hundreds of them, it was said. The unloading was due this morning on the branch railroad.

The mare had long since caught up to Milford's horse. She walked close to his heels, anxious for a swifter pace. Tom rode herd with her on the Milford stock, and she liked to have his spurs touch her lightly, to be allowed to break into a long, smooth gallop across open wire grass. She jerked her head impatiently to the ground and snorted. Tom touched her mane. "No use to run when you're headin' toward the enemy," he said to her.

Doney was suddenly depressed. Old Milford hated everybody, and his curses no longer disturbed her. But if Tom felt danger, nothing was secure.

She said, "Will this here sure enough harm us?"

He hesitated. "There's so much harm to it, honey," he said, "I just don't know where it's like to stop. Pa just ain't of a mind to let no stranger block his pastures."

"But 'twa'n't his land."

"No, but seems like what folks have always used belongs to them."

"What can he do?"

"I reckon he'll try to make trouble for this here Dixon."

"What kind of trouble?"

"Can't never tell, with pa."

The woods road came out onto the highway, and heat rolled over the riders as though the gravel were the top of a cookstove. Milford's feather-pillow back was soaked with sweat. Tom was too lean for sweating, but his young body was feverish to Doney's touch. A mile before they reached the railroad, they heard the cattle.

Milford shouted, "They're done a'ready unloadin'!"

He kicked clumsily, and his horse, sagging under its burden, went into a jig trot. In the distance the cattle lowed deeply. Half a mile on, they met the first of the herd. Strange riders kept them hemmed on the highway, cutting in deftly when a spry yearling broke and ran. The cattle were white-faced Herefords, sleek for all their journey, half again the size of local animals. Milford eyed them enviously and spat.

The family rode along the edge of the ditch to the railroad. They drew rein to one side of the line of freight cars, tumultuous with the cattle that now smelled freedom. A single file of the animals was being driven down a runway from an open car door. The watching crowd of countryfolk was sullen. Yet the men talked among themselves with unwilling admiration for the Herefords. They greeted the Milfords, opening the talk to include their opinions. Doney poked Tom's back.

"Yonder. See. Be that Dixon?"

A gray-haired man with a clipped mustache, mounted erect on a bay horse, was directing the opening of the next freight car. Tom stared at him, then caught his father's eye and jerked his head in the stranger's direction. Old Milford turned heavily in his saddle. He, too, stared. The venom in his face was tangible, as though a wave of angry blood shifted back and forth through its coarse veins. He tugged a plug of tobacco from his pocket and pared off a shaving, easing it into his mouth from the knife blade.

"Looks like he'd fight," he said.

Dixon moved with a cold assurance. He ignored the local cattlemen. Doney was disappointed that there was no jostling and joking, as was usual in a crowd. She had pictured the unloading as a festivity, like the arrival of a tent show. Suddenly a ripple spread from the men nearest the newly opened boxcar. The Dixon crew moved quickly and shouted to one another. The Brahman bull was guided carefully down the runway. He made no effort to stampede, like the nervous cows and yearlings. He moved slowly and ponderously, felt the solid earth under him, and paused a moment to paw it with one great hoof, as though in salute to his only equal. The pent interest of the watchers broke loose.

"Whooey! Look at him! That ain't no bull, that's a elephant."

One of the Mills boys ran close to the beast and swept his hat to the ground.

"I got respect for a better man than me," he shouted, and the crowd roared in laughter.

Old Milford's face was purple. He bellowed above the tumult, "Laugh, you yellow-bellies! That there bull is takin' the rations right out of your mouths!"

The crowd hushed. Milford dug his heels into his horse's flanks and rode up to Dixon.

"You cain't do this to honest men just because they're poor! We've ranged our stock in these woods since before your ma changed your didies. You cain't take a pocketful of dirty Yankee money and run our cattle outen our own woods!"

Dixon stared at the gross and apoplectic figure overflowing its saddle. He looked Milford up and down, then swung his horse and moved away. He was heard giving orders for the handling of the Brahman.

Doney caught her breath. He had ignored old man Milford, whom all men reckoned with. Milford headed out of the crowd, and Tom followed. The men lifted their hands to him. They spoke approvingly as he passed along.

"That's tellin' him!"

The Milfords made the highway and slowed down. The old man mopped the sweat from his neck. "Block our pastures!" He turned sideways in his saddle and gaped at his son. He roared, "The pastures ain't the half of it! He's got us blocked from the river!"

"Mebbe the ponds'll hold out."

"Do this drought keep up, they'll not. They'll go dry as a haystack. Then we'll see. We'll just natchelly see."

Tom said over his shoulder to Doney, "Looks to me like Dixon better pray for rain. And pray quick."

The drought was implacable. Old Milford wrote Dixon three times, "Get your cattle out of here or we will cut your fences. Signed, a Cattleman, speaking for All." The Dixon herds continued to graze over the fenced acres of fast-drying wire grass. It was as though the owner had turned indifferently away from the anonymous letters as he had turned from Milford himself. There was no one to threaten about the drought, although Milford once shook his fist at the sky on a red and breathless evening.

On the morning of the tenth day after the unloading, Doney and the old man sat together on the porch, waiting for Tom. A dry, hot breeze, like air from the oven, stirred the boughs of the chinaberry over the roof. One bough lifted and fell with a steady thudding, so that it sounded like the hoofs of the mare in the sand. Doney had sometimes thought of climbing to the roof and sawing off the bough, for there had been other times when it interfered with the sound of her husband's coming. She stretched her bare legs on the hard pine floor of the porch to cool them, but the boards were hot against her skin. She brushed back a strand of hair from her forehead and her hand came away wet.

Milford stirred in his cushioned rocker. "If that last pond's dried up, I got my mind made up what to do," he said. "Nobody livin' can keep my stock from water."

She looked at him admiringly. It had taken her some time to accustom herself to his puffy body, the paunch lapping in folds over his thighs; to his bald redness; to the tobacco stains down the shirts she tried to keep washed and ironed; to the unwashed smell of him. She had come to accept it along with his rages and his closeness about money. He was old man Milford, with money in the bank and a word in the county like a whip. No candidate went to the legislature without the cattle vote, and the cattle vote was Milford's. The storekeeper's wife had once asked her what the old man paid his son for riding herd on his cattle. With no thought of betrayal, she had told the truth. He paid six dollars a week, and out of that Tom must buy half of the family rations, and pay for the feed of the mare. His father gave him one calf out of every ten for his own.

The storekeeper's wife said, "He couldn't hire him a nigger for that. And you doing for him, cooking for him, cleaning up his old man's dirtiness. How long since you had a new dress or a pair of shoes?"

Doney had withdrawn into silence. She was sorry she had answered. She and Tom lived rent free, as Milford reminded them. In time, Tom would have a herd of his own. She decided not to tattle again about the family business. A new dress was nothing. What were shoes to a girl who had Tom for her true love? Nothing was of importance but Tom, coming home from the range, eating food she had cooked, washing his feet in the basin of water she brought, lying beside her, holding her in his lean hard arms until she fell asleep.

Milford said, "The man ain't come to this county can interfere with my stock."

Above the thumping of the chinaberry bough she heard the hoofs of the mare. Milford heard, too, and sat straight. Tom rode into the yard and dismounted. His face had the one look she dreaded; the look for which she did not exist, being concerned with a man's worldly business.

He said, "Well, the pond's dry. The cattle's licking the mud. All the herds is bunched up there, against Dixon's fence."

Old Milford rose from his rocker. "Fetch me my horse," he said.

"What you fixin' to do?"

"Fixin' to do a plenty. And fetch me the wire cutters."

"Pa, there belongs to be a way to settle this without such as that."

"You heered me."

Tom turned away.

Milford said to Doney, "Fetch me my rifle and the box of cartridges."

She dared not question him as Tom had done. She brought the gun. He loaded it and slipped the extra cartridges in the pocket of his shirt. Tom brought the horse, saddled, to the porch.

Milford mounted. He said, "All right. Let's go."

Tom said, "I ain't goin'."

Milford pushed out his lips like a mudfish. "And I say you be."

The boy shook his head. "What you're fixin' to do ain't right."

Milford raised the butt of his rifle as though to strike. He lowered it. "All right. Stay home and hide. You ain't got the guts of a sapsucker." He clicked to the horse and rode away.

Tom said, "I've sure done it now. But how's a man to be a man if he don't do what he knows is right?"

Waiting with Tom was not like waiting with old Milford. It was good to be alone with him in the daytime.

Doney said, "I got dinner ready, do you want to eat now?"

"Honey, I cain't eat, with a mess like this un goin' on."

"You figure pa's aimin' to do somethin' fearful?"

"Fearful or no, it's wrong."

It was a new thought to have old Milford wrong.

"Reckon you hadn't ought to of gone with him?"

He shook his head. "There comes a time when a man knows."

They sat unhappily. There was no sound but the chinaberry bough scraping the roof. Midday was cruel with its heat. Waves of it vibrated from the sand. The chickens lifted their wings and parted their bills, and their trips for water to the cypress trough were of no help in cooling.

Tom said, "Hark!" In the distance there was a bellowing. Here and there a shrill animal scream tore across it. "He's done it. He's cut Dixon's fences and the cattle is stampeding to the river."

He paced back and forth. Doney thought that he looked as he would look when he was old. It stabbed her to think of him growing old, shortening their time together.

He said, "There belonged to be some other way to settle it. Pa should of gone to Dixon."

The sound of the stampeding cattle faded to a thin roll like far thunder. Stillness and heat took over the pine woods. A dirt dauber buzzing in the rafters was suddenly noisy. Then, violating the peace, Milford's rifle cracked in the distance. It popped thinly again and again, like a string of firecrackers.

"Tom, what's he shootin'?"

"Ain't no earthly tellin'. But it won't settle nothin'. It'll begin a bitter thing."

She ached to smooth away the furrows between his eyebrows. All the cattle in the county were not worth the distress in his face.

"Dixon'll fight back, and there'll be no peace for nary one." His face lightened. "Mebbe t'other cattlemen won't back pa."

"They always do back him, don't they?"

"They always have. There's got to be a first time for everything." His face darkened again. "Even if they don't back him, pa'll not give in till hell freezes. Dixon couldn't even have the law on him. Pa'd shoot ary sheriff come to arrest him."

Doney pictured the house in siege. They would have to barricade the doors and windows. The enemy would ride into the yard. There would be Dixon in the lead, with the high sheriff behind him, and an army of deputies. Old Milford would shoot first, and then bullets from the attackers would rain like hail over the house. Tom would be killed, because old Milford would never surrender. She began to cry. Tom reached out his hand and tousled her hair.

"Honey girl, quit that. I hadn't ought to of worried you about it. Go put our dinner on the table. We'll mebbe both feel better once we've et."

She could not control her tears, but she moved about the kitchen automatically. Everything was cold, but Tom was never particular about hot food. She laid out the cow peas and bacon, the cold corn pone, and poured the thick coffee and chicory into the cups. She ate blindly. She was grateful when Tom asked for a second helping. There was comfort in feeding him. It seemed the only thing she could do for him. She cleared the table and washed the dishes. Tom went to smoke on the porch and she joined him with Milford's mending. The big man burst through the seams of shirts and trousers as fast as she could bind them. The afternoon was so still that she thought she heard a limpkin crying from the river.

Tom said, "He's had time to do all the devilment he wanted to. He'd ought to be back by now."

Two hours before sundown the two Mills boys rode into the yard. There was no trace of the lighthearted nonsense they usually brought with them on a visit. Their dark, carefree faces were almost as grave as Tom's. They hitched their horses to the chinaberry and came to the porch.

Joe Mills said, "Your daddy told us to come here and wait on him. What's he up to?"

"I don't know. Him and me don't see this the same. What's he done a'ready?"

"Cut Dixon's fences and let all our cattle in. They stampeded for the river. We heered shootin', but don't know was it somebody shootin' at him, or did he shoot Dixon."

Jerry Mills said, "Mebbe he got jealous and shot the Barnum bull."

They laughed then, and settled themselves, rolling cigarettes. The three Wilsons arrived with the same meager information, then the Hobkirks and the Dibbles. Within an hour, cattlemen from a ten-mile radius had gathered. At last old Milford rode in. His horse was as wet with sweat as he, its tongue lolling under the bit. Milford shook with fatigue as he dropped from the saddle, but he eyed the group of men with satisfaction.

"I reckon they's enough of us to settle this our way," he said.

There was no answer.

Old man Wilson said, "You best tell us what you've been a-doin'."

Milford dropped into his rocker. He reached for his tobacco. "Doney, cain't you see I'm burnin' up?"

She scurried to the well and pumped him a dipper of fresh water. He drank in noisy gulps. As he drank, she mopped his face with a wet cloth. He pushed her away. The men leaned forward to listen.

"Well," he said, "first I cut them damned fences. The stock didn't need no second look. They lit out for the river and they went into it one on top of t'other. They was twenty drowned." He cut a shaving of tobacco and eased it into his mouth. "So when I come out again, why, I killed off twenty of Dixon's herd, just to start things off even."

The listeners looked at one another.

"Just as I rode back out of the gap I'd cut, two of Dixon's riders come gallopin' down inside the fence. One of 'em hollered, 'So you're the man, calls hisself a man, been writin' them letters to the boss?' And I said, 'You damned right. Mebbe he'll wish he'd read 'em more careful.' The feller said, 'He didn't believe nobody'd be fool enough to mean such as that. You're on public land, so we don't aim to kill you. But ary one of you low-down sons we catches trespassin' on this property—and the line lies ten feet outside this fence—why, we aim to shoot on sight.'

"So I goes on and rounds up all you men, and here you be. And now we'll set a whiles and figure the quickest way to get Dixon and his cattle outen our territory."

The Mills brothers exchanged a glance. The group seemed absorbed in its own bootlaces. Here a man dug his toe in the sand, as though in a moment he would turn up something expected but startling. Will Dibble whittled his knife idly on the edge of his sole leather. No one looked at Milford. The silence was a vacuum.

Milford said impatiently, "Well, who's the first with a good idee?"

Old man Wilson looked up from where he squatted on his heels. "We've had the use of that land a long time, ain't we?" he asked.

The question contained its answer. The group focused on him, as though he were a hook on which to hang their thoughts.

"We've used it, and our daddies, and our granddaddies before us, back to the Injun days. And who's paid a cent of taxes on it?"

The blue and gray eyes were leeches clinging to him.

"Nobody's paid a cent of taxes on that land. We've had it all our own way. We've sent men to the legislature that kept this open range, so's we could use that land for our stock and not have to pay no taxes on it. Ary man could of come in, ary time, and grazed his stock on them acres, on account of it was free. That right?"

Men nodded.

"We could of bought them four thousand acres among us, for taxes, ary time we wanted to. Didn't amount to scarcely nothing, the price. But we figured what had always done been free, always would be free right on. Be I lyin'?"

Men shook their heads.

"All right. Times has changed. Florida ain't the wild free place 'twere in my daddy's time nor even my time. Folks is buyin' up land and buildin' houses on it and farmin' land that ain't had nothin' on it for a thousand years but polecats and coons and possums and wildcats. And they got just as good a right to do it as we got to be settin' here."

Old Milford lurched from his rocking chair. "What you gettin' at?" he shouted. "You got the guts to go stand up for a blasted Yankee comes in and blocks our stock from water?"

"I got the guts to stand up for him," Wilson said.

Milford dropped back heavily. He wiped the back of his hand across his mouth. "I never figured I'd live to see the day when a Yankee lover'd stand in front of my doorstep."

"Yankee lovin' has got nothin' to do with it," Wilson said. "All I say is, Dixon had the right to buy that land and the right to put his cattle on it. If it's got us blocked from water, it's a accident, just like the drought is a accident. We got to do somethin' and do it quick. But I sure as hell ain't goin' to cut no lawful owner's fences nor kill no lawful owner's cattle."

Milford swung his head like a turtle's. He looked from one man to the next. "Who here's man enough to say I'm right and Wilson's wrong?"

There was no answer. He leaned forward.

"I don't care do every yellow-bellied one of you go hide under your bed quilt. I'll fight Dixon till he ain't got a cow nor a bull nor a calf nor yearling left on them acres. And how you fixin' to get back your cattle? They're on Dixon's land this minute. And them riders of his is furriners, but they meant it when they said they'd shoot on sight." He rocked violently. "Them riders'll herd our stock out again. What you got left to do but slip in and pick off them riders one by one? Cut the rest of his fence, nighttimes, and let Dixon's cattle out. Herd 'em off some'eres and leave them perish for water. 'Twon't take long to make him turn tail and get out."

Wilson said, "You reckon the law'll sit off quiet in Ocala and leave you do such as that?"

"The law!" Milford spat over the side of the porch. "I'm too old a man to begin obeyin' the law." He pounded his fat knee. "What you got left to do but fight?"

"We got this left to do," Wilson said, "and we should of done it a week ago. We can go to Dixon and talk it over like men. Show him the fix we're in for water. Ask him to let us leave our stock on his land, where they can get to the river, 'til we can locate new land to move to."

Milford threw back his head and laughed from his belly. "I can see the whole fool passel of you ridin' into Dixon's gate and gettin' shot down like a covey of quail catched on the rise."

"I been studyin' on that," Wilson said. "Now you've got us in this fix, some one man had ought to take the risk and ride in alone. Ride in to Dixon and tell him 'tain't nobody but you raisin' the hell, and we ain't with you. Tell him the rest of us aims to play fair and square. Tell him we don't want nary thing but a mite of time to get our cattle moved. One man ride in alone and tell him."

Doney stirred from her paralysis behind the house door. She saw Tom's boots feel for the floor. She saw him stand and stretch, tightening his belt. He walked across the porch and down the steps. She wanted to cry out after him, but no sound would come.

"I'm the one to go," he said. "I'll ride alone to Dixon."

She edged around the door and darted to the side of Milford's chair. It was rocking violently back and forth. He was trying to rise. His face was purple. She put a hand to help him and he knocked it away. He heaved to his feet. He called to Tom, "You've got too big for you breeches! Get back here where you belong!"

Tom went across the sand to the corral. Doney heard the mare snort. She heard the sound of the saddle and stirrups. The group of men rose and drifted to their horses with uneasy casualness. Tom rode to the porch. Milford was choking for speech.

Tom said, "I hate this, pa, but I got it to do."

Milford gathered his strength.

He bellowed, "Get goin' and keep goin'! Don't come back if you want to hold your hide! If Dixon don't kill you, 'y gee, I will!"

Tom fumbled with the reins. He looked at Doney.

He said, "I'll get you word."

Before she could speak from her numbness, he had touched the mare with his spurs. The men fell in behind him and they were gone. Doney stared down the empty lane. Milford gasped for breath.

He sputtered, "Get in the house!"

She did not move.

He roared, "Gape after him! You've seed the last of him! Dixon'll fill him so full of lead he'll be too heavy to tote to the graveyard. Serve him right! Saves me the shootin'!"

She jumped from the porch to the sand yard. Nothing could keep her from following wherever he had gone.

The sun was setting below the pine trees, but the sand road was still hot and harsh. It burned through the thin soles of Doney's shoes. The heels turned under her in the loose sand. If they had already shot Tom, they could kill her, too, and it would be better so. She had the feeling that he was alive, and if she begged Dixon, he would spare him. She began to run again. Shadows were long across the road, and through the twilight of the pine woods bats darted, and doves went, wings whistling, to their roosts. Small things scurried across the dry pine needles. The woods were alive with rustlings in preparation for the night, some creatures on their way to bed, others awakening from the day's sleep.

The sun set suddenly, and its going was followed by a grayness in the sky that might mean rain tomorrow. Why could not the drought have broken before this happened? She would at this instant be listening for the hoofs of the mare. In a few minutes Tom would have been on the porch and into the kitchen with his loping stride, lifting pot lids to see what she had cooked for supper, kissing the back of her neck if old Milford were not looking. The road became a crossroads. The broader one led to Dixon's lodge. She took a deep breath like a swimmer in the surf, and forced herself to run a little faster.

The high gates of the lodge were open. She had imagined a sentry posted there to stop her, and had thought of what she would say to him, to let her pass. There was no one in sight. She hesitated, then moved up the path. Oleanders were newly set out along its borders. The door of the lodge stood open. She almost wished for someone standing beside it, to prepare her, to break time in two. Then nothing existed but the need to know, to follow through this door where Tom perhaps had gone. She ran inside, across a dusky hall, and stumbled into a great room where voices sounded. Dixon stood at one side of the high fireplace, and Tom, living, thin and straight, at the other. He turned and looked at her, and there was not even Dixon to terrify her. There was only Tom. She threw herself against him.

He said to Dixon, "You'll have to excuse her."

He stroked her hair, then turned her by the shoulders. "Don't shame me, honey girl. Speak to Mr. Dixon."

She could not, but covered her face with her hands.

"This is my wife," Tom said. "She thinks a heap of me. I reckon she got worried."

Dixon said, "I can imagine. Well, it's settled then."

"Yes, sir. I can speak for the men, to say they'll be plumb grateful."

Dixon said, "I'd like to avoid bad blood in the community. I'm not going to prosecute your father for the damage he's done. Peace is worth more to me than the price of the cattle. What can I expect from him?"

Tom did not answer.

Dixon said, "I understand perfectly that this is a quarrel between the old and the new. But certainly even a man who's always been his own law, as you say of him, will mind his own business when he isn't bothered."

Tom said slowly, "I hate to say it, but you got a right to know. Pa's been mean all his life, but this is more'n meanness. He figures he's right. And he'll fight 'til he ain't got breath to fight with."

Dixon tapped the hearth with one toe.

"Well, I'll put the burden on him. The next overt act, I'll put him under a peace bond. Then his fight will be with modern law, not with me."

Tom was silent. Dixon held out his hand. Tom shook it and turned away. He linked his arm through Doney's and led her across the room, through the hall, and out of the house. The mare was at the side, cropping the soft green grass. Tom swung into the saddle and pulled Doney up behind him.

She reached for a corner of her skirt and dried her eyes. "I shouldn't of follered you," she said. "I know I shamed you. But seemed like I'd die if I didn't."

"Ne' mind now."

He turned the mare into the road.

"Honey," he said, "Dixon didn't have no idee we was blocked from water. He said if ary one had of come to him right off, nothin' need of happened. You know what he aims to do? He aims to sell us cattle people the south thousand of that land, at what he paid for it, and buy hisself another thousand to the north."

"What'll your pa say?"

"I ain't even studyin' on seein' him, to tell. I'm done."

"Ain't we goin' home now?"

"We can't never call it home again. We'll spend the night at Dibbles'. Tomorrow, Dixon's got a house for us. He's give me a job as woods rider. He's got jobs for ten. The men he carried down here with him ain't satisfied with the country. Millses'll take it, and Kelceys, and five-six more. He pays good wages."

She puzzled in silence.

"Ain't you pleased, Doney?"

"I got to get used to thinkin' about it," she apologized. "Seems like more'n I can think about, you workin' for a enemy."

He slowed the mare to a walk and turned his head.

"Well, honey, you better get it straight right now. Pa won't never change. We're in for it. The law don't mean no more to him than a last year's calf to a cow. I hate to go against my blood, but I got no choice. Dixon's a white man. We got a chancet to live independent and decent. Dixon's a friend. It's pa, now, is the enemy."

The world was upside down. Her mind was a loose bag full of unsorted patchwork pieces. Nothing hung together. She had tried to be a good daughter to old Milford. Her goodness had included, even, acceptance of him. Who would mend now the bursted seams in his shirts and trousers? Who would run to him with a cup of cold water when his whole obese mass gasped for breath? It would not be she, because he was become an enemy.

She said, "It's mighty hard to figure. Last week Dixon was the enemy, and now it's pa. Ain't none of you done a thing but what you thought was right."

He said grimly, "If you aim to figure thataway, just as good to say the drought was wrong. Things would likely have worked out peaceable, had rain come. Just as good to say the drought was the enemy."

Suddenly the truth stood stark and clear. Every man was at the

mercy of the winds of chance. The danger was so great that it frightened her that all men did not see it and stand together. Life was
the enemy.

She said, "Tom! I'm a-feered!"

He closed one hand over her fingers at his waist. "Why, sugar," he
said, "don't do me thataway. Don't you reckon I'll look out for you?"

What was one man, thin and young, against the huge menace of
living?

"Ain't you got your old Tom that loves you, and you love him?"

She caught her breath. She laughed against his bony back in her
relief. It was true. Her love was a lean, hard bulwark against the foe.

IN THE HEART

I TOOK the Negro directly from the chain gang. I do not believe it was that fact, however, that filled my colored man and woman, Joe and Etta, with the same unreasoning fear that a dog shows in the presence of an unidentified danger. I think it was the sheer look of the man. I have never seen a bigger black, nor an uglier one. I myself was startled when I saw him at the pump stand and heard his deep rumble, requesting water.

I remember that Joe, close behind him, and Etta and I on the back porch, all stared in hypnosis at his bulk; at his head like a square block of creosote; his winglike ears, cut straight across, ending in points; at his arms, hanging loose like a pair of cottonmouth moccasins; and finally, jointed to the arms, as though they had a unique life of their own, a pair of paws like a gorilla's—huge, sinewy, not quite believable.

I said to Etta, "Give him a cup."

We watched him pump. The heavy handle lifted and fell like a twig in his hand. He drank again and again. He was wet with sweat from long walking. He wiped his jowls on his sleeve. I heard him grunt. Something had attracted his apelike attention. He shuffled with a peculiar directness to my garden and leaned his arms on the five-foot fence.

He said, "This ain't no kind of a garden."

Joe looked at me uncertainly, as though for my order to the intruder to move on. A moment's perversity made me withhold it. Joe's distaste for garden work, his stubborn neglect of my flowers and vegetables, had long been a sore point between us.

I said, solely for the effect on Joe, "My man doesn't know anything about garden work."

The strange black gripped the fence and turned his face toward me. It had the intensity of a gargoyle.

He said, "I got to get me a piece o' work. I'm fresh off the gang. Leave me make you a garden."

Joe said furiously, "Nigger, get goin'."

His presumption precipitated a decision I should not otherwise have made. I saw the situation as made to order for shaming him into future attention to my garden plot.

The stranger said, "I kin make a garden. I got the livin' hand."

I said, "Good. You can get to work right away. The hoe and the hand plow are in the first room in the barn. The fertilizer is under the shed."

He ambled toward the barn. Joe threw out his arms.

"Missy, 'fore God, you hirin' us trouble. Livin' hand! You look at them hands? I'se seed that kind before. He got the killin' hand."

I was as angry as he. My anger, I know now, was not for his challenge to my judgment and my authority, but a cover for my own uneasiness before the fear in the eyes of the black man and woman who looked, with the prescience of their race, into a terrible unseen.

I said, "Get back to your grove work." I called after the newcomer, "What's your name?"

"Calls me Black Bat," he said.

I had no intention of keeping Bat more than two or three days, to make my point and serve my disciplinary purpose. But when I saw my garden rouse, and breathe, and come to green, new life, I weakened. The rows were straight and clean. As though blessing his labor, the first rain in weeks followed his weeding and fertilizing. The feathered tops of the young carrots stood up with vigor. The spindling broccoli stretched and spread out sturdy arms.

In the section of the garden that I kept for my flowers, the change was even more miraculous. Rosebushes that had been lank and famished were in a few days ruddy with the new growth that presaged bloom. Bat asked for seedling plants. I bought snapdragon and stock, larkspur and schizanthus, all the fragile flowers I had longed for. He set them out, and they seemed never to have known another home than the soil of my garden. I could not endure the thought of their drooping and finally dying, like their neglected predecessors, and Bat stayed on.

Joe and Etta were sullen. They looked at me with the unhappiness of dogs that have been whipped unjustly. I kept my own uncertainty stubbornly to myself. They had nothing to do with the intruder. They kept the door of the tenant house shut at night against him. By day, Etta wore the key of her house pinned on the front of her uniform. Bat slept in the barn. He came to the back door for his plates of food which Etta handed him with a darting gesture, stepping away from him quickly, as though she fed a thing that would slash before she could avoid it.

I left the three of them alone on the place together over a week end. As I drove away, Joe and Etta watched after my car with a look of helpless betrayal. I felt a moment's temptation to relieve them, to take Bat to the quarters in the neighboring village while I should be gone. But it seemed to me that it would be an admission of error to acknowledge their fear.

The sheriff called me long distance on Sunday afternoon at an East Coast café. My man, Joe Wilkins, he shouted over the buzzing wire, had shot another Negro.

"It was a big buck he called Bat," the sheriff said. "I'd've shot a nigger looked like that one, myself. It looks like a clean case of self-defense. I figured you wouldn't want your help locked up, so I didn't bother Joe. You can go bond for him when you get back."

I heard his breathing, waiting for my thanks for the courtesy often extended landowners in our section, whereby the local law puts the seignorial rights over Negro workers ahead of such meaningless abstractions as justice.

I said, "Thanks so much. I'll see you tomorrow. The other man— Bat. Is he dead?"

"No, Ma'am. He's in the hospital. A few shots in his ribs. Them big hands caught most of the load."

I went back, half sick and guilty, to the festive clatter of the café.

There are times when one's confusion as to right and wrong seems to run in a desperate and unbreakable circle. On my return to my grove, I was torn between the feeling that Joe had perhaps acted precipitously, shooting out of panic rather than necessity, and his own quiet statement that Bat had "come at him."

"With them big hands," he said. "I done tol' you he had the killin' hand. Sheriff say I done right."

Again I could only say, "Get on with your grove work."

But I could not set aside a feeling of responsibility to Bat himself. I went to the hospital to see him; to make arrangements for his care and for the rudiments of comfort that it seemed to me I owed him in payment of my own obstinacy.

It was impossible for me to read the expression on the grotesque mask that was his face. It grimaced, with what feeling I could not tell. His huge hands were bandaged. In their wrappings they were as big as hams. A few inches of fingers protruded from the gauze, and these he was manipulating. He pulled each finger in turn, crooked it, then massaged it with a circular motion.

"Doc say maybe I ain't goin' to get to use these no more. Doc wrong." He dropped one finger after the other, like a practicing piano player. "I got use for these hands," he said. "I got somethin' I'm fixin' to do."

I hurried from the room. I drove home in a chill numbness, study-ing my way out of the maze of danger I had so carelessly established. Joe was right— By the time I turned up the drive to my house, I had thought myself clear. I had been the medium of damage, above all to my own people's trust in me. There need be no final, cataclysmic harm. Two weeks for Bat's recovery, the hospital said. Within the week, I would pay the bill and send him money to go away. I would ask the sheriff to see him definitely on the train.

I said to Joe, "The grove is looking fine," and he understood my assurance and my apology.

I shall never recall the morning that Black Bat reached my place without a moment of the old shaken feeling. I walked out into the grove and there he stood. I think I have never felt so terrifying a sense of my fallibility. He stood as still as the trunks of the orange trees.

Then Joe walked casually from behind the powerhouse. He looked at me, and turned to where I stared. Black Bat moved toward us. He lifted his hands. The nightmare was complete.

I would not live those moments of paralysis over again for an added year of life. Joe moved a step closer to me, as though there might be a brief respite under the shelter of my white authority. Bat turned the palms of his hands upward. Their grayness was scarred with livid, half-healed wounds.

"I still got my hands," he said.

I think Joe screamed. I'm not sure.

"Keep them hands off me— Don't touch me— Don't— "

Bat sighed. The sound came from his deep chest like wind in the grove.

"You puts me low in my mind," he said. He made a hopeless gesture toward me. "All my life things has been this-a-way. I ain't never harmed nobody. Everybody feered of me. All my life. Niggers misentrustin'. White folks shuttin' me up. Cain't git me no friend, cain't git me no wife, cain't git me no chillun. Folks jest looks at me, never asks what I got in my heart."

He threw back his head.

"Please lemme git to my garden. I been frettin'. Layin' up in the bed. 'Got to git my hands right,' I says. 'All them little young things in that garden hongry for Black Bat's hands.' "

He walked past us and pushed open the garden gate. He dropped to his knees beside the seedling marigolds. His fingers felt among them.

"Wind and rain got you beat down," he grumbled. "How they 'spect you to grow up, dirt and weeds 'round yo' necks? Lemme turn you loose—"

I stared at his hands. They were the hands of a black father, cradling the helpless children of the earth.

JESSAMINE SPRINGS

THE Reverend Thomas J. Pressiker watched the road signs abstractedly. He was lonely. His loneliness puzzled and disturbed him. God was enough for any man. God's Son was enough. He was a trifle confused in his loyalty since the night the old lady at the revival meeting had arisen and demanded to know, "If God is All, why do we have to go around worshipping two of them?"

His talk to the Kiwanis Club in Elvinsport had been a great success. He had talked on "God Is My Buddy," and the Kiwanians had understood and had slapped him afterward on his back. Yet, after they had slapped, they had turned away and formed into small, tight groups and had told stories that had evidently little to do with divinity or buddying. Their hoarse laughter was a wall shutting him off from contact with his fellow-man. He liked to laugh. When he was a little boy he had had his first taste of public acclaim, telling funny stories. Of course, they were good, clean stories, which those of the Kiwanians probably were not. Yet for all he knew, these Kiwanians' stories were as innocuous as those he had recited for public acclaim in his childhood. He had never heard one of them. Only the laughter afterward.

It seemed to him sometimes that men actually did not like him. Yet they were cordial, they were gracious, they frequently gave "a good, hot cheer for the Reverend" when he addressed them. And he liked them. He liked everybody. He had begun his storytelling, he had gone into the ministry, because he liked people and wanted them, terribly, to like him. Yet today, on this hot Florida afternoon, driving his Ford from Elvinsport to Kenoha, where he would speak again on "God Is My Buddy," he sat not only behind the wheel of the car but behind a barricade. On the one side were the Kiwanians, cheering him with a sound that seemed to come from a great distance, and then going off into space to talk and laugh together. On the other side was the Reverend Pressiker, lonely, loving, and wanting to belong.

He wondered often whether the gap might not be because he was an itinerant preacher. If he had his own church, his own regular congregation, he would have a home—an earthly home, a cozy counterpart of the heavenly one, where the good and kind all gathered. His denomination was famously poor. In the small Florida villages where he filled in for the more fortunate circuit preachers, they had preaching Sunday only once or twice a month, and then had to scramble to get together a collection that would not shame them to offer and him to receive. The poverty was nothing. His text was very likely to be "Inasmuch as ye have done it unto one of the least of these my children," and he had in mind, as he preached, their poverty and their leastness. Yet even among the simple backwoods folk, with their bare, freshly washed, lifted faces, he was an alien. They shook hands with him stiffly and hurried home to their noon dinners—chicken on Sundays, unless it was hog-killing time and a fat peanut ham was on the table. He was always invited to go home to dinner with one of them, and usually he accepted. Occasionally he had to refuse after he had seen a group arguing together. He knew then that he was not wanted and that the invitation came from the unhappy combination of courtesy and pressure.

His weekday talks, he assured himself, were actually in a larger field. He put aside the thought, the knowledge, that the small-town Rotarians and Kiwanians had a time of it getting speakers for nothing. He was glad to serve. He told himself every night and every morning, kneeling by whatever hard bed was his for the moment, that he was glad to serve. All men were brothers, and as his kin listened and applauded and slapped and then went away and talked of other matters, he reminded himself that he was doing the best he could.

"Jessamine Springs. Where the County Swims."

He liked the sign and its consciousness of county. He liked the consciousness of all group formations. That was why his heart warmed and beat fast when he arose to speak in places like Elvinsport and Kenoha. He was part of a group. He belonged.

"Jessamine Springs. One Mile to the Left."

He had not had a swim since the Missionary Auxiliary at Luther had had a fish fry several years ago. He had borrowed a bathing suit and had gone in the muddy pond with the rest of them. He had said, splashing about in the warm, shallow water, "We should have a community baptizing in this fine pool." He had wondered then if he looked ridiculous in the borrowed suit, for even there, as he paddled around among them, the other swimmers had ignored him.

"Here You Are. Jessamine Springs. Everybody Welcome. 10c."

He liked that "Everybody Welcome. 10c." It was the kind of sign he would put up if he owned a swimming pool. Why, even he could go in there and swim, and nobody would know that he was any different from anyone else. His heart thumped.

A line of cars was coming out of the Springs entrance onto the highway. It was almost sunset. He turned left toward the cement-lined pool. It was fed by underground springs, and the overflow trailed off into a narrow run. There was a shed at one side. Suits could be rented. A man ahead of him was paying the dime admission fee, and another dime for the suit and towel.

The Reverend Pressiker said, "The suits are—quite sanitary, I suppose?"

"They go to the laundry," the proprietor said. "Boiled."

Pressiker pushed his change across the counter and followed his fellow-swimmer into the bathhouse marked "Men." He heard his neighbor taking off his shoes and hanging up his trousers. It was a good sound, another human's clothes being hung on the other side of the thin wall. He undressed hurriedly and arranged his own garments on the rusty nails. The cement walk seemed harsh under the soft soles of his feet. He reached the pool in time to see the man ahead of him dive from the edge. Except for the two of them, the pool was empty. He was slightly disappointed.

He had never dived, and he walked, one foot cautiously ahead of the other, down the steps into the shallow end of the pool. He splashed the water, surprisingly cold, across his chest and stomach. He stooped and gave himself to the water, spreading himself out across its receptive surface. He fluttered his legs and then stood up. The shock of the cold water was delightful. He looked about for his companion. He was swimming toward him with a lazy side stroke. The Reverend Pressiker swam to meet him. They stood up at the same moment.

The other man said, "Jeez, it's cold."

Pressiker said, "A cooling fount, indeed."

The man shook his hair back from his face. "I been meaning to stop and swim here. This is on my route."

Pressiker was delighted. He said, "And on mine also."

"You on the road?"

Pressiker was often asked this question. His businesslike briefcase and civilian clothes made him appear a travelling salesman, and it pleased him to think of himself as a travelling salesman for the Lord. Usually he said, "I am on the road on the Lord's business." Now, with his longing for simple community, he said, "Indeed, yes. On the road. On the broad highway."

"Books?"

"In a way. One book. Only one."

"Kind of limited, eh? But they say this is the age of specialization."

The man dived under the water and came up some feet away, then struck out for the deep end of the pool. The Reverend Pressiker followed, swimming with a careful breast stroke. He was a little panicky as he advanced, and headed in toward the side railing. The other man turned at the deep end and swam back and joined him.

Pressiker said, "I saw many cars departing as I entered. A multitude."

"That's why I turned in—because they were leaving. I'm not so keen about swimming with a couple of dozen Boy Scouts."

"Ah, yes. The little—" he hesitated. Ordinarily he would have said, "The little ones." He said, "The little shavers."

The man said, "When I swim, I like to swim. Want to race?"

"Thank you. That's good of you. I'm afraid I might falter in a— no, not foot race. It isn't a foot race, is it? I have done very little of an athletic nature in a long, arduous life given to the—I have swum very little. I use the breast stroke. I think it develops the physique, don't you?"

"I don't know about the physique, but it's damn slow."

The man stroked away, hand over hand. Pressiker watched him, then floated into the water. He counted aloud.

"One, two, kick. One, two, kick."

"You sure haven't done much of this." The man was resting his back against the far edge of the pool.

"Indeed, no. My—my work takes my—my all."

The man submerged like a porpoise, swam the length of the pool and back again, and came up blowing.

"Headed for Kenoha?"

"Yes. Yes, Kenoha."

"Where you stopping?"

"I don't know. I have not, you might say, where to lay my head. I hope to rest with friends."

"Lucky. I got an expense account, but it don't pay for beer."

Pressiker lowered himself in the water, bounced up, and lowered himself again. He was tremendously happy. He was immersed not in water but in a fluid fellowship.

"Look not on the wine when it is red," he said gaily, "but nothing is said about beer!"

He felt devilish and free. He thought of asking the man to have a beer with him in Kenoha.

"Well, I've had enough exercise for a guy that doesn't get much," said the other man. He swung himself over the edge of the pool and shook himself like a dog. "Be seeing you, Reverend," he said.

"Be seeing you." Pressiker waved a wet arm after his friend.

The man sloshed into the bathhouse. Pressiker stood up in the shallow water and stared after him.

"Now, how could he possibly know I was a preacher?"

He hitched up the straps of the rented bathing suit and looked about the empty pool. His throat tightened as it had done when he was a little boy, trying not to cry.

THE PROVIDER

THE Georgia land bordering the railroad tracks was rich and poor by turns. North of Masonville, No. 9 roared through waist-high cotton. White puffs of engine smoke drifted over the fields. Big Joe leaned on his fireman's shovel and looked behind him out of the cab window.

He said, "Looks like the smoke catches in them cotton bushes and makes the bolls."

The engineer slacked speed to take a curve. The soil changed abruptly. It turned with the roadbed from tawny loam to a parched red clay. A rise to the right was fissured with gullies. Pines grew sparsely. The banks along the tracks were dense with honeysuckle which asked, not richness, but only a foothold. Here and there a bank was bare, as though a poor proud soil rejected the charity of the honeysuckle. Beyond the curve a straightaway cut through pine forest. No. 9 gathered its speed for the run to Atlanta. The pines broke and a clearing showed. There was a cabin in the center of the clearing. The yard was naked and on the baked clay two children, a boy and a girl, leaned their heads together over a circle that was a game.

Big Joe said, "I be dogged how them people makes a living."

Bill said, "You keep my pressure up or you'll be figuring on a new job to try to make you a living."

Joe bent to the coal. His long arms swung like the pistons of the

326

engine. The boiler flames flared. Sweat coated his muscles. He rolled two cigarettes and handed one to the engineer.

He said, "Don't look to me like them kids goes to school. In Jacksonville the kids is all in school again. It's near about November."

"It's a wonder to me you ain't got a family. You watch kids the way I watch the barman drawing beer."

"I never seemed to think about it when Ma was living. A guy lives with his Ma, and her all he's got, and he don't think about a family."

"But a guy thinks about women, and women mean kids. That's the way I got to be a family man."

Big Joe's face turned as red as his chest.

"Women purely scares the chitlings outen me."

Winter lay over Georgia. No. 9 hummed north into frost. The cotton plantation beyond Masonville was as bleak as though the big house within sight of the tracks had not had a sea of white bolls to pick, to send them to the gin and take its profit. The fissures in the red clay around the curve were silvered with ice. The train throbbed toward the clearing.

Joe said, "Them kids ain't in school. There they be."

He leaned from the cab window and threw a lump of coal at them and waved his hand. He looked back. The boy jumped to the piece of coal and pounced on it. He held it in small hands and ran into the cabin.

Joe said, "I bet them kids is cold. They ain't no smoke coming outen the chimney."

"Never you mind them kids. We're running late and if I don't get smoke you and me will catch it in Atlanta."

"Cold don't bother me. Nor heat, neither. But kids is little. They got to keep warm."

"You and your kids. You get you a houseful, like me, and you'll find out all they got to have is a licking now and again."

"I wouldn't lick no kid. Kids is little."

Joe watched anxiously for the clearing. December had come in with an icy venom. On his last run the boy and girl had not been in sight. He could picture them under the bed covers or huddled close to the hearth inside the cabin. He had pitched a whole shovelful of coal toward the yard. He had not gauged well and when he had looked back he could see the coal scattered along the bank. But children ran all over, like squirrels, and they would surely have found it. The speed of the train seemed like a knife, cutting one place sharply from another. It sliced into the pines and the clearing flashed, bare and open. The sun lay in bars across the cabin.

The boy and girl were in the yard. His heart jumped. The boy flapped his thin arms and the girl waved one hand, high over her head. Joe had his shovelful of coal ready, but he was afraid to pitch it where they stood. He waited a moment and heaved it. It scattered among the trees north of the clearing. He leaned far out to wave and point. The children were scrambling along the bank toward the coal. Before he could tell whether they had waved again, they were gone, merged with the line of pines behind him.

He said excitedly, "Them kids was waiting for me. They was waiting."

Bill said, "You just as good to get some young uns. You just as good to get hitched to your woman."

"I told you, I got no woman. I wouldn't know what to say to a woman. They look at me and I ain't got a word to say."

Joe sat on the edge of his cot in the railroad boarding house. The unshaded bulb of the ceiling light made a poor light on the mail-order catalogue. He shifted it, trying to see the sizes under the description of the child's dress. The dress came in taffeta, in rose, blue or yellow. If his mother were still alive, she would be able to tell the ages of the boy and girl from his description.

He turned to the boy's section of the catalogue. He tried to remember how old he had been when he was the size of the boy in the clearing. It was hard to tell the height of either of the children, for they stood small against the cabin and under the pine trees and were out of sight almost as soon as he had seen them and waved to them and they had waved back at him. He could tell only that the lumps of coal looked very large in their hands.

He marked items in the catalogue and laid it beside his clothes for the next day's run.

Bill swung into the engine cab. He grunted when he looked at the pressure.

"What's the rush? You won't get back any quicker."

He pulled on his gloves and looked at his watch. He hung out of the cab window and talked with the brakeman. Joe looked at his watch. The signal was due and they could just as well get going. Bill lifted his hand and No. 9 puffed and slid slowly backward out of the terminal.

Joe said, "I want you should look at something in the catalogue when we get out a ways."

He waited impatiently. Past the switch he brought out the catalogue.

"Christmas is about due," he said, "and I figured I'd order me some things for them kids at the clearing, where I been chunking coal. They ain't got no daddy to look out for them and I figured they wouldn't be looking for no Christmas."

"I reckon you'll be spending Christmas with them. I suppose when we go through here Christmas Day you'll just jump off the train."

"I can't figure the sizes. You got kids and I figured you could help me tell the sizes."

"Hold the catalogue where I can see the pictures."

"I don't know whether I should get the taffeta—that's a kind of silk, ain't it? A kid likes things that ain't too useful. I remember, somebody give me a comb and brush once, and I wanted a train of cars. I figured on a train of cars for the boy and a silk dress for the girl."

"How you aim to pitch a train of cars out the cab? It'd bust to bits."

"That's right. A cowboy suit, maybe now. Kids like to play Indians."

"What their folks going to think when silk dresses and cowboy suits come flying out of the air? They're going to think there's something funny about it. They've got a ma or somebody and they ain't going to like it."

"Like I figured they was poor? Poor folks is proud, I know. Maybe I better just go on pitching out the coal and they'll figure that's an accident."

"The company hears of it and there'll be an accident."

Joe sat with the catalogue on his knees. He couldn't make up his mind about the presents. When he passed the clearing a woman was with the boy and girl in the yard. She was young and looked not much bigger than the children. She was too young and small to be tormented and worried with having to look out for a family. He was afraid to pitch out the coal. She wouldn't know what to make of it. Maybe Bill was right. She might not like having a stranger throw things out to them. But it did not seem to him that he was a stranger.

He knew the kids and they knew him. They watched for him and waited for him and jumped up and down and waved to him.

He stoked the fire and rolled a cigarette and thought about the children's mother. She looked the way their mother ought to look. He would not even be afraid of a woman who looked like that, small and frail with no one to take care of her. She must be a widow. They must be hard put to it, for many a day there was no smoke coming out of the chimney. Maybe she just let the fire die down in the afternoon and saved the coal he pitched out to cook supper. That was a good thought. It warmed him to think she saved the coal he threw to them to cook their supper. Probably she was a good cook. The children were thin but they looked healthy. They played hard, because sometimes he saw them running around in a game like tag. If they belonged to him he would teach them mumbledepeg and duck on the rock. If they were his, he would play with them in the late afternoon and then they would all three go into the cabin and the woman would have supper ready. They would all sit together after supper and the kids would sit on his lap and the woman would wash the dishes in the lamplight.

Bill bellowed, "Joe, give me steam!"

He jumped to the coal and shoveled furiously. He was in a sweat when he sat down. It gave a man the jerks to be snatched away from lamplight and supper dishes that quickly. At the end of the run he carried the catalogue with him to his room and sat late.

On Christmas morning he was uneasy. At the last moment he had almost bought things from the long list. But there was plenty of time, and it would be better to get the woman used to him. He had seen her several times and he felt that he knew her almost as well as he knew the kids, but she had never waved to him. He packed candy in a shoebox and around it a knife and ball for the boy, a soft calico doll for the girl and, in a separate box, three handkerchiefs for the woman. On the box he wrote, "For the Lady." No one could think he was acting as if they were poor with a box like that. He wrapped the shoebox in several layers of newspaper, to cushion it when it should fall on the hard clay of the clearing.

Bill was grumpy and took his train out with a jerk. Joe wondered if his wife and kids had not been satisfied with their Christmas. If he had his own family he would give them exactly what they wanted, once a year at least. It didn't hurt anybody to have the things they longed for once in a while. He was torn between regret that he had not bought the things he had planned for the woman and the children in the clearing, and relief that he had not done something they might not understand. Both men were silent past Masonville. It occurred to him that he could have a shovelful of coal ready as usual, with the shoebox on top of it. That way they would find the box when they picked up the coal.

His heart thumped. The clearing always came too quickly. As the light broke through the pines, he saw that a man was sitting on the stoop of the cabin. He wondered for an instant if he had been watching so eagerly that he had mistaken the place. But the children were on the stoop too, and the woman. The woman had her hand on the man's shoulder. He was so confused that he could not lift his shovel. No. 9 roared past the clearing.

It seemed to Joe that something inside him was going three ways at once. What was a man doing on the stoop of the cabin and the woman's hand on his shoulder? But it could be her brother. That was it. Her brother had come from a long ways to be with his sister and her children at Christmas. He probably had a family of his own and couldn't do much to help them, but he had come to be with them at Christmas. Joe wiped the sweat from his chest. He shouldn't have been upset about the man. No matter who the man was, he should have thrown out the box for the kids' Christmas.

He could throw out the box some other time. It would seem even better to the kids to have it come when Christmas was over. In his room at the end of the run he went through the catalogue again.

On his next run the man was still there. He sat this day in a rocking chair on the small porch with the afternoon sun on him. He was wrapped in a quilt. In the brief sight Joe had of him, he seemed to have his head leaned backward as though he were ill. Joe had his shovelful of coal with the box on top, poised and ready, but he dared not throw it. The man could be the father. He was resentful. The kids were entitled to things. Children couldn't go without things just because a man was a no-account. They seemed more ragged every time he saw them. He thought the girl was looking a little peaked. Probably the man was too sorry to keep a job and they were actually hungry.

He was obliged to decide that the man was the father. It made him angry to acknowledge it. Yet his concern for the children was even greater, as though the man were an intruder, standing in the way of their proper care. On every run when it was fair and sunny the father sat wrapped up on the porch. On rainy days he was not to be seen, though even then the children sometimes were playing on the porch. Joe looked forward to the rainy days, for he had more time then to watch for the children and throw out the coal and wave to them. When the man was there it wasted a part of the flash of the train's passing to look at him. He bought cookies twice to throw out to them, but both times the man was there and he did not throw them. He and Bill ate the cookies. They seemed drier to him and less tasty than when he had eaten the same kind with his mother's cocoa. Nothing that he ate seemed to taste as good as when his mother was alive. Home cooking was the trick. He was sure that the children's mother was a fine cook. A woman as trim and clean as she was bound to be a cook. All she needed was a good provider to bring home the food.

In March the man appeared only two or three times. Once Joe saw the woman and children helping him out of his chair to lead him into the cabin. He was stooped over and seemed to have no strength at all. It would be all right if he had made provision for his family. Joe thought that if he had kids he would carry all kinds of insurance.

He had carried insurance for his mother, but then it had turned out he didn't need to.

On his first run in April he knew almost before he reached the clearing that something was wrong. He had a lemon coconut cake that he intended to throw out if the man was not there, but it was not the cake that made him feel strange as No. 9 slashed through the pines. Thinking it over afterward, he thought that perhaps he had caught a glimpse of the car in the clearing. The train swept by. The car was a hearse. A wreath of dark leaves hung on the closed door of the cabin. He did not even throw out the coal. He sat down on his bench. He was dizzy. It could only be the father. Neither of the kids could be dead, nor the woman.

On his next run, both the boy and the girl were in the yard. A wave of relief swept over him so that he wanted to shout. Then he found that he settled down again to anxiety. If the mother was dead and not the father, it would be worse than before.

On the second Thursday in April the woman was in the yard. He leaned out of the cab window and shouted and waved his arm violently. She did not see him but it did not matter. They were all alive. He whistled all the way to Atlanta. In the yards a boy handed him a message. He was wanted in the superintendent's office the next morning.

He said to Bill, "Bet they give me a raise. I'm due."

Bill looked at him.

"You wouldn't listen to me about that coal," he said.

The superintendent said, "I'm sorry, Joe. This is the only complaint we've ever had against you. I wouldn't fire you if I had my way."

Big Joe was neat for the interview, as his mother had taught him. His thick tawny hair was slicked back. His big hands hung down under a clean white shirt and the hands were scrubbed so that they were red. His blue eyes looked directly into the eyes of the man who was doing this to him, like the honest eyes of a dog, punished unjustly.

Joe said, "I never figured on the cost of the coal to the railroad. I'll pay for it. I got money saved."

"It's too late, Joe. The order came through when we found you were short three quarters of a ton. We asked Bill about it. He had to tell. Joe, I just wondered. That family you've been throwing out the coal to. I just wondered. Are they your own people?"

Joe stared at him. He lifted his eyes from the superintendent's face. They looked off down the far tracks through the pines and rested on the clearing. He saw the woman come down the steps of the cabin and go to the children in the yard. Excitement seized him. The whole thing was suddenly clear.

"Why, yes," he said. He drew a deep breath. "Why, yes. They was my own people. I was looking out for them."

Joe closed the mail order catalogue on his knees. He turned out the light and got into bed. He chuckled. It was strange that it hadn't occurred to him right away not to mind being fired. It made everything simpler. A fireman's job was no good for a family man anyway. How could he have gone on looking out for his folks, living the way a fireman had to live, in one town one night and in another the next? And his home right in between the two terminals. Just giving a woman your money and buying things for children wasn't enough. A man had to be right with them, to get the kids to a doctor if they were sick, to cook supper and wash the dishes if a woman was tired. Being fired fixed everything. He had often thought he would make a good farmer. His father had been a farmer and even as a boy he hadn't minded the chores. He shifted his pillow and drifted off into a pleasant half-sleep in which the furniture in the catalogue arranged itself around a cabin room. The first thing to do was get new furniture for the cabin.

When he awoke he was out of bed at once. He had to move fast. There might not be a thing to eat in the cabin kitchen. He packed his clothes in his cardboard suitcase. There were a few left over and he made a bundle of them. He made sure he had his bankbook and the money he had drawn in his pocket. He called the landlady and paid his rent. He hurried out of the boarding house and across the tracks. He thought of asking Bill for a ride in the engine cab but somehow he didn't want Bill to know his business. He bought a ticket to Masonville in the day coach and went in and sat down on the plush seat. When the train jerked and subsided and jerked again, his throat tightened so that he could not swallow. He could scarcely see the familiar signal tower as No. 9 pulled out.

Masonville had always seemed to come very quickly after the three o'clock stop at the water tower. He fretted when they were delayed at the switch. When the conductor called, "Masonville, next stop," he was half blind and stumbled to the door. He swung off the train at the depot before it quite stopped, pushing past the conductor. He hesitated a moment, deciding between cutting to the east out of the village and then north, or following the tracks. He could not tell how far the clearing lay from Masonville. The next train came along in two hours. He might have trouble getting off a trestle or a bridge in time, but the tracks were the most direct. He fell in behind the blown cinders of No. 9 and set out.

The clearing was farther north than he had realized. His knees ached from the unaccustomed walking. He shifted his suitcase from one hand to the other. He reached a cotton field that he remembered. A hedge of sassafras lay beyond it. He pushed through it and the clearing was in front of him. The hard clay yard was there, familiar yet now somehow strange, the cabin, the steps where he had first seen the woman with the children, the porch above on which the man had sat in his quilts and from which he had gone inside the house to die.

Joe set down the suitcase and pushed back his hat to wipe his forehead. A panic came over him, so that it seemed he was caught in a whirlpool and could move neither back nor forward. This was the place. Now that his feet were on the yard, it was unexpected to be truly here. What should he say? Their names—he did not know their names. His pulse pounded and he heard a roaring in his ears. But a spring that had been tightly wound in him was not yet unwound and he picked up his suitcase and was compelled forward to the cabin door.

The door was shut. His knocking made an echo inside the cabin. He knocked again, then shook the door and it rattled to his shaking. He called, "Is anybody here?" and there was no answer. He tried the front window and it lifted. He stepped inside. The cabin was dusky. It was filled with the litter of departure. The front room had dust over the floor and a broken chair in one corner. He went into the kitchen. A rusty pot was on the sagging wood stove. A pile of papers lay on a rough table. Old envelopes were strewn near the stove. He took one in his hands. He went to the small window and held it to the light. "Mrs. Vangie Watters." Her name was Vangie. He looked around. They were gone. Vangie—Vangie and the kids were gone. He tried the front door from the inside and it opened. He went outside and sat down on the stoop. People couldn't just go off this way.

He looked around the yard. This was where the kids had played. It was poor playing because they had had no one to teach them better. A slow angry burning filled him. He felt a resentment that he had not felt when the superintendent fired him. He was betrayed. They should not have gone. Vangie should not have picked up like this and gone away. He heard a whistle from the south. He sat up, listening. He heard the distant throbbing that was the power of a limited train. He heard the clunk, clunk that was wheels on rails. A roaring filled the clearing and the crack express shot through.

He was bewildered by the speed of its passing. It seemed to him that he had no more than heard the whistle when the train was gone so fast that anyone watching from a cabin's steps, as he watched now, could recognize nothing except the train's passing and a flash of its various units. Why, when he had been fireman on No. 9, he must have gone by as rapidly, as unrecognizably, as the fireman on the express. Standing in the clearing, as Vangie and the kids had done, No. 9 must have gone by like a flash of lightning. Coal thrown from the cab must have showered down as from a swift-moving cloud. No one standing here, no one sitting on the steps, could have had more than a glimpse of a shovel out of a cab window, scattering its gift of heat for the stove. He must have passed like a dark bird flying.

He had had a Christmas box ready for them but he had not thrown it. He had had cookies from the bakery ready to toss out but he had not tossed them. He had picked out furniture from the catalogue with which to furnish the cabin, but they had not known. He had thought of them all day, and at night he had sat on the edge of his bed and thought of them, and in his sleep they had moved across his dreams and were a part of him. But how could they have known? His resentment left him. How could they have known that they belonged to him and that he would come to them?

A man's thoughts, a man's dreams—Why, they were thoughts and dreams, and there was a long bridge between them and the world of fact. He had never thought about other people, except his mother and the mythical folk of the movies. He wondered now if all men dreamed and found the pain of this bridge separating the dream from the reality. He turned over in his hands the envelope he had taken from near the stove. "Mrs. Vangie Watters." There was a return address. It was from a rural route in Alabama. The date was recent. It might be from her kinfolks in Alabama. He stood up. He picked up his suitcase and his bundle. The sun was setting across the railroad tracks and long shadows lay across the clay yard of the clearing. There was time to reach the nearest village, to inquire of the storekeeper and the postmaster.

Surely a man in his loneliness and his great need might cross that bridge. Surely he could find his own and come to them. He tucked the envelope carefully in his pocket and set out southward in the sunset.

THE SHELL

AFTER the message came, she spent most of the time on the beach picking up sea shells. Sometimes she made piles of all kinds. Sometimes she passed by the common shells and picked up only the rare ones. She waited for three days, as though the mere passage of time would make the message clear. Then she remembered that Bill had told her to get on the beach bus and go to the Red Cross in the city if she was in trouble. The message seemed to be trouble, so she walked from the cottage on the dune to the coastal highway and stood there with her hands folded over her purse, and a bus stopped for her, as Bill had said it would do. She was so young and so pretty that people on the bus smiled at her, and she smiled back, like a shy but amiable child. She got off the bus at the terminal. She stood still. The driver passed her on his way to the office and turned back.

He asked, "Where did you want to go?"

"I want to go to the Red Cross."

"It's right across the street. There."

Inside the office she stood in front of a desk while many people came and went and talked with a plain, capable woman. After a long time the woman said, without looking up, "Can I do something for you?"

"Please, can you tell me what it means when it says he is missing?"

The woman looked up in amazement. She hardened before the gentle face with china-blue eyes, loose blond hair, and an infuriating innocence.

She said, "Really now, just what do you think it means?"

"I think it means they don't know where he is. Not right now."

"Not right now?"

"No, not the same as lost. I thought maybe you'd know how long it will take them to find him, if it isn't the same as lost."

"Really! I can assure you it is the same as lost. It means he may possibly be found but that probably he won't."

"Probably he won't?"

"Almost certainly not. Is it someone close to you?"

"Oh, no. He's a long way away. He said it would be a long way."

"Is there anything we can do for you?"

"I don't know."

She returned to the bus station and stood until the same driver asked her if she wanted to go back to the beach. When she opened her purse to pay her fare, she saw Bill's picture and took it out. It was not the same as when she looked at him, himself, but it was tangible, and she held it in her lap as a child holds a doll. She remembered with pleasure that Bill had her picture, too, and had written her— she had had to ask the colored girl to explain only a few of the words—that he had showed it to the men on his ship and they had said she was very pretty. He knew that it pleased her to be told she was pretty, though she was without vanity, and she kept her silky hair brushed and her dainty body neat and clean as instinctively as a kitten washes its fur. She understood Bill's showing the picture, but she would not have understood what followed.

Even in the picture, the exquisite wistful face was entirely vacuous. One man had said maliciously, "Smart, too?"

Bill had eyed the questioner. "My wife," he had said gravely, "is a moron. She's a moron the way a wild rose is a moron."

The man, shocked, had said gruffly, "She got anybody to look out for her while you're over?"

"A colored girl I've had several years. She understands. She'll take care of her until I get back. We don't either of us have any family."

On the bus, forgetting to watch for her stop, she thought about the colored girl. The girl had left a week before the message came. She had cooked a great many things and filled the icebox and said, "I hates to fail you. I hates to fail him, when I promised. But I cain't live this lonesome life no more. It was all right, summers, when we had gas to go and he took me backards and fowards. Nobody cain't come to see me, I cain't git no place, excusin' goin' on the bus oncet a week marketin'. My boy friend he said he couldn't fool with me no more, didn't I git to town. He hadn't ought to of left you in this lonesome place."

He had left her in the cottage on the dune because she was happy at the seashore in the summer. The shells kept her occupied for hours at a time. And too, he would be on the ocean most of the time, he told her, and she might look at it and know that somewhere he was there. The rent on the cottage was paid, and the rent on the small apartment in the city for the winter, and the colored girl understood that they were to move to the city when the fall storms began.

She did not notice her stop, but the bus driver remembered, and when he stopped the bus and looked back at her she got off and walked up to the cottage. She felt hungry and went to the icebox. There did not seem to be very much left in it, and it occurred to her that she should have bought something while she was in the city. She had used most of her money, but there were two government checks in her purse. The colored girl had cashed the previous ones for her, since she found the bank confusing, although everyone was always kind and helpful. She ate some crackers and peanut butter and walked automatically down to the beach.

The tide was low and the sea calm. She wished she had put on her bathing suit, even though she understood that she was not to go out in the water any deeper than her knees. A fisherman had told the colored girl that the sharks were bad. They were seldom seen so far north on the coast, but the colored girl explained to her that the sinking of ships had disposed dead bodies of sailors through the water and the sharks had followed. One day she had found a pair of blue dungarees on the beach, the cuffs tied with string. She stared at them a long time, since she thought there was probably a dead sailor in them. On approaching closer she saw that they were empty.

Now she gathered a few shells idly and sat down on the sand and arranged them in a circular pattern. She tried to think. Bill had often urged her, "Try to think, honey. Try real hard." She asked herself what she should think about, and the answer came easily, "About Bill." She could remember a great deal, although it was spread in a diffused fog, with only the memory of his smile and his always being there standing clear. There had been perhaps a few years when she had not known him, but they were lost in the haze that veiled the same years when her mother and father were alive. She had been six years old when she went to live with her older sister. Long after she and Bill were married and the sister had moved somewhere across the country, she had heard Bill say, "I don't know whether she was born like that, or whether her sister did it to her. Her sister hated her because she was so pretty, and because she didn't want her, and she beat her as I wouldn't beat a dog. It seems to me you can hurt a child's mind that way. But I don't know."

She had known Bill was talking about her, but she had felt no special interest. The beatings had faded into the fog, too. But she remembered Bill in the first grade at school. She remembered standing in the center of a ring of children who were jostling her as animals jostle the unnatural or injured before they attack, and then Bill came into the ring and the animal-children melted away. After that, down the years, there was only Bill. He walked with her to and from school, carrying her books and her lunch basket. The lunch basket usually had cruelly little in it, and he shared his with her, sitting in the play yard beside her. When he found that she did not understand the lessons, and turned in blank copybooks for her homework, he wrote out her lessons. He was unable to protect her in the classroom, where she only smiled and shook her head when called on. He managed the homework cleverly, and in a different handwriting, so that only one of the teachers guessed the strange condition, the strange protection, the strange love, and her he bearded, telling her that what she took for stupidity was a great shyness, because of the beatings at home. The disparity between the homework and the class lessons puzzled the teachers, but they passed her from grade to grade until the eighth grade was done and she could read and write a little, and Bill could carry her no further. He went on to high school alone, working in the afternoons and late at night, saving his money. Although he was offered a scholarship, he would not go to college but took a job and married her, and all the years had been as sweet as a south wind blowing over wild roses.

There were not many shells on the beach, for the last high tide had been a gentle one and there was no debris, either from the sea or the lands beyond the sea. She walked a way and gathered a few angel's wings and a mossy conch. Then she saw the little shell, a shell for a doll house, minute, white, turned in lovely spirals. She picked it up and spoke to it, and saw that it was broken and imperfect. It was too small and fragile, now that it was empty, to have survived the buffeting of great forces. There were tiny holes along its infinitesimal length, where the roaring seas had pounded it against the implacable sands. She nestled it against her face and when it pricked her looked closely again and saw that the tip was sharp and pointed. It was a fine pencil to write with, and she sat down and in the sand began to draw loops and circles with delight. A memory touched her and she drew a heart, as Bill had taught her, and she put inside the heart their initials, as he had also showed her.

She laughed. She looked up with surprise when a ripple of water washed over the curve of the heart. The tide was coming in. The wind was from the east and against the sky the ocean heaved and formed breakers that rolled in from a long way away. That was where Bill was, she thought, a long way away, beyond the breakers. A paw of water slapped in and wiped out half the heart on the sand. Bill was lost, he was missing, and this was what it meant. He would almost certainly not come back, for the lady had said so. But certainly he could not be altogether lost; he was only out there against the horizon. He had told her to watch the sea, for he would be there. If no one was looking for him to find him, she might look for him. "Try to think, honey. Try real hard." Oh, she would try, and she would find him, for he had never been far away.

She stood up, clutching the shell, and waded into the cool water. He could not possibly be so far away that she could not find him.

The tide surged about her waist and above her small breasts. A wave washed over her face. The undertow lifted her feet and there was under her no more the earth but a fluid force of great power, swaying her like seaweed. A smooth body brushed past her, nudging her with a hard nose, and then another. She opened her hand and the little empty shell dropped from it and spiralled down through the water, to reach the sand and be thrown by the tide on the beach again, still further to be broken. The shell was worthless, and had been even when there was life within it. But it was a pretty little thing and it was a pity that it should be quite destroyed.

BLACK SECRET

THE shutters were drawn in the parlor against the afternoon sun. June lay heavy on the street outside, but the room was dark and cool. Hummingbirds droned in the honeysuckle over the window. The fragrance filtered through the shutters. Dickie flattened his face against the rose-patterned Brussels carpet. It was pleasantly harsh and faintly dusty. He moved his cheek to the smoothness of his picture book. The page was smooth and slippery. He lay comfortably, imagining that the painted lion under him was alive and his friend. He shook his loose, tucked blouse and pretended that the lion was breathing against him. He wished that it was night, when the new gas lights would flare from their brass pipes on the wall, for their yellow flickering made the lion's eyes move and shine. He lifted his head. The double doors of the parlor were sliding open. He heard his mother speak.

"The garden party was lovely, Mrs. Tipton. But aren't you exhausted?"

Dickie thinned himself to a shadow. If he were quiet, they might let him stay while they talked. There was an excitement in his mother's talk in this room with Mrs. Tipton that he heard no other place and with no other person. The women came into the parlor and Mammy Dee closed the folding doors after them. His mother saw him. She had on her flowered organdie with the ruffled flounces. They touched his ankle as she rustled past him.

344

She said, "Speak to Mrs. Tipton, Dickie."

He scrambled to his feet and jerked his head and put out his hand.

Mrs. Tipton said, "Precious. And how is Master Merrill today?"

"I'm reading my book," he said.

She said, "Precious."

He flopped down hurriedly on the rug and began turning the pages of the book. He sank himself in it, hopefully.

His mother said, "Straight chairs are more comfortable when it's warm, aren't they? Take this one. . . . Oh, the party was beautiful!"

The room was an empty box waiting to be filled.

"Thank you."

His mother said, "I see you had Lulu Wilson again to help."

His heart beat rapidly. They were beginning. They would forget him.

Mrs. Tipton said, "She's marvellous help for that sort of thing. Of course, no one could have her around steadily. You know—"

"I know."

His mother's voice held the vibration of the secret.

Mrs. Tipton said, "You couldn't have Judge Wimberley knocking at your back door."

His mother said, breathlessly, "Judge Wimberley?"

"He's the latest."

Turning his head casually, Dickie saw Mrs. Tipton lean forward in the cool, straight chair.

She said, "Oh, Mrs. Merrill, it's incredible, isn't it?"

"Mrs. Tipton, not Judge Wimberley!"

"Yes."

The parlor hummed, as though the birds in the honeysuckle had flown inside. He heard the soft sound of the women's bosoms rising and falling.

His mother said, "It seems as though something could be done."

Mrs. Tipton said, "If we sent them away, there'd only be others."

He knew exactly whom she meant. She meant Creecy and Long Tom and Lulu Wilson. They were nigger women, and something about them was different, even from other nigger women. Creecy was a Geechee, short and fat and blacker than the soot in the fireplace. Long Tom was as black, but tall and thin and bony. Lulu

Wilson was the color of his mother's coffee when the cream and sugar were in it. She was young and slim and pretty. They were the secret. Not quite all of it, for Judy Lane was a part of it. But Judy had moved away.

Mrs. Tipton said, "I learned enough from Lulu this time to run half the men out of town."

His mother rose from her chair and walked up and down the rug. She said, "Oh, Mrs. Tipton, somehow it doesn't seem right, knowing these things."

Her voice had the sick sound that he hated and that made him weak all over. Yet he wanted to hear.

Mrs. Tipton rose too. The two women stood in the center of the dark coolness, like birds fresh caught in a cage.

Mrs. Tipton said, "Well, I want to know. That's why I have her. Women are blind. Women are stupid. I want to know."

His mother said, "Perhaps she's lying."

Her voice sounded the way it sounded when she had a headache.

"She's not lying. I tell you, Mrs. Merrill, men are beasts."

His mother sat down again, and Mrs. Tipton sat too.

Mrs. Tipton said in a low voice, "Dickie?"

His mother said, "Oh, my dear, he's only seven."

"But little pitchers have big ears."

His mother said, "Dickie, dear, wouldn't you like to go out and play?"

He pretended not to hear her.

"Dickie, dear."

He looked up from the picture book. "Mummy, do lions have long tails?"

His mother smiled at Mrs. Tipton. "You see."

They settled back.

Mrs. Tipton said, "I don't tell all this to everyone."

"I know."

"Some women—I just couldn't. Poor things. And never knowing. Oh, men, Mrs. Merrill! Men . . ."

His mother said, "The rest of us must just thank God for ours."

"If anyone could be sure, Mrs. Merrill."

His mother's voice fluttered like a butterfly.

"You mustn't say such things, Mrs. Tipton. My Richard . . . I thank God every night. I don't know what I've done to deserve such—such devotion. I suppose any woman is fortunate to be truly loved."

Dickie wanted to run and bury his head in the lace and ribbons over her soft breast. He wanted to cry out, "I love you, too." Her breast smelled of the sweet lavender that Mammy Dee raised in the herb garden and dried and laid away in all the dresser drawers.

She said, "Mrs. Tipton—it's no excuse, I know—but do you suppose the wives could be in any way to blame?"

Mrs. Tipton said coldly, "I'm sure Judge Wimberley's wife has always done her duty."

"Oh, not duty!"

His mother's voice was a cry.

Mrs. Tipton said, "I tell you, Mrs. Merrill, men are beasts."

The sun found an opening in the shutters. Dickie turned on his side and watched the dust motes dancing across the bright bar.

His mother said, "Only God can judge. . . . Tell me, do they say the cotton has had enough rain?"

Mrs. Tipton said, "I think so. At the bank, they're making more loans."

"I feel guilty sometimes, Richard being in timber and lumber—things already there, so stable—and the people dependent on their annual crops have so much anxiety."

Mrs. Tipton said, "Your husband's uncle, Mr. Baxter Merrill—I believe he has a fine stand of cotton."

"Oh, dear Uncle Baxter. He always prospers. We were at the plantation last Sunday. Everything was beautiful. We have such a gay time when we go there. We depend on Uncle Baxter to be gay. Dickie adores him."

A chime sounded in the depths of the house.

Mrs. Merrill said, "You'll have cake and sherry with me, won't you, Mrs. Tipton?"

"Thank you, Mrs. Merrill."

"Dickie, dear."

He rose in seeming abstraction and went to her. Now he might sink into her laces and her fragrance. She stroked his hair.

"Dickie, darling, I was to take you to Robert to have your hair cut.

Dearest, you're such a big boy, couldn't you go alone?"

His heart was pounding.

"Yes, Mummy."

He longed for the hot sunlight outside the parlor.

"Then have Mammy Dee give you a quarter and go to Robert. Cross the streets very carefully, won't you, lamb?"

"Yes, Mummy. Goodbye."

Mrs. Tipton murmured, "Precious."

He ran from the parlor. Mammy Dee was singing in the kitchen.

"I'm old enough to have my hair cut by myself," he said. "Mummy says you're to give me a quarter."

The vast black woman fumbled in a sugar sack on the wall. "You mind how you cross the railroad tracks."

"I'll be careful."

Dickie tightened his fingers over the coin and ran from the house. He was faint from the secret. It had something to do with black women and white men. It was remote and fascinating and more sickening than too much syrup candy. The lawn grass was green, for it was watered every evening, but beyond it the grass that bordered the town sidewalks was parched and brown. He ran west for three blocks and at the corner by Mrs. Tipton's big house he turned and ran south. He had never crossed the tracks alone before.

He was afraid for a moment that he would not find the barbershop, but the striped pole lifted ahead of him like a lighted lamp. He darted inside the open door and stood an instant, catching his breath. Black Robert rose lazily from a stool, and he was at home again.

Robert said, "I declare, Mastuh Dickie. All by yo'self."

Dickie looked about him. The barbershop lay in its summer stupor. The two chairs stood a little separated, one empty, the far one filled with the shapeless form of a man buried under a white apron. Black Perchy scraped at the face of the chair's occupant. Two other white men sat nearby. They were talking together. Now and then the man in the chair joined in with them, his voice muffled by the lather and the apron. They glanced at Dickie and went on talking.

Black Robert said, "Missy know you come alone?"

Dickie nodded and held out the quarter and Robert laid it on the shelf under the glass case where lotions and tonics glittered in the sunlight.

Robert whispered, "Yo' ma ain't changed yo' haircut, is she?"

Dickie understood that he was to be quiet, so the men talking would not be interrupted.

"She's got company," he whispered in return.

Robert nodded. Dickie climbed into the great chair. The headrest was too high and Robert lowered it for him. He leaned back, feeling mature and important. Robert drew a clean white apron around him and tied it behind his neck. He turned to the case and took out a thin comb and a pair of shining scissors. The comb ran through Dickie's hair, lifting it away from his scalp with the feeling of strong wind. The scissors snipped through his upper hair, then lay suddenly, cool and ticklish, against the back of his neck.

The man in the other chair said, "What's new since I've been here?"

One man said, "What do you think? Nothing."

The other said, "We've got a new bridge over the mill creek. Progress!"

All three laughed together.

One man said, "By God, Beck, you didn't tell him Judy Lane was back in town."

The man in the chair said under his soapsuds, "That good-looking high yellow that married the white man in Chicago?"

"That's the one. Breezed into town in one of those electric broughams, dressed in ostrich feathers long enough to cover her yellow shanks."

"I'll swear. Do you suppose the Chicago guy knows?"

"Probably not."

Robert leaned close to run the scissors around Dickie's right ear.

The man in the chair said, "Strikes me she's right bold, coming back here. Was she raised here?"

"Right here. Her mammy was blacker'n coal'll ever be. One of our leading lights is her daddy."

"Who's that?"

"Baxter Merrill."

"The cotton man?"

"Baxter Merrill, the cotton man. Cotton's the only white crop he's ever raised."

For a moment Dickie saw the secret lie shadowy, as always, in the distance. Then it rose and swelled. It rushed at him with a great roaring, shouting "Uncle Baxter!" He could not breathe. He clawed at the apron around his neck.

Robert murmured, "I'll fix it, Mastuh Dickie."

The glass case of lotions glittered. The barber's chair heaved up and down. He felt something wet on his mouth and splashing on his hands. He was a big boy and he never cried. He was crying.

Robert moved in front of him and planted his bulk between him and the rest of the barbershop. The round ebony face was furrowed and strained.

He said in a low voice, "Hol' still, Mastuh Dickie."

Dickie lifted his fists and beat them on Robert's chest. He twisted his mouth and blinked his eyelids rapidly. It was no use. A sob tore from him. It ripped flesh with it, somewhere in his chest. Two drops of sweat rolled down Robert's face and sank into the white apron.

Dickie said, "I'm sick."

Suddenly Robert gathered him from the chair and wrapped the white apron around him. The black man carried him in the apron to the door and set him on his feet on the sidewalk.

Robert said, "You go down the street a while, Mastuh Dickie." He untied the apron from around his neck. "You come back about traintime. The gemmuns'll be gone then, at traintime."

Dickie drew a deep breath against the coming cyclone.

Robert said, "You come back, now, to get finished." The sweat ran down the black face like rain. "You come back. You cain't go home to yo' ma part done. A li'l man got to go home to his ma all done."

Dickie wavered on his feet. Robert reached into a pocket under his barber's smock and pulled out a penny. He put it in Dickie's palm and closed his fingers over it.

"You go down the next block and get you a ice ball. They got ras'br'y an' cherry today. Then you come back at traintime."

Dickie began to run down the street. The cyclone was on him. He sobbed so deeply that his side ached before he had gone half a block. The tears washed down his face and over his blue dimity blouse. He clutched the penny tightly. It was wet and sticky with sweat from the black hand and from his own.

MIRIAM'S HOUSES

IT seems strange, the way in maturity one sometimes recalls from childhood a long-forgotten incident, or chain of incidents, and finds the memory flooded with a brilliant light of understanding. It is as though one comes across a box of old playthings in the attic, among them a lump of modeling clay half formed into a figure, and one moistens the clay again and the proper shape comes at once, as the child could not have managed it years before. Or as though one reads a book that had been read without comprehension when young, and it is now, of course, crystal-clear. That happened to me when I suddenly remembered Miriam's houses.

Mother liked me to bring Miriam home from school with me for an afternoon's play. She did not approve of all my playmates, but Miriam, she said, was a little lady. Children have a strong sense of caste, but it is based on quite different standards from those of their elders. For instance, the most admired girl in our class came to school dressed not in the neat blue serge and Peter Pan collars of most of us but in obviously shortened adult satin skirts and open-work lace or eyelet blouses run with wide bands of pink ribbon and so large that the shoulder seams came halfway down her scrawny arms. So Mother's approval of Miriam's gentility was meaningless at best, and irksome, for it bound me to be quiet and mannerly, too, and I was a boisterous child. I liked Miriam because she lived in so many houses.

I am still fascinated by strange houses. If they are vacant, one can people them with the proper family, happy or murderous as the place may suggest. If occupied, the glimpses of life within are more intriguing than the known lives of friends. When I was a little girl I was considered most courageous, for I begged to be sent on errands after dark, the longer the better. I skipped indifferently past the homes of immediate neighbors, for there was no wonder there, then walked slowly, often stopping altogether, before the lighted houses of strangers. The gas street lamps were far apart, and the house windows were squares of gold in the darkness. Here a large family sat late at the dinner table. Here a man and woman were quarrelling, their faces angrily close together, the woman with hands on her hips. Here a boy and girl embraced.

In one isolated house the shades were drawn. A narrow slit of light showed at the bottom, and it seemed to me that I must see within, and I slipped over the low barberry hedge and crept close and peered inside. An old, old woman sat alone by a hearth fire, her hands folded on the head of a cane. Her lips were moving, and I looked for the person to whom she was speaking, but there was no one. I was shattered by the sight of age and loneliness so great that she must speak with the dead.

Strange furnishings charmed me, too, and I noticed positions of tables, of chairs and sofas, of bookcases and lamps, and whether there was a piano and flowers or potted plants. I longed to live in all these houses, one by one, to learn their secrets and then move on to others. So, having such an obsession, it was natural that Miriam should seem to me the most desirable friend it was possible to possess. For in the time that I knew her, she never lived in one house longer than three months. The period was more likely to be a single month. I did not bring her home except when my mother insisted. I wanted to go to her house, to her houses. Each morning when I went to school, swinging my books and pencil box strapped together, I thought with excitement, today may be the day Miriam lives in another house. I cannot now remember them all. There were too many, and some must have made little impression even at the time.

I recall the first day Miriam appeared at school, in the middle of the morning, in the middle of the term. The principal led her in to our third-grade teacher and handed over a note from, we guessed, Miriam's mother. All this was unusual, and we stared at the little girl with pale skin and soft dark hair who came to school at such a time, and without her mother. We whispered back and forth and agreed that the family must have moved to our city from a very great distance. When we questioned Miriam during the noon recess, in the blunt way of children, we found that she and her mother had moved to our suburb the day before from one only a mile away.

The first house in our neighborhood in which Miriam lived had not been occupied for many years. It had been Colonel Brook's mansion and I had longed to prowl inside. I had once climbed a mulberry tree outside the high brick wall, hoping to reach the grounds, but my short legs would not quite extend to the wall from the nearest bough. A few days after Miriam's first appearance in our classroom, she asked me to walk home with her from school, and I was able to satisfy my curiosity about the place. The huge, high-ceilinged rooms had a minimum of furniture—a faded brocade sofa here, a gilt chair there. The windows were curtained with heavy red damask and the very bleakness seemed to me elegant. The great ballroom, empty except for two tall gilt mirrors, the billiard room, and a dozen other large rooms were closed and unused. Miriam and her mother used only a small sitting room and the kitchen downstairs, and two bedrooms upstairs. I did not meet her mother while they were in this house. Miriam was plainly disappointed not to find her at home.

"You'll just love my mother," she said. "She's *perfect*."

I had only begun to know well the weed-tangled gardens, the attic filled with old trunks and dressers, when one afternoon, as I accompanied her home, Miriam led me in a new direction. They were living in a shabby house at the end of a street.

I said, "You didn't tell me you were going to move."

She said, "I didn't know."

This house, a tall, narrow, wooden box with turrets, had long attracted me because the windows caught the full blaze of the westerly sun, and toward evening seemed to be on fire. I was delighted now to make its acquaintance. It was dark within, crowded with gloomy black furniture and thick with dust, which was not removed in the two months that I went there. It was in this house that I met Miriam's mother. She wandered vaguely into the kitchen, where we were making cocoa over a spirit lamp, late one afternoon. I looked up from my stirring and saw her in the doorway, twisting her hands. She was like a ghost in that dark place, and I was startled by her frailty, for I came of robust people. Miriam ran to her and took her hand and looked at her with a passionate adoration. Even to a child she seemed very young, prettier than Miriam, with pale, curling hair and light-blue eyes with a frightened expression. She was thin and somehow translucent. She looked at me and tried to smile, and because she was so timid, I was bold and said brightly, "I'm Helen. I'm Miriam's friend."

She said, "I'm glad Miriam has a friend," and she turned uncertainly and wandered away. I heard her coughing in the hall.

I understood that my mother would say of her, too, that she was a lady. I asked my mother to go to see her, and Mother did so, but, as it happened, they had moved again that day and Mother could not find her, and was rather provoked with me. Mother tried to call on her later, in one of the more respectable houses, but was obliged to leave cards, as Miriam's mother was not at home.

"I'm sure the mother is as genteel as the child," she said to me. "Now, those are the kind of people I like you to know. I look forward to her call."

But Miriam's mother never did return the call.

I settled down to the pleasure of Miriam's houses, waiting eagerly for each new move. As time went on, I noticed that she and her mother had very few belongings of their own: a spinet so small that even Miriam's mother could have lifted it, a set of fragile china, linens, and two suitcases for their clothes. Miriam was always neat and clean and properly dressed, but she had only two jumpers, with which she wore different blouses or sweaters.

After the first two houses, there was an assortment of others— some small, some large, some new, most of them old and long unoccupied, some of them far enough away so that Miriam did not come to our school for a month or two, until they moved back nearer. It was at some time during this succession that I began to see now and again an item belonging to a man. I had supposed that Miriam had no father, an unfortunate accident that I knew sometimes happened to children. Once I saw a pipe and a pouch of tobacco on the top of the little spinet.

I said, "Oh, Miriam, you have a father, and he's home."

Her white forehead puckered. "Yes, but I never see my papa," she said sadly. "He's away on business most of the time, and when he does come home, it's at night, after I'm asleep, and then he's gone in the morning, no matter how early I wake up." Her soft brown eyes filled with tears. "I love my mother so very much. But I wish I had a papa who was home in the evening, like yours."

I threw my arms around her and hugged her tight. "You can come home with me and spend the night, and sit on my father's lap with me, and he'll tell us stories."

She returned my embrace. "Oh, thank you, Helen. I'd love to."

But it never came about.

Another time I saw a man's hat and coat hanging on a hall rack, and occasionally I saw pipes or the ends of cigars or cigarettes. My sharp nose sometimes took in the unique scent of a man fresh from the barber. I decided that Miriam's father must be a fine gentleman, and thought no more about him. And then, toward the end of the summer vacation, she moved to the last house in which I knew her, and its memory is clear, for it was the most attractive one of them all.

It was the only house that seemed suitable for the delicate lady mother and the gentle little worshipping daughter. It was small, so that they lived all over it, instead of in two or three rooms out of many. It was Colonial, of soft cream brick, with windows to the floor, deep carpets, and lovely old mahogany furniture, and the little spinet was at home for the first time. There was a tiny garden filled with late yellow roses and asters and chrysanthemums, and Miriam's mother had bowls of flowers on the spinet and through all the house. I saw more of her here than at any other time, and she seemed happier and less harassed and frightened, but she coughed even more than at first. School began again, and I could hardly wait for three o'clock, when Miriam and I would skip, hand in hand, to her house in the crisp October air. Her mother played the spinet, and we sang together, and for once I hoped that Miriam would not move for a long, long time.

Then, one day in November, she did not come to school. The days passed, and the weeks, and the months, and she did not come at all. I looked for her wherever I went. Once, in the heart of the city, I saw her mother, half a block away, and ran to try to speak to her. She was walking slowly and timidly, turning her head now and then, it seemed to me, to look at someone, and I thought she was smiling. She turned into a shop before I could reach her. I never saw Miriam or her mother again.

Not long ago I made a call on a new acquaintance. Her living room was charming—Colonial, with windows to the floor and antique mahogany furniture, and on a little spinet stood a low bowl of yellow roses. It seemed to me that I had been in this room before, but that was impossible. Yet the sense of familiarity haunted me, and I was abstracted through talk and tea. I walked away, puzzling. Then, from forty years ago, it came to me. Miriam. Miriam and her houses. Miriam and her mother. I saw them in the room so like the one I had just left. My memory raced, and I remembered now the first house and the second, and a few of the others, and, above all, the last. Miriam. Miriam's houses. What had become of her? I could not recall her last name. Her frail mother, surely so ill. How strange to have moved so often! I stopped and leaned against a fence.

Understanding like a great light played over that long-forgotten mother and child, over the many houses. It was so clear now that it amazed me that even as a little girl of long ago I should not have known. They had moved so often, naturally, because the rent was never paid. They stayed until the owner or agent would have no more of it and then moved on. When a neighborhood was exhausted, they left it altogether. Miriam's beloved mother, shunted from pillar to post. Miriam's father, so infrequently home, and in the nighttime only. What had been wrong with him, to have allowed it? I saw again the occasional hat or coat, the pipe, the cigar, the cigarette, smelled the barbershop fragrance. But of course. They had all belonged to different men.

I laughed out loud. The fragile little frightened lady had not even been a good streetwalker. The papas who came in the night had not done so often enough to pay the rent. And my prudish mother had never guessed. It was all most amusing. My knowledge had come to me after forty years.

Ah, but when had it come to Miriam?

MISS MOFFATT STEPS OUT

MISS Moffatt went to bed excited. She had corrected all the history papers, and the next day, Saturday, was to be festive. She had decided definitely to go downtown to watch the parade. History was being made, and she could bring a greater enthusiasm to her classes if she shared in the city's moment of glory. The state division was home from the wars. She expected to be wakeful; but she slept soundly after all. The band woke her up at nine o'clock. She put on her rayon dressing gown and took the curlpapers out of her hair before going to the window.

The parade itself would not leave the courthouse until eleven. She moved the burlap screen from one corner of her bedroom, unscrewed the light bulb in a standing lamp and screwed in the two-cup coffee percolator. She looked out in the hall to see if her neighbor, Mrs. Gwynn, who went to her office at eight o'clock, had put out her newspaper for her. The newspaper was not in sight. The morning paper with her breakfast, on holidays, was a luxury, and she could not help being disappointed. She thought, If I get a raise some day, I'll *subscribe* to the paper. She made her bed and cleared the rickety card table on which she worked and ate, made two pieces of toast on a grill over the single-burner gas plate, hesitated, then spread the table with her best linen cloth and brought from the clothes cupboard the jar of strawberry jam she had brought back from her week in the country.

If only she had the newspaper, breakfast would be a real party. But Miss Moffatt would not allow her disappointment to spoil the morning. And what a lovely October morning! The maples were turning, and one branch, yellow and red, stretched close enough to her window so that by sitting a little to one side she could see it. The sky was robin's-egg blue, the air was crisp without being cold, the sun touched one corner of the window sill, and sparrows twittered as though the season were spring. She pulled the card table to the far side of the window so that she could watch the maple bough, then she set the percolator and the plate of toast on the table, and replaced the screen to hide the corner.

I do like things *nice,* she thought, and she had a moment of pride that she managed to live so nicely. She considered combing her hair before sitting down, but decided that was carrying things too far. She ate slowly, greatly enjoying the strawberry jam. It was a very small jar indeed, and reluctantly she ate only half of it, saving the rest for another occasion. "Something else may happen, and I'd feel so badly if I had eaten *all* the jam."

She changed to her old wool dressing gown before washing the dishes. The roominghouse maid would probably skip her room, as she often did on Saturday, and she brought out her broom and dustpan from the cupboard and brushed up and dusted, although there was really no dirt in the room. But she would hate to come back from the parade and not have things neat. She took clean underwear from the dresser and tiptoed down the hall to the bathroom, since others might be sleeping late on Saturday. The hot water had had time to catch up after the early baths. She scrubbed the tub, then drew it full of steaming water. She tied her hand towel around her head so that her hair would not come uncurled.

She dressed carefully, hesitating between her brown everyday suit and her print dress. She decided on the print, although her topcoat was shabby. The day would probably be warm and she could carry the coat over her arm. She was ready a little after ten. If she had had the paper to read, she would have come out exactly even. She looked at herself in the small mirror over the dresser. She felt pleasant, she felt almost pretty, and then the mirror betrayed her. The gold spectacles were unbecoming, no question of it, but buying new ones was unthinkable. The hair was so thin that she seemed all face. The face was bony, gray from the years of eating cheap foods that could be warmed up over the one gas burner. She thought, I just don't believe I eat properly. I'm such a strange *color*. But her salary was small, and fear of losing her job always hung over her, so that she saved most of her pay for a rainy day. She seemed to remember a time when she had been pretty. That had been in grade school, at the age of the children she now instructed. She had even had two beaus who competed to walk home with her and carry her books. It was a long time ago. She was fifty-two. That would make it more than forty years ago.

Interrupting her soliloquy, suddenly she thought, Why, I don't have to wait! I can go now.

She gave a final straightening to the tufted bedspread, locked the door behind her, and set out to walk downtown. She strolled along slowly, looking in shop windows. The day was surely warming up, and she took off her coat and hung it over her left arm and felt neat and proper in her print dress. She decided not to go all the way to the courthouse. It seemed as though the parade would last longer if she met it halfway. It would be horrid to see it start out, then trail away into nothingness. The crowd was gathering and she took a place at the front of the curb. Two of her pupils raced by. She called gaily, "Hello!" The boys seemed not to recognize her. One jostled the other and they laughed boisterously. One did not speak at all. The other said, "Hey, Miss Moffatt," and they ran on.

She heard a thumping of drums far up the street. Then a flute began an air, thin and high, and the heavier instruments of the band came in, and there was music, a march of Sousa's. Miss Moffatt shivered with pleasure. It seemed ages before the parade appeared, but it was enough to know it was coming and to listen to the stirring march. A drum major came first, twirling his baton. Then the band. Then a group of WACs, trim and marching well. And now—now, the home division was coming! She should have noticed, being a history teacher, whether they were in battle garb or in dress uniform, but she saw only that they were grinning from ear to ear as the crowds cheered.

People pressed close behind her, and she was pushed off the curb into the street.

Ordinarily she would have been in a panic, to be out alone, practically with the parade, but there were such roars, such hand clapping, that she was caught up in the tumult. She pulled her handkerchief from her coat pocket and waved it wildly. The marching columns passed her. She called out, "Hurray! Hurray!" From the mass of men a sergeant noticed her, alone on the street, waving, calling. He was a little drunk and extremely happy. He stepped out of formation, bowed in front of her, chuckled, "Hiya, babe," and stepped back.

She was suddenly conscious of her position and pushed back against the people on the curb. They yielded, for the parade was almost over, and they were already turning away. Her heart was pounding. She felt her way through the crowd and walked, unseeing, home to her room. She sat down on the edge of the bed. Oh, I am so silly, she thought. I'm trembling, and she leaned back on the pillow and took off her stiff felt hat. "It didn't mean anything. Why am I so upset?"

As she lay, and her pulse slowed, it seemed to her that she began to understand.

"It's my own fault that I'm so lonely. I don't *go out* to people. When I did, today, it happened. Someone *responded* to me. I must *participate*."

Why, she had found the answer to everything. She sat up straight.

"I'll go to a hotel for dinner. A *good* hotel. Everyone will be celebrating, and I'll celebrate too."

She did try to be honest with herself, and so she inquired if she had it in mind that a man would speak to her, perhaps the sergeant again, but she denied it indignantly.

"It's only that I'm going to stop being such a *hermit*."

She took off the print dress and put on faded gingham and made a pot of tea and a peanut-butter sandwich for her lunch. She washed the cup and teapot, putting the tea leaves in a paper bag and then in the wastebasket. She lay down to take a nap, to be fresh for the evening. Sleep would not come, and she was suddenly alert, deciding what to wear. Her one evening dress, of course. All the women would be dressed. The dress was many years old, but she had worn it only once, at the Board of Education banquet, and there was really nothing about it to go out of style.

She was glad to have something to occupy her and she got up and took the dress out of its cotton bag, brought out the ironing board, and pressed it carefully. It was an uglier gray than she had remembered. The afternoon dragged. At four o'clock she had another bath. She dressed as slowly as possible. Her white summer purse would have to do, and there was nothing for it but to wear the shabby topcoat. She would take it off and carry it the moment she reached the hotel door. And she would take a taxi. She took five dollars from an envelope hidden under her flannel nightgowns.

"I sha'n't even *think* about money tonight."

She put a few drops of perfume on her handkerchief. The perfume was old and brown and had a peculiar smell. Her class had given it to her for Christmas ten years ago, the only class ever to give her a present. Why, some of those boys were probably in the parade today. Perhaps they had thought of her as they fought through Africa, Italy, France, and Germany. She put another drop of perfume under the net ruching outlining the neck of the gray evening dress. Six thirty would surely not be too early to arrive at the hotel. At six she sauntered, elegantly, she felt, down the stairs, and called a cab from the telephone in the lower hall. It came almost at once.

"The Buckingham Hotel," she said, but the driver did not seem at all surprised.

It was a magnificent hotel. The striped awning reached out to the cab to welcome her. The doorman rushed out to swing open the door. She fumbled in her purse and paid her fare and tipped the driver five cents. She was in the lobby before she realized that she had forgotten to take off her coat. She struggled with it and dropped her purse. A bellboy picked it up for her.

"Check your coat, ma'am?"

"Oh, yes. Thank you." It was such a relief to see him take it away.

"I should have tipped him, too," and she looked around, but he was not in sight.

The hotel was a confusion of large rooms, gilt and crystal and elegant. The dining room could be any one of them. She wandered around and found it in a distant wing. It was empty, except for dozens of waiters, white-coated, idle, and arrogant. She had strayed halfway across the great room before one appeared beside her and inquired, "Madam is alone?"

Yes, she was quite alone. Yes, a table just anywhere. Thank you. Thank you so much. The table was in the farthest corner. Far away was the raised stand for the orchestra. But it was better not to be too near the music. The waiter flourished a menu and laid it in front of her.

She said firmly, "I'll have a cocktail first, please."

"Yes, madam. What will madam have?"

He was probably deaf.

She said loudly, "A cocktail, please."

"Madam, there are a hundred cocktails, a thousand. A Martini, a Manhattan, a Daiquiri—"

"Yes, yes, please. Any one. Thank you."

She was red and hot. Her spectacles were opaque with steam. She took them off and wiped them with her handkerchief. Of course, she knew there was more than one kind of cocktail. How stupid. The cocktail was before her. They did have quick service, but she would have liked a little time to get herself together. The drink was pale and a trifle bitter. There was an olive at the bottom of the glass and she ate it gratefully to take away the horrid taste. So that was a cocktail. How could anyone get down enough to be drunk? But she felt a warm glow and was calm when the waiter leaned over with pencil and order pad. She would have liked to choose slowly, for there was a long list of wonderful dishes, all unbelievably expensive. Three dollars and a half for steak, two dollars and a half for broiled chicken. Against her will, she looked hurriedly down the column of prices. There, a dollar and a half, which was not so appalling.

"I'll have the country sausage with apple rings," she said.

"And what else, madam?"

"Oh, nothing, nothing at all. That's all I care for."

Why, if she had anything else, her five dollars might not be enough. She really was not hungry, anyway. She saw with pleasure that a man and woman had come into the dining room and were headed her way. They took a table near her, the only one more remote than hers. She had felt for an instant that her being there had attracted them to the corner, out of the vast empty room, but they were lovers and leaned their heads together and began to murmur softly. When she caught their eyes, she smiled brightly, but they looked through her and once they kissed. She might not have been there at all, sitting stiffly in the old-fashioned gray dress with net ruching, her streaked gray hair coming out of curl and hanging limply.

There was a candle on her table. She struggled to light it, looking forward to dinner by candlelight, but a draft kept blowing out the matches. "Oh, dear," she said, and gave it up. The waiter put a plate before her. On it were two small patties of dark brown sausage, each topped with a pale fried apple ring. How could they have cooked the sausage so quickly? It almost seemed as though the waiter were trying to hurry her away. Well, she would not be hurried. She was paying for this and she intended to enjoy it.

The waiter said, "Madam understood that the price of the entree included other things, soup, vegetables, rolls, dessert?"

His tone was bland but his eyes were malevolent. She believed he knew she had not understood. He could have told her in time. She could not send him back now across that great room. And she was hungry, terribly hungry.

"Nothing else. I'll have dessert—and coffee," and she bent her head over her plate. Her eyes smarted.

She thought, If I went out oftener, I wouldn't be so *foolish*.

She ate as slowly as possible and drank all her water, but the waiter did not come to fill up the glass again. She didn't even have bread and butter, and she was accustomed to eating a great deal of bread. It was too provoking. The dining room was beginning to fill. The sausage was good and she felt more cheerful. She looked up between minute bites to watch the people coming in, laughing and joking. Not one of the women had on an evening dress. They were either in sports clothes or wore very brief black dresses. She looked up and smiled when a party passed her table. No one noticed. She could not divide the last morsel again. The waiter took away her plate and handed her the menu. She was hungrier than when she began, and she would have the richest dessert possible.

"Biskit Tortinny," she said, "and coffee."

"Bisquee Tortoni," said the waiter. "Coffee." And again it was before her before she could say Jack Robinson. The dessert was a tiny thing in a fluted paper basket. The coffee was good and she used all the cream and four teaspoons of sugar. She sipped slowly. For a moment she thought it was her sergeant of the morning who sat down at the table next to her, but of course it was not. He was a much younger sergeant. He looked around uncertainly. The coincidence raised her spirits.

Why, he was alone, too! He was probably far from home and feeling as forlorn as she. I don't *have* to let myself be cheated, she thought. All I have to do is *go out* to people. Like this morning. Her heart beat rapidly. I'll invite him to have dinner as my guest, and I'll have ice cream. She wiped her forehead. Now. Speak to him now.

The young sergeant lifted one hand high and his face shone. A girl with a corsage and a little perky hat was making her way to him, smiling as luminously as he. Miss Moffatt felt suddenly faint and dizzy. The cocktail, of course, was responsible for this dreadful feeling of collapse. She looked about desperately and the waiter shoved before her the check on a silver tray. The cocktail had cost a dollar. She counted out two dollar bills and two quarters. There was fifteen cents left in change in her purse. She added that to the tray and pushed back her chair clumsily. The waiter ignored her.

The crossing of the room was endless. The long gray dress wrapped itself around her ankles. The dining room was nearly full, the orchestra came in, the violinist tuned his fiddle, and applause sounded from the gay company. The music began as she reached the lobby. She found her way to the checkroom and described her coat. She folded it over her arm.

The doorman said, "Taxi, madam?"

She hesitated. Another thirty-five cents would be an insane extravagance. Then she lifted her chin and pulled the shabby coat around her.

"If you please," she said.

She would go home in glory, as the state division had returned. She had shared in history, and she would tell her class on Monday that they had shared, too. And she would tell them—oh, she would tell them again and again—that the battle was not yet won, that one human being must be kind to another, one race, one nation to another, or the world was lost.

THE FRIENDSHIP

THE little boy had a policeman for a friend. He acquired him out of a clear sky. He ran out of the schoolyard to go home for his noon lunch, tripped over a rough spot on the sidewalk, and fell so hard and so flat that for gasping moments he could not draw a breath. The policeman happened to be passing by. Robert felt himself being lifted and pounded on the back. The first breath that came was agony and wonder, for drawing it had seemed impossible. It was only with the third that he realized his knees were hurting, and he looked down to see them torn and bleeding. He became aware of the policeman and then it was unthinkable to cry.

He was not afraid, like the defiant older boys who gave themselves away by bragging of what they had done and intended to do to policemen. His father had often told him that the law was a protector, and if he ever found himself lost, for he was something of a roamer, he was to ask for a policeman and give his name and address. This seemed appropriate now.

He said, "My name is Robert Wilkinson and I live on Newton Street. I've forgotten the number."

The policeman nodded his head gravely. "I know your father," he said. "Isn't your house the large green-and-white one?"

"Oh, yes. With a big snow-apple tree in the yard."

The policeman again inclined his head. "My duties take me that way, Robert. I'll walk along with you."

The little boy was enchanted. The policeman's gravity was pleasing and complimentary.

"That was a bad tumble, young man. Are your knees painful?"

"Yes, sir, they hurt terribly."

"Will there be someone at home to fix you up?"

"Oh, yes; my mother. She's always there when I come home for lunch."

"You're lucky, Robert. I didn't have a mother when I was your age. Eight, I'd guess?"

"Just six. I almost wasn't old enough to begin the first grade." He glowed with pride that the policeman thought he was eight years old. "I thought everybody had a mother."

"Everybody has a mother to begin with."

"Even kittens and puppies and little birds."

"And colts and calves and baby elephants," said the policeman, and smiled. "But sometimes a mother can be lost."

Robert was puzzled. "I thought only little boys got lost. I never have been, quite, but my father says he's always expecting it."

"Just ask for me if you're lost. I am Sergeant Masters."

"That's what my father told me, to ask for a policeman and tell my name and where I live. But I can't ever remember the number."

"The name and the street are what matter. Your father is well known in the area where you would presumably stray."

Robert did not quite understand all the words, but he was charmed with the truly adult conversation, with his father's being well known, and above all with the policeman. He sighed happily, and when the policeman took his hand in crossing a street, his cup of joy ran over, and he left his small hand inside the vast one. They walked in silence down another block.

He asked, "Do you have a little boy?"

"No, Robert. I should have liked a dozen, but I shall never have a single one."

"How can you tell?"

"Sometimes," the policeman said, "it is possible to know."

The sergeant at once took third place in omniscience behind God and his father, and it occurred to Robert that perhaps he should put him first. The only flaw in everything was that his protector had been unimpressed by his not crying when his knees did hurt so intensely. They reached the gate of his house. His mother stood anxiously on the front porch, since the accident had delayed him. He waved to her and she waved back.

The policeman said, "You might say to your mother that I suggest hot water first, and then an antiseptic and bandages." He cleared his throat. "You are a very brave young man. Many boys would have cried. I usually pass your school during the noon recess, and when we meet again, I hope we may walk together."

"Oh, I hope so too." He recalled his manners. "Thank you, sir," he said.

"And you are polite too. I'm sure we shall be friends."

He tipped his cap to the lady coming down the path and strolled impressively away.

Robert cried out, "Mother, I fell down and I couldn't breathe, and see my knees, all bleeding, and a policeman picked me up and came home with me."

"How nice of him. Oh, darling, this is dreadful. You can't go back to school this afternoon."

"Of course I can go back. I'm a very brave young man."

His mother laughed and hugged him to her, and treated his injuries as the policeman had suggested, although he forgot to tell her.

He was a little late for the afternoon session, but he went boldly into the classroom with his bandaged knees. They were their own apology, and the teacher nodded to him and went on with the lesson. He was disappointed that she did not ask him any questions, so that he could tell of his peril and of his friend.

In the evening he could hardly wait for his father to come home. He hung on the gate, watching for him. When he saw him coming down the street, he ran to him and clasped him around the legs.

"Father, I fell down and hurt myself, and a policeman brought me home."

His father lifted quizzical eyebrows. "A policeman brought you home? Well, well. In chains, no doubt. What bad thing had you done?"

"Oh, father." He was accustomed to his father's jokes, and nothing could spoil his pleasure. "The policeman is my friend."

"Well, that may come in handy someday when you've done something really bad."

"Father." The jesting was adult, too, and he ate his vegetables at dinner without his mother's urging.

He was unable to avoid boasting at school, just a little, for Sergeant Masters was waiting for him almost every noon.

The tough boys sneered, "Who wants a cop for a friend? Yah. Bet your mamma pays him to take baby home. Yah. 'Fraid we'll beat you up. We don't beat up babies. Bet she pays him a dollar a week."

The idea had its unspeakable possibilities. His mother was often unduly solicitous. He did not dare approach her on the subject, but he did sound out the sergeant.

"Do you know my mother?" he asked one day.

"I don't have that pleasure. But as I said before, I am acquainted with your father."

Perhaps his father had hired the policeman. Perhaps his father had enemies and was threatened with the kidnaping of his son. This thought was exciting and acceptable, but it invalidated the friendship. He pondered over his next question. He felt very sly and clever as he asked it.

"A good policeman wouldn't take money for walking home with anybody, would he?"

The sergeant stopped and stared down at him. "Somebody has been putting ideas in your head. No, Robert, a good policeman doesn't take money for anything." He laid a huge gentle hand on the little boy's shoulder. "I am your friend. Always remember that friendship is a noble thing."

He was comforted. And then the snow apples on the tree in the yard began to ripen and fall. They lay each morning like rosy flowers in the soft grass. By family custom these were his own, the windfalls. He invited the policeman into the yard every day and insisted on his putting an apple in all his pockets.

Sergeant Masters said invariably, "Thank you, Robert. I wish I had a little boy to take them home to. But I'll think of you and enjoy them."

One day the windfalls were scarce and the policeman would not take any, but said that he would prefer to think of Robert's eating them. The next noon there was only one snow apple on the ground. This was unreasonable, as the tree was still loaded. Robert watched from behind the hedge that evening, and saw Jimmy Thomas and his sister dash into the yard and swoop to the grass and dash away again. He was in a rage. It was his apple tree, his apples. He not only liked to use them as tribute to his friend but he was passionately fond of snow apples himself.

He ran toward the house to tell his father, then halted, and in triumph decided on a superior plan. Of what avail to have a policeman for a friend, if not to use him for his vengeance?

The next noon he prayed there would be no apples on the ground. There was a disappointingly large number, but still, he was sure, not nearly so many as usual. He turned haughtily to Sergeant Masters.

"Well," he said, "those Thomases have been over here again, stealing. I want you to arrest them and put them in jail. Right now."

"Arrest the Thomases for stealing? Who are the Thomases?"

"A horrid boy across the street and his nasty little sister. They've been stealing my snow apples."

"I see. Robert, do they have an apple tree?"

"No. But they don't have any right to mine."

"Have you ever given them any of your apples?"

"I don't have to. I don't like them. And you're my friend, you said so, and I want you to arrest them."

Sergeant Masters slowly took out from his pockets the apples that Robert had pressed on him and dropped them to the autumn earth.

"It's a very large tree, Robert," he said, "but perhaps you'd better just keep all the apples for yourself."

Robert stared at the gift apples discarded on the ground, then up at the beloved face far above him. It was sad and stern. He drew a gasping breath more painful than the one when he had fallen flat and the policeman had pounded him on the back and had become his friend. In a moment now Sergeant Masters would walk out of the gate and be lost to him forever. He threw his arms around the strong legs and gripped them tight and hid his face against them.

A sparrow flew into the tree and chirped cheerfully in the dreadful silence. An apple dropped with a thump. A cloud drifted across the sun and the autumn air was chill. He shivered. The big hand of the policeman dropped slowly to his head and ruffled his hair. A great arm encircled him.

"It's all right, Robert."

The little boy burst into loud sobs of relief and shame. Friendship was a noble thing and he had proved unworthy.

PUBLICATION NOTES

"Cracker Chidlings," *Scribner's Magazine* 89 (February 1931): 127–34.

"Jacob's Ladder": *Scribner's Magazine* 89 (April 1931): 351–66, 446–64. Reprinted in *When the Whippoorwill* (New York: Charles Scribner's Sons, 1940), 41–118; *Jacob's Ladder* (Miami, Fla.: University of Miami Press, 1950); *The Marjorie Rawlings Reader*, ed. Julia Scribner Bigham (New York: Charles Scribner's Sons, 1956), 436–504.

"Lord Bill of the Suwannee River," ed. Gordon E. Bigelow, *Southern Folklore Quarterly* 27, no. 2 (June 1963): 113–31; ed. Kevin M. McCarthy in "The History of Gilchrist County," 218–32, Trenton, Fla., Historical Committee of the Trenton Women's Club, 1986. Bigelow's text is incomplete; thus McCarthy's is used here. The story was written in early 1931.

"A Plumb Clare Conscience," *Scribner's Magazine* 90 (December 1931): 622–26. Reprinted in *When the Whippoorwill*, 233–40.

"A Crop of Beans," *Scribner's Magazine* 91 (May 1932): 283–90. Reprinted in *When the Whippoorwill*, 1–19.

"Gal Young Un," *Harper's Monthly Magazine* 165 (June 1932): 21–33; 165 (July 1932): 225–34. Reprinted in *When the Whippoorwill*, 175–216; *The Marjorie Rawlings Reader*, 377–413.

"Alligators," *Saturday Evening Post* 206 (23 September 1933): 16–17, 36, 38. Reprinted in *When the Whippoorwill*, 217–32.

"Benny and the Bird Dogs," *Scribner's Magazine* 94 (October 1933): 193–200. Reprinted in *When the Whippoorwill*, 20–40.

"The Pardon," *Scribner's Magazine* 96 (August 1934): 95–98. Reprinted in *When the Whippoorwill*, 119–29.

"Varmints," *Scribner's Magazine* 100 (December 1936): 26–32, 84–85. Reprinted in *When the Whippoorwill*, 130–55.

"A Mother in Mannville," *Saturday Evening Post* 209 (12 December 1936): 7, 33. Reprinted in *When the Whippoorwill*, 241–50.

"Cocks Must Crow," *Saturday Evening Post* 212 (25 November 1939): 5–7, 58, 60, 62–64. Reprinted in *When the Whippoorwill*, 251–75; *The Marjorie Rawlings Reader*, 414–35.

"Fish Fry and Fireworks," *Florida Quarterly* 1 (Summer 1967): 1–18. Edited by Gordon E. Bigelow, this story was written circa 1940.

"The Pelican's Shadow," *New Yorker* 15 (6 January 1940): 17–19. Reprinted in *The Marjorie Rawlings Reader*, 361–68.

"The Enemy," *Saturday Evening Post* 212 (20 January 1940): 12–13, 32, 36, 39. Reprinted in *When the Whippoorwill*, 156–74.

"In the Heart," *Collier's* 105 (3 February 1940): 19, 39.

"Jessamine Springs," *New Yorker* 17 (22 February 1941): 19–20. Reprinted in *The Marjorie Rawlings Reader*, 355–60.

"The Provider," *Woman's Home Companion* 68 (June 1941): 20–21, 44, 46, 48, 60, 61.

"The Shell," *New Yorker* 20 (9 December 1944): 29–31. Reprinted in *The Marjorie Rawlings Reader*, 369–74.

"Black Secret," *New Yorker* 21 (8 September 1945): 20–23.

"Miriam's Houses," *New Yorker* 21 (24 November 1945): 29–31.

"Miss Moffatt Steps Out," *Liberty Magazine* 23 (16 February 1946): 31, 58–61.

"The Friendship," *Saturday Evening Post* 221 (1 January 1949): 14–15, 44.